BEOWULF

A TRANSLATION AND COMMENTARY

together with

SELLIC SPELL

Works by J.R.R. Tolkien

THE HOBBIT
LEAF BY NIGGLE
ON FAIRY-STORIES
FARMER GILES OF HAM
THE HOMECOMING OF BEORHTNOTH
THE LORD OF THE RINGS
THE ADVENTURES OF TOM BOMBADIL
THE ROAD GOES EVER ON (WITH DONALD SWANN)
SMITH OF WOOTTON MAJOR

Works published posthumously

SIR GAWAIN AND THE GREEN KNIGHT, PEARL AND SIR ORFEO*
THE FATHER CHRISTMAS LETTERS
THE SILMARILLION*
PICTURES BY J.R.R. TOLKIEN*
UNFINISHED TALES*
THE LETTERS OF J.R.R. TOLKIEN*
FINN AND HENGEST
MR BLISS
THE MONSTERS AND THE CRITICS & OTHER ESSAYS*
ROVERANDOM
THE CHILDREN OF HÚRIN*
THE LEGEND OF SIGURD AND GUDRÚN*
THE FALL OF ARTHUR*

The History of Middle-earth – by Christopher Tolkien

I THE BOOK OF LOST TALES, PART ONE
II THE BOOK OF LOST TALES, PART TWO
III THE LAYS OF BELERIAND
IV THE SHAPING OF MIDDLE-EARTH
V THE LOST ROAD AND OTHER WRITINGS
VI THE RETURN OF THE SHADOW
VII THE TREASON OF ISENGARD
VIII THE WAR OF THE RING
IX SAURON DEFEATED
X MORGOTH'S RING
XI THE WAR OF THE JEWELS
XII THE PEOPLES OF MIDDLE-EARTH

* Edited by Christopher Tolkien

BEOWULF

A TRANSLATION AND COMMENTARY

together with

SELLIC SPELL

BY

J.R.R. TOLKIEN

Edited by Christopher Tolkien

HarperCollins*Publishers*

HarperCollins*Publishers*
77–85 Fulham Palace Road,
Hammersmith, London W6 8JB
www.tolkien.co.uk

www.tolkienestate.com

Published by HarperCollins*Publishers* 2014

I

A CIP catalogue record for this book
is available from the British Library

ISBN 978-0-00-759006-3

Printed and bound in Great Britain by
Clays Ltd, St Ives plc

CONTENTS

PREFACE

Since the nature and purpose of this book could very easily be misunderstood I offer here an explanation, which I hope will also be a justification.

It is well-known that there exists a translation of *Beowulf* into modern English prose made by J.R.R. Tolkien; and in view of his reputation and eminence in Old English literary and linguistic scholarship the fact that it has remained unpublished for so many years has even become a matter of reproach.

I am responsible for this; and the primary reason, or explanation, is fairly simple. The translation was completed by 1926, when my father was 34; before him lay two decades as the professor of Anglo-Saxon at Oxford, two decades of further study of Old English poetry, together with an arduous programme of lectures and classes, and reflection most especially on *Beowulf*. From his lectures of those years there survives a great deal of writing on the poem, including much on the interpretation of the detail of the text. Clearly, there was no step-by-step relationship between the lectures and the translation, but changes made to the translation (and there are many) at different times can often be seen to accord with discussion of the questions in his lectures. In other cases he did not alter the translation in the light of his later, revised opinion.

There seemed no obvious way in which to present a text that was in one sense complete, but at the same time evidently 'unfinished'. Merely to print what appears to have been his latest choice in the translation of a word, a phrase, or a passage and to leave it at that seemed misleading and mistaken. To alter the translation in order to accommodate a later opinion was out of the question. It would of course have been possible to attach my own explanatory notes, but it seemed very much better to include in this book actual passages from the lectures in which he expounded his views on the textual problems in question.

He did indeed explicitly intend that the series of lectures on *Beowulf* which I have used in this book should be a 'textual commentary', closely concerned with verbal detail. In practice however he found this restriction confining: he was very often led from the discussion of a word or phrase to more far-reaching exposition of the characteristics of the Old English poet, his thought and his style and his purpose; and in the course of the lectures there are many short but illuminating 'essays', arising from specific points in the text. As he wrote, 'I try to do it, yet it is not really possible or satisfactory, to separate one's commentary into "legendary content" and "text".'

There is here, amid the huge library of *Beowulf* criticism, a very evident individuality of conception and insight; and in these characteristically expressed observations and arguments there can be seen the closeness of his attention to the text, his knowledge of the ancient diction and idiom, and his visualization of scenes thus derived. There emerges, as it seems to me, his vivid personal evocation of a long-vanished world – as it was perceived by the author of *Beowulf*; the philological detail exists to clarify the meaning and intention of that poet.

Thus after much reflection I have thought to enlarge and very greatly extend the scope of this book by extracting a good deal of material from the written form of those lectures, providing (as I hope) a readily comprehensible commentary arising in express relationship with the actual text of the poem, and yet often extending beyond those immediate limits into expositions of such matters as the conception of the *wrecca*, or the relation of the characters in the poem to the power of 'fate'.

But such a use of these abundant writings, in a way that was of course by no means intended, necessarily raises problems of presentation that are not easy to resolve. In the first place, this is a work of my father's (distinct in this from all save one of the editions of his unpublished writings that I have made) which is not of his own conceiving, but is concerned with a specific work, of great celebrity and with a massive history of criticism extending over two centuries. And in the second place, the lectures in question were addressed to an audience of students whose work on Old English was in part based on the demanding language of *Beowulf*, and his purpose was to elucidate and illuminate, often in precise detail, that part of the original text that was prescribed for study. But his translation would of course have been addressed primarily, though not exclusively, to readers with little or no knowledge of the original language.

In this book thus conceived I have tried to serve the different interests of possible readers; and in this connection there is a curious and interesting partial parallel with my father's dilemma that he expressed in a letter to Rayner Unwin of November 1965, concerning his inability to compose the 'editorial' matter to accompany his completed translation of *Sir Gawain and the Green Knight*:

> I am finding the selection of notes, and compressing them, and the introduction, difficult. Too much to say, and not sure of my target. The main target is, of course, the general reader of literary bent but with no knowledge of Middle English; but it cannot be doubted that the book will be read by students, and by academic folk of 'English Departments'. Some of the latter have their pistols loose in their holsters. I have, of course, had to do an enormous amount of editorial work, unshown, in order to arrive at a version; and I have, as I think, made important discoveries with regard to certain words, and some passages (as 'importance' in the little world of Middle English goes). . . . I think it desirable to indicate to those who possess the original where and how my readings differ from the received.

Years later, in 1974, soon after my father's death, I referred to this letter of his when writing to Rayner Unwin on the subject of a posthumous publication of his translation of *Sir Gawain*. I said that I had searched through his notes on *Gawain*, but 'I can find no trace of any that would be remotely suitable for "the general reader of literary bent but with no knowledge of Middle English" – or for most students, for that matter'; and I wondered 'whether it was not his complete inability to resolve this question that prevented him from ever finishing the book.' I said that the solution that I (doubtfully) favoured was to have no 'learned' commentary at all; and continued:

> But quite apart from this, and assuming that the philological gunmen whom my father was anxious about can be safely neglected, what of 'the general reader of literary bent but no knowledge of Middle English'? The situation is so highly individual that I find it difficult to analyse. In general I would assume that a book of translations of mediaeval poems of this order published without any commentary on the text at all would be so odd as to arouse hostility.

My solution in the present case is of course based on different materials standing in different relationships, in origin going back some three quarters of a century and more, but it is certainly open to criticism: the commentary as here presented is and can only be a *personal selection* from a much larger body of writing, in places disordered and very difficult, and strongly concentrated on the earlier part of the poem. But it goes no further than that; and it has therefore no more than a very superficial resemblance to an 'edition'. It does not aim at any degree of general inclusiveness, any more than my father's lectures did: as he himself said, he was largely restricting himself to matter where he had something personal to say or to add. I have not added explanations or information that a reader might look for in an edition; such very minor additions as I have made are mostly those that seem needed by elements in the commentary itself. And I have not myself related his views and observations to the work of other scholars before him or after him. In making this selection I have been guided by relevance to features of the translation, by my own estimate of the general interest of the subject-matter, and by the need to keep within limits of length. I have included a number of notes from the lectures on very minor points in the text that illustrate how from a small grammatical or etymological detail he would derive larger conclusions; and a few elaborate discussions of textual emendations to show how he presented his arguments and evidences. A fuller account of these lectures as they survive in written form, and of my treatment of them, will be found in the introduction to the commentary, pp. 131 ff.

In his lecture-commentary he assumed (perhaps too readily) some knowledge of the elements of Old English, and the possession of or at any rate easy access to a copy of 'Klaeber' (the major and generally used edition of *Beowulf*, by Frederic Klaeber, of which he was often critical but which he also esteemed). I on the other hand have throughout this book treated the translation as primary; but side by side with those line-references I have invariably given the corresponding references to the Old English text for those who wish to have it immediately accessible without a search.

In my foreword to *The Legend of Sigurd and Gudrún* I said: 'Of its nature it is not to be judged by views prevailing in contemporary scholarship. It is intended rather as a presentation and record of his perceptions, in his own day, of a literature that he greatly admired.' The same could be said of this book. I have most emphatically not seen my role in the editions of *Sigurd and Gudrún* or *The Fall of Arthur* as the offering of a critical survey of his views, as some seem to have thought that it should be. The present work should best be regarded as a 'memorial volume', a 'portrait' (as it were) of the scholar in his time, in words of his own, hitherto unpublished.

As a further element it thus seems especially appropriate to include his work *Sellic Spell*, also now first published, an imagined story of Beowulf in an early form; so also at the end of the book I have printed the two versions of his *Lay of Beowulf*, a rendering of the story in the form of a ballad to be sung. His singing of the *Lay* remains for me a clear memory after more than eighty years, my first acquaintance with Beowulf and the golden hall of Heorot.

The four illustrations that are reproduced as part of this book are all the work of J.R.R. Tolkien. Beneath the painting of the dragon on the front cover he wrote these words from *Beowulf*, line 2561, (*ðá wæs*) *hringbogan heorte gefýsed*, which he translated as '(now was) the heart of the coiling beast stirred (to come out to fight)' (2153–4). The drawing on the back cover is of Grendel's mere: the words *wudu wyrtum fæst* that appear beneath this are from *Beowulf*, line 1364; in the translation (1136–9) 'It is not far hence . . . that that mere lies, over which there hang rimy thickets, and *a wood clinging by its roots* overshadows the water.' Another drawing of the mere, made at the same time (1928), is reproduced on the rear flap. The drawing on the first page of this book, showing a dragon attacking a warrior, was done in the same year.

All four illustrations are reproduced, with interesting observations, in *J.R.R. Tolkien: Artist and Illustrator* by Wayne G. Hammond and Christina Scull, pp. 52–5.

INTRODUCTION TO THE TRANSLATION

The textual history

The texts of my father's prose translation of *Beowulf* are, superficially at least, easily described. There is, first, a typescript, made on very thin paper and using what he called his 'midget' type on his Hammond typewriter; this I will call 'B'. It extends as far as line 1773 in the translation (line 2112 in the Old English text), 'warrior of old wars, in age's fetters did lament his': the last word stands at the end of the last line on the page, at its foot.

The 32 pages of B are in very poor condition, the right-hand edges being darkly discoloured and in some cases badly broken or torn away, with the text at that point lost. In appearance it bears an odd resemblance to the *Beowulf* manuscript itself, which was badly damaged in the ruinous fire at Ashburnham House in Westminster in 1731: the edges of the leaves were scorched and subsequently crumbled away. But whatever caused the damage to the text B of my father's translation, he wrote in most of the lost words in the margins (though occasionally this is not so).

There is no trace of any other sheets of the typescript B, but a manuscript takes up with the words (following 'did lament his' where B ends) 'youth and strength in arms'. I will refer to the typescript therefore as **B(i)** and the manuscript, which continues to the end of the poem, as **B(ii)**.

The translation had been completed by the end of April 1926, as is seen from a letter in the archive of Oxford University Press from my father to Kenneth Sisam:

> I have all Beowulf translated, but in much hardly to my liking. I will send you a specimen for your free criticism – though tastes differ, and indeed it is hard to make up one's own mind ... [1]

(My father took up his appointment to the professorship of Anglo-Saxon at Oxford in the winter of 1925 and my family moved from Leeds in January 1926.)

Following B(i) and B(ii) is a further typescript (extant also in a carbon copy) which I made, and which can be dated to about 1940–2.[2] This typescript I will call 'C'. There are no other texts.

The typescript B(i) was fairly heavily emended, most substantially in the passage describing Grendel's coming

---

1 I am grateful to Wayne Hammond and Christina Scull for this reference.
2 At that time I did various 'amanuensis' tasks to assist my father: recently I came upon a forgotten map of *The Silmarillion*, very carefully drawn and coloured, signed with my initials and the date 1940, though I have no recollection now of its making. Other indications suggest 1942: see the Notes on the Text of the translation, pp. 126–7, note on lines 2260–2.)

to Heorot and his fight with Beowulf (in the translation lines 574–632), which my father after preliminary emendation struck through and replaced with a rewritten passage in another type; but curiously, from this point onwards the emendations become very few and far between, to the end of the B(i)-typescript.

Turning to the manuscript B(ii), which takes up in the middle of the last sentence in B(i), this was written fluently and fairly quickly, legibly enough for the most part to one familiar with my father's handwriting, but here and there presenting difficulty. There are a good many emendations, but the majority were made at the time of the writing of the manuscript. Some of these corrections were much altered in the making and difficult to interpret; while there are notes here and there in this text of an explanatory nature or suggesting alternative interpretations of the Old English text.

The typescript C contains the whole text of the translation. The great mass of the corrections to B(i) were incorporated in C, but a few were made to B(i) later. In the case of B(ii) the manuscript had virtually reached its latest form when my father gave it to me to make a copy.

When I typed C the text of B(i) had become in places difficult to make out, but I made a surprisingly accurate rendering of it (no doubt with requests for assistance here and there). In the latter part of the translation, the handwritten B(ii), on the other hand, I made a fair number of mistakes (it is strange to look back over three-quarters of a century at my earliest struggles with the famous handwriting).

3

Finally, at some date(s) unknown, my father went quickly, even cursorily (as with other works of his) through the C typescript and jotted down – in some cases scarcely legibly – many further changes of wording. If at that stage he compared my text with its antecedents he seems not to have done so very closely (at any rate he did not observe cases where I had plainly misread the B(ii) text).

Thus, while the series of texts, B(i), B(ii), C, is simply stated, the layers of textual correction constitute an extremely intricate history. To present it all would be out of place in this book; but following the translation I have provided a substantial list of notable textual features, and in order to give some idea of the process I print here a much emended passage as it appears in different stages. This is in the translation lines 263–79, in the Old English text lines 325–43.

(a)   The text as originally typed in B(i).

Weary of the sea they set their tall shields [*word lost*]. . .
ed and wondrous hard, against that mansion's wall, then
turned they to the benches. Corslets clanged, the war-
harness of those warriors; their spears were piled together,
weapons with ashen haft each grey-tipped with steel. Well
furnished with weapons was [*words lost*: the iron-]clad
company. There a proud knight then asked those men of
battle concerning their lineage: 'Whence bear ye your gold-
plated shields, your grey shirts of mail, your vizored helms
and throng of warlike spears? I am Hrothgar's herald and
esquire. Never have I seen so many men of alien folk more

proud of heart! Methinks that in pride, not in the ways of banished men, nay, with valiant purpose are you come seeking Hrothgar.' To him then made answer, strong and bold, the proud prince of the Weder-Geats; these words he spake in turn, grim beneath his helm: 'Companions of Hygelac's table are we; Beowulf is my name.'

(b)   The text of B(i) as emended

Weary of the sea they set their tall shields and bucklers wondrous hard against the wall of the house, and sat then on the bench. Corslets rang, war-harness of men. Their spears were piled together, seamen's gear, ash-wood steel-tipped with grey. Well furnished with weapons was the iron-mailed company. There then a knight in proud array asked those men of battle concerning their lineage: 'Whence bear ye your gold-plated shields, your grey shirts of mail, your vizored helms and throng of warlike spears? I am Hrothgar's herald and esquire. Never have I seen so many men of alien folk more proud of heart! I deem that with proud purpose, not in the ways of banished men, nay, in greatness of heart you are come seeking Hrothgar.' To him then, strong and bold, the proud prince of the Weder-Geats replied, these words he spake in answer, stern beneath his helm: 'We are companions of Hygelac's board; Beowulf is my name.'

The text of C as typed was identical with (b) except that the words 'with grey' were omitted, obviously a mere oversight (Old English *æscholt ufan græg*), and I typed 'with greatness' in error for 'in greatness'.

(c) The text of C as emended (the further changes are underlined)

> Weary of the sea they set their tall shields, bucklers won-drous hard, against the wall of the house, and sat then on the bench. Corslets rang, war-harness of men. Their spears <u>stood</u> piled together, seamen's gear, <u>ash-hafted</u>, <u>grey-tipped with steel</u>. Well furnished with weapons was the iron-mailed company. There then a knight in proud array asked those men of battle concerning their lineage: 'Whence bear ye your <u>plated</u> shields, your grey shirts of mail, your <u>masked</u> helms and throng of warlike <u>shafts</u>? I am Hrothgar's herald and <u>servant</u>. Never have I seen so many men of <u>outland</u> folk more proud of <u>bearing</u>! I deem that <u>in pride</u>, not in the ways of banished men, nay, with greatness of heart you <u>have</u> come seeking Hrothgar!' To him then, strong and bold, the proud prince of the <u>Windloving folk</u> replied, words he spake in answer, stern beneath his helm: 'We are companions of Hygelac's <u>table</u>; Beowulf is my name.'

It will be seen that among these revisions 'grey-tipped with steel', 'in pride' for 'with proud purpose', and 'table' for 'board' return the text to B(i) before emendation. The only differences in this text from the passage as printed in this book occur in line 275: 'in greatness' restores the correct

6

reading (see above), and 'ye have come' is my correction of my father's obvious slip 'you have come' (cf. 315–20).

There seem to be two superficially simple explanations of the relationship between the two very different texts B(i) and B(ii) that are conjoined so neatly, with the first words of a sentence on the last page of the typescript and the rest of it on the first page of the manuscript. Thus it could be supposed that the typescript B(i) was immediately continued in the manuscript B(ii) for some external cause or other (e.g. the typewriter had to be repaired); or else that the manuscript was the primary text and that it was in the course of being overtaken by the typescript when the typewriter was for whatever reason withdrawn. On this supposition the putative manuscript up to the point where it now begins was lost or destroyed.

The latter seems much the less probable of the two; but I doubt that the first explanation is correct either. The manner of composition of the two texts is very different. The typescript B(i), before heavy subsequent correction, was a finished text (even if regarded at the time of its making as provisional), whereas the manuscript B(ii) gives a strong impression of being a work still in progress, with corrections made in the act of writing, and marginal notes which may leave one in doubt whether the reading is intended as a replacement or a possibility to be considered.

On the whole I am inclined to think that the relationship cannot be unravelled on the basis of the material that has survived, but in any case it is clear that it was the unhappy state of B(i) and the abundant corrections of both texts that explains why – many years after he had said that his prose translation of *Beowulf* was completed – my father invited me to make a new typescript text of the whole.

*

Abandoning his fragmentary work on a fully alliterative translation of *Beowulf*, imitating the regularities of the old poetry, my father, as it seems to me, determined to make a translation as close as he could to the exact meaning in detail of the Old English poem, far closer than could ever be attained by translation into 'alliterative verse', but nonetheless with some suggestion of the rhythm of the original.

Of Old English verse he wrote: 'In essence it is made by taking the half-dozen commonest and most compact phrase-patterns of the ordinary language that have two main elements or stresses. Two of these [phrase-patterns], usually different, are balanced against one another to make a full line.' I have found nowhere among his papers any reference to the rhythmical aspect of his prose translation of *Beowulf*, nor indeed to any other aspect, but it seems to me that he designedly wrote quite largely in rhythms founded on 'common and compact prose-patterns of ordinary language', with no trace of alliteration, and without the prescription of specific patterns.

> upon the morrow they lay upon the shore in the flotsam of the waves, wounded with sword-thrusts, by blades done to death, so that never thereafter might they about the steep straits molest the passage of seafaring men.   (459–63)

8

In care and sorrow he sees in his son's dwelling the hall of feasting, the resting places swept by the wind robbed of laughter – the riders sleep, mighty men gone down into the dark; there is no sound of harp, no mirth in those courts, such as once there were. Then he goes back unto his couch, alone for the one beloved he sings a lay of sorrow: all too wide and void did seem to him those fields and dwelling places. (2064–70)

It is interesting to compare his translation into alliterative verse of the description in *Beowulf*, lines 210–24, of the voyage of Beowulf and his companions to Denmark (given in the section 'On Metre' in his *Prefatory Remarks* to the translation by J.R. Clark Hall, revised by C.L. Wrenn, 1940), with the prose translation in this book, lines 171–82.

> Time passed away.   On the tide floated
> under bank their boat.   In her bows mounted
> brave men blithely.   Breakers turning
> spurned the shingle.   Splendid armour
> they bore aboard,   in her bosom piling
> well-forged weapons,   then away thrust her
> to voyage gladly   valiant-timbered.
> She went then over wave-tops,   wind pursued her,
> fleet, foam-throated,   like a flying bird;
> and her curving prow   on its course waded,
> till in due season   on the day after
> those seafarers   saw before them

shore-cliffs shimmering   and sheer mountains,
wide capes by the waves;   to water's end
the ship had journeyed.

Time passed on. Afloat upon the waves was the boat beneath the cliffs. Eagerly the warriors mounted the prow, and the streaming seas swirled upon the sand. Men-at arms bore to the bosom of the ship their bright harness, their cunning gear of war; they then, men on a glad voyage, thrust her forth with her well-joined timbers. Over the waves of the deep she went sped by the wind, sailing with foam at throat most like unto a bird, until in due hour upon the second day her curving beak had made such way that those sailors saw the land, the cliffs beside the ocean gleaming, and sheer headlands and capes thrust far to sea. Then for that sailing ship the journey was at an end.

This rhythm, so to call it, can be perceived throughout. It is a quality of the prose, by no means inviting analysis, but sufficiently pervasive to give a marked and characteristic tone to the whole work. And this rhythmic character will be found to account for such features of the diction as the ending -*ed* being in some cases written -*éd*, to provide an extra syllable, as 'renowned' 753, 833, but 'renownéd' 649, 704, or 'prized' 1712, but 'prizéd' 1721, and similarly often elsewhere; or the use of 'unto' for 'to' in such cases as 'a thousand knights will I bring <u>to</u> thee, mighty men <u>unto</u> thy aid' 1534–5. Verbal endings -*s* and archaic -*eth* can be seen varying for rhythmical reasons, very notably in the passage 1452–76; inversion of word-order can often be similarly explained, and choice of word scarcely noticeable (as 'helmet' for the more usual 'helm' 839). Many of the corrections to the typescript 'C' were of this nature.

*

From what I have said earlier it can be seen that the text of the translation given in this book has been based throughout on the latest readings of the author, represented by the typescript C as corrected by him; and as I have already mentioned many features are amplified in the section *Notes on the text* following the translation (pp. 107 ff.), which in turn is linked to discussions in the commentary.

My guiding principle has been to introduce no readings that are not actually present in one of the texts B(i), B(ii), and C, except in one or two obvious cases that are recorded in the *Notes on the text of the translation*.

In the matter of proper names my father was inconsistent and sometimes found it difficult to decide between several possibilities – a notable example is *Weder-Geatas*, on which see the note to lines 182–3 in the *Notes on the text*. On the spelling of Old English names see the end of the introductory note to the commentary, p. 135.

I should mention here that I have not altered any archaic usages, letting for instance the once common form *corse* stand, for modern *corpse*.

*

BEOWULF

Lo! the glory of the kings of the people of the Spear-Danes in days of old we have heard tell, how those princes did deeds of valour. Oft Scyld Scefing robbed the hosts of foemen, many peoples, of the seats where they drank their mead, laid
5 fear upon men, he who first was found forlorn; comfort for that he lived to know, mighty grew under heaven, throve in honour, until all that dwelt nigh about, over the sea where the whale rides, must hearken to him and yield him tribute – a good king was he!
10 To him was an heir afterwards born, a young child in his courts whom God sent for the comfort of the people: perceiving the dire need which they long while endured aforetime being without a prince. To him therefore the Lord of Life who rules in glory granted honour among men: Beow
15 was renowned – far and wide his glory sprang – the heir of Scyld in Scedeland. Thus doth a young man bring it to pass with good deed and gallant gifts, while he dwells in his father's bosom, that after in his age there cleave to him loyal knights of his table, and the people stand by him when war
20 comes. By worthy deeds in every folk is a man ennobled.

Then at his allotted hour Scyld the valiant passed into the keeping of the Lord; and to the flowing sea his dear comrades bore him, even as he himself had bidden them, while yet, their prince, he ruled the Scyldings with his words: beloved

25 lord of the land, long was he master. There at the haven stood with ringéd prow, ice-hung, eager to be gone, the prince's bark; they laid then their beloved king, giver of rings, in the bosom of the ship, in glory by the mast. There were many precious things and treasures brought from regions far away;

30 nor have I heard tell that men ever in more seemly wise arrayed a boat with weapons of war and harness of battle; on his lap lay treasures heaped that now must go with him far into the dominion of the sea. With lesser gifts no whit did they adorn him, with treasures of that people, than did those

35 that in the beginning sent him forth alone over the waves, a little child. Moreover, high above his head they set a golden standard and gave him to Ocean, let the sea bear him. Sad was their heart and mourning in their soul. None can report with truth, nor lords in their halls, nor mighty men beneath the

40 sky, who received that load.

Then in the strongholds long was Beow of the Scyldings, beloved king of men, renowned among peoples – elsewhere had the prince his father departed from his home – until thereafter he begat Healfdene the high, who held the lord-

45 ship while he lived, aged and fierce in war, over the fair Scyldings. To him were children four born in the world, in order named: captains of the hosts, Heorogar, and Hrothgar, and Halga the good; and [a daughter] I have heard that was Onela's queen, dear consort of the warrior Scylfing.

50   Thereafter was fortune in war vouchsafed to Hrothgar, and glory in battle, that the vassals of his own kindred hearkened willingly unto him and the numbers of his young warriors grew to a mighty company of men. Then it came into his heart that he would command men to fashion a hall and a
55   mansion, a mightier house for their mead-drinking than the children of men had ever known, and there-within would he apportion all things to young and old such as God had granted him, save the people's land and the lives of men.

    Then have I heard that far and wide to many a kindred
60   on this middle-earth was that work proclaimed, the adorning of that dwelling of men. In a while, swiftly among men, it came to pass for him that it was all made ready, the greatest of houses and of halls. For it he devised the name of Heorot, even he whose word far and wide was law. His vow he belied
65   not: the rings he dealt and treasure at the feast. The hall towered high with hornéd gables wide, awaiting the warring billows of destroying fire: the time was not far off that between father and daughter's spouse murderous hate in memory of a deadly feud should awake again.

70   Then the fierce spirit that abode in darkness grievously endured a time of torment, in that day after day he heard the din of revelry echoing in the hall. There was the sound of harp and the clear singing of the minstrel; there spake he that had knowledge to unfold from far-off days the first begin-
75   ning of men, telling how the Almighty wrought the earth, a vale of bright loveliness that the waters encircle; how triumphant He set the radiance of the sun and moon as a light

for the dwellers in the lands, and adorned the regions of the world with boughs and with leaves, life too he devised for

80 every kind that moves and lives.

Even thus did the men of that company live in mirth and happiness, until one began to work deeds of wrong, a fiend of hell. Grendel was that grim creature called, the ill-famed haunter of the marches of the land, who kept the moors, the

85 fastness of the fens, and, unhappy one, inhabited long while the troll-kind's home; for the Maker had proscribed him with the race of Cain. That bloodshed, for that Cain slew Abel, the Eternal Lord avenged: no joy had he of that violent deed, but God drove him for that crime far from mankind. Of him all

90 evil broods were born, ogres and goblins and haunting shapes of hell, and the giants too, that long time warred with God – for that he gave them their reward.

Then went Grendel forth when night was come to spy on that lofty house, to see how the Ring-Danes after the ale-

95 drinking had ordered their abode in it; and he found therein a lordly company after their feasting sleeping, sorrow they knew not, the unhappy fate of men. That accursèd thing, ravenous and grim, swift was ready; thirty knights he seized upon their couch. Thence back he got him gloating over his prey,

100 faring homeward with his glut of murder to seek his lairs.

Thereafter at dawn with the first light of day was Grendel's strength in battle made plain to men; then was weeping after feasting upraised, a mighty cry at morn. The glorious king, their prince proven of old, joyless sat: his stout and valiant

105 heart suffered and endured sorrow for his knights, when men had scanned the footprints of that foe, that demon cursed;

too bitter was that strife, too dire and weary to endure! Nor
was it longer space than but one night ere he wrought again
cruel murders more, and grieved not for them, his deeds of
110 enmity and wrong – too deep was he therein. Thereafter not
far to seek was the man who elsewhere more remote sought
him his couch and a bed among the lesser chambers, since
now was manifested and declared thus truly to him with
token plain the hatred of that hall-keeper; thereafter he who
115 escaped the foe kept him more distant and more safe.

Even thus did one lord it and against right make war, alone
against them all, until empty stood that best of houses. Long
was the while; twelve winters' space the Scyldings' dear lord
endured anguish and every woe and sorrow deep. So it was
120 made known to men and revealed to the children of mankind
sadly in songs that Grendel strove a while with Hrothgar,
wrought hate and malice, evil deeds and enmity, for many
a year, a strife unceasing; truce would he not have with any
man of the Danish host, nor would withhold his deadly cru-
125 elty, nor accept terms of payment; and there no cause had any
of the counsellors to look for golden recompense from the
slayer's hands; nay, the fierce killer pursued them still, both
knights and young, a dark shadow of death, lurking, lying in
wait, in long night keeping the misty moors: men know not
130 whither sorcerers of hell in their wanderings roam.

Thus many a deed of evil that foe of men stalking dread-
fully alone did often work, many a grievous outrage; in
Heorot's hall bright with gems in the dark nights he dwelt.
(Never might he approach the precious Throne of grace in
135 the presence of God, nor did he know His will). That was

great torment to the Scyldings' lord, anguish of heart. Many a mighty one sat oft communing, counsel they took what it were best for stouthearted men to do against these dire terrors. At times they vowed sacrifices to idols in their heathen
140 tabernacles, in prayers implored the slayer of souls to afford them help against the sufferings of the people. Such was their wont, the hope of heathens; they were mindful in their hearts of hell, (nor knew they the Creator, the Judge of deeds, nor had heard of the Lord God, nor verily had learned to praise
145 the Guardian of the heavens and the King of glory. Woe shall be to him that through fiendish malice shall thrust down his soul into the fire's embrace, to look for no comfort, in no wise to change his lot! Blessed shall be he that may after his death-day go unto the lord and seek peace in the bosom of
150 the Father!)

Even thus over the sorrows of that time did the son of Healfdene brood unceasingly, nor could that wise prince put aside his grief; too strong was that strife, too dire and weary to endure, that had come upon that folk, torment fierce and
155 cruel that they needs must bear, the greatest of miseries that came by night.

Of this, of Grendel's deeds, the knight of Hygelac, esteemed among the Geats, heard in his home afar; in that day of man's life here in might the strongest of mankind was
160 he, noble and of stature beyond man's measure. He bade men prepare for him a good craft upon the waves, saying that over the waters where the swan rides he would seek the warrior-king, that prince renowned, since he had need of men. With

165 that voyage little fault did wise men find, dear though he
were to them; they encouraged his valiant heart, and they
observed the omens.

Champions of the people of the Geats that good man had
chosen from the boldest that he could find, and fifteen in
all they sought now their timbered ship, while that warrior,
170 skilled in the ways of the sea, led them to the margins of the
land. Time passed on. Afloat upon the waves was the boat
beneath the cliffs. Eagerly the warriors mounted the prow,
and the streaming seas swirled upon the sand. Men-at-arms
bore to the bosom of the ship their bright harness, their cun-
175 ning gear of war; they then, men on a glad voyage, thrust her
forth with her well-joined timbers. Over the waves of the
deep she went sped by the wind, sailing with foam at throat
most like unto a bird, until in due hour upon the second day
her curving beak had made such way that those sailors saw
180 the land, the cliffs beside the ocean gleaming, and sheer head-
lands and capes thrust far to sea. Then for that sailing ship the
journey was at an end. Thence the men of the Windloving
folk climbed swiftly up upon the beach, and made fast the
sea-borne timbers of their ship; their mail-shirts they shook,
185 their raiment of war. They gave thanks to God that the pas-
sage of the waves had been made easy for them.

Then from the high shore the watchman of the Scyldings,
who of duty guarded the cliffs by the sea, saw them bearing
over the gangway bright shields and gallant harness; anxiety
190 smote him in his heart to learn what these men might be.
He went then to the strand riding on his horse, Hrothgar's
knight, and mightily he brandished in his hands his stout

spear-shaft, and in words of parley he asked: 'What warriors are ye, clad in corslets, that have come thus steering your tall ship over the streets of the sea, hither over deep waters? Lo! I long while have dwelt at the ends of the land, keeping watch over the water, that in the land of the Danes no foeman might come harrying with raiding fleet. Never have armed men more openly here essayed to land, knowing not at all the pass-word of men in array of war, nor having the consent of kinsmen. Never have I seen on earth a greater among men than is one of you, a warrior in arms; no hall-servant is he in brave show of weapons, if his fair countenance lie not and his peerless mien. Now must I learn of what people you are sprung, rather than ye should pass on hence, false spies, into the land of the Danes. Come now, ye dwellers afar, voyagers of the sea, hear my thought plainly spoken: in haste it is best that ye declare whence your ways have led!'

To him then the chief made answer, the leader of the company, opened his store of words: 'We are by race men of the Geats and hearth-comrades of Hygelac. Famed among peoples was my father, a noble warrior in the forefront of battle; Ecgtheow was he called. Many a winter he endured ere in age he departed from his courts; full well doth every wise man remember him far and wide over the earth. With friendly purpose are we now come seeking thy master, the son of Healfdene, defender of his people. Be thou kindly in counsel to us! A mighty errand have we to him renowned, the lord of the Danes; and there a certain matter shall not be kept secret, as I think. Thou knowest if so it be, as in truth we have heard tell, that among the Scyldings I know not what

deadly thing, a doer of deeds of secret hatred, on dark nights
in dreadful wise makes plain his monstrous malice, shame of
men, and felling of the dead. Concerning that with ungrudg-
225   ing heart I can give counsel to Hrothgar how he, wise and
good, will overcome his enemy – should there ever come
change or betterment in the torment of his woes – how those
burning griefs will be assuaged; or else for ever after he will
endure a time of tribulation and dire need, while there in its
230   high place abides the best of houses.'

The watchman spake, sitting there upon his steed, fear-
less servant of the king: 'A man of keen wit who takes good
heed will discern the truth in both words and deeds: my ears
assure me that here is a company of friendly mind towards
235   the Lord of the Scyldings. Go ye forward bearing your weap-
ons and your armour! I will guide you! My young esquires,
moreover, I will command honourably to guard your ship,
your new-tarred vessel upon the sand, against every foe,
until with its timbers and its wreathéd prow it bears back
240   again over the streams of the sea its beloved master to the
Weather-mark. To such a doer of good deeds it shall surely
be granted that he will come sound and whole through this
onset of war!'

They went then marching forth. Their fleet vessel
245   remained now still, deep-bosomed ship it rode upon its
hawser fast to the anchor. Figures of the boar shone above
cheek-guards, adorned with gold, glittering, fire-tempered;
fierce and challenging war-mask kept guard over life. The
men hastened striding together until they could descry the
250   builded hall adorned bright with gold, foremost it was in

fame of all houses under heaven among the dwellers upon
earth, wherein the mighty one abode; the light of it shone
over many a land. Then that warrior bold pointed out to
them, clear to see, the court of proud men, that they might
255 march straight thither.

Then that warrior turned his horse, and thereupon spake
these words: 'Time it is for me to go. May the Almighty
Father in his grace keep you safe upon your quests! To the
sea will I go, against unfriendly hosts my watch to keep.'

260 The street was paved in stone patterns; the path guided
those men together. There shone corslet of war, hard, hand-
linked, bright ring of iron rang in their harness, as in their
dread gear they went striding straight unto the hall. Weary
of the sea they set their tall shields, bucklers wondrous hard,
265 against the wall of the house, and sat then on the bench.
Corslets rang, war-harness of men. Their spears stood piled
together, seamen's gear, ash-hafted, grey-tipped with steel.
Well furnished with weapons was the iron-mailed company.
There then a knight in proud array asked those men of battle
270 concerning their lineage: 'Whence bear ye your plated shields,
your grey shirts of mail, your masked helms and throng of
warlike shafts? I am Hrothgar's herald and servant. Never
have I seen so many men of outland folk more proud of bear-
ing! I deem that in pride, not in the ways of banished men,
275 nay, in greatness of heart ye have come seeking Hrothgar!'

To him then, strong and bold, the proud prince of the
Windloving folk replied, words he spake in answer, stern
beneath his helm: 'We are companions of Hygelac's table;

22

Beowulf is my name. To the son of Healfdene, glorious king,
280 I wish to tell mine errand, to thy lord, if he will vouchsafe
to us that we may approach him in his excellence.' Wulfgar
spake – noble prince of the Wendels was he, his heart's
temper, his prowess and wisdom, were known to many a
man: 'This will I enquire of the Friend of the Danes, lord of
285 the Scyldings, giver of rings, concerning thy quest, even as
thou prayest, and such answer quickly declare to thee as he
in his goodness is minded to give.'

Then swiftly he returned to where Hrothgar sat, old and
hoar-headed, amid his company of knights; valiant he strode
290 until he stood by the shoulder of the lord of the Danes, well
he knew the customs of courtly men. Wulfgar spake to his
beloved lord: 'Here are now landed, come from afar over the
encircling sea, noble men of the Geats; the chiefest of them
men of arms name Beowulf. They beg to exchange words with
295 thee, my king. Do not make denial to them of thy fair answer,
O gracious Hrothgar! In their harness of war they seem well
to merit the esteem of men; assuredly a man of worth is the
captain, who hath led these men of battle to this land.'

Hrothgar spake, protector of the Scyldings: 'I knew him
300 while he was yet a boy. His sire of old was called Ecgtheow;
to him Hrethel of the Geats gave as bride his only daughter;
it is his son that has now here come dauntless seeking a friend
and patron. Voyagers by sea, such as have borne gifts and
treasures for the Geats thither in token of good will, have
305 since reported that he hath in the grasp of his hand the might
and power of thirty men, valiant in battle. Holy God hath
sent him to us in his mercy, even to the West Danes, as is

23

my hope, against the terror of Grendel. To this good knight
I shall offer precious gifts to reward the valour of his heart.
310 Make haste now! Bid them enter here and look upon the
proud company of our kin here gathered together; tell them
too in words of greeting that they are welcome to the people
of the Danes!'

[Then Wulfgar went toward the door of the hall, and]
315 standing within he pronounced these words: 'My victori-
ous lord, chieftain of the East Danes bade me say to you
that he knows your lineage, and that with your dauntless
hearts ye come as welcome guests to him over the surges of
the sea. Now may ye go in your harness of battle beneath
320 your masked helms to look upon Hrothgar. Leave here your
warlike shields and deadly shafted spears to await the issue
of your words.' Then that lordly man arose, and about him
many a warrior, a valiant company of knights. Some remained
behind guarding their gear of war, even as the bold captain
325 commanded. They went with speed together, the knight guid-
ing them, beneath the roof of Heorot. Stern beneath his helm
[strode Beowulf] until he stood beside the hearth. Words he
spake – his mail gleamed upon him, woven like stuff in crafty
web by the cunning of smiths: 'Hail to thee, Hrothgar! I am
330 Hygelac's kinsman and vassal; on many a renownéd deed I
ventured in my youth. To me on my native soil the matter of
Grendel became known and revealed; travellers upon the sea
report that this hall, fairest of houses, stands empty and to
all men useless, as soon as the light of evening is hid beneath
335 heaven's pale. Thereupon the worthiest of my people and
wise men counselled me to come to thee, King Hrothgar; for

they had learned the power of my body's strength; they had themselves observed it, when I returned from the toils of my foes, earning their enmity, where five I bound, making deso-
340 late the race of monsters, and when I slew amid the waves by night the water-demons, enduring bitter need, avenging the afflictions of the windloving Geats, destroying those hostile things – woe they had asked for. And now I shall with Grendel, with that fierce slayer, hold debate alone with the
345 ogre. Now therefore will I ask of thee, prince of the glorious Danes, defender of the Scyldings, this one boon, that thou deny not to me, O protector of warriors, fair lord of peoples, since I have come from so far away, that only I may, and my proud company of men, this dauntless company, make
350 Heorot clean. I have learned, too, that this fierce slayer in his savagery to weapons gives no heed. I too then will disdain (so love me Hygelac, my liege lord!) to bear either sword, or wide shield, yellow-bossed, to battle, nay, with my gripe I shall seize upon the foe, and engage in mortal contest with
355 hate against hate – there to the judgement of the Lord shall he resign himself whom death doth take. Methinks he will, if he is permitted to have the mastery, in this hall of battle devour without fear the Gothic knights, the strong band of Hrethmen, as he oft hath done. No need wilt thou have in
360 burial to shroud my head, but he will hold me reddened with gore, if death takes me; a bloody corse will bear, will think to taste it, and departing alone will eat unpitying, staining the hollows of the moors. No need wilt thou have any longer to care for my body's sustenance! Send back to Hygelac, should
365 battle take me, the mail-shirt most excellent that defends my

breast, fairest of raiment. Hrethel bequeathed it, the work of Wayland. Fate goeth ever as she must!'

Hrothgar made answer, protector of the Scyldings: 'My friend Beowulf, for my deserts and for the grace that once
370 I showed thou hast now come to us. Thy father with the sword ended one of the greatest feuds: Heatholaf with his own hands he slew among the Wylfings. Then the kindred of the Wederas could no longer keep him for the dread of war. Thence he sought the South-Danish folk over the surges
375 of the sea, even the glorious Scyldings, when first I ruled the people of the Danes and in youth governed a spacious realm, treasury and stronghold of mighty men. Heorogar was then dead, mine elder brother, no longer lived the son of Healfdene; better was he than I! Thereafter that feud I settled
380 with payment, sending [to the Wylfings] over the backs of the sea ancient treasures; oaths he swore to me. Grievous to my heart is it to recount to any among men what humiliations in Heorot, what dreadful deeds of malice Grendel hath wrought for me in the hatred of his heart. Diminished is the
385 company of my hall, the ranks of my warriors; Fate hath swept them into the dire clutch of Grendel. God (alone) may easily hinder from his deeds that savage foe! Full often have champions of war flushed with drink over the goblets of ale made vaunt that in the drinking hall they would meet
390 the warlike might of Grendel with the terror of their blades. Thereafter was this mead-hall, my royal house, on the morrow-tide red with dripping blood when day shone forth, all the bench-boards drenched with blood and the hall with dew of swords. The fewer loyal hearts and bold men tried

395 in war had I, for death had taken them. Sit now at the feast, and when the time comes turn thy thought to victory for the Hrethmen, as thy heart may urge thee.'

Then for the young Geatish knights together in company a bench was made free in the drinking hall; there to their seats 400 went those stout of heart resplendent in their strength. An esquire his office heeded, he that bore in hand the jewelled ale-goblet and poured gleaming out the sweet drink. Ever and anon the minstrel sang clear in Heorot. There was mirth of mighty men, no little assembly of the tried valour of Danes 405 and Wederas.

Unferth spake, son of Ecglaf, who sat at the feet of the lord of the Scyldings, a spell to bring forth strife he loosed – the quest of Beowulf come thus boldly over the sea gave to him great displeasure, for it was not to his liking that 410 any other man in this world below should ever accomplish more honour under heaven than he himself: 'Art thou that Beowulf who strove with Breca in swimming upon the wide sea, that time when ye two in pride made trial of the waters and for a rash vaunt hazarded your lives upon the deep? No 415 man, friend nor foe, could dissuade you two from that venture fraught with woe, when with limbs ye rowed the sea. There ye embraced with your arms the streaming tide, measuring out the streets of the sea with swift play of hands, gliding over the ocean. The abyss was in tumult with the waves and 420 the surges of the winter. Seven nights ye two laboured in the waters' realm. He overmatched thee in swimming, he had greater strength! Then on the morrow-tide the billows

bore him up away to the Heathoreamas' land; whence he,
beloved of his people, sought his own dear soil, the land of
425 the Brandings and his fair stronghold, where a folk he ruled,
his strong town and his rings. All his vaunt truly did he, the
son of Beanstan, accomplish against thee. Wherefore I expect
for thee a yet worse encounter, though thou mayest in every
place have proved valiant in the rush of battle and grim war,
430 if thou darest all the nightlong hour nigh at hand to wait for
Grendel.'

Beowulf spake, the son of Ecgtheow: 'Lo! my friend
Unferth, flushed with drink thou hast spent much speech,
telling of Breca and his feat! Truth I account it that greater
435 prowess in the sea had I, more labour in the waves than any
other man. We two agreed, being boys, and made our vaunt,
being yet both in the youth of life, that we would hazard our
lives out upon the ocean; and that we accomplished even so.
Naked we held our swords, hard in our hands, when we two
440 rowed the sea; we thought thus to defend us against mon-
strous fish. Never at all could he swim away from me afar
upon the streaming waves, more swift than I upon the deep;
from him I would not go. Then we two were together in the
sea five nights' space, until the tide drove us asunder, and
445 the boiling waters. The coldest of storms, glooming night,
a wind from the north came with cruel onslaught against
us; rough were the waves. The hearts of the fishes of the sea
were stirred, and there the corslet on my flesh, links stoutly
wrought by hand, gave me aid against my foes; my woven
450 raiment of battle lapped my breast adorned with gold. To the
abyss drew me a destroying foe accurséd, fast the grim thing

held me in its gripe. Nonetheless, it was granted to me to find
that fell slayer with point of warlike sword; the battle's onset
destroyed that strong beast of the sea through this my hand.
455   Thus many a time deadly assailants menaced me grievously.
With my beloved sword I ministered to them, as it was meet.
In no wise had they joy in that banqueting, foul doers of ill
deeds, that they should devour me sitting round in feast nigh
to the bottoms of the sea; nay, upon the morrow they lay
460   upon the shore in the flotsam of the waves, wounded with
sword-thrusts, by blades done to death, so that never there-
after might they about the steep straits molest the passage
of seafaring men. Light came from the East, God's beacon
bright; the waves were lulled, so that I could descry the
465   headlands out to sea and windy cliffs. Fate oft saveth a man
not doomed to die, when his valour fails not. Howbeit it was
my lot with sword to slay nine sea-demons. Never have I
heard beneath the vault of heaven of more bitter fighting by
night, nor of a man more unhappy in the torrents of the sea,
470   and nonetheless from the grappling of accurséd creatures my
life I saved weary of my venture. Then the sea, the tide upon
the flood, with boiling waters swept me away to the land of
the Finns. Never have I heard men tell of thee any such cruel
deeds of war and dreadful work of swords. Breca never yet
475   in the play of battle, nay, neither of you twain, hath accom-
plished so daring a deed with blood-stained blades – yet little
do I glory in it – not though thou wert the slayer of thine own
brethren, thy nearest kin. For that thou shalt in Hell suffer
damnation, though thy wit be good. I tell thee for a truth, son
480   of Ecglaf, that never would Grendel have achieved so many

a deed of horror, fierce slayer and dire, in thy lord's despite, humbling him in Heorot, if they heart and soul were thus fell in war as thou thyself accountest. Nay, he hath found that he need not greatly dread avenging wrath nor dire pursuit of swords from your people of the conquering Scyldings! Forced toll he levies, none he spares of the folk of the Danes, but followeth his lust, slays and ravishes, for no vengeance looking from the Spear-Danes. But I shall now ere long in battle oppose to him the might and valour of the Geats. He will return who may, triumphant to the mead, when the light of the morning on the following day, the sun in skiey robes, shines from the south over the children of men!'

Then in joyful hour was the giver of rich gifts, greyhaired, bold in battle; prince of the glorious Danes he believed that succour was at hand. Shepherd of his people he had discerned in Beowulf's words the moveless purpose of his mind.

There was laughter of mighty men, the din of singing; sweet were the words. Wealhtheow went forth, Hrothgar's queen, mindful of courtesy; with gold adorned she greeted the men in the hall, and then the cup she offered, noble lady, first to the guardian of the East Danes' realm, and wished him joy at the ale-quaffing and his lieges' love. He, king victorious, in delight partook of feast and flowing bowl. Then the lady of the Helmings went to and fro to every part of that host, to tried men and young proffering the jewelled vessels, until in due time it chanced that she, ring-laden queen of courteous heart, to Beowulf bore the cup of mead, and hailed the Geatish knight, and gave thanks to God in words of wisdom that her desire was granted to her that she might

510 trust in any man for comfort in their miseries. That cup
he then received, grim warrior at Wealhtheow's hand, and
thereupon, his heart being kindled with desire of battle, fair
words he said. Thus Beowulf, son of Ecgtheow, spake: 'This
did I purpose when I went up upon the sea and sat me in my
515 sea-boat amid my company of knights, that I wholly would
accomplish the desire of your people or would fall among
the slain fast in the clutches of the foe. A deed of knightly
valour I shall achieve, or else in this mead-hall await my latest
day!' These words well pleased that lady, the proud utterance
520 of the Geat; with gold adorned she went, fair queen of the
people, to her seat beside her lord.

Then again as before were valiant words spoken within
the hall, the host was in joyful hour, there was clamour of
folk triumphant, until on a sudden the son of Healfdene
525 desired to seek his nightly couch. He knew that onslaught
against that lofty hall had been purposed in the demon's
heart from the hours when they could see the light of the sun
until darkling night and the shapes of mantling shadow came
gliding over the world, dark beneath the clouds. All the host
530 arose. Then man saluted man, Hrothgar and Beowulf; all hail
the king him wished, giving to him the keeping of his house
of wine, and this word he spake: 'Never have I ere this, since
I could lift hand and shield, to any other man save thee here
and now entrusted the mighty dwelling of the Danes. Have
535 it now and hold it, fairest of houses! Remember thy renown,
show forth thy might and valour, keep watch against our
foes! No lack shall there be to thee of thy desires, if thou dost
achieve this deed of valour and yet live.'

Then Hrothgar departed, defender of the Scyldings, with
540 his company of knights forth from the hall ; their warrior
lord would follow Wealhtheow his queen as the companion
of his couch. The King of Glory, as men now heard, had
appointed one to guard the hall against Grendel; now a special
office he held in the service of the Danes, having taken on
545 himself a watch against monstrous things. Verily the Geatish
knight trusted confidently in his valiant strength, God's
grace to him. Then his corslet of iron things he doffed, and
the helm from his head, and gave his jewelled sword, best of
iron-wrought things, to his esquire, and bade him have care
550 of his gear of battle. Then the brave man spake, Beowulf of
the Geats, a speech of proud words, ere he climbed upon his
bed: 'No whit do I account myself in my warlike stature a
man more despicable in deeds of battle than Grendel doth
himself. Therefore I will not with sword give him the sleep
555 of death, although I well could. Nought doth he know of
gentle arms that he should wield weapon against me or hew
my shield, fierce though he be in savage deeds. Nay, we two
shall this night reject the blade, if he dare have recourse to
warfare without weapons, and then let the foreseeing God,
560 the Holy Lord, adjudge the glory to whichever side him
seemeth meet.'
Then he laid him down, that valiant man, and his face was
buried in the pillow at his cheek; and about him many a gal-
lant rover was stretched upon his couch within the hall. None
565 of them believed that he would ever return to the sweetness
of his home, to the strong places of the free people where he
was nurtured. Nay, they had learned that a bloody death had

ere now in that hall of wine swept away all too many of the
Danish folk. Yet God granted them a victorious fortune in
570   battle, even to those Geatish warriors, yea succour and aid,
that they, through the prowess of one and through his single
might, overcame their enemy. Manifest is this truth, that
mighty God hath ruled the race of men through all the ages.

There came, in darkling night passing, a shadow walk-
575   ing. The spearmen slept whose duty was to guard the gabled
hall. All except one. Well-known it was to men that, if God
willed it not, the robber-fiend no power had to drag them to
the shades; but he there wakeful in his foe's despite abode
grimhearted the debate of war.

580   He came now from the moor under misty fells, Grendel
walking. The wrath of God was on him. Foul thief, he pur-
posed of the race of men someone to snare within that lofty
hall. Under cloud he went to where he knew full well that
house of wine was, hall of men with gold bright-plated.
585   Not the first adventure that, that he had made, seeking for
Hrothgar's home. Never in days of life before nor later with
harder fortune guards in hall he found.

He came now to the house, a man-shape journeying of
men's mirth shorn. The door at once sprang back, barred
590   with forgéd iron, when claws he laid on it. He wrenched then
wide, baleful with raging heart, the gaping entrance of the
house; then swift on the bright-patterned floor the demon
paced. In angry mood he went, and from his eyes stood forth
most like to flame unholy light. He in the house espied there
595   many a man asleep, a throng of kinsmen side by side, a band
of youthful knights. Then his heart laughed. He thought that

33

he would sever, ere daylight came, dread slayer, for each
one of these life from their flesh, since now such hope had
chanced of feasting full. It was no longer doomed that he yet
600   more might of the race of men devour beyond that night.

There stern and strong the kinsman of Hygelac watched
how that foul thief with his fell clutches would now play his
part. And that the slayer was not minded to delay, not he,
but swiftly at the first turn seized a sleeping man, rending
605   him unopposed, biting the bone-joints, drinking blood from
veins, great gobbets gorging down. Quickly he took all of
that lifeless thing to be his food, even feet and hands.

Onward and nearer he stepped, seized then with hand the
valiant-hearted man upon his bed. Against him the demon
610   stretched his claw; and swiftly he laid hold on it, and with hate
in heart he propped him on his arm. Straightway that master of
evil deeds perceived that never had he met within this world in
earth's four corners on any other man a mightier gripe of hand.
In heart and soul he grew afraid, yet none the sooner could
615   escape. His desire would haste away, he would to hiding flee,
seeking the devils' throng. Not now were his dealings there
such as he ever before in the days of his life had found.

Then the good knight, kinsman of Hygelac, remembered
his words at evening. Upright he stood and grappled fast
620   against him. Fingers cracked. Out would the ogre go. Forth
strode the knight. The accursèd thing would fain, could he
have done so, go free afar and thence flee away to hollows
in the fens. He felt the power of his fingers in his fierce foe's
grasp. It was a woeful journey that the fell robber had to
625   Heorot made!

The royal hall rang. On all the Danes, dwellers in the town about, on each bold heart there fell a ghastly fear. Wroth were they both, fierce rivals in the keeping of the house. The hall was full of noise. Great wonder was it then that that house of

630 wine endured their battling, so that it fell not to the ground, fair dwelling upon earth; but stout was it smithied within and without with bonds of iron cunningly contrived. There, where they fought in wrath, was many a bench adorned with gold for the drinking of mead cast from its place upon the

635 floor, so the tale tells. Never aforetime had the Scyldings' counsellors foreseen that any among men could in any wise shatter it its goodliness adorned with ivory, nor dismember it with craft, unless the embrace of fire should engulf it in swathing smoke. Clamour new arose ever and anon. Dread

640 fear came upon the northern Danes, upon each of those that from the wall heard the cries, the adversary of God singing his ghastly song, no chant of victory, the prisoner of hell bewailing his grievous hurt. Fast was he held by that most strong in body's might in that day of men's life here.

645 In no wise would that captain of men permit that deadly guest to go forth alive, nor did he account the days of his life of use to any man. There many a knight of Beowulf drew swift his ancient blade, wishing to defend the life of his lord and master and renownéd prince, if so he might. They knew

650 it not, young warriors brave-hearted, as they fought that fight, and on each side sought to hew the foe and pierce his vitals: that doer of evil none upon earth of swords of war would touch, not the most excellent of things of iron; not so, for he had laid a spell upon all victorious arms and upon

655 every blade. On that day of this life on earth unhappy was
fated to be the sending forth of his soul, and far was that
alien spirit to fare into the realm of fiends. Now did he per-
ceive who aforetime had wrought the race of men many a
grief of heart and wrong – he had a feud with God – that his
660 body's might would not avail him, but the valiant kinsman
of Hygelac had him by the arm – hateful to each was the
other's life. A grievous hurt of body that fierce slayer and
dire now endured; a mighty wound was seen upon his shoul-
der; the sinews sprang apart, the joints of his bones burst. To
665 Beowulf was vouchsafed triumph in battle; thence now must
Grendel flee stricken to death to hide beneath the slopes of
the fens, seeking his joyless haunts. Thereby the more surely
did he know that the end of his life was come to pass and the
hours of his days were numbered. That deadly contest was
670 over and achieved was the desire of all the Danes; in that hour
had one come from afar, wise and stout of heart, purged the
hall of Hrothgar and redeemed it from the malice of Grendel.
He rejoiced in his deeds that night and in the glory of his
prowess. The chief of those Geatish men had accomplished
675 all his proud vaunt before the East Danes, and had healed,
moreover, all the woe and the tormenting sorrow that they
had erewhile suffered and must of necessity endure, no little
bitterness. Of this a clear token it was when that warrior bold
had set the hand, the arm and shoulder, beneath the wide-
680 spread roof – there was all Grendel's clutching limb entire.

Then have I heard that in the morning many a warlike
knight was gathered about his patron's hall; the chieftains of

the people had come from far and near over the distant ways
that marvel to behold, and the footprints of that hated one.
685 No grief for his departure from life felt any of those men
who looked upon the trail of his inglorious flight, marking
how sick at heart he had dragged his footsteps, bleeding out
his life, from thence away defeated and death-doomed to the
water-demons' mere. There the waters boiled with blood,
690 and the dread turmoil of the waves was all blended with hot
gore, and seethed with battle's crimson. Therein doomed to
die he plunged, and bereft of joys in his retreat amid the fens
yielded up his life and heathen soul; there Hell received him.
Thence the ancient men of the court, and many a young man
695 too, fared back from their joyous journey riding from the
mere upon their steeds in pride, knights upon horses white.
There was the renown of Beowulf recalled; many a man and
oft declared that South or North the Two Seas between was
there no other beneath the encircling sky more excellent
700 among bearers of the shield, more worthy of kingly rule. Yet
verily they did not in any thing belittle their lord and patron,
gracious Hrothgar; nay, a good king was he.

At whiles those warriors bold set their bay horses of
renownéd excellence to gallop and run in rivalry, where the
705 paths over earth seemed good to them. At whiles a servant of
the king, a man laden with proud memories who had lays in
mind and recalled a host and multitude of tales of old – word
followed word, each truly linked to each – this man in his
turn began with skill to treat the quest of Beowulf and in
710 flowing verse to utter his ready tale, interweaving words. He
recounted all that he had heard tell concerning Sigemund's

37

works of prowess, many a strange tale, the arduous deeds of the Wælsing and his adventures far and wide, deeds of vengeance and of enmity, things that the children of men

715 knew not fully, save only Fitela who was with him. In those days he was wont to tell something of such matters, brother to his sister's son, even as they were ever comrades in need in every desperate strait – many and many of the giant race had they laid low with swords. For Sigemund was noised afar

720 after his dying day no little fame, since he, staunch in battle, had slain the serpent, the guardian of the Hoard. Yea, he, the son of noble house, beneath the hoar rock alone had dared a perilous deed. Fitela was not with him; nonetheless it was his fortune that the sword pierced through the serpent of strange

725 shape and stood fixed in the wall, goodly blade of iron; the dragon died a cruel death. The fierce slayer had achieved by his valour that he might at his own will enjoy that hoard of rings; the boat upon the sea he laded and bore to the bosom of his ship the bright treasures, the offspring of Wæls was he.

730 The dragon melted in its heat.

He was far and wide of adventurers the most renowned throughout the people of mankind for his works of prowess, that prince of warriors – thereby did he aforetime grow great – after the valour of Heremod, his might and prowess,

735 had failed, and he, in the land of the Jutes, was betrayed into the power of his enemies and swiftly sent to death. Too long did the surges of sorrow beat upon him; a mortal affliction he became unto his people and to all his nobles; yet in time gone by many a wise man had oft lamented the exile of that

740 stouthearted one, to whom they looked for the cure of their

ills, believing that this son of their king was like to advance
in virtue and inherit the qualities of his father, to keep well
the people, the treasures and the fencéd stronghold and the
realm of his vassals, the land of the Scyldings. But he there
745 now among them, the kinsman of Hygelac, had proved more
pleasing in the eyes of all men and of his friends; on that
other's heart wickedness had seized.

Again at whiles in rivalry upon their steeds they measured
the dusty roads. Now the light of morning was advanced in
750 haste far upon its course. Many a knight of stout heart went
unto that lofty hall to see that marvel strange; so too the king
himself from his bedchamber, guardian of hoards of rings
renowned for his largesse, strode in majesty amid a great
company, and with him the queen with her train of maidens
755 paced the path unto the mead-hall. Hrothgar spake – he was
come to the hall and stood upon the steps and looked upon
the steep roof bright with gold and upon Grendel's hand:
'For this sight be thanks swiftly given to Almighty God.
Much evil and many woes have I endured from Grendel.
760 Ever may God perform marvel upon marvel, Lord of glory!
It was but little while ago that I hoped never in all my life
to find healing of any of my woes, when this best of houses
stood stained with blood and dripping with fresh gore: that
was a grief far-reaching to every one of my counsellors,
765 who hoped not that they ever in the world should defend
this stronghold of the people of the land from the malice of
demons and of devils. Now hath one young man through the
might of the Lord wrought a deed that we none of us with
our wisdom were able to compass. Lo! this may she say, if

39

770 yet she lives, whosoever among women did bring forth this
son among the peoples of earth, that the eternal God was gra-
cious to her in her childbearing! Now, Beowulf, best of men,
I will cherish thee in my heart even as a son; hereafter keep
thou well this new kinship. Lack shalt thou have of none of
775 thy desires in the world, of such as lie in my power. Full oft
for less have I granted a reward and honourable gifts from
my treasure to a humbler man and to one less eager in battle.
Thou hast achieved for thyself with thine own deeds that thy
glory shall live for ever to all ages. The Almighty reward thee
780 with good, even as He hitherto hath done!'

Beowulf spake, the son of Ecgtheow: 'We with all good
will achieved that deed of prowess in battle and the perilous
strength of the unknown thing we dared. Yet rather had I
wished that thou might see him here, Grendel himself, thy
785 foe in his array sick unto death! I purposed in hard bonds
swiftly to bind him upon his deathbed, that by the grasp of
my hands he should be forced to lie struggling for life, had
not his body escaped me. I might not, since it was not the will
of God, restrain his flight; I did not cleave fast enough for
790 that unto my mortal foe; too overwhelming was the might
of that fiend in body's movement. Nonetheless he hath left
behind upon his trail his hand and arm and shoulder. Yet in
no wise thus hath that unhappy one purchased him relief;
none the longer thereby will he live, that doer of evil wrong,
795 burdened by his sins; nay, pain hath him closely gripped in
a grasp he cannot flee, in bonds of anguish – there must he,
stained with sin, await the great Day of Doom and the sen-
tence that the bright Judge will pronounce on him.'

Then was the son of Ecglaf a man more sparing of his
800 words and vaunting speech concerning his deeds in war,
now that the royal company through the valour of Beowulf
looked up to the lofty roof at the hand and fingers of their
foe. At the tip was each one of the stout nails most like unto
steel, grievous and cruel were the spurs upon the hand of that
805 savage thing. All agreed that there was naught so hard, no
iron proven of old, that would touch him in such wise as to
hurt that demon's bloodstained murdering hand.

Then was it ordered that Heorot should swiftly be
adorned within by the hands of men; many were there, men
810 and women, who arrayed that hall of revelry and welcome.
Glittering with gold tapestries shone along the walls, many
a marvellous thing to see for every one of those that on such
things love to look. Sorely shattered was all that shining
house within, from their iron bars the hinges of the doors
815 were wrenched away; the roof alone was preserved free from
all injury, when that fierce slayer stained with deeds of wrong
had turned to flee despairing of his life. No easy thing is it to
escape – let him strive who will; nay, he shall come at last to
a place appointed by inevitable fate, made ready for all those
820 who have life, the sons of men dwelling upon earth, where
his body still upon its bed of rest shall sleep after the feast.

Now was it the time and hour and the son of Healfdene
went to the hall; the king himself would partake of the feast.
Never have I heard tell that a people was thronged more
825 numerous or bore itself more gallantly than they did then
about their lord and friend. They went then in splendour to
their seats, rejoicing in plenty, meetly they partook of many

a cup of mead. High of heart were the kinsmen in that lofty
hall, Hrothgar and Hrothulf. Heorot was filled with friends;
830   in no wise did the Scyldings work treachery as yet. Then
did the son of Healfdene give to Beowulf a golden ensign as
reward of his victory, an embroidered banner upon a staff,
and a helm and corslet; a renowned and treasured sword
there many saw laid before that warrior. The cup Beowulf
835   received there in the hall; no need had he to feel shamed by
the riches given unto him before the assembled bowmen.
Few men, have I heard tell, gave ever to another seated at
the drinking in more loving wise four such precious gifts.
Round the helmet's crown the wale wound about with wire
840   kept guard without over the head, that no sword that leaves
the file of smith, hardened in the rain of blows, might cruelly
injure it, when the eager warrior beneath his shield should
go against his foes. Then the lord of men commanded that
eight horses with gold-plated bit and bridle be led into the
845   hall, in amid the courts. Upon one of these there lay a saddle
adorned with cunning colours and rich with gems – the seat
in battle had it been of the high-king, in days when the son
of Healfdene would play the play of swords; never had the
valour of that far-famed lord failed in the front of war, when
850   slain men fell. And thereupon the warden of the Servants of
Ing (Danes) granted unto Beowulf possession of both, of
weapons and of steeds; he bade him use them well. Thus right
manfully did the renownéd king, rich lord of men, reward
the impetuous deeds of battle with treasures and with horses,
855   in such wise that no man finds fault in him who will justly
speak the truth. Moreover the lord of men to each of those

that with Beowulf had made the passage of the sea gave as
they sat at their mead a rich gift and heirloom, and com-
manded that atonement should be paid with gold for that one
860 whom Grendel wickedly had slain – even as he would have
more, had not the foreseeing God and the courage of that
man fended fate from them. God was lord then of all the race
of men, even as He yet is. Wherefore is understanding and
the heart that taketh thought in every time and place the best.
865 Much must he endure of sweet and bitter, who long time here
in these days of trouble enjoyeth life in the world!

There was song, and the voices of men gathered together
before the leader of the host of Healfdene, there the harp
was touched to mirth, and many a lay recalled. Then accord-
870 ing to his office Hrothgar's minstrel touched upon a tale to
the liking of those upon the benches drinking their mead
within the hall. He told of the sons of Finn. When the sudden
onslaught came upon them the hero of the Half-Danes,
Hnæf of the Scyldings, fell by fate in the Frisian slaughter.
875 Of a truth Hildeburg had little cause to praise the loyalty
of the Jutes; by no fault of hers she was robbed of her loved
ones in the clash of shields, of brothers and of sons. They fell
according to their doom slain by the spear. A woeful lady
she! Not without cause did that daughter of Hoc lament the
880 decree of fate, when that morning came, whereon she might
behold beneath the light of day the cruel slaying of her kin.
Where he aforetime had possessed the greatest earthly joy,
there had war taken all Finn's champions, save few alone;
so that he might by no means on that field of meeting wage

885 to an end the fight with Hengest, nor in battle wrest the sad
remnant from the captain of the prince. Nay, they offered
terms to him, that he would make all free for them another
court, both hall and throne; that they should have possession
of the half thereof, sharing with the sons of the Jutes, and at
890 the giving of treasure the son of Folcwalda should each day
honour the Danes, should with the rings and hoarded jewels
of plated gold rejoice the company of Hengest no whit less
than he was wont in the drinking-hall to enhearten the men
of Frisian race.

895 Thus on both sides they confirmed a binding treaty of
peace. To Hengest Finn in full and without reserve declared
with solemn oaths that he would with the advice of his coun-
sellors honourably entreat the sad remnant (of the fight); and
that there should no man ever recall it to mind, not though
900 they served the slayer of him who before had given them
rings, being now without a lord; for such was their necessity.
If moreover any of the men of Frisia should with grievous
words recall to memory that deadly feud, then should it be
expiated by the edge of sword.

905 A pyre was made ready, and the gleaming gold brought
forth from the treasury. That best of the heroes in battle of
the warrior Scyldings was arrayed upon the funeral pile.
Upon that pyre was plain to see blood-drenched corslet,
swine-crest all made of gold, boar hard as iron, many a lord
910 by wounds destroyed – one and all they had fallen in that
slaughter! Then Hildeburg bade that her own son be com-
mitted to the flames upon the pyre of Hnæf, there to burn
their bones, setting him upon the funeral pile at his uncle's

side. The lady mourned bewailing them in song. The war-
915 rior was mounted upon high. Up to the clouds swirled
that mightiest of destroying fires, roaring before the burial
mound. Consumed were their heads, their gaping wounds
burst open, the cruel hurts of the body, and the blood sprang
forth. Flame devoured them all, hungriest of spirits, all that
920 in that place war had taken of either people: their glory had
passed away.

Then the warriors bereft of their friends departed to look
upon their dwellings, to see the Frisian land, their homes
and mighty town. Still Hengest abode with Finn that blood-
925 stained winter, keeping fully to his word. He thought of his
own land, even though he could not speed upon the sea his
ship with curving beak. The deep was tossed in storm and
battled with the wind; winter locked the waves in icy bond,
until another year came to the dwellings of men, even as it
930 doth yet, those weathers gloriously fair that unchangingly
observe the seasons. Now past was winter, and fair the
bosom of the earth. The exile, the guest of Finn, was eager
to be gone from those courts. Therein more thought did he
give to vengeance for his sorrow than to the passage of the
935 sea, pondering if he might again achieve a clash of wrath,
wherein he would in his heart remember the children of the
Jutes. Wherefore he did not refuse the homage (that binds all
men), when Hunlaf's son laid the Light of Battle, that best of
swords, upon his lap. The edges thereof the Jutes knew full
940 well! And so too in turn cruel destruction by the sword came
upon Finn in his very hall, when Guthlaf and Oslaf after
their journey over the sea had recounted their sorrow and

that deadly onslaught, and complained their woeful lot; the
restless spirit within the breast might not be restrained. Then
945 was that hall reddened with the life-blood of their foes, and
Finn, too, slain, the king amid his company, and the queen
was taken. The bowmen of the Scyldings bore to their ships
all the wealth of the house of that king of earth, all such as
they could find of jewels and cunning gems. Over the ways
950 of the sea they bore that royal lady to the land of the Danes,
and brought her to her people.

The lay was sung, the minstrel's tale at an end. Merry
noise arose once more, loud and clear the sound of revelry
upon the seats; the cup-bearers gave out wine from vessels
955 wondrous wrought. Now came Wealhtheow forth, and
wearing many a golden ring she went to where those proud
men sat, both uncle and brother's son. Still was their kin-
ship's love between them, and each to the other true. There
too Unferth, the king's sage, sat at the feet of the Scyldings'
960 lord. Each man among them trusted in his mind's temper,
that he had a mighty heart, albeit he had not in the play of
swords dealt mercy to his kin.

Then spake the lady of the Scyldings: 'Receive now this
cup, dear lord of mine, giver of rich gifts. In happy hour
965 be thou, from whom men get love and gifts of gold, and
to the Geats speak with kindly words, as behoves a man.
To the Geats be gracious, and forget not to give of those
things that now thou hast, gathered from near and far. I
have heard men say that thou wert in mind to take this
970 warrior for thy son. Lo! Heorot is cleansed, this shining

hall where rings are dealt; dispose while yet thou mayest of
many a reward, and to thy kin after thee leave thy people
and thy realm, when thou must go forth to look upon thy
fate. Hrothulf I know well, my nephew fair, that he will in
975   honour cherish these our youths, if thou, dear master of the
Scyldings, sooner than he do leave this world. Methinks that
he will with good repay our sons, if he recalleth all those
deeds of grace that we did unto him, to his pleasure and his
honour, while yet he was a child.'
980   Then turned she to the seat where sat her sons, Hrethric
and Hrothmund, and the children of mighty men, young
warriors all, were gathered together. There beside those
brethren twain that brave heart sat, Beowulf of the Geats.
To him was the cup borne, and friendship offered in fair
985   words; and the twisted gold was brought forth with all good
will, two armlets, a mantle, and rings, and the mightiest of
torques that I have heard was ever upon the neck of man
on earth. Beneath the light of day I heard never men tell of
any better treasure in the hoards of the mighty, since Hama
990   bore away to the bright city the necklace of the Brosings,
jewel and precious vessel. He fled from the ensnaring hate of
Eormenric, and chose the counsels of the eternal faith. This
circlet Hygelac, King of the Geats, of the blood of Swerting,
had with him on that last day when beneath his standard he
995   defended his treasures, and fought for the spoil of battle.
Fate took him, for that he in his pride had challenged his
own ruin and the enmity of the Frisian folk. This fair thing
of precious stones he bore now over the bowl of the seas, a
king in his might. Beneath his shield he fell. Thus into the

47

1000 grasp of the Frank came now the life of the king, the armour
upon his breast, and that necklet too; and warriors, albeit of
less prowess in arms, there stripped the slain, when the blows
of battle were done. The people of the Geats were left upon
the field of slain.

1005 The hall was filled with clamour. These words did
Wealhtheow utter, before all that host she spake: 'Have and
use well to thy good this precious thing, Beowulf, young and
dear, and for thine own joy take this mantle, a thing treasured
among this people, and prosper well! Show forth thyself in
1010 valour, and to these my sons be thou gracious in thy coun-
sels. For that my heart will remember to reward thee. Thou
hast achieved that far and near all the ages long shall men
esteem thee, as wide as the sea encircleth the windy walls of
the land. Be thou blessed, O prince, while thy life endures!
1015 A wealth of precious things I wish thee with good heart. Be
thou to my sons kindly in deeds, possessing days of mirth!
In this place is each good man to his fellow true, friendly in
heart, loyal unto his liegelord, of one mind the servants of the
king, the people all ready to his will, his warriors filled with
1020 wine. Do thou as I bid!'

She went then to her seat. There was the very choice of
banquets, there men drank their wine; fate they knew not
grim, appointed of old, as it had gone already forth for many
of those good men, so soon as evening came, and Hrothgar
1025 the mighty departed to his lodging and to his couch. The hall
was guarded by a host of men uncounted, even as it was oft
before. They stripped the benches of wooden board, and all
along the hall were beds and pillows spread. Over those who

48

had there drunk the ale fate hung now nigh at hand, as they
1030 laid them upon their couches on the floor. At their heads
they set their warlike shields, targes fashioned of wood and
blazoned bright. There upon each bench was plain to see
above each knight the helm that he had borne aloft in battle,
and his coat of ringéd mail, his spear valiant in the press of
1035 war. Their manner was it that seldom were they unprepared
for the onslaught, be it at home or amid the host, or in either
case, even at all such times as upon their liegelord need
should come – a worthy company was that!

Now they sank into sleep. One there was who paid
1040 grievously for his rest that eve, even as full oft had befallen
them, in time when Grendel had dwelt in that golden hall
and wrought evil there, even until his end came and death
after his deeds of wrong. Plain was it made and published
abroad among men that an avenger to succeed their foe
1045 lived yet long while after that woeful strife – Grendel's
mother, ogress, fierce destroyer in the form of woman.
Misery was in her heart, she who must abide in the dread-
ful waters and the cold streams, since Cain with the sword
became the slayer of his only brother, his kinsman by his
1050 father's blood. Thereafter he departed an outlaw branded
with murder, shunning the mirth of men, abiding in the
wilderness. From thence sprang many creatures doomed of
old; of whom was Grendel one, outlawed by hate as is the
deadly wolf, who at Heorot had found one who unsleep-
1055 ing awaited battle. There had the fierce slayer seized upon
him, but he remembered the might of his valour, that gift

49

which God had bounteously bestowed upon him, and he trusted in the One God for mercy, for succour and for aid. Therewith did he vanquish that fiend and brought low the creature of hell. Wherefore that enemy of man departed humbled, robbed of his triumph, to look upon his house of death. And now once more his mother grimhearted, ravenous, was minded to go upon a journey full of woe to avenge the slaying of her son.

1060

Now was she come to Heorot, where the Ring-Danes slept along the hall. There suddenly now old ills returned upon those knights when into their midst crept Grendel's mother. Less indeed was the terror, even by so much as is the might of women, the terror of a woman in battle compared with arméd man, when the sword with wire-bound hilt, hammer-forged, its blade stained with dripping blood, trusty of edge, cleaves the opposing boar-crest high upon the helm. Lo! in the hall along the benches stoutedged swords were drawn, many a tall shield was gripped in hand and held aloft. Of his helm no man bethought him, nor of long corslet, when that horror came upon him. She was in haste. Out and away she would be gone for the saving of her life, now that she was discovered. Swift and close had she clutched one of those noble knights as she departed to the fen. He was unto Hrothgar of all his men of might, holding high place in his court, the one most dear the Two Seas between; proudly had he borne his shield in battle, whom now she rent upon his bed, a man established in renown. Not there was Beowulf, but to that glorious Geatish knight had other lodging been assigned after the giving of gifts.

1065

1070

1075

1080

1085

Clamour arose in Heorot. Under the covering dark she took the arm she knew so well. Grief was renewed, and was come again to those dwelling places. An evil barter was that, wherein they must on either side exchange the lives of men
1090 beloved! Now was that king aged in wisdom, warrior grey of hair, in mournful mood, knowing that his princely servant lived no more, and that most beloved of his men was dead. Swiftly was Beowulf, that warrior whom victory had blessed, summoned to the king's chamber. With the break of day he
1095 went, a noble champion with his good men about him, himself and his companions, to where that wise king abode pondering whether haply the Almighty God will ever after these grievous tidings bring some betterment to pass. Now strode across the floor that man well-tried in arms amid his retinue
1100 – the timbers of the hall echoed – and there he addressed in speech the wise lord of the Friends of Ing, asking if he had known repose according to his desire.

Hrothgar made answer, the guardian of the Scyldings: 'Ask not for news of happy hours! Sorrow is come anew
1105 upon the people of the Danes. Dead is Æschere, the elder brother of Yrmenlaf; my counsels were his and his wisdom mine, at my right hand he stood when on fatal field we fended our lives, as the ranks clashed in battle and the boar-crests rang. Such should a good man be, of noble birth long
1110 tried in deeds, even as was Æschere! In Heorot has death come upon him at the hands of a wandering murderous thing. I know not whither she hath turned her backward steps, as dreadfully she gloats over her prey, exulting in her belly's fill. That deed of war she hath avenged, that last night thou

1115 didst slay in violent wise Grendel with thy gripings hard, for
that he too long had minished and destroyed my folk. He
fell in battle forfeiting his life, and now another hath come,
a mighty doer of cruel wrong. She purposed to avenge her
kin, and indeed hath carried far the feud, as may well seem
1120 to many a knight who mourns in his heart for him that gave
him bounty: a heartpiercing grief and bitter. Now lieth still
that hand that aforetime availed to accomplish for you (O
knights) all things of your desire.

'This have I heard dwellers in the land, lieges of mine,
1125 vassals in their halls, recount, telling how they saw two such
mighty stalkers of the outer places, who kept the moors,
alien creatures. Of these was one, in so far as they might clear
discern, a shape as of a woman; the other, miscreated thing,
in man's form trod the ways of exile, albeit he was greater
1130 than any other human thing. Him in days of old the dwell-
ers on earth named Grendel; of a father they knew not, nor
whether any such was ever before begotten for him among
the demons of the dark. In a hidden land they dwell upon
highlands wolfhaunted, and windy cliffs, and the perilous
1135 passes of the fens, where the mountain-stream goes down
beneath the shadows of the cliffs, a river beneath the earth. It
is not far hence in measurement of miles that that mere lies,
over which there hang rimy thickets, and a wood clinging
by its roots overshadows the water. There may each night
1140 be seen a wonder grim, fire upon the flood. There lives not
of the children of men one so wise that he should know the
depth of it. Even though harried by the hounds the ranger of
the heath, the hart strong in his horns, may seek that wood

being hunted from afar, sooner will he yield his life and
1145 breath upon the shore, than he will enter to hide his head
therein: no pleasant place is that! Thence doth the tumult
of the waves arise darkly to the clouds, when wind arouses
tempests foul, until the airs are murky and the heavens weep.

'Now once more doth hope of help depend on thee alone.
1150 The abode as yet thou knowest not nor the perilous place
where thou canst find that creature stained with sin. Seek it
if thou durst! For that assault I will with riches reward thee,
with old and precious things, even as I did ere now, yea with
twisted gold, if thou comest safe away.'

1155 Beowulf made answer, the son of Ecgtheow: 'Grieve
not, O wise one! Better it is for every man that he should
avenge his friend than he should much lament. To each one
of us shall come in time the end of life in the world; let him
who may earn glory ere his death. No better thing can brave
1160 knight leave behind when he lies dead. Arise, O lord of
this realm! Swiftly let us go and look upon the footprint of
Grendel's kin. This I vow to thee: in no refuge shall he ever
hide, neither in bosom of earth nor in mountain-forest, nor
in the deeps of the sea, go where he will! For this day have
1165 patience in every woe, even as I know thou wilt!'

Then did the aged king leap up, and God, the Mighty
Lord, he thanked for that other's words. Now a horse was
bridled for Hrothgar, a steed with plaited mane, and forth the
wise prince went with seemly array, forth went the company
1170 of his warriors bearing shields. Far over the paths across the
wolds the print of her feet, her course over the lands, was
plain to see, as straight on she strode over the darkling moor,

53

bearing the best of knights who by Hrothgar's side had ruled his house, a lifeless corse. And now those men of noble race, steep stony slopes they overpassed, narrow tracks and one-man paths, down unfamiliar trails, past headlong crags, and many a house of demons of the deep. One with a few men of hunting-craft went on before to spy the land, until on a sudden he came upon the mountain-trees leaning o'er the hoar rock, a joyless forest. Bloodstained and troubled water loomed beneath.

To all the Danes, vassals of the Scylding lords, to the hearts of many a knight, grievous was it endure, and pain to all good men, when there upon the cliff above the deep they found the head of Æschere. The water surged with gore, with blood yet hot. The people gazed thereon. Ever and anon the horn cried an eager call unto the host. There sat them down the ranks of men. Now they saw about the water many of the serpent-kind, strange dragons of the sea, ranging the flood, and demons of the deep lying upon the jutting slopes, even such as in the middle hours watch for those journeying anxious upon the sailing paths, serpents and beasts untamed.

Back they dived filled with wrath and hate; they had heard the clangour of the war-horns braying. One the Geatish chief with an arrow from his bow bereft of life and his labour in the waves, that in his vitals stood the hard and deadly dart. Therefore less swift to swim in the deeps was he, for death took him. Straightway amid the waves with boar-spears cruelly barbed sorely was he pressed and grievously assailed, and dragged upon the jutting cliff, monstrous upheaver of the waves. Men there gazed upon this strange and terrible thing.

In warrior's harness Beowulf clad him, no whit recked he of his life. Now must his long corslet woven for battle by the hands of smiths and cunningly adorned make trial 1205 of the flood, raiment skilled to guard his body's frame, that the grappling of war and the fell clutch of angry foe should not harm his life. But his head the white helm guarded, that now must stir the deep places of the mere, searching out the eddying floods, adorned with gold and clasped with rich 1210 chains, even as in days of old a weapon-smith had wrought it, marvellously fashioning it, setting thereon images of the boar, so that thereafter never blade nor swords of strife might cleave it. Nor yet was that thing to be misprized among his mighty aids which to him in his need Hrothgar's 1215 sage had lent. Hrunting was the name of that hafted blade; pre-eminent among old and precious things was that, of iron was the blade stained with a device of branching venom, made hard in the blood of battle. Never had it in warfare betrayed any man of those that had wielded it with hands, 1220 who had dared to achieve adventures perilous upon battle-fields against their foes. This was not the first time that it was required to accomplish valorous deeds. Verily the son of Ecglaf mighty of valour remembered not that which he had before spoken being filled with wine, when he lent that 1225 weapon to a swordsman worthier than was he. He durst not himself beneath the warring waves adventure his life and deeds of prowess perform. There he forfeited glory for heroic deeds. Not so that other, who now had arrayed him for battle. Beowulf spake, the son of Ecgtheow: 'Forget not, 1230 O thou the son renowned of Healfdene, wise prince from whom men get love and gifts of gold, now that I haste to mine adventure, that which was aforetime spoken between us: if I should at thy need lay down my life, that thou wouldst ever be to me when I was gone in father's stead. Be

1235 thou protector of the knights that follow me, the companions at my side, if battle take me. And send thou, too, those precious gifts that thou hast given me, beloved Hrothgar, unto Hygelac. Then by that gold may the son of Hrethel, Lord of the Geats, when he gazeth upon that treasure, per-

1240 ceive and understand that, finding a giver of rings, a lord endowed with generous virtue, I earned his bounty while I might. And let Unferth, that man of wide renown, receive back his olden heirloom, his sword cunningly adorned with flowing lines and hard of edge. For myself glory will I earn

1245 with Hrunting, or death shall take me!'

After these words the prince of the windloving Geats hastened dauntless forth, for no answer would he wait. The surging sea engulfed that warrior bold. Thereafter a long hour of the day it was ere he could descry the level floor.

1250 Straightway that creature that with cruel lust, ravenous and grim, had a hundred seasons held the watery realm, perceived that there from on high some man was come to espy the dwelling of inhuman things. She clutched then at him, seized in her dire claws the warrior bold. No whit the sooner did

1255 she hurt his body unharmed within; the ring-mail fended him about, that she might not pierce with cruel fingers the supple-linkéd shirt that clad him in the fray. Then that she-wolf of the waves to the sea-bottom coming bore the mail-clad prince unto her own abode. Even so, in no wise could

1260 he wield his weapons – wroth was he thereat! – so many a
monster strange beset him sorely as they swam, and many
a beast of the sea with fell tusks at his hauberk tore; fierce
destroyers pressed upon him.

    Now then the good man perceived that he was in some
1265 abysmal hall, he knew not what, wherein no water did him
any hurt, nor might the sudden onrush of the flood touch
him by reason of the vaulted chamber. A light as of fire he
saw with gleaming flames there shining bright. Then did that
gallant one perceive the monstrous woman of the sea, she-
1270 wolvish outlaw of the deep. To his warlike sword he lent a
mighty force, nor did his hand hold back the blow; and on
her head the weapon ring-adorned sang out its lusting song
of war. Soon did the invader learn that in battle shining it
would bite not there nor harm her life; nay, that blade failed
1275 the prince at need, which aforetime had endured many a
clash of blows, oft-times had cloven helm and harness of the
doomed. This was the first venture for that dearly-prizéd
thing wherein its glory fell.

    Again he made on, no laggard in valour, remembering his
1280 renownéd deeds, that kinsman of Hygelac. As he fought in
ire he cast away that blade with twisted ornament and curi-
ously bound, and upon the earth it lay steeledged and strong.
He trusted in his strength and the grasp of his own mighty
hands. Such shall a man's faith be, when he thinks to win
1285 enduring fame in war: no care for his life will trouble him.
Then seized the prince of Geatish warriors Grendel's mother
by her locks, ruing not the cruel deed, and his mortal foe he
threw, for now he grim in war was filled with wrath, and she

1290 was bowed unto the floor. Again she swiftly answered him with like, and grappling cruelly she clutched at him. Then stumbled, desperate at heart, that warrior most strong, that champion of the host, and he in turn was thrown. Then did she bestride the invader of her hall, and drew her knife with broad and burnished blade: she thought to avenge her son 1295 and only child. Upon his shoulders hung the woven net of mail about his breast; this now his life defended, and withstood the entry of both point and edge. In that hour had the son of Ecgtheow, champion of the Geats, come to ill end beneath the widespread earth, had not his corslet, the stout 1300 net of rings, furnished him help in fight and fray – there Holy God did rule the victory in battle. The allseeing Lord who governeth the heavens on high with ease did give decision to the right, when Beowulf again sprang up.

Lo! among the war-gear there he beheld a sword endowed 1305 with charms of victory, a blade gigantic, old, with edges stern, the pride of men of arms: the choicest of weapons that, albeit greater than any other man might have borne unto the play of war, a good and costly thing, the work of giants. Now he grasped its linkéd hilt, that champion of the 1310 Scyldings' cause, in fierce mood and fell he flashed forth the ring-adornéd blade; despairing of his life with ire he smote, and on her neck it bitter seized, and shivered the bony joints. Through and through the sword pierced her body doomed. She sank upon the floor. The sword was wet. The knight 1315 rejoiced him in the deed.

The flame flashed forth, light there blazed within, even as of heaven radiantly shines the candle of the sky. He gazed

about that house, then turning went along the wall, grasping upraised that hard weapon by the hilt, in ire undaunted
1320 the knight of Hygelac. That blade the warrior bold did not despise; nay, he thought now swiftly to requite Grendel for those many dire assaults that he had made upon the Western Danes, far oftener than that one last time, slaying in slumber the companions of Hrothgar's hearth, devouring as they
1325 slept fifteen of the people of the Danes, and others as many bearing forth away, a plunder hideous. For that he had given him his reward, that champion in his wrath, so that on his couch he saw now Grendel lying weary of war, bereft of life, such hurt had he erewhile in battle got at Heorot. Far
1330 asunder sprang the corpse, when Grendel in death endured a stroke of hard sword fiercely swung; his head was cloven from him.

Soon did the wise men, who about Hrothgar kept watch upon the deep, this sight behold, that the sea's confuséd
1335 waves were all mingled and were stained with blood. About their good lord old men with greying hair then said with one accord that never again they hoped to see that noble knight, or that he would come in triumph and victory to see their king renowned; of one mind in this were many then, that the
1340 she-wolf of the sea had broken him.

Now came the ninth hour of the day. The gallant Scyldings forsook the headland; he from whom they had love and gifts of gold departed thence. The strangers sat sick at heart and gazed upon the mere. They wished, and hoped not, that they
1345 might see the dear form of their lord. In that hour the valiant sword began, after the hot blood of battle touched it, to drip

away in fearful icicles. A thing of wonder that; for it melted all, most like unto ice when the Father looseneth the bonds of frost and unlocks the enchainéd pools, even He who hath

1350 the governance of seasons and of times, who is the steadfast designer of the world. In those abodes no more did the prince of the windloving Geats take of the hoarded treasures, though many such he looked upon, save that head alone, and the hilt too, all bright with gems; the sword had melted now

1355 away, and all its woven ornament was consumed; so hot that blood, so venomous was that alien creature that there had perished in the hall. Soon was he swimming swift, who had erewhile lived to see his enemies fall in war. Up dived he through the water. The confuséd waves, those regions vast,

1360 all were purged, now that the alien creature had given up the days of life and this swift-passing world.

Lo! to the land came swimming, dauntless of heart, the chieftain of seafaring men, rejoicing in the plunder of the sea and the huge burden of the things he bore. Then the

1365 proud company of his knights went forth to meet him, giving thanks to God, welcoming their prince with joy, that they might look upon him there unharmed. Swiftly then were loosed the helm and corslet from that valiant one. The waters of the lake lay dark and still beneath the clouds stained

1370 with deadly gore. Thence in heart rejoicing they measured with their marching feet the way across the land, the road well-known. Royalhearted men from that cliff beside the deep they bore the head – a weary task for each of those most brave: four must on a spear-shaft there with labour

1375 grievous carry to the golden hall the head of Grendel, until anon they came striding thither, gallant, eager in arms, those fourteen Geats. Their liege lord with them, proudly among his company, trod the level ways about the hall of mead. Now in came striding that prince of knights daring in deeds, 1380   honoured with men's praise, a mighty man of valour greeting Hrothgar. Now Grendel's head by its locks was borne upon the hall's floor where men were drinking, hideous in the sight of men and of the lady in their midst, a marvellous thing to look upon with eyes. Men gazed thereon.

1385   Beowulf spake, the son of Ecgtheow: 'Lo! this plunder of the sea, O son of Healfdene, Scyldings' prince, we gladly have brought to thee, the token of my triumph which here thou lookest on. Hardly did I save my life therein, in war beneath the water, perilously did dare that deed. Well nigh were there 1390   my days of battle ended, were not God my shield. Nor might I in that combat with Hrunting aught achieve, good though that weapon be. Nay, the Lord of men vouchsafed to me that on the wall I saw hanging fair a mighty sword and old – oft and again hath He guided those bereft of friends – and that 1395   weapon now I drew, slew then in that strife, when space was granted me, the guardians of the house. Thereupon that blade of war with woven ornament was all consumed, even as the blood sprang out, gore most hot in battle. The hilt I bore thence from my foes, their evil deeds avenged, the 1400   death and torment of the Danes, even as was meet. This do I promise thee henceforth, that thou mayest in Heorot sleep untroubled amid the proud host of thy men, thou and each one of thy knights and captains, the proven and the young

that thou wilt not from that quarter have need to fear for
1405 them, King of the Scyldings, the bane of good men's lives, as
once thou didst.'

Then was the golden hilt given to the aged chieftain's
hand, to the grey-haired leader of the host, the work of trolls
of old. After the demons' fall it passed to the dominion of
1410 the Lord of Danes, that fabric of wondrous smiths; and since
that fellhearted foe, the enemy of God, had left this world
stained with murder's guilt, yea and his mother too, it passed
into the keeping of that most excellent of earthly kings the
Two Seas between, who aforetime dealt out their wealth on
1415 Sceden-isle.

Hrothgar made answer, looking close upon the hilt,
the relic of old days, whereon was writ the beginning of
that ancient strife, whereafter the flood of pouring ocean
destroyed the Giants' race; evilly did they fare. That was
1420 a people alien to the eternal Lord; for that a final payment
with surging water the Almighty made to them. There too
upon the plates of purest gold was it duly marked in let-
tered runes, set forth and declared, for whom that sword was
fashioned first, that best of things of iron with wirewrapped
1425 hilt and snakelike ornament. Now spake the wise king, son
of Healfdene – all were silent: 'Lo! this may he say who
furthereth truth and justice among men and, aged ruler of
his home, recalleth all things long ago, that this good knight
was born to mastery. Thy glory is uplifted to pass down the
1430 distant ways, Beowulf my friend, thy glory over every folk.
All which unmoved by pride thou dost possess, keeping thy
valour with discerning heart. I shall to thee my vow of love

accomplish, even as at first we spake together. Thou shalt
unto thy lieges prove a comfort destined to endure, the help
1435 of men of might. Not such did Heremod prove to Ecgwela's
sons, the Scyldings proud; he grew not to their joy, but to
their bane and fall, to death and destruction of the chief-
tains of the Danes. In the fury of his heart he destroyed the
companions of his board, the followers at his side, until he
1440 passed forth alone, renownéd king, the mirth of men forsak-
ing. Albeit the almighty God had advanced him beyond all
in the glad gifts of prowess and in might, nonetheless the
secret heart within his breast grew cruel and bloody. He
gave not things of gold unto the Danes to earn him praise;
1445 joyless he lived on to suffer misery for that strife, the tor-
ment long-lasting of his folk. Learn thou from this, and
understand what generous virtue is! These considered words
on thy account have I here uttered to whom have the winters
wisdom brought.
1450   'Wondrous 'tis to tell how the mighty God doth apportion
in His purpose deep unto the race of men wisdom, lands, and
noble estate: of all things He is Lord. At whiles the heart's
thought of man of famous house He suffereth in delight to
walk, granteth him in his realm earthly joy ruling over men
1455 within his walléd town, maketh the regions of the earth as
his to sway, a kingdom vast, so that the end thereof in his
unwisdom he cannot himself conceive. He dwells in plenty;
no whit do age or sickness thwart him, nor doth black care
grieve his soul, nor strife in any place bring murderous hatred
1460 forth; nay, all the world goeth to his desire. He knows noth-
ing of worse fate, until within him a measure of arrogance

doth grow and spread. Now sleeps the watchman, guardian
of his soul: too sound that sleep in troubles wrapped; the
slayer is very nigh who in malice shooteth arrows from his
1465 bow. Then beneath his guard he is smitten to the heart with
bitter shaft, the strange and crooked biddings of the accurséd
spirit; he cannot himself defend. Too little now him seems
what long he hath enjoyed, his grim heart fills with greed;
in no wise doth he deal gold-plated rings to earn him praise,
1470 and the doom that cometh he forgets and heeds not, because
God, the Lord of glory, hath before granted him a portion of
honour high. Thereafter in the final end it cometh to pass that
his fleshly garb being mortal faileth, falls in death ordained.
Another succeeds to all, who unrecking scattereth his pre-
1475 cious things, the old-hoarded treasures of that man: his wrath
he fears not. Defend thee from that deadly malice, dear
Beowulf, best of knights, and choose for thyself the better
part, counsels of everlasting worth; countenance no pride, O
champion in thy renown! Now for a little while thy valour is
1480 in flower; but soon shall it be that sickness or the sword rob
thee of thy might, or fire's embrace, or water's wave, or bite
of blade, or flight of spear, or dreadful age; or the flashing of
thine eyes shall fail and fade; very soon 'twill come that thee,
proud knight, shall death lay low.

1485 'Even so did I for half a hundred years beneath heaven
rule the ring-proud Danes, and with my battle fenced them
round from many a neighbour over all this earth below, with
swords and spears, so that I counted no man beneath the
compass of the sky my likely foe. Lo! a change of this for-
1490 tune in my very home befell me, grief after gladness, when

64

Grendel, ancient enemy, became the invader of my house,
and I for that trespass unceasingly endured deep sorrow in
my heart. For this be to the Creator thanks, to the everlasting
Lord, that I have lived in my life, that long strife over, to gaze
1495   on this head dyed with cruel gore! Go now to thy seat, use
the gladness of the feast, war's honour with thee! Between us
shall many a host of treasures pass when morn shall come.'

Glad was the heart of the Geat; swift went he to his place,
seeking his seat as the wise king bade. Then was again once
1500   more for the bold and valiant sitting in that hall fair feasting
made anew. The hood of night fell darkling black upon the
proud men there. All the fair host arose. The aged Scylding
with grey-sprinkled hair desired to seek his bed. Longing
immeasurably sweet for rest there took the Geatish knight,
1505   bold bearer of the shield. Straightway there led him forth,
that man of distant folk now weary of his quest, a chamber-
lain who in courtesy to the knight's need ministered, in such
things as in that day were due for men on warlike errantry
to have.
1510   Now rested that mighty heart. The hall loomed high,
wide-vaulted, gold-adorned. The stranger slept within, until
the raven black announced with merry heart the heaven's
gladness. Then came speeding bright a radiance above the
gloom. The warriors were in haste; eager were those noble
1515   men to journey back unto their people; far from thence that
guest proud-hearted now wished to seek his ship.
Then the bold son of Ecglaf bade men Hrunting bring,
bade him take the sword, dear thing of iron. For that offered

gift he spake his thanks, saying that a good friend in war he
1520 deemed it, a power in battle, nor uttered any words belittling
the edges of that sword – a gallant knight was he! And now
those warriors were in their armour dight for journey long-
ing. Honoured among the Danes their prince to the high seat
went where the other sat, a mighty man of valour Hrothgar
1525 greeted. Beowulf spake, the son of Ecgtheow: 'Now we who
came from far away voyaging over the sea desire to say that
we are eager to be gone to seek King Hygelac. Here have we
right well been cherished in delight; good hast thou been to
us. Wherefore if I may in any matter upon this earth deserve
1530 thy greater love beyond what I yet have done in way of
valiant works, swift will I be at hand. If news be brought to
me over the encompassing seas that thy neighbours threaten
thee with war's alarm, as on a time those did that hated thee,
a thousand knights will I bring to thee, mighty men unto thy
1535 aid. This do I know of Hygelac, lord of Geats, though young
he be, the shepherd of his folk, that in word and deed he will
further me, that I may meetly honour thee, and to thy sup-
port lead throng of spears, the succour of thy might, when
thou hast need of men. If Hrethric, king's son, moreover, do
1540 purpose to seek the Geatish courts, there may he find many
friends. To profit are far countries visited by him that in
himself hath worth.'

Hrothgar then spake thus answering him: 'These words
that thou hast spoken the all-knowing Lord hath set within
1545 thy heart. Never heard I of years so young a man discourse
more wise. Thou art in valour strong and in thy mind prudent,
knowledge is in thy uttered words. Likely it is, methinks, if it

should come to pass that the spear in battle grim and deadly take Hrethel's son, thy prince, the shepherd of his folk, sick-

1550 ness or the sword, and thou dost keep thy life, that then the sea-loving Geats would have no better one to choose for king and keeper of the wealth of mighty men, if thou wilt rule the kingdom of thy kin. The temper of thy mind pleaseth me the better the longer known, Beowulf beloved! Thou hast

1555 accomplished that between these peoples, the Geatish folk and spearmen of the Danes, a mutual peace shall be, and strife and hateful enmities shall sleep which erewhile they used, and long as I my wide realm rule, shall precious things between us pass, and many a man shall send over the water

1560 where the gannet dives greeting to another with goodly gifts, and vessels ring-adorned over the high seas shall bring offer-ings and tokens of our love. That people do I know to be formed in steadfast mould, be it toward foe or friend, in all things without reproach after the good ways of old.'

1565 Then the son of Healfdene, protector of good men, in that hall again twelve costly things gave unto him, bade him with those gifts in safety seek now his own dear people, and swiftly again return. Then the prince of the Scyldings, that king of noble line, kissed there the best of knights, clasping

1570 him about the neck. Tears ran down his face beneath his grey-strewn hair. Two thoughts were in his heart old with the wisdom of years, but this thought more, that never might they meet again proudly in high discourse. To him the other was so dear that he might not restrain that upwelling of the

1575 heart, but twined in the heartstrings in his breast longing profound for that beloved one now burned within his blood.

Thence Beowulf went, a warrior bold in golden splendour, treading the grassy sward, his heart uplifted with rich gifts. The traverser of the sea awaited its lord and master there on 1580 the anchor riding; and as they went oft was the bounty of Hrothgar praised: unrivalled king was he in all things without reproach, until age robbed him of his joyous strength – oft hath it stricken many a man.

Now to the flowing sea came that band of young men 1585 most proud wearing their netlike mail, their supple-linkéd shirts. The watchman of the shore descried the warriors' return, as he had before. Not with unfriendly words from the cliff's brow did he hail the guests, but rode to meet them, and said to the men of the windloving Geats that welcome 1590 they came, warlike men in gleaming raiment, to their ship. Then upon the beach was their deep-draughted vessel of the sea with curving beak laden with gear of war, with horses and with precious things. The mast stood tall above Hrothgar's hoarded wealth. To the keeper of his ship Beowulf gave a 1595 sword, bound with golden wire, so that thereafter sitting at the mead he was the more honoured by reason of that rich gift and heirloom old.

Forth sped the bark troubling the deep waters and forsook the land of the Danes. Then upon the mast was the 1600 raiment of the sea, the sail, with rope made fast. The watery timbers groaned. Nought did the wind upon the waves keep her from her course as she rode the billows. A traveller upon the sea she fared, fleeting on with foam about her throat over the waves, over the ocean-streams with wreathéd prow, until

1605 they might espy the Geatish cliffs and headlands that they knew. Urged by the airs up drove the bark. It rested upon the land.

Swiftly was the portreeve ready beside the sea, who long while now had anxious upon the shore looked out afar for 1610 those men beloved. The deep-bosomed ship he moored unto the beach, made fast with anchor-ropes, lest the might of the waves should wrest from them their fair-builded craft. Then he bade men bear to land the wealth of princes, the jewelled work and plated gold. Not far thence must they go to find 1615 Hygelac Hrethel's son giver of rich gifts, where he dwelleth in his own house, chief amid his champions, nigh to the walls of the sea.

Good was that mansion, a brave king was its lord, lofty were his halls; very young was Hygd, wise and of virtue 1620 seemly, though winters few she had known within the castle courts; Hæreth was her sire. Yet no niggard was she, nor too sparing of gifts and precious treasures to the Geatish men. The fierce mood of Thryth she did not show, good queen of men, nor her dire wickedness. None was there of the dear 1625 companions of the court, save her lord alone, who dared in his hardihood to gaze openly with eyes upon her. Nay, then he might count on deadly bonds woven by hands in store for him; then swift when he was seized and held the sword was called upon that with its figured blade it might make an end 1630 and deal the agony of death. No course is this for queens, for woman to pursue, peerless though she be, that she who should weave men's peace should compass the life of man beloved with lying tales of wrong. Verily he of Hemming's

race made light of that; yea, men at their ale-drinking have
1635 further told that less injuries to men, less cruel wickedness
she wrought, since first she was given a bride of noble line
adorned with gold to that young champion, since first at her
father's bidding she had come unto Offa's hall over the wan
waters journeying. There did she afterward use well her life's
1640 estate upon the royal throne, renowned for goodness while
she lived; her loving duty she observed toward that prince
of mighty men, of all mankind, as I have learned, the one
most excellent the Two Seas between of wide earth's race.
For Offa in his bounty and his wars was honoured far and
1645 wide, a man bold amid the spears who with wisdom ruled his
rightful land. Of him was begotten Eomer for the comfort of
men of might, valiant in fell deeds, of the race of Hemming,
Garmund's grandson.

Now that valiant one, Beowulf himself, his retinue about
1650 him, went forth along the sand, treading the level beach and
the wide shores. The lamp of the world shone down, the sun
hasting from the south. Their journey to its end they brought
bravely marching to where, as they had learned, the protector
of good men, the young warrior-king, slayer of Ongentheow,
1655 within his fast dwelling dealt out the rings, a worthy lord.
To Hygelac was word of Beowulf's coming told in haste,
how there to the outer courts that lord of warriors, stout
beneath the shield, was come striding to the court alive and
whole from the play of war. Swift, as the mighty king them
1660 bade, was room in the hall within made for the new-come
warriors. He who that strife had safely passed now sat him

beside the very king, kinsman at kinsman's side, when he with solemn words and gracious utterance had greeted his good liege-lord. Now Hæreth's daughter down that high hall
1665 passed for the pouring of the mead, cherished the good men there, bearing the cup of strong sweet drink to the hands of mighty men. Then Hygelac began in that lofty house with fair words to question the companion at his side; eagerness pierced his heart to know of what sort the adventures of the
1670 sealoving Geats had been: 'What fortune befell you on your voyage, Beowulf beloved, since thou didst on a sudden take the mind to seek strife far away over the salt waters, deeds of arms in Heorot? And, come! didst thou for Hrothgar king renowned in any wise amend his grief so widely noised? On
1675 this account did care about my heart well ever up in surging sorrow; I feared the hazard of my man beloved. Thee long I prayed that thou shouldst in no wise approach that deadly creature, but shouldst suffer the South-Danes look them-selves to their war with Grendel. To God I render thanks that
1680 I can now see thee safe returned.'

Beowulf made answer, the son of Ecgtheow: 'Lord Hygelac, no secret is it to many among mortal men in what sort our warlike bout, the mighty duel of Grendel and of me, fell out upon that field, where many a host of wrongs and
1685 agelong misery he wrought against the victorious Scyldings. These did I all avenge, so that none upon earth of Grendel's kin hath cause to boast of that encounter at grey dawn, who-so of that fell brood yet longest liveth in the encircling fens. First then I came there to the hall of rings greeting
1690 Hrothgar. Straightway did the renownéd son of Healfdene,

as soon as he learned the temper of my mind, beside his own son appoint my seat. The company was in mirth, nor saw I ever in life beneath the vault of heaven greater revelry of men that sit at mead within the hall. At whiles the glorious queen, 1695 peace and goodwill of peoples, did traverse all that floor about, enheartening the young esquires; oft to some knight she gave a twisted ring ere she went unto her seat. At whiles before the host Hrothgar's daughter bore the goblet of ale to all goodmen in turn. Her did I hear men sitting in that hall 1700 name Freawaru, as the gem-studded vessel to mighty men she gave. Betrothed is she, that young maid gold-adorned to Froda's gallant son. This hath the Scyldings' lord, the shepherd of his realm, determined, and accounts it policy that through that woman he may set to rest long tale of deadly 1705 deeds of enmity and strife. Oft do we see that seldom in any place, even for the briefest time, when a prince falleth, doth the murderous spear relent, good though the bride may be! This, maybe, will in that purposed time displease the Heathobardish king and each knight of that folk, when 1710 one walks down their hall beside the lady, a noble scion of the Danes amid their host. On him will gaily gleam things prized by their sires of old, a stout sword ring-adorned once treasure of the Heathobards, while yet their weapons they could yield, until they led their comrades dear and their own 1715 lives to ruin in the clash of shields. Then will one speak at the ale, seeing that costly thing, a soldier old who remembers all, recalling the slaying of men with spears – grim is the heart of him, with gloomy thought he will begin to try the young warrior's temper searching the secrets of his breast, to wake

1720 again cruel war, and these words will he say: "Canst thou not, my lord, the sword recall which thy father bore, his prizéd blade, unto the fray wearing his vizored helm upon that latest day whereon the Danes slew him, the eager Scyldings, and were masters of the stricken field, after Withergyld was slain 1725 and the downfall of mighty men? Now here the son of one, I know not who, among those slayers walks in this hall, his heart uplifted with fair things, boasteth of the slaying and weareth that treasure which thou shouldst by right possess."

'Thus at each occasion will he stir remembrance, prompt-1730 ing with wounding words, until the hour cometh when that lady's knight shall sleep, red with his blood from the bite of sword, forfeiting his life for his father's deeds. The other fleeing thence will with his life escape, knowing the land full well. Then will on either hand the sworn oaths of men 1735 be broken; thereafter will cruel thoughts of hate surge up in Ingeld's heart, and for this tide of woe cooler will wax his love of wife. For this cause I count the good will of the Heathobards, their part in this royal truce, filled with menace for the Danes, their friendship insecure.

1740 'I shall speak on once more concerning Grendel, that thou mayst fully know, O giver of rich gifts, to what end it came when we mighty ones did rush to grips. So soon as the jewel of the sky had glided over the world, that creature came in ire, bringing fierce horror in the dusk, to seek us 1745 out where yet unharmed that hall we guarded. There did slaughter upon Handscioh fall, a cruel ending to his dooméd life; sword-girt warrior he was the first to fall. Death came to that young knight renowned by Grendel's jaws, who all

the flesh devoured of him we loved. And yet none the more
1750 did he desire to go forth from that golden hall with empty
hand, that murderer with bloody tooth bethinking him of
evil deeds. Nay, he in his strength glorying of me made trial,
seized upon me with eager clutch. His pouch hung down;
deep was it and strange, made fast with curious thongs; with
1755 subtle skill it was all contrived by fiends' craft wrought of
dragon-hides. Therein did he, doer of deadly deeds, desire to
thrust me all unoffending, adding one more to many. That
might not be done, when I in ire stood upright upon my feet.
Too long it is to tell how I to that destroyer of men gave due
1760 reward for each of his foul deeds. There I, my lord, brought
honour on thy people by my works. To hiding he escaped, a
little while possessed the joys of life. And yet his right hand
remained to mark his trail behind in Heorot, and he hum-
bled, misery in his heart, far thence did cast him to the mere's
1765 abyss. For that deadly combat the Scyldings' lord granted me
a manifold reward of plated gold and many precious things,
when morn was come and we had sat us at the feasting. There
was mirth and minstrelsy: the aged Scylding, full of ancient
lore, told tales of long ago; now did he, once bold in battle,
1770 touch the harp to mirth, the instrument of music; now a lay
recited true and bitter; or again, greathearted king, some
wondrous tale rehearsed in order due; or yet again, warrior
of old wars, in age's fetters did lament his youth and strength
in arms. His heart heaved within him, when he wise with
1775 many years recalled a host of memories.

'Thus did we within that hall all the long day take our
delight until another night came upon this world. Then

was Grendel's mother swiftly ready to revenge her woe
once more. Full of anguish she took the road. Death had
1780 taken her son, the wrathful valour of the windloving Geats.
Inhuman troll-wife she avenged her child, and daringly a
man she slew. There was from Æschere the life sped forth,
a sage wise in old lore. Nor could they, the Danish lords,
when morn was come, burn him sleeping in death upon the
1785 blazing wood, nor lift upon the pyre that man beloved. She
had borne away that corse in her fiend's clutches beneath
the mountain-stream. That was for Hrothgar the most
grievous of those his sorrows that he, lord of his folk, long
while had known.

'Then the king gloomy-hearted implored me by thy life
1790 that I would in the tumult of the deeps accomplish deeds
of prowess, adventure my life achieving glory. Reward he
vowed me. Then, as is noised abroad, I sought out the grim
and dreadful guardian of the whirling gulf. There awhile were
1795 our hands in duel joined. The deep swirled with blood, and
in that abysmal hall I hewed the head of Grendel's mother
with the edges of a mighty sword. Thence hardly did I
retrieve my life; but not yet was I doomed to die. Nay, the
son of Healfdene, protector of good men, gave me thereaf-
1800 ter a multitude of precious things. Thus did the king of that
people live according to kingly virtue – no whit did I fail to
find those rewards , my valour's meed; nay, to me the son of
Healfdene gave costly things at mine own choice. These, O
warrior king, I will bring to thee, offering them in all good
1805 heart. To thee belongeth still all that share of joys. Few have
I of kinsmen near and dear, O Hygelac, save thee!'

He bade now the men bring in the banner charged with a boar's head, the helm towering in war, the grey corslet, the sword of battle cunning-wrought; and thereupon uttered
1810 these appointed words: 'To me did the wise prince Hrothgar give this raiment of war, and spake bidding me that I should first describe to thee his gracious gift. He said that King Heorogar, lord of the Scyldings, long while possessed it; and yet he would not for that the rather bestow it upon his son,
1815 the gallant Heoroweard, for the clothing of his breast, loyal to him though he was. Use all the gifts with honour (said he).'

I have heard that to those fair things four steeds dapple-grey swift and well-matched were added. Beowulf to Hygelac granted the sweet possession of horses and of precious things.
1820 Even so shall a kinsman do, nor in any wise shall spread with secret craft a net of malice for another, death devising for the comrade at his side. To Hygelac, dauntless in fell deeds, his nephew was exceeding true, and each was mindful of the other's honour. I have heard too that to Hygd he gave that
1825 necklace, a costly thing of intricate and marvellous fashion, which Wealhtheow, king's daughter, had bestowed on him, and therewith three horses, lithe limbed with gleaming saddles. Nobly arrayed was her breast thereafter by that necklet she received.

1830 Thus did the son of Ecgtheow, renowned in battle, show his manhood in fair deeds, bearing himself honourably. Never did he at the drinking strike down the comrades of his hearth; no grim heart was his – nay, with greatest might among mankind he maintained those lavish gifts which God had granted
1835 him, a warrior bold. Long was he contemned, for the sons of

the Geats did not account him worthy, nor would the king of the windloving folk accord him a place of much honour upon the seats where men drank mead. They much misdoubted that he was of sluggish mood, without eager spirit though of noble birth. A change and end of all his heart's griefs had come for him, a man now blessed with glory.

1840

Then the king, in battle valiant, protector of good men, commanded that a fair thing bequeathed by Hrethel, adorned with gold, should be brought into the hall. In that time there was not among the Geats a treasure or rich gift more excellent in form of sword. This now on Beowulf's lap he laid, and granted unto him seven thousand (hides of land), a hall and princely throne. To both of them alike had land by blood descended in that realm, estates and rightful heritage, but in greater measure to the one that was higher in the land, a kingdom wide.

1845

1850

*

This after came to pass in later days in the clash of wars, when Hygelac was fallen, and swords of battle had been Heardred's bane amid the shielded ranks, what time the warlike Scyldings, dauntless men of arms, sought him out amid his glorious people, and came upon him, nephew of Hereric, with fell assault, then into Beowulf's hands came that broad realm. Well he ruled it for fifty winters – now was he a king of many years, aged guardian of his rightful land – until a certain one in the dark nights began to hold sway, a dragon, even he who on the high heath watched his hoard, his steep stone-barrow: below lay a path little known

1855

1860

77

to men. Therein went some nameless man, creeping in nigh
to the pagan treasure; his hand seized a goblet deep, bright
1865   with gems. This the dragon did not after in silence bear, albeit
he had been cheated in his sleep by thief's cunning. This the
people learned, men of the neighbouring folk, that he was
wroth indeed.

By no means of intent had that man broken the dragon's
1870   hoard of his own will, he who thus wronged him griev-
ously; but in dire need, being the thrall of some one among
the sons of mighty men, he had fled from the lashes of
wrath, and having no house he crept therein, a man bur-
dened with guilt.

1875   Soon did the dragon bestir himself . . . that (swiftly) upon
the trespasser dire terror fell; yet nonetheless illfated one . . .
when the sudden danger came on him, (he saw) a treasure
chest . . .

There was in that house of earth many of such olden
1880   treasures, as someone, I know not who, among men in days
of yore had there prudently concealed, jewels of price and
mighty heirlooms of a noble race. All of them death had
taken in times before, and now he too alone of the proven
warriors of his people, who longest walked the earth, watch-
1885   ing, grieving for his friends, hoped but for the same fate, that
he might only a little space enjoy those longhoarded things.

A barrow all ready waited upon the earth nigh to the
watery waves, new-made upon a headland, secured by bind-
ing spells. Therein did the keeper of the rings lade a portion
1890   right worthy to be treasured of the wealth of noble men, of
plated gold; and a few words he spake:

78

'Keep thou now, Earth, since mighty men could not, the wealth of warriors. Lo! aforetime in thee it was that good men found it! Death in battle, cruel and deadly evil, hath taken each mortal man of my people, who have forsaken this life, the mirth of warriors in the hall. I have none that may bear sword, or burnish plated cup and precious drinking vessel. The proud host hath vanished away. Now shall the hard helm, gold-adorned, be stripped of its plates; those who should burnish it, who should polish its vizor for battle are asleep, and the armour too that stood well the bite of iron swords in war amid bursting shields now followeth its wearer to decay. The ringéd corslet no more may widely fare in company of a prince of war, upon the side of mighty men. There is no glad sound of harp, no mirth of instrument of music, nor doth good hawk sweep through the hall, nor the swift horse tramp the castle-court. Ruinous death hath banished hence many a one of living men.'

Even thus in woe of heart he mourned his sorrow, alone when all had gone; joyless he cried aloud by day and night, until the tide of death touched at his heart.

This hoarded loveliness did the old despoiler wandering in the gloom find standing unprotected, even he who filled with fire seeks out mounds (of burial), the naked dragon of fell heart that flies wrapped about in flame: him do earth's dwellers greatly dread. Treasure in the ground it is ever his wont to seize, and there wise with many years he guards the heathen gold – no whit doth it profit him.

Even thus had that despoiler of men for three hundred winters kept beneath the earth that house of treasure, waxing strong; until one filled his heart with rage, a man, who bore to his liege-lord a goldplated goblet, beseeching truce and pardon of his master. Then was the hoard laid bare, the hoard of rings minished, and his boon granted to the man 1925 forlorn. The lord for the first time gazed now on the olden work of men. Then the serpent woke! New strife arose. He smelt now along the rock, and grimhearted he perceived the footprint of his foe, who in his stealth had stepped right nigh, yea, close to the dragon's head. Thus may indeed one whose 1930 fate is not to die with ease escape woe and evil lot, if he have the favour of the Lord! The Guardian of the Hoard searched eagerly about the ground, desiring to discover the man who had thus wrought him injury as he lay in sleep. Burning, woeful at heart, ofttimes he compassed all the circuit of the 1935 mound, but no man was there in the waste. Nonetheless he thought with joy of battle, of making war. Ever and anon he turned him back into the barrow, seeking the jewelled vessel. Quickly had he discovered this, that some one among men had explored the gold and mighty treasures. In torment the 1940 Guardian of the Hoard abode until evening came. Then was the keeper of the barrow swollen with wrath, purposing, fell beast, with fire to avenge his precious drinking-vessel. Now was the day faded to the serpent's joy. No longer would he tarry on the mountain-side, but went blazing forth, sped with 1945 fire. Terrible for the people in that land was the beginning (of that war), even as swift and bitter came its end upon their lord and patron. Now the invader did begin to spew forth glowing fires and set ablaze the shining halls – the light of the burning leapt forth to the woe of men. No creature there did

1950 that fell winger of the air purpose to leave alive. Wide might it be seen how the serpent went to war, the malice of that fell oppressor, from near and far be seen how that destroyer in battle pursued and humbled the people of the Geats. Back to his Hoard he sped to his dark hall ere the time of day. He had
1955 wrapped the dwellers in the land in flame, in fire and burning; he trusted in his barrow, in its wall and his own warlike might, and his trust cheated him.

Now to Beowulf were the dread tidings told, swift and true, that his own homestead, best of houses, was crumbling
1960 in the whirling blaze, even the royal seat of the Geats. Grief was that to the good man's heart, the greatest of sorrows in his breast. Wise though he was he thought that he had bitterly angered the eternal Lord, Ruler of all, against the ancient law. His breast within was whelmed in dark boding thought, as
1965 was unwonted for him. The flaming dragon from without that seabordered land with glowing fires had crushed to ruin the stronghold of the folk, the guarded realm. For him did the king of war, lord of the windloving Geats, ponder vengeance therefore. He then, protector of warriors, lord of good men,
1970 bade fashion for him a shield for battle curiously wrought, all made of iron: full well he knew that no wood of the forest, no linden shield, would avail him against the flame. Appointed was it that the prince proven of old should find now the end of his fleeting days, of life in this world, and the serpent with
1975 him, albeit he had long possessed his hoarded wealth.
Lo! the lord of gold disdained with a host and mighty army to go against that creature flying far abroad. For

himself he did not fear the contest, nor account as anything the valour of the serpent, nor his might and courage. For 1980 he, daring many a grievous strait, had aforetime come safe through many a deadly deed and clash of war, since the time when, champion victory-crowned, he had purged Hrothgar's hall and in battle crushed the kin of Grendel of hated race.

Not the least of these encounters was that wherein 1985 Hygelac was slain, when in the onslaughts of war blades drank the blood of the King of the Geats, the gracious prince of peoples, Hrethel's son, in the Frisian lands by the broadsword beaten down. Thence Beowulf got him by his own prowess, using his craft of swimming; he alone upon his arm 1990 had thirty coats of mail as he strode into the deep. Little cause in sooth had the Hetware who bore forth their shields against him to exult in that fight on foot – few came back from that fierce warrior to see their home! Then the son of Ecgtheow over the expanse of the salt sea, unhappy and alone, swam 1995 back unto his people. There Hygd offered to him treasury and realm, rings and kingly throne. She trusted not in her son that he was yet wise enow to defend the seats of his fathers against alien hosts, since Hygelac was dead. Yet never the more could the bereaved people obtain in any wise from the 2000 prince that he would be lord over Heardred, or accept the kingship. Rather he upheld him among his folk with friendly counsel in love and honour, until he grew older and ruled the windloving Geats. To Heardred came banished men over the sea, the sons of Ohthere; they had set at nought the lord 2005 of the Scylfings, that best of sea-kings that ever in Sweden dealt out precious gifts, a king renowned. That marked his

end – there to the son of Hygelac for his harbouring was allotted a deadly wound by stroke of sword. But the son of Ongentheow, when Heardred was slain, returned to seek his
2010   home, suffering Beowulf to hold the kingly throne and rule the Geats – a good king was he!

He did not forget the requital of his prince's fall in later days: to Eadgils in his need he was found a friend, with a host he supported Ohthere's son, with warriors and weap-
2015   ons beyond the broad lake, and later in cold and grievous marches achieved revenge, the king he reft of life.

Even thus had he, the son of Ecgtheow, been preserved in every deadly strait and cruel slaying and desperate deed, until that one day when he must fight the serpent.
2020   Then filled with grief and rage the lord of the Geats with eleven companions went to look upon the dragon: already he had learned whence those deeds of enmity and dire hatred of men had sprung – into his possession had come the splendid and precious vessel by the hand of the spy: he was in that
2025   company the thirteenth man who had wrought the beginning of that warfare, a captive with gloomy heart he now must in shame show the way thence over the land. Against his will he went to where he knew a solitary hall of earth, a vault under ground, nigh to the surges of the deep and the warring waves.
2030   All filled within was it with cunning work and golden wire. The monstrous guardian eager and ready in battle ancient beneath the earth kept those golden treasures – no easy bargain that for any among men to win. Now upon the headland sat the war-proven king from whom the Geats had love and
2035   gifts of gold while he bade farewell unto the companions of

his hearth. Heavy was his mood, restless hastening toward death: the fate very nigh indeed that was to assail that aged one, to attack the guarded soul within and sunder life from body – not for long thereafter was the spirit of the prince in flesh entrammelled.

2040

Beowulf spake, the son of Ecgtheow: 'In youth from many an onslaught of war I came back safe, from many a day of battle. I do recall it all. Seven winters old was I, when the king of wealth, gracious prince of peoples, received me of my father. King Hrethel it was, who guarded me and kept me and gave me rich gift and fair feast, remembering our kinship. No whit was I while he lived less beloved by him within his house than any of his sons, even Herebeald, and Hæthcyn, and Hygelac my lord. For the eldest, as never should it have been, by a kinsman's deed the bed of cruel death was made, when Hæthcyn with arrow from his horn-tipped bow smote grievously his lord – he missed his mark and shot to death his kinsman, brother slew brother with a bloody shaft. That was an assault inexpiable, a wrong most evilly wrought, heart-wearying to the soul; and yet the prince must depart from life all unavenged.

2045

2050

2055

'In like wise is it grievous for an old man to endure that his son yet young should swing upon the gallows, that he should utter a dirge, a lamentable song, while his child hangs a sport unto the raven, and he old and weighed with years cannot devise him any aid. Ever is he reminded, each morning, of his son's passing; little he cares to await within his courts another heir, now that this one hath tasted evil deeds through the violence of death. In care and sorrow he sees in his son's dwelling

2060

2065 the hall of feasting, the resting places swept by the wind robbed
of laughter – the riders sleep, mighty men gone down into the
dark; there is no sound of harp, no mirth in those courts, such
as once there were. Then he goes back unto his couch, alone
for the one beloved he sings a lay of sorrow: all too wide and
2070 void did seem to him those fields and dwelling places.

'Even so did the lord of the windloving folk bear the surg-
ing sorrow of his heart for Herebeald – in no wise could he
exact atonement for the evil deed from the slayer of life; none
the more might he pursue with deeds of hate that warrior,
2075 though little was his love. Then beneath that sorrow that had
fallen thus too grievously upon him he forsook the joys of
men, God's light he sought: to his heirs, as rich man doth, he
left his lands and populous towns, departing from this life.
Soon was deed of hate and strife betwixt Swede and Geat and
2080 feud on either hand across the water wide, bitter enmity in
war, since Hrethel was dead, or else the sons of Ongentheow
were bold in war, eager to advance, and desired not to keep
the peace across the sea, but about Hreosnabeorg they oft-
times wrought cruel slaughter in their hate.

2085 'That did my kinsmen avenge, the deeds of enmity and
wrong, as has been famed, albeit one of them paid for it with
his life in grim barter: upon Hæthcyn, lord of the Geats, war
fell disastrous. That day, as I have heard, at morn one kins-
man with the edges of his sword brought home to the slayer
2090 the other's death, when Ongentheow met Eofer. The helm of
battle sprang asunder and the aged Scylfing fell, death-pale
in the fray. His hand remembered fell deeds enow, but it
warded not the fatal stroke.

'Hygelac I repaid in battle for those precious gifts that he
2095   gave me, even as was permitted me, with my shining sword;
he gave me lands and the joyous possession of my fathers'
home. No need was there for him that he should seek among
the Gifethas or the spearmen of the Danes or in the Swedish
realm a warrior less doughty or hire such with pay; ever in
2100   the marching hosts I would go before him alone in the front
of war, and thus shall through life do battle, while this sword
endures that has oft, early and late, served me well, since
before the proven hosts my hands were Dæghrefn's death,
the champion of the Franks. In no wise might he bring that
2105   fair-wrought ornament of the breast unto the Frisian king;
nay, he fell in battle, the keeper of their banner, that prince in
his pride. No sword-edge was his slayer, but a warrior's gripe
it was that quenched his beating heart crushing his frame
of bones. Now shall this sword's edge, hard and tempered
2110   blade, do battle for the hoard.'

Beowulf spake, for the last time proud words he uttered:
'In youth many a deed of war I dared and still I will, aged
protector of my people, seek strife and achieve renown, if
that worker of evil and ruin comes forth from his house of
2115   earth to find me.' Then he addressed each of those men, bold
warriors bearing their shields, his dear comrades for the latest
time. 'I would not bear sword or weapon against the serpent,
if I knew how else I might grapple with the fierce destroyer
to mine honour, as aforetime I did with Grendel. But here
2120   do I look for fell fire's heat, for blast and venom; wherefore I
have upon me shield and corslet. Yet I will not from the bar-
row's keeper flee one foot's pace, but to us twain hereafter

86

shall it be done at the mound's side, even as Fate, the Portion of each man, decrees to us. Fearless is my heart, wherefore I forbear from vaunting threat against this wingéd foe.

'Wait now on the hill, clad in your corslets, ye knights in harness, to see which of us two may better endure his wounds when the combat is over. This is not an errand for you, nor is it within the measure of any man save me alone that he should put forth his might against the fierce destroyer, doing deeds of knighthood. I shall with my valour win the gold, or else shall war, cruel and deadly evil, take your prince.'

Then the bold warrior stood up beside his shield, resolute beneath his helm. Wearing his grim mail he strode up to the stony cliffs, trusting in the strength of one man alone – such is no craven's feat! Then he who, endowed with manly virtue, had passed through many a host of battles and a clash of war, when the ranks of men smote together, saw now at the mound's side a stone-arch standing from whence a stream came hurrying from the hill. The boiling water of that spring was hot with deadly fires; no man could long while endure unscorched that deep place nigh the hoard by reason of the dragon's flame.

Now in his wrath the prince of the windloving Geats let words speed from his breast; grim of heart he shouted loud, so that his voice came ringing clear as a war-cry in beneath the hoary rock. Hatred was aroused. The Guardian of the Hoard perceived the voice of man. No longer was there space for the sueing of peace. Forth came first the blast of the fierce destroyer from out the rock, hot vapour threatening battle. The earth rang. The Lord of the Geats beneath the mound

87

flung round his warrior's shield to meet the dreadful comer. Now was the heart of the coiling beast stirred to come out to fight. His sword had already the good king drawn for battle, 2155 his ancient heirloom, quick of edge. Each with fell purpose in their hearts knew dread of [the] other; but undaunted stood the prince of vassals with his tall shield against him, while the serpent swiftly coiled itself together. In his armour he awaited it. Now it came blazing, gliding in loopéd curves, hastening 2160 to its fate. The shield well protected the life and limbs of the king renowned a lesser while than his desire had asked, if he were permitted to possess victory in battle, as that time, on that first occasion of his life, for him fate decreed it not. The Lord of the Geats flung up his arm and with his ancient sword 2165 smote the dread foe and the burnished edge turned on the bony body, but less keenly than its king had need, thus sore oppressed. Then was the guardian of the barrow after that warlike stroke in fell mood; murderous fire he flung – wide the flames of battle sprang. No triumphant cry of victory then 2170 uttered he from whom the Geats had love and gifts of gold: his naked blade had failed him in the cruel deeds of battle, as never should it have done, that iron tried of old. No pleasant fare was his that day, (nor such) that the renownéd son of Ecgtheow should of his own will forsake that field on earth; 2175 against his will must he inhabit a dwelling otherwhere, even as each man must, leaving the brief days of life.

Not long was it now before those fierce slayers together came again. The Guardian of the Hoard took heart afresh, his breast heaved with gasping breath. Anguish he endured 2180 oppressed with fire who aforetime was ruler of his folk. In no wise did his companions in arms, sons of princes, stand about him, a company proved in war; nay, they had retreated to a wood for the saving of their lives. In one alone of them the heart was moved with grief. Kinship may nothing set

2185 aside in virtuous mind. Wiglaf was he called, Wihstan's son, that fair warrior beneath his shield, a lord of Scylfing race of Ælfhere's line. He saw his liege-lord beneath his vizored helm of war in torment of heat. He remembered then those favours which Beowulf had granted to him, the rich dwell-

2190 ing-place of the Wægmundings, and all the landed rights which his father before had held. Then he could hold back no more: his hand wielded shield of yellow linden, ancient sword he drew – among men was it known as plunder of Eanmund Ohthere's son. Him, a lordless exile, did Wihstan

2195 in battle slay with edge of sword, and to Eanmund's kin bore off his bright burnished helm, ringéd corslet, and old gigantic sword. All which did Onela return to him, the battle-harness of his nephew, and gallant gear of war; nor did he speak of the injury to his house, albeit Wihstan had laid low his

2200 brother's son. These fair things he kept for many a year, both sword and corslet, until his son might accomplish deeds of knightly valour, as his father had before him. Then he gave unto him in the land of the Geats of harness of battle an uncounted store, when he departed life full of years upon his

2205 journey hence. This was the first venture in which that champion young was destined to make onslaught in battle beside his good lord. His heart turned not to water within him, nor did the weapon his sire bequeathed betray him in the fight. And that indeed the serpent found when they came together.

2210   Wiglaf spake many a right fitting word, saying to his comrades (for heavy was his heart): 'I do not forget the time when, where we took our mead in the hall of revelry, we vowed to our master, who gave us these precious things, that we would repay him for that raiment of warriors, the helmets

2215 and stout swords, if ever on him such need as this should fall. For this of his own choice he chose us amid the host, for this adventure, considering us worthy of glorious deeds; for this he gave to me those costly gifts, for he accounted us spear-men valiant, bold bearers of the helm – yea, even though our

2220 lord, shepherd of his people, purposed alone on our behalf to achieve this work of prowess, for he hath above all men wrought feats of renown and deeds of daring. Now is the day come when our liege-lord hath need of valour and of war-riors good. Come! Let us go to him! Let us help our leader

2225 in arms, while the heat endures, the glowing terror grim. God knoweth that for my part far sweeter is it for me that glowing fire should embrace my body beside the lord that gave me gold. Nor seems it fitting to me that we bear back our shields unto our home, unless we can first smite down the foe, and

2230 defend the life of the king of the windloving people. Verily I know that his deserts of old were not such that he alone of proven Geatish men should suffer anguish, and fall in battle. With him my sword and helm, my corslet and my armour, shall be joined in league!'

2235   Then strode he though the deadly reek, his head armed for war, to the succour of his lord, and these brief words he spake: 'Beowulf beloved, do all things well unto the end, even as thou didst vow aforetime in the days of youth that thou

wouldst not while living suffer thy honour to fall low. Now
2240 must thou, brave in deeds, thy noble heart unwavering, with
all thy might thy life defend. To the uttermost I will aid thee.'

Upon these words the serpent came on in wrath a second
time, alien creature fierce and evil, assailing with swirling
fires, drawing nigh unto his foes, these hated men. His buck-
2245 ler in the billowing flames was burned even to the boss, his
corslet could afford no help to that young wielder of the
spear; but beneath his kinsman's shield stoutly fared that
warrior young, when his own was crumbled in the glow-
ing fires. Now once more the king of battles recalled his
2250 renownéd deeds, with mighty strength he smote with his
warlike sword, and fast in the head it stood driven by fierce
hate. Nægling burst asunder! Beowulf's sword, old, grey-
bladed, had failed him in the fight. It was not vouchsafed to
him that blades of iron might be his aid in war: too strong
2255 that hand, that as I have heard with its swing overtaxed each
sword, when he to the battle bore weapons marvellously
hard; no whit did it profit him.

Then for the third time the destroyer of the folk, the fell
fire-dragon, bethought him of deeds of enmity, and rushed
2260 upon that valiant man, now that a clear field was given him,
burning and fierce in battle. His neck with his sharp bony
teeth he seized now all about, and Beowulf was reddened
with his own life-blood; it welled forth in gushing streams.
I have heard tell that in that hour of his king's need the
2265 good man unbowed showed forth his valour, his might and
courage, as was the manner of his kin. He heeded not those
jaws; nay, his hand was burned, as valiant he aided now his

kinsman, and smote that alien creature fierce a little lower down – a knight in arms was he! – so that bright and golden-
2270 hilted his sword plunged in, and the fire began thereafter to abate. Once more the king himself mastered his senses; drew forth a deadly dagger keen and whetted for the fray, that he wore against his mail; Lord of the windloving folk he ripped up the serpent in the midst. They had slain their foe – valour
2275 had vanquished life; yea, together they had destroyed him, those two princes of one house – of such sort should a man be, a loyal liege at need! That for the king was the last of his hours of triumph by his own deed, last of his labours in the world.

2280 Now the wound that the dragon of the cave had wrought on him began to burn and swell. Swiftly did he this perceive, that in his breast within the venom seethed with deadly malice. Then the prince went and sat him upon a seat beside the mound, full of deep thought. He gazed upon that work of
2285 giants, marking how that everlasting vault of earth contained within it those stony arches on their pillars fast upheld.

Then that knight surpassing good with his hands sprin-kled him with water, that king renowned all dreadly bloody, his own liege-lord, weary of war; his helmet he unclasped.
2290 Beowulf spake – despite his hurt, his grievous mortal wound, he spake – verily he knew that he had accomplished his hours of life, his joys upon the earth; now was departed all the number of his days, and Death exceeding near.

'Now to a son of mine I should have wished to give my
2295 harness of battle, had it been granted unto me that any heir of my body should follow me. This people have I ruled for

fifty winters – no king was there, not one among the peoples
dwelling nigh, who dared with allied swords approach me,
or threaten me with war's alarm. In mine own land I faced
2300 what time brought forth, held well mine own, nor pursued
with treachery cruel ends, nor swore me many an oath
unrighteously. In all this may I now, sick of mortal wounds,
have joy, for that the Ruler of men hath not cause to charge
me with cruel murder of my kin, when my life departeth
2305 from my body. Now go thou swiftly and survey the Hoard
beneath the hoary rock, Wiglaf beloved, now that the serpent
lieth dead, sleepeth wounded sore, robbed of his treasure.
Make now haste, that I may behold the wealth of long ago,
the golden riches, may plain survey the clear jewels cun-
2310 ning-wrought, and so may I, the wealth of precious things
achieved, the softer leave my life and the lordship which long
time I held.'

Then I have heard that speedily the son of Wihstan, when
these words were spoken, did hearken to his wounded lord
2315 in combat stricken, striding in his netlike mail, his corslet
for battle woven, under the barrow's vault. Then, passing by
the seat, that young knight proudhearted, filled with the joy
of victory, beheld a host of hoarded jewels, gold glistening
that lay upon the ground, marvellous things upon the wall,
2320 the very lair of that old serpent in the dim light flying, and
ewers standing there, vessels of men of bygone days, reft
of those who cared for them, their fair adornment crum-
bling. There was many a helm old and rusted, a multitude
of twisted armlets in strange devices twined. Treasure, gold
2325 hidden in the earth, easily may overtake the heart of any of

the race of men – let him beware who will! There too he saw
a banner hanging all wrought of gold, high above the hoard,
the chiefest of all marvellous things of handicraft, woven by
skill of fingers. Therefrom a radiance issued, that he might
2330   plain perceive that space beneath the earth, and all the pre-
cious things survey. Of the serpent there was nought to see;
nay, the sword had taken him. Then, as I have heard, within
that mound the Hoard and ancient work of giants did one
man plunder, lading his bosom with dish and goblet at his
2335   own sweet will; the banner, too, he seized, of standards the
most shining-fair. The broad-sword of his aged lord – iron
was its edge – had brought to ruin him that in his sway these
precious things had kept long while, the terror of his flame
wielding hot before the Hoard, swirling fiercely in the mid-
2340   most night, until he died a bitter death.

    In haste was the messenger, eager to return, urged by the
precious spoils. Anxiety pierced his uplifted heart to know
whether he should yet living find the prince of the windlov-
ing people upon that level place where he had erewhile left
2345   him, his valour ebbing. Now bearing these precious things
he found that prince renowned, his lord, bleeding, nigh to
his life's end. Once more he began to sprinkle him with
water, until speech like a sharp pang burst from the prison
of his breast. Thus spake the aged warrior king in anguish,
2350   looking upon the gold: 'To the Master of all, the Glorious
King and everlasting Lord, I speak now my words of thanks
for these fair things, that I here gaze upon, for that I have
been suffered ere my death's hour such wealth to gather for
my people. Now that I have for the hoard of precious things

2355 bartered the span of mine old life, do ye henceforth furnish
the people's needs. No longer may I here remain. Bid ye men
renowned in war to make a mound for me plain to see when
the pyre is done upon a headland out to sea. It shall tower on
high upon Hronesnæs, a memorial to my folk, that voyagers
2360 upon the sea shall hereafter name it Beowulf's Barrow, even
they who speed from afar their steep ships over the shadows
of the deeps.' From his neck that prince of valiant heart undid
a golden circlet and gave it to his knight, young wielder of
the spear, and his helm, gleaming with gold, his corslet and a
2365 ring, bidding him use them well. 'Thou art the end and latest
of our house of Wægmund's line. All hath fate swept away of
my kinsfolk to their appointed doom, good men of valour – I
must follow them!' That was the latest word that issued from
that aged heart and breast, ere he betook him to the pyre and
2370 the hot surge of warring flames. From his bosom did the soul
depart to seek the judgement of the just.

Then grievous was the lot of that man little tried in
years, seeing upon the earth that most beloved of men at
his life's end suffering miserably. His slayer, too, lay dead,
2375 the dire dragon of the cave bereft of life, whom torment had
oppressed. Those hoarded rings no longer might he rule, that
serpent crooked-coiling; nay, blades of iron had seized him,
hard, forged by hammers, notched in war; that he who had
winged afar by wounds was stilled, fallen upon the ground
2380 beside his treasure-house. Never more in his disport did he
wander through the air at midmost night, nor proud in the
possession of fair things reveal his form to men, but was cast
upon the earth by the hand and deed of that leader of the

host. In sooth few among men that possessed great valour
2385 in that land, as I have learned, had luck therein, when daring
though he were in every deed, he hurled him against the
blast of that envenomed foe, or troubled with his hands his
hall of rings, if he therein had found the Guardian dwelling
watchful in his mound. Even by Beowulf was his portion of
2390 those kingly treasures paid for with his death. Both now had
journeyed to the end of passing life.

Now it was not long ere those laggards in battle, who
before had not dared to wield their shafts in the great need
of their sovereign lord, forsook the wood, ten faint hearts
2395 together, breakers of their vows. But now in shame they
came bearing their shields and harness of war to where the
aged king lay dead. They looked upon Wiglaf. Wearied he
sat, that champion of the host, close to the side of his lord,
seeking with water to revive him – nought did it avail him.
2400 He could not, dearly though he wished it, keep upon the
earth his captain's life, nor any whit avert the Almighty's
will. God's Doom was ever the master then of every man in
deeds fulfilled, even as yet now it is.

Then did each man that had forgot his valour with little
2405 seeking get a grim rebuke from Wiglaf the young, the son of
Wihstan. He now spake, a man with pain at heart, looking on
those men unloved: 'Lo! this indeed may he say, who wishes
the truth to tell, that this liege-lord (who gave you those
costly gifts and soldier's gear, arrayed wherein ye now stand
2410 here, in that time when he oft did grant to you, sitting drink-
ing ale upon the benches in his hall, both helm and corslet,

even the most splendid of such things as he, a king for his knights, might get for you from far or near) that in the hour when war came upon him all that harness of war he utterly 2415 had cast away, ruinously. Little cause indeed had the king of this people for pride in his comrades in arms. Nonetheless God who ruleth victories vouchsafed to him that he unaided avenged himself with his sword, when he had need of valour. Little succour of his life could I afford him in that combat, 2420 and yet essayed beyond the measure of my power to help my kinsman. Thereafter ever was that deadly adversary in vigour less, when I had smitten him with sword, less violent then the fire surged from the gateways of his head. Too few the defenders that thronged about their prince, when that evil 2425 hour was come upon him! Behold! receiving of rich gifts, the giving of swords, all joy in the homes of your fathers, and hope shall fail for all your kin. Stripped of lands and rights shall each man of that house and line depart, when good men learn from afar of your retreat and deed inglorious. Death 2430 is more sweet for every man of worth than life with scorn!'

Then he bade men up over the cliff by the sea to bring news of the deeds of war to the fencéd camp, wherein good men assembled, having their shields beside them, sat the long morning of the day, gloom in their hearts, pondering either 2435 chance, the last day or the home-coming of the man they loved. Little of these tidings new did he in silence keep who rode that seaward slope, but faithfully he said for all to hear: 'Now is he who to the windloving people furnished their delight, the lord of the Geats, bound upon the bed of death; 2440 he abides upon a bloody couch through the serpent's deed.

Beside him his mortal adversary lies stricken with strokes of knife; sword could in no wise to that fierce slayer do grievous hurt. Wiglaf, Wihstan's son, by Beowulf sits, the brave living watching the brave dead; in weariness of soul he holds wake 2445 beside the body of both friend and foe.

'Now must our people look for time of war, as soon as afar to Frisian and to Frank the king's fall is revealed. Bitter was the feud decreed against the Húgas (Franks), when Hygelac came sailing with his raiding fleet to Frisian land. 2450 There the Hetware in battle assailed him, and valiantly with overwhelming strength achieved that the mailéd warrior should lay him down: he fell amid the host, not one fair thing did that lord to his good men give. From us hath been ever since the favour of the Merovingian lord withheld. Nor do 2455 I from the Swedish realm look for any peace or truce at all: rather has it been reported far and wide that Ongentheow reft of life Hæthcyn Hrethel's son beside Hrefnawudu (Ravenswood), when the Geatish folk in arrogance had first attacked the warlike Scylfings. Quickly did the aged father 2460 of Ohthere, old and dread, deliver him an answering stroke; the sea-chieftain he destroyed, and his wife aged as he was he rescued, his lady revered, of her gold bereaved, the mother of Onela and Ohthere; and then pursued his mortal foes until they escaped hard-pressed, leaderless, into Hrefnesholt 2465 (Ravensholt). Then with all his great host he besieged the survivors of his swords, weary of their wounds; grievous things often did he vow to that unhappy band through the long night, saying that he at morn would spill their lives with edge of sword or some would do upon gallows-trees to be

2470 the sport of crows. Relief thereafter came for those unhappy
hearts with the first light of day, when they heard the horns
and trumpets of Hygelac for battle ringing, as that good man
came marching on their trail with the proven valour of his
people. Plain to see was far and wide the bloody swath of
2475 Geats and Swedes, the murderous assault of men, how those
peoples between them stirred up deeds of enmity.

'Then the good king (Ongentheow) – full of years was
he and many sorrows – betook him with his bodyguard to a
fast place; yea, the warrior Ongentheow gave back to higher
2480 ground. He had heard of the valour of Hygelac and the might
in war of that proud prince; he hoped not to withstand him,
nor to strive against those men of the sea, to defend from
those fierce rovers treasure, child, nor wife. Back he gave
from that place, the old king, behind an earthen wall. There
2485 attack was ordered upon the people of the Swedes; the ban-
ners of Hygelac marched forth over that defended space,
when Hrethel's people came crowding upon the fencéd
camp. There was Ongentheow with grey-strewn hair driven
to bay with edge of sword, and there must that king of (his)
2490 people endure the single will of Eofor. Him in wrath had
Wulf Wonreding with his weapon found, so that at the stroke
from veins forth spouted blood beneath the hair. And yet
daunted was he not, the aged Scylfing; nay, swiftly requited
that deadly blow with exchange more fell, when he, the king
2495 of his people, turned upon his foe. Now could the eager son
of Wonred no answering blow return; nay, he had cloven the
helm upon his head, so that dyed with blood he must sink
down: he fell upon the earth. Not yet was he doomed to die;

99

nay, he recovered, albeit the wound had touched him nigh.
2500 Lo! Hygelac's bold knight, since his brother was laid low, let
now the broad blade of ancient giant-forgéd sword above the
wall of shields shatter the helm gigantic. Now the king gave
back, the shepherd of his people, he was stricken mortally.
Many then were those that bound up Eofor's brother and
2505 swiftly lifted him, since it was granted them that they should
be masters of the stricken field. Whereupon the knight
despoiled his adversary, from Ongentheow he took the iron
corslet, the hilted sword hard-tempered, and the helm too;
the harness of the greyhaired lord he bore to Hygelac.
2510 'These fair things he received, and graciously vowed to
him rewards amid his people, and even so fulfilled his word.
For their onslaught in that battle the lord of the Geats,
Hrethel's heir, when he came to his home Eofor and Wulf
repaid with gifts beyond measure; to each of them he gave
2515 one hundred thousand (silver pence) in land and linkéd
rings – no cause had any man on earth to reproach him with
those rewards, since they had with their swords achieved
such glorious deeds. Moreover to Eofor he gave his only
daughter, as a pledge of his favour, for the honouring of his
2520 house.
'Such is the feud and enmity, the cruel malice of men, for
which I look, in which the Swedish people will come against
us, when they learn that our lord is reft of life, who aforetime
did guard against those that hated him his treasury and realm,
2525 after the fall of mighty men did rule the sealoving Geats,
accomplishing the profit of his people, yea, and before all did
knightly deeds.

'Now is all speed the best, that we should look upon the king of this people where he lies, and bring that one who gave us rings upon his funeral way. Nor is it due that some solitary thing should be consumed beside that proud heart; nay, there is a hoard of precious things, gold beyond count grimly purchased, and rings now at this last paid for with his very life – these is it right that the blazing wood devour, the fire enfold. Not for him shall good man wear a thing of price in memory, nor maiden fare about her neck have ring to deck her; rather woeful-hearted, stripped of gold, long time and again shall she tread the lands of exile, now that the captain of our host hath laid aside his laughter, his mirth and merriment. For this shall many a spear cold at morn be grasped and seized, lifted in hand; nor shall the music of the harp awake the warriors, but the dusky raven gloating above the doomed shall speak many things, shall to the eagle tell how it sped him at the carrion-feast, when he vied with the wolf in picking bare the slain.'

Thus was that gallant man a teller of tidings bitter; little did he report amiss of what had chanced or had been said. All the host arose. Joyless they went with welling tears to the foot of Earnanæs (Eagles' Head) that monstrous sight to see. So found they keeping his bed of ease, lifeless upon the earth, him who in former times had given rings to them. Now was his last day passed for that good man, and the king of battles, the prince of the windloving people had died a monstrous death. Already had they seen a thing there yet more strange: the loathly serpent lying there stretched out before them on the ground. Grim to see, dreadly-hued, the flaming dragon had been scorched with his own glowing fires; fifty measured feet in length he lay at rest. Joy in the air aforetime had he had by night, then back was wont to go seeking his lair; now was he bound in death, for the last time had he used his earthy

2560 caves. Beside them goblets and ewers stood, and dishes lay and precious swords, rusty and eaten through, as had they dwelt there a thousand winters in the earth's embrace. In that day that heritage had been endowed with mighty power; the gold of bygone men was wound about with spells, so that

2565 none among them might lay hand upon that hall of rings, unless God himself, true King of Victories, granted to the man he chose the enchanter's secret and the hoard to open, to even such among men as seemed meet to Him.

Now all could see that to evil fortune had he sallied forth

2570 who wrongfully had kept concealed therein the precious things beneath the builded mound. One only, and none beside, had the Guardian slain, before his deeds of enmity were bitterly avenged. A mystery it is where a man of prowess and good heart shall meet the end of his allotted life, when

2575 no longer may he among his kin dwell in the hall, his mead drinking. Even thus it was with Beowulf: when he sought out the barrow's guardian, his guile and malice, he knew not himself through what means his parting from the world should come about. To this end had the mighty chieftains,

2580 those that there had laid it, set a deep curse upon it even until the Day of Doom, that that man should be for his crimes condemned, shut in the houses of devils, fast in the bonds of hell, tormented with clinging evil, who should that place despoil. Alas, Beowulf ere he went had not more carefully

2585 considered the old possessor's will that cursed the gold.

Wiglaf spake, the son of Wihstan: 'Oft must it be that many men through one man's will shall suffer woe, even as is now befallen us. We could not advise our king beloved, the shepherd of this realm, to any well-counselled course, that he should not approach the keeper of the gold, but should let him lie where long time he had been, abiding in his dwellings unto the world's end, pursuing his mighty fate. The hoard is laid bare, grimly was it gained. Too mighty was the doom that thither drew this mortal man. I have been therein and all of it have I surveyed, the treasures of that house, when leave was given me – in no kindly wise was my entry welcomed in beneath the earthy mound. In haste I seized with hands a mighty burden huge of hoarded treasures, and hither did I bear them out unto my king. Yet living was he then, clear in mind and conscious, and all those many things he spake, aged and in anguish; and he bade me greet you, commanding that ye should fashion in memory of your good lord's deeds upon the place of his pyre such a lofty tomb, mighty and splendid, even as he was among men the most renowned in war over the wide earth, while yet it was his lot to use the wealth within his courts.

'Let us now haste, going once again to find and look upon that press of fair-wrought gems, the marvellous things beneath the builded mound. I will guide you, that ye from nigh at hand shall gaze there upon rings in plenty and on massive gold. Let the bier be ready, swiftly arrayed, when we come out; then let us bear our prince, our dear-beloved, where he shall long abide in the keeping of the Lord!'

Then the son of Wihstan, mighty man of valour, bade them summons send to many among men that homesteads

2615 ruled, that they being masters of men should bring from afar wood for the pyre to their good lord's need. 'Now shall the smoking flame be fed, the glowing fire devour the prince of men, even him who oft endured the iron hail, when the storm of arrows urged by bowstrings fled above the wall of shields, 2620 and the shaft performed its task sped by its feathered raiment, following the arrowhead.'

Moreover the wise son of Wihstan summoned from the host the king's own knights, seven in company, men most excellent; now eight warriors in all they went under the 2625 accurséd roof, one bearing in his hand a fiery torch, going forward at their head. No need then to cast lots who should despoil that hoard, when keeperless those men espied still any portion lying crumbling there; little did any grieve that they in haste brought forth those treasures of great price. The 2630 serpent too they thrust over the towering cliff, let the tide the dragon take, the flowing sea engulf the keeper of fair things. Then was the wreathéd gold laded upon a wain, beyond all count, and the prince borne away to Hronesnæs (Whale's Head), their chieftain hoar.

2635 For him then the Geatish lords a pyre prepared upon the earth, not niggardly, with helms o'erhung and shields of war and corslets shining, as his prayer had been. Now laid they amidmost their glorious king, mighty men lamenting their lord beloved. Then upon the hill warriors began the mighti-2640 est of funeral fires to waken. Woodsmoke mounted black above the burning, a roaring flame ringed with weeping, till the swirling wind sank quiet, and the body's bony house

was crumbled in the blazing [?core]. Unhappy in heart they
mourned their misery and their liege-lord slain. There too a
2645 lamentable lay many a Geatish maiden with braided tresses
for Beowulf made, singing in sorrow, oft repeating that days
of evil she sorely feared, many a slaying cruel and terror
armed, ruin and thraldom's bond. The smoke faded in the
sky. Then the lords of the windloving people upon a seaward
2650 slope a tomb wrought that was high and broad, to voyagers
on the waves clear seen afar; and in ten days they builded the
memorial of the brave in war, encompassed with a wall what
the fires had left, in such most splendid wise as men of chief
wisdom could contrive. In that mound they laid armlets and
2655 jewels and all such ornament as erewhile daring-hearted men
had taken from the hoard, abandoning the treasure of mighty
men to earth to keep, gold to the ground where yet it dwells
as profitless to men as it proved of old.

Then about the tomb rode warriors valiant, sons of
2660 princes, twelve men in all, who would their woe bewail, their
king lament, a dirge upraising, that man praising, honouring
his prowess and his mighty deeds, his worth esteeming – even
as is meet that a man should his lord beloved in words extol,
in heart cherish, when forth he must from the raiment of
2665 flesh be taken far away.

Thus bemourned the Geatish folk their master's fall, com-
rades of his hearth, crying that he was ever of the kings of
earth of men most generous and to men most gracious, to his
people most tender and for praise most eager.

*

NOTES ON THE TEXT
OF THE TRANSLATION

These notes are largely but not exclusively concerned with the varying interpretations, found in the texts of the translation, of words and passages in *Beowulf*. Many of these are discussed in the commentary, and the words in a textual note 'See the commentary' without line-reference means that it is the same in both cases; but the page-number of the note in the commentary, or of the particular passage in the note, is usually given to make it easier to find quickly.

The letters LT ('latest text') stand for the text of the translation of *Beowulf* given in this book.

14 (*18) *Beow*: this (and again at 41 (*53)) is almost the only case in the translation where I have altered a clear reading without justification in any of the texts, all of which have *Beowulf*. The matter is discussed in the commentary on pp. 144–8.

17–18 (*21) On the translation 'he dwells in his father's bosom' see the commentary, p. 149.

60 (*74) In B(i) against the word 'proclaimed' is written in pencil in another hand 'summoned?' This is the first of several suggestions certainly in the hand of C.S. Lewis, in this case not adopted.

67 (*83) B(i) had 'the time was not yet come'; in C 'come' was changed to 'at hand', together with another alternative 'was not far off', which I have adopted; see the commentary, p. 158.

94–5 (*117) 'ale-drinking': B(i) had 'ale-quaffing'; 'ale-drinking' was the suggestion of C.S. Lewis.

97 (*120) For Old English *Wiht unhǽlo* B(i) and C had 'That ruinous thing', later emended in C to 'That accurséd thing'. In a note on *Wiht unhǽlo*, taken to mean 'creature of evil', my father wrote that he favoured the emendation *unfǽlo*, 'since elsewhere *unhǽlo* means "bad health, illness", and *unfǽle* is precisely the right adjective: it means unnatural, sinister, unclean, evil – and ridding Heorot of Grendel is said to be making it *fǽle* again (*Heorot fǽlsian*, 350, *432).'

97–9 (*121–3) The Old English text reads: . . . *grim ond grǽdig, gearo sóna wæs, réoc ond réþe, ond on ræste genam þrítig þegna*; in the translation, 'ravenous and grim, swift was ready; thirty knights he seized . . .' Thus there is no translation of the words *réoc ond réþe* (both adjectives mean 'fierce, savage, cruel'). This was lacking in the earliest text B(i), and was never noticed subsequently.

107–8 (*134–5) On the translation 'Nor was it longer space than but one night' see the commentary, p. 164.

110 (*137) 'wrong' (O.E. *fyrene*): suggested by C.S. Lewis for B(i) 'sin'.

123–5 (*154–6) 'truce would he not have with any man of the Danish host, nor would withhold his deadly cruelty, nor accept terms of payment': on this translation see the commentary, pp. 164–6.

'nor accept terms of payment' is an emendation in C for 'nor make amends with gold'.

127–8 (*160) 'both knights and young' (O.E. *duguþe ond geogoþe*): this is apparently a clear example of a correction made to B(i) after the making of the typescript C, which retained the original reading 'both old and young'. On the translation of *duguð* see the commentary on p. 189 and pp. 204–5.

134–5 (*168–9) These lines were enclosed in brackets in both B(i) and C. Both texts had 'Who took no thought of him', but this was emended in C to 'nor did he know His will'. See the commentary pp. 181 ff.

135–50 (*170–88) See the commentary, where p. 173 appears a closely similar version of this passage in the translation.

140 (*175) 'tabernacles': emendation in C of 'fanes'; see the commentary pp. 179–80.

140 (*177) 'the slayer of souls' (O.E. *gástbona*): suggested by C.S. Lewis for B(i) 'destroyer of souls'.

143–50 (*180–8) The brackets enclosing these lines are editorial: see the commentary, p. 186, footnote.

146 (*184) 'fiendish malice': emendation in C of 'rebellious malice'. On the translation of *sliðne nið* see the commentary, pp. 175–6.

163–4 (*202–3) 'With that voyage little fault did wise men find': pencilled here on C: '[i.e. they applauded it]'. See the commentary, pp. 187–8.

181–2 (*223–4) The original reading of B(i) 'The waters were overpassed; they were at their sea-way's end' was changed on the text to 'Then for that sailing ship the voyage was at an end' (on C 'voyage' emended to 'journey'). See the commentary, pp. 193–4.

182–3 (*225) 'the Windloving folk' (O.E. *Wedera léode*). My father found it difficult to decide on a rendering of the names of the Geats, who in *Beowulf* are called also *Weder-Geatas*, *Wederas*, *Sæ-Geatas*. In the texts of the translation are found, in addition to simple preservation of the Old English names, 'Storm-folk', 'Storm-Geats', 'Windloving folk', 'Windloving

Geats'. His cursory correction of the C text left inconsistencies, but it is plain nonetheless that his final decision was 'windloving folk, windloving Geats' (perhaps following 'sealoving Geats' for *Sæ-Geatas*). I have therefore given 'windloving (folk, Geats)' at all occurrences of *Wederas* and *Weder-Geatas* in the poem.

184 (*226) B(i) 'their mail-shirts clashed' was changed on the text to 'their mail-shirts they shook'; see the commentary, pp. 194–5.

189 (*232) The word *fyrwyt* was translated 'eagerness' in B(i) and corrected in C to 'anxiety'; see the commentary, pp. 195–6. At 1668 (*1985) 'eagerness' remained; while at 2342 (*2784) 'anxiety' was the original translation in B(ii).

202 (*249) O.E. *seldguma*: B(i) and C 'minion', corrected in C to 'hall-servant'. See the commentary, pp. 196–7.

210 (*259) 'opened his store of words' (O.E. *wordhord onléac*): suggested by C.S. Lewis for B(i) 'unlocked his prisoned words'.

219–20 (*271–2) 'nor shall there in his court be aught kept secret' was emended in C to 'and there a certain matter shall not be kept secret'.

223 (*276) 'monstrous' (O.E. *uncúðne*): emendation in B(i) of 'inhuman'.

232–4 (*287–9) In B(i) and C the text 'it behoves a warrior that is bold of heart and right-minded to discern what truth there is in both words and deeds' was not part of the coast-guard's speech, which begins "This have I heard . . ." This was emended in C to '"A man of keen wit who takes good heed will discern the truth in both words and deeds: my ears assure me . . ."' See the commentary, pp. 200–1.

240 (*297) 'streams' (O.E. *lagustréamas*): suggested by C.S. Lewis for B(i) 'currents'.

246–8 (*303–6) B(i) after emendation and C had here: 'Images of the boar shone above the cheek-guards, adorned with gold, gleaming, fire-tempered; grim of mood the vizored helm kept guard over life'; this was corrected in C to LT (the text given in this book). See the commentary, pp. 201–4.

334–5 (*413–14) 'as soon as the light of evening is hid beneath heaven's pale': on this translation see the commentary, pp. 225–7.

338–9 (*419–20) B(i) and C: 'when I returned all stained with blood from the dangerous toils of my foes'; my father was treating *fáh* as the distinct word ('decorated, coloured, stained'), taken (as widely) to mean here '(blood)-stained'; but he made no reference to this interpretation in his commentary. Later, in pencil on 'C', he changed his original version to the translation in LT, 'when I returned from the toils of my foes, earning their enmity'. See the commentary, pp. 227–8.

339–40 (*420–1) B(i) and C: 'when five I bound, and made desolate the race of monsters, and when I slew. . .' On the changes made to C here see the commentary on 290–5, pp. 228–32.

344 (*426) O.E. *ðing wið þyrse*: B(i) and C: 'keep appointed tryst'; corrected in C to 'hold debate'.

346 (*428) In the poem Beowulf addresses Hrothgar as *brego Beorht-Dena, eodor Scyldinga,* but *eodor Scyldinga* is omitted in the translation. I have introduced this into the text, 'defender of the Scyldings' (as in line 539, *663).

348–9 (*431–2) B(i) and C: '. . . that I (be permitted B(i) >) may, unaided, I and my proud company', corrected in C to 'only I may, and my proud company'; see the commentary, pp. 232–5.

356–9 (*442–5) B(i) and C: 'Methinks he will, if he may so contrive it, in this hall of strife devour without fear the Geatish folk, as oft he hath the proud hosts of your men'. On the B(i) typescript my father pencilled now scarcely legibly above 'Geatish folk' the words 'folk of the Goths', and above 'the proud hosts of your men' some words were struck through and are illegible except for 'Hreðmen'. These corrections do not appear in C as typed, but the text as given in this book was entered subsequently. On this passage see the commentary, pp. 237–40.

380–1 (*471–2) B(i) and C: 'sending over the backs of the sea ancient treasures': the O.E. text has *sende ic Wylfingum ofer wæteres hrycg ealde mádmas*, but 'to the Wylfings' was omitted and its absence not noticed in C.

386–7 (*478) 'God (alone) may easily', O.E. *God éaþe mæg*: the word 'alone' was struck through but then marked with a tick of acceptance in B(i); typed in C it was subsequently bracketed. In his copy of Klaeber's third edition my father noted against line 478: 'A cry of despair: Only God can help me'. See the commentary, pp. 247–8.

395–7 (*489–90) B(i): 'Sit now at the feast, and unlock the thoughts of thy mind, thy victories and triumph, unto men, even as thy heart moveth thee'; emended on the typescript to 'Sit now at the feast, and in due time turn thy thought to victory for thy men, as thy heart may urge thee.' This was the form in C as I typed it; later my father changed 'in due time' to 'when the time comes', and scribbled, just legibly, '*or* for the Hrethmen' against 'for thy men'. See the commentary, pp. 251–2.

398 (*491) O.E. *Géatmæcgum*: C 'the Geatish knights', corrected to 'the young Geatish knights', with 'not B' (i.e. 'not Beowulf') written at the same time in the margin: see the commentary, p. 229.

398–405 (*491–8) This passage in the translation appears in almost identical form in the commentary on 163–4, pp. 188–9.

452 (*555) O.E. *hwæþre mé gyfeþe wearð*: B(i) 'it was decreed by fate that I found', emended to 'as my fate willed I found'; emended in C to 'it was granted to me to find'. See the commentary, pp. 255–6.

524–30 (*644–51) See the commentary pp. 262–4 on the translation of these lines.

555–6 (*681) O.E. *þára góda* 'of gentle arms': see the commentary, p. 265.

635 (*776) O.E. *míne gefrǽge* 'as I have heard' B(i) and C; in B(i) (only) with 'so the tale tells' written above, which I have adopted.

687–8 (*846) O.E. *feorhlastas bær* 'his desperate footsteps' B(i) and C, changed in C to 'his footsteps, bleeding out his life'; see the commentary, p. 279.

691–2 (*850) O.E. *déaðfǽge déog* 'doomed to die he plunged': see the commentary, pp. 279–80.

707–8 (*870–1) O.E. *word óþer fand sóðe gebunden*: 'word followed word, each truly linked to each'. This rendering goes back to B(i); my father did not change it later, despite the view that he expressed in the commentary on 705–10; see pp. 280 ff.

709 (*871–2) B(i) and C have 'began with skill to treat in poetry the quest of Beowulf; 'in poetry' was later bracketed in C, and I have omitted it from LT.

735 (*902) 'in the land of the Jutes' (O.E. *mid Éotenum*): the form 'Eotens' appears in B(i) and C; in the latter my father pencilled above it a name that I am unable to decipher. See further the textual note below on 875–6 'Jutes'.

791–2 (*971) On the omission of the words *tó lífwraþe* ('to save his life') in the translation see the commentary p. 297.

803–5 (*984–7) See the commentary, pp. 298–301.

813–15 (*997–9) B(i) and C: 'Sorely shattered was that shining house, all bound as it was within with bonds of iron, the hinges of the doors were wrenched apart'; in C emended later to the wording in LT. See the commentary, pp. 301–2.

850–1 (*1044) O.E. *eodor Ingwina*: 'the warden of the Servants of Ing (Danes)': 'warden' was a late change from 'bulwark' in C, and the explanatory 'Danes' in brackets is present in B(i) and C.

875–6 (*1072) 'the loyalty of the Jutes' (O.E. *Éotena tréowe*): here as in 735 and in the subsequent references, 889 (*1088), 937 (*1141), 939 (*1145), the name in B(i) and C is 'Eotens'. At 735 as already noted the name was changed in C to an illegible form, but in the other cases it was changed to 'Eote'; at line 876 (only) 'Jutes' was written above 'Eote'.

In LT I have printed 'Jutes' in all cases. There is a substantial discussion of this question in J.R.R. Tolkien, *Finn and Hengest*, ed. Alan Bliss, 1982, entry *Eotena* in the Glossary of Names, where also will be found an explanation of the form *Eote*, and a translation of the *Fréswæl* (as my father termed the minstrel's lay in Heorot: 'the Frisian slaughter', *Beowulf* 874, *1070) distinct from that in this book.

877 (*1074) 'of brothers and of sons': see the commentary p. 303, and my father's discussion in *Finn and Hengest* p. 96.

898 (*1098) 'the sad remnant (of the fight)' (O.E. *þá wéaláfe*): the explanatory words in brackets are found in B(i) and C.

917–19 (*1121–3) B(i) and C: 'their gaping wounds burst open, the cruel hurts of the body, and the blood sprang forth. Flame devoured them all, hungriest of spirits . . .' O.E. *bengeato burston, ðonne blód ætspranc, láðbite líces. Líg ealle forswealg, gǽsta gífrost . . .*

Very rapidly in barely legible pencil my father changed this in C to 'their gaping wounds burst open, the cruel hurts of the body, and the blood sprang away from the cruel devouring of the flame. Flame swallowed up them all . . .' This translation depends on his view (*Finn and Hengest*, see note to 875–6 above) that by scribal error *líg* 'flame' and *líc* 'body' were reversed, hence his translation in *Finn and Hengest*, pp. 152–3, 'gaping wounds burst open, when the blood sprang away from the cruel bite of flame (*láðbite líges*). That greediest of spirits consumed all the flesh (*líc eall forswealg*) of those ...' He compared *2080 (1748–9) *líc eall forswealg* 'all the flesh devoured'.

Since the emendation in C was clearly at an early stage I have left the original reading to stand in LT.

1102 (*1320) 'according to his desire'; pencilled here in B(i): 'seeing that he was summoned thus earnestly'.

1191 (*1428) 'in the middle hours' (O.E. *on undernmǽl*). B(i) as typed had 'in the very morning time', corrected to 'the underntide' with 'middle hours' written by the side; C 'in the middle hours'.

1216 (*1458) 'old and precious things' (O.E. *ealdgestréona*). B(i) 'prizéd', C 'precious'; the reading in B(i) was not corrected, but 'precious' appears in C as if it had been present in the previous text; presumably my father communicated this to me, perhaps on account of 'misprized' in line 1213.

1217 (*1459) O.E. *átertánum fáh*; B(i) and C 'stained with a device of branching venom', with a footnote in B(i) and in C (as usual bracketed and incorporated in the text) 'or "deadly with venom from poisoned shoots".'

1227–8 (*1470–1) O.E. *þér hé dóme forléas, ellenmǽrðum*. In B(i) there is no translation of these words, but the need for it is marked in the text, and at the foot of the page is written in an unknown and unformed handwriting (one of the many small oddities of these texts) 'There he forfeited glory for heroic deeds', with 'lost' written above 'forfeited' as an alternative. This I typed (with 'forfeited') in C.

1261 (*1510) 'as they swam', O.E. *on sunde*: there is a footnote in B(i) and C 'or "in the flood" (*on sunde*, cf. *1618).' At *1618 (1357) *Sóna wæs on sunde* is translated 'Soon was he swimming'.

1264–5 (*1513) 'that he was in some abysmal hall': a footnote to 'abysmal' in B(i) and C suggests 'hostile, evil' as a translation for O.E. *niðsele.*

1287 (*1537) 'by her locks': this translates *be feaxe*, which is an emendation of the manuscript *be eaxle*; a footnote here in B(i) and C has 'or (manuscript) "shoulder"', but alliteration and the next words are against this.'

1299 (*1551) 'beneath the widespread earth' (O.E. *under gynne grund*): footnote in B(i) and C 'or "under the vasty deep"; "under" is rather against the sense "earth".'

1304–5 (*1557) 'a sword endowed with charms of victory', O.E. *sigeéadig bil*: B(i) and C have 'a sword endowed with victory's might', with 'magic?' pencilled over 'victory's' in B(i) and taken up in C, later changed in that text to 'with charms of victory'.

1414–15 (*1686) 'on Sceden-isle', O.E. *on Scedenigge*: see the commentary on p. 148.

1444 (*1720) O.E. *æfter dóme* 'to earn him praise': footnote in B(i) and C: '*æfter dóme* may mean "according to honourable use".' See the note to 1831 below.

1481 (*1764) O.E. *oððe flódes wylm* was missed out in B(i); 'or water's wave' was supplied in C as if it had been present in B(i).

1549 (*1847) 'Hrethel's son' (O.E. *Hréþles eaferan*): footnote in B(i) and C: 'or, if the reference is fully prophetic, "descendant", i.e. Heardred' (son of Hygelac; see 1853–4).

1551 (*1850) O.E. *Sǽ-Géatas,* 'sea-loving Geats': see the note to 182–3 above.

1554–62 (*1855–63) Another translation of these lines appears in the commentary on 303–4, p. 217.

1666–7 (*1983) 'to the hands of mighty men', O.E. *hæleðum tó handa* (*hæleðum* is an emendation of the manuscript *hæ[ð]num*): footnote in B(i) and C: 'or *Hæthenas,* name of a people.' See the commentary, pp. 318 ff.

1711 (*2035) At the words 'amid their host' a footnote in B(i) and C says 'passage corrupt and doubtful'. See the commentary on 1708 ff., pp. 338 ff.

1773 (*2112) 'in age's fetters did lament his': the B(i) type-script stops here at the foot of a page, and the B(ii) manu-script begins a new page with 'youth and strength in arms'.

(From this point the textual changes, alternatives, and explanations referred to are those made to the manuscript B(ii). Many of these, as noted, were taken up into the C typescript.)

1788–9 (*2130) '(most grievous of those his sorrows) that he, lord of his folk, long while had known', O.E. *þára þe léodfruman lange begéate*: marginal note 'literally, had long while befallen the people's prince'.

1796 (*2139) 'in that abysmal hall'. The word 'abysmal' (cf. note to 1264–5 above) is bracketed, with a marginal note '[grund]sele'. The O.E. manuscript has *in ðám sele* with no gap. The meaning is 'the hall at the bottom of the mere.'

1801 (*2144) O.E. *þéawum*: 'kingly virtue': in B(ii) and C 'ancient virtue', but in B(ii) 'ancient' was bracketed with 'kingly' written above.

1810 (*2154) O.E. *gyd*: 'these fitting words' changed – at the time of writing (there are many such instances in B(ii) – to 'these appointed words'. On *gyd* see the commentary pp. 260–1, 347–8.

1816 (*2162) O.E. *Brúc ealles well!* Beside 'Use all the gifts with honour' is written in very faint pencil 'Blessed be thy use of all the gifts'.

1831 (*2179) 'bearing himself honourably', O.E. *dréah æfter dóme*: in a bracketed addition to the text other renderings are suggested: 'according to [?worthy] tradition' > 'according to honourable use', or 'so as to earn praise'; with a reference to *1720, see textual note to 1444 above.

1834–5 (*2182) 'those lavish gifts which God had granted him': added in the manuscript: '*sc.* gifts of prowess, manhood, strength, and prudence, loyalty, &c.'

1882 (*2236) Added after 'All of them': '(that kin)'; repeated in C.

1885 (*2239) O.E. *winegeómor* 'grieving for his friends': added: '(or "lord")'.

1888–9 (*2243) 'secured by binding spells', O.E. *nearocræftum fæst*: added: '(or "inaccessible (confining) arts")'; repeated in C.

1908 (*2266) 'many a one of living men', O.E. *fela feorhcynna*: added in brackets: 'life's kindred'; repeated in C.

1909–10 (*2267–8) O.E. *Swá giómormód giohðo mǽnde án æfter eallum*, 'Even thus in woe of heart he mourned his sorrow, alone when all had gone': following this in brackets 'alone mourning for them all'.

1910 (*2268) 'joyless he cried aloud', marginal note 'or "walked abroad"', repeated in C. Only the first three letters of the O.E. verb could even many years ago be certainly read in the manuscript; my father's two translations reflect different proposals, the first being *hwéop* (*hwópan*) in a doubtful sense 'lamented', the second *hwearf* (*hweorfan*), 'moved, went about, wandered'.

1912–14 (*2270–2) O.E. *Hordwynne fond eald úhtsceaða opene standan, sé ðe byrnende biorgas séceð*, 'This hoarded loveliness did the old despoiler wandering in the gloom find standing unprotected, even he who filled with fire seeks out mounds (of burial)': against this my father wrote: 'Can this be done more concisely?'

1934–5 (*2296–7) O.E. *hléw oft ymbehwearf ealne útan-weardne*, 'he compassed all the circuit of the mound': footnote 'literally, turned about all the outward mound'.

1944 (*2307) 'on the mountain-side', O.E. *on wealle*: marginal note 'possibly, "by the mound's wall",' repeated in C.

1947 (*2312) 'the invader', O.E. *se gæst*: marginal note 'or "creature"?'; repeated in C.

1963 (*2330) O.E. *ofer ealde riht*, 'against the ancient law': marginal note 'i.e. that laid down of old'.

2063 (*2454) 'evil deeds' (O.E. *dǽda*): following this in the manuscript: '(sc. men's cruelty)'; repeated in C.

2103 (*2501) O.E. *for dugeðum*, 'before the proven hosts'; marginal note 'or "by reason of my valour"?'

2124–5 (*2527–8) 'Fearless is my heart, wherefore I forbear from vaunting threat against this wingéd foe'; O.E. *Ic eom on móde from, þæt ic wið þone gúðflogan gylp ofersitte*. In margin: 'referring to his modest words that "the result is in the hands of fate" – whereas he might have said: "I shall defeat the dragon, as I have all others".'

2133–4 (*2538–9) 'Then the bold warrior stood up beside his shield, resolute beneath his helm' (O.E. *Árás ðá bí ronde, róf óretta, heard under helme*). Following this in the manuscript: 'or "arose, resolute in heart, his shield at side, his helm at head"', repeated in C.

2140–3 (*2546–9) Here there is a marginal note: 'The dragon was on fire now with wrath, formerly (when the hoard was plundered) he was asleep.'

2147 (*2554) Added after 'Hatred was aroused': '(within)'; repeated in C.

2161–3 (*2573–5) The translation in the manuscript B(ii) as I have given it was allowed to stand, but my father introduced a distinct interpretation in a footnote: 'when he had chance on that occasion for its first day of battle to wield it [the shield, see 1970-2] – for fate did not appoint him triumph in that combat'. This footnote looks very much as if it were added at the time of writing the page, which of course carries the text in the main body of the translation, but C does not include this second version. I have found no note of my father's on this difficult passage.

2164–5 (*2576–7) O.E. *gryrefáhne slóh incgeláfe,* 'with his ancient sword smote the dread foe'. After 'sword' follows in the manuscript '(exact sense unknown of *incgeláfe*)'. Against the word 'dread foe' there is a marginal note with a query: 'that thing of dreadful hue: that dreadfully shining thing'; this was repeated in C.

2172–4 (*2586–8) O.E. *Ne wæs þæt éðe síð, þæt se mæra   maga Ecgðéowes grundwong þone   ofgyfan wolde.* The translation first written here ran: 'No pleasant fare was his that . . . the son of Ecgtheow should witting leave that field on earth'. This was struck through immediately and replaced by 'No easy task was his that day (nor such) that the son of Ecgtheow should of his own will forsake that field on earth'. Subsequently 'pleasant fare' was retrieved from the rejected sentence and written above 'easy task', and the word 'renowned' was entered in pencil before 'son of Ecgtheow' in my handwriting of that time (but without the needed accent 'renownéd'!). It translates *mæra* in *se mæra maga Ecgðéowes* *2587. It seems possible that I was following the Old English text and pointed out its absence to my father. The word 'renowned' appears in the C text, but 'easy task' was still retained.

2258–9 (*2688–9) 'the destroyer of the folk, the fell fire-dragon' (O.E. *þéodsceaða . . . frécne fýrdraca*). In the margin my father wrote: 'CH the public scourge, the dreadful salamander!' And at 2309–10 (*2749) he wrote against 'clear jewels cunning-wrought' (O.E. *swegle searogimmas*) 'bright artistic gems!'

Both of these absurd expressions in the original translation of *Beowulf* by J.R. Clark Hall (1911) appeared in my father's 'Prefatory Remarks' to the revised edition of Clark Hall by C.L. Wrenn, 1940, p. xiii.

2260–2 (*2690–2) O.E. *þá him rúm ágeald, hát ond heaðogrim, heals ealne ymbeféng biteran bánum.* The translation as written read '(the dragon rushed upon Beowulf) now that a clear field was given him. His neck with his sharp bony teeth he seized now all about'. The words *hát ond heaðogrim* were thus omitted, but they are written in the margin of the manuscript in my handwriting, and their translation 'burning and fierce in battle' appear in the C text as typed.

Whether I observed this and pointed it out to my father cannot be said, but I note in passing that I did to some extent at any rate follow the poem in Old English when making the typescript C of the manuscript B(ii): this is seen from my pencilled '(*giong*)' over the word 'went' at line 2283 (*Ðá se æðeling gíong* *2715, 'Then the prince went'). Why I did this I don't know: perhaps I thought that *giong* here was the adjective 'young', and didn't realise that it could also be the past tense of *gangan* 'to go'. I mention this trifling matter here (and also in the note to 2172–4) because it probably casts light on the date of my typescript. I was briefly an undergraduate at Oxford in 1942, when a very reduced form of examination was introduced for an unclassed 'wartime B.A.', and one of the elements in this was a part of *Beowulf*.

2265 (*2695) 'unbowed' (O.E. *andlongne*): marginal note 'or "steadfast throughout".'

2271–2 (*2703) 'drew forth a deadly dagger' (O.E. *wæll-seaxe gebræd*): marginal note 'It is Beowulf [who] gives the *coup de grace*'.

2274–5 (*2706) 'valour had vanquished life' (O.E. *ferh ellen wræc*): marginal note against 'vanquished': 'driven forth his'.

2284–5 (*2717) 'that work of giants' (O.E. *enta geweorc*): marginal note '*sc.* the tomb'.

2402–3 (*2858–9) O.E. *wolde dóm Godes dǽdum rǽdan gumena gehwylcum, swá hé nú gén déð*. This was first translated: 'God's doom was ever the master then of every man in deeds fulfilled, even as yet now it is' as in LT; but a footnote was appended in the manuscript: 'God would then in deed accomplish his decrees for each and every man, even as yet now he doth.'

2423 (*2882) 'the gateways of his head', O.E. *of gewitte*. Footnote to B(ii): 'highflown, but so is the odd expression *of gewitte* = eyes, ears, nose, mouth.'

2489–90 (*2963) 'king of (his) people' (O.E. *þéodcyning*): I have inserted 'his' which is absent from both B(ii) and C.

2548 (*3031) The manuscript B(ii) and text C have '*Earnanæs* (Eagle's Head)'; I have substituted 'Eagles' Head'.

2559–60 (*3046) 'his earthy caves', O.E. *eorðscrafa*. The word in B(ii) is certainly 'earthy', not 'earthly' as in C; so also at 2597, where *eorðweall* (*3090) is translated 'the earthy mound' (again 'earthly' in C). (Incidentally, at 2114–15, (*2515), where Clark Hall has Beowulf referring to the habitation of 'the destructive miscreant' [the dragon] as 'his earthly vault' (O.E. *eorðsele*, 'his house of earth', 2114–15) my father placed an exclamation mark in his copy against 'earthly'.)

2600 (*3094) 'and all those many things he spake', O.E. *worn eall gespræc*: after 'many things' there is an explanatory addition: '*sc.* which ye have been told'.

2626–7 (*3126) 'No need then to cast lots who should despoil that hoard': footnote in B(ii): '*sc.* there was no hanging back – the dragon was dead.'

2644–6 (*3150) 'There too a lamentable lay many a Geatish maiden with braided tresses for Beowulf made'. As first written the translation reads here: 'a lamentable lay his lady aged with braided tresses for Beowulf made'. This was widely accepted as the best solution of a very badly damaged passage in the *Beowulf* manuscript. Of this leaf my father wrote: 'This is most unfortunate, as *3137–82 [the last line] are in many respects the finest part of the poem (especially in technical composition).'

The words 'his lady aged' translated a damaged Old English word read as *g .. méowle* (with the Latin word *ănus* 'old woman' written above it). In a fairly brief note on this in his commentary he said that 'the conjectured *geo-méowle* is excellent in sense and metre and goes with the Latin gloss over it. The word occurs elsewhere (only) in *Beowulf* *2931 (2461), *ióméowlan*, of the aged queen of Ongentheow. It means here therefore "aged lady", Beowulf's unnamed queen (who may be Hygd).'

In the manuscript B(ii) the words 'his lady aged' were replaced by 'many a Geatish maiden', and this is present in the typescript C as typed. I have found no comment on this among my father's papers, but in a text of the conclusion of *Beowulf* that seems to have been intended for recitation occur the words *Géatisc méowle*. It may also be mentioned that an illustrative text associated with one of the versions of his 1938 lecture on 'Anglo-Saxon verse' (see the Appendix to *The Fall of Arthur*) is an alliterative translation of the last lines of *Beowulf*, in which occurs this passage:

              Woeful-hearted
men mourned sadly   their master slain
while grieving song   Gothland-maiden
with braided hair   for Beowulf made,
sang sorrowladen,   saying oft anew
that days of evil   she dreaded sorely
dire deeds of war,   deaths and slaughter,
shameful serfdom.   Smoke rose and passed.

Against the third line my father wrote subsequently 'while her grievous dirge the grey lady', perhaps suggesting that he regretted the loss of this last appearance of Hygd, if indeed it was she.

*

INTRODUCTORY NOTE TO
THE COMMENTARY

At Oxford University, in the years when my father was the Professor of Anglo-Saxon, candidates for the degree of bachelor of arts in the English faculty were obliged to follow a course, or courses, of varying scope, in the oldest English literature ('Anglo-Saxon'). Few indeed were those ('the philologists') who elected to take the course in which the emphasis was expressly and extensively 'mediaeval'; the very great majority of undergraduates took what was known as the 'general course' in English literature. In this, one of the nine papers that constituted the final examination was concerned with Old English; and for this there was a requirement to read a substantial part of *Beowulf* in the original language, and translation of passages from it was compulsory in the examination.

The portion prescribed was from the beginning to line 1650, that being just over half the poem, a halting place that my father thought mistaken. The lectures from which the commentary in this book is largely derived were in their written form headed 'Lectures for the general school, Text,

1–1650'. I hope that I have found, by putting a selection of them into company with his translation of *Beowulf*, a suitable setting in which to bring them to light.

It must be said that the preparatory writings, and often subsequent rewritings, for these lectures, taken as a whole, offer many intrinsic difficulties and complexities hard to disentangle, and I doubt that any final ordering would be possible. But most notable is the fact that the earlier parts of the commentary have a distinct character. They were written fairly carefully and legibly with sufficient uniformity to suggest that it was all done more or less at the same time: there are many later additions and alterations, but relatively very little correction or hesitation in the course of the original writing. This work does not end sharply, but after some thousand lines of the Old English text it becomes by degrees rougher and much less uniform: hasty notes in pencil rather than ink, clipped, abbreviated and allusive in manner, often very hard to read, and ultimately petering out. (There is thus a long gap (p. 302) in the commentary as it appears in this book, and the notes that follow it are derived from another set of lectures, addressed to the 'philologists', clearly written and lengthy discussions of major problems in the interpretation of the text of *Beowulf*: these lectures I have also used occasionally elsewhere in the commentary.)

The conclusion seems to me to be unavoidable that the well-written earlier parts of his commentary was an abandoned undertaking of my father's based on earlier (and no doubt rougher) material, although the evidence for this is limited to a few pages where erased pencilled text can be seen beneath the well-written text in ink. There is no indication of his purpose, but it seems to me very unlikely that he had in mind some possible publication: I think it much more probable that his intention was simply to clarify his material, grown complex and confused from repetition and alteration of these lectures over the years.

I append here some indications of the ways in which I have treated these lectures for their place in this book. In the first place I must make it clear that my selection from the lectures was dictated not only by considerations of suitability for this purpose, but also by the need to keep within limits of length.

Additions. My notes of all kinds, appearing chiefly in footnotes, are set within square brackets; but citations of the *translation*, which are of course additions to the lectures, are not as a rule distinguished. As I have noted in the preface, I have throughout given the line-references in two forms, those of the translation and those of the Old English; this has of course entailed a great many doubled references, and I have attempted to avoid confusion by printing those to the poem itself in smaller type and with an asterisk. It should be noted that, unless indicated otherwise, in the heading to each separate note in the commentary the translated word or phrase is almost always that found in the translation, irrespective of any rendering that may be advocated in the note. (It must be borne in mind that when writing the lectures my father did not consult his translation in any consistent fashion.) The Old English citation in the heading is the text found in Klaeber's edition, unless shown otherwise.

The only extraneous addition of mine of substance is the introduction of extracts from my father's tale of King Sheave in the notes on line 3, Scyld Scefing, and 21, the ship-burial.

Omissions and Alterations. In his edition *Finn and Hengest* (1982) of my father's lectures on the episode of 'Finnsburg' in *Beowulf* Professor Alan Bliss wrote: 'I have not attempted to alter the colloquial style appropriate to lectures, though occasionally it reads oddly in print. If Tolkien himself had revised his work for publication, no doubt he would have made many stylistic changes.' In this case I think that the tone of a speaking voice – the direct, spontaneous, and accessible style – is an essential character of these written lectures, and the texts are printed precisely as he wrote them.

In general I have applied no unvarying principles, but have treated each note, long or short, as I thought best for the purpose. I have quite often thought it necessary or desirable to make omissions in the case of my father's introduction of difficult etymological detail, and of syntactic, grammatical, and metrical detail that does not affect the translation, or have given brief summaries. Here and there, where there has been an omission, sentences have been lightly remodelled, but I have taken pains to ensure that I have not modified the sense.

In the course of these lectures my father sometimes repeated, more or less, views that he had already expressed in another context. In such cases I have retained the repetition, for to remove it might spoil the later argument. And I have not 'improved' the text where there are infelicities in the expression such as arise in rapidly written compositions (for example, the use of the word 'mysterious' three times in quick succession, pp. 138–9), for that is a slippery slope.

In the difficult matter of the use of accents or markings of length in the printing of Old English, my father's writing varied so constantly that I have decided to follow his usage in his Old English text of *Sellic Spell* (pp. 407 ff.), acute accent rather than macron, e.g. ó not ō, throughout.

As regards the spelling of Old English names, both in the translation and in the body of the commentary, he used th beside ð or þ (which he used indiscriminately), so *Hrothgar, Hroðgar*. I see no advantage in keeping these variations, and thus I print *Hrothgar, Ecgtheow, Sigeferth*, etc., without accents; but I give in all cases (rather than ae and Ae) æ and Æ: *Hæðcyn, Æschere*.

COMMENTARY ACCOMPANYING THE TRANSLATION OF *BEOWULF*

1   *Lo!* [This translates *Hwæt*, the first word of the poem.]

A genuine *anacrusis* – or a note 'striking up' at the beginning of a poem. Deriving from minstrel tradition: in origin a call for attention. It is 'outside the metre'. It occurs at the beginning of other poems; but it is not confined to the beginnings of poems nor to verse.

3; *4   *Scyld Scefing*

Scyld is the eponymous ancestor of the *Scyldingas*, the Danish royal house to which Hrothgar King of the Danes in this poem belongs. His name is simply 'Shield': and he is a 'fiction', that is a name deduced from the 'heraldic' family name *Scyldingas* after they became famous. This process was aided by the fact that the Old English (and Germanic) ending *-ing*, which could mean 'connected with, associated with, provided with', etc., was also the usual patronymic ending. The invention of the eponymous 'Shield' was probably

Danish, that is actually the work of Danish *þylas* and *scopas*[1] in the lifetime of the kings of whom we hear in *Beowulf*, the certainly historical Healfdene and Hrothgar.

As for *Scefing*, it can thus, as we see, mean 'provided with a sheaf', 'connected in some way with a sheaf of corn', or son of a figure called Sheaf. In favour of the latter is the fact that there *are* English traditions of a mythical (not the same as eponymous and fictitious) ancestor called *Scéaf* or *Scéafa*, belonging to ancient culture-myths of the North; and of his special association with Danes. In favour of the former is the fact that Scyld comes out of the unknown, a babe, and the name of his father, if he had any, could not be known by him or the Danes who received him. But such poetic matters are not strictly logical. Only in *Beowulf* are the two divergent traditions about the Danes blended in this way, the heraldic and the mythical. I think the poet meant (Shield) Sheafing as a patronymic. He was blending the vague and fictitious warlike glory of the eponymous ancestor of the conquering house with the more mysterious, far older and more poetical myth of the mysterious arrival of the babe, the corn-god or the culture-hero his descendant, at the beginning of a

---

1 [The word *scop* meant 'poet, minstrel'; the meaning of *þyle* was very various and can be uncertain in particular cases. Elsewhere in these lectures my father wrote:

> To learn by heart from other and older members of his craft was part of the occupation of the *scop* or minstrel, and the *þyle*, 'recorder' of genealogies, and stories in prose. But also it was his duty to make lays or tales or mnemonic lists concerning matters that came under his own contemporary observation, or came to him personally, as news from afar.]

people's history, and adding to it a mysterious Arthurian departure, *back into the unknown*, enriched by traditions of ship-burials in the not very remote heathen past – to make a magnificent and suggestive *exordium*, and background to his tale.

[In 1964 my father wrote in a letter (*The Letters of J.R.R. Tolkien*, no. 257) of 'an abortive book on time-travel [*The Lost Road*] . . . It started with a father-son affinity between Edwin and Elwin of the present, and was supposed to go back into legendary time by way of Eädwine and Ælfwine of circa A.D. 918, and Audoin and Alboin of Lombardic legend, and so to the traditions of the North Sea concerning the coming of corn and culture heroes, ancestors of kingly lines, in boats (and their departure in funeral ships).' I published what he wrote of *Sheaf* ('King Sheave') in *The Lost Road and Other Writings*, 1987 (*The History of Middle-earth* vol.V), pp. 85 ff.), to which the reader is referred. I gave there the text of the lecture reprinted above, and it seems to me appropriate to cite again here portions of the tale of King Sheave in prose version and in alliterative verse that he wrote at that time. The former (*ibid.* p. 85) begins thus:

To the shore the ship came and strode upon the sand, grinding upon the broken shingle. In the twilight as the sun sank men came down to it, and looked within. A boy lay there, asleep. He was fair of face and limb, dark-haired, white-skinned, but clad in gold. The inner parts of the boat were gold-adorned, a vessel of gold filled with clear water at his side, at his right was a harp, beneath his head was a sheaf of corn, the stalks and ears of which gleamed like gold in the dusk. Men knew not what it was. In wonder they drew the boat high upon the beach, and lifted the boy and bore him up, and laid him sleeping in a wooden house in their burh.

From the poem, which runs to 153 lines (*ibid.* pp. 87–91), I cite the passage corresponding to that in the prose version just given:

The ship came shining   to the shore driven
and strode upon the sand,   till its stem rested

on sand and shingle.   The sun went down.
The clouds overcame   the cold heavens.
In fear and wonder   to the fallow water
sadhearted men   swiftly hastened
to the broken beaches   the boat seeking,
gleaming-timbered   in the grey twilight.
They looked within,   and there laid sleeping
a boy they saw   breathing softly:
his face was fair,   his form lovely,
his limbs were white,   his locks raven
golden-braided.   Gilt and carven
with wondrous work   was the wood about him.
In golden vessel   gleaming water
stood beside him;   strung with silver
a harp of gold   neath his hand rested;
his sleeping head   was soft pillowed
on a sheaf of corn   shimmering palely
as the fallow gold   doth from far countries
west of Angol.   Wonder filled them.
The boat they hauled   and on the beach moored it
high above the breakers;   then with hands lifted
from the bosom its burden.   The boy slumbered.
On his bed they bore him   to their bleak dwellings
darkwalled and drear   in a dim region
between waste and sea.

This work on 'Sheaf' or 'King Sheave' probably dates from 1937;
and it would reappear some eight years later in *The Notion Club
Papers* (*Sauron Defeated*, 1992 (*The History of Middle-earth* vol.IX),
pp. 269–76).]

4   *the seats where they drank their mead*; *5 *meodosetla*

The Old English word *meodosetl* is a compendious
expression for 'benches in the hall where knights sat feast-
ing'. The symbolism and emotional connotations of *mead*

and *ale* are very different in Old English verse, especially what survives of heroic and courtly verse, from the modern associations. 'Scyld denied the mead-benches to men', i.e. he destroyed the kings of lesser tribes and their halls. [See the note to 627, p. 278.]

7–8   *over the sea where the whale rides*; *10 *ofer hronráde*

hronráde is a 'kenning' for the 'sea'. What is a 'kenning'? (See my introduction to the Clark Hall translation revised by Wrenn [1940]). A *kenning* is an Icelandic word meaning (in this particular technical use) 'description'. From Old Icelandic criticism of Norse alliterative verse it has been borrowed and used by us as a technical term for those *pictorial descriptive compounds* or *brief expressions* which can be *used in place of the normal plain word*. Thus to say 'he sailed over the gannet's bath' (O.E. *ganotes bæþ*) is to use a kenning for the sea. You could, of course, strike out a kenning for yourself, and all must at some time have been struck out by some poet; but the tradition of Old English verse-language contained a number of well-established kennings for such things as the sea, battle, warriors, and so on. They were part of its 'poetic diction' just as 'wave' for 'water' (based on poetic Latin use of *unda*) is part of 18th century 'diction'.

Several of the sea-kennings refer to the sea as the place where seabirds or animals dive or travel. Thus *ganotes bæþ* (which in full means 'the place where the gannet dives, like a man bathing'); or *hwælweg* ('the place where whales go on their journeys' as horses or men or waggons go over the plains of the land); or the 'seal paths' (*seolhpaþu*) or 'seal's baths' (*seolhbaþu*).

hronrád is evidently related to these expressions. Nonetheless it is quite *incorrect* to translate it (as it is all too frequently translated) 'whale road'. It is incorrect stylistically since compounds of this sort sound in themselves clumsy or bizarre in modern English, even when their components are correctly selected. In this particular instance the unfortunate sound-association with 'railroad' increases the ineptitude.

It is incorrect in fact. *rád* is the ancestor of our modern word 'road', but it does not mean 'road'. Etymology is not a safe guide to sense. *rád* is the noun of action to *rídan* 'ride' and means *riding* – i.e. 'riding on horseback; moving as a horse does (or a chariot), or as a ship does at anchor'; and hence 'a journey on horseback' (or more seldom by ship), 'a course (however vagrant)'. It does not mean the actual 'track' – still less the hard paved permanent and more or less straight tracks that we associate with the 'road'.

Also *hron* (*hran*) is a word peculiar to Old English. It means some kind of a 'whale', that is of that family of fish-like mammals. What precisely is not known: but it was something of the porpoise or dolphin kind, probably; at any rate less than a real *hwæl*. There is a statement in Old English that a *hron* was about seven times the size of a seal, and a *hwæl* about seven times the size of a *hron*.

The word as 'kenning' therefore means *dolphin's riding*, i.e. in full, the watery fields where you can see dolphins and lesser members of the whale-tribe playing, or seeming to gallop like a line of riders on the plains. That is the picture and comparison the kenning was meant to evoke. It is not evoked by 'whale road' – which suggests a sort of semi-submarine steam-engine running along submerged metal rails over the Atlantic.

13 *being without a prince*; *15 *aldorléase*

I think that this reference to an 'interregnum' before the founding of the Scylding house is clearly connected with the downfall of Heremod referred to later, 731 ff. (*898 ff.), 1435 ff. (*1709 ff.). Heremod occurs in the genealogies of English kings that also use the Scyld and/or Sceaf traditions, above Sceaf and/or Scyld.

13–14 *the Lord of Life*; *16 *Líffréa*

The use of *Líffré(g)a* as a kenning for God is probably a piece of Christian poetic diction. *Beowulf* was not composed in the form we now have (however ancient may be some of the traditions it enshrines) until much Christian verse had already been written: i.e. after Cædmon's time.[1]

---

[1] ['Cædmon's Hymn is famous as the only authentic piece that survives of the once renowned sacred poetry of the Whitby cowherd, Cædmon, who lived in the seventh century. The nine lines of the hymn were recorded by the Venerable Bede, and are found in an eighth century copy of his Latin *Ecclesiastical History;* they are thus among the very earliest recorded fragments of English.'

'Cædmon lived to make a great mass of verse on Scriptural

14; *18   *Beow*

[Both here and again in line 41 (*53) the O.E. manuscript has *Beowulf*, not *Beow*. But this Beowulf, son of Scyld, is *not* the hero of the poem. In other lectures my father studied at great length and with great subtlety the fearsomely tangled history of this ancient genealogy, in far too great detail for the purpose of this book; but in more concise lectures concerned primarily with the actual text of *Beowulf* he discussed the question of 'the two Beowulfs' in the form that follows here.]

This poem – it has no title in the manuscript – has by a modern consensus quite rightly been called *Beowulf*: Beowulf is indeed the 'hero', absolutely: no poem could be more about one exclusive hero than this poem. Here we learn that Beowulf was the son and heir of Scyld, and at 41 ff. (*53 ff.) that he succeeded his father, and that he was succeeded by his son, Healfdene. The Beowulf of the *exordium* (*1–52, 1–40), therefore, is not the hero of the poem! One of

---

themes of the Old and New Testament and also to have many imitators. Bede says that none of them could compare with him. But we can no longer judge for ourselves for practically all have perished. Of Cædmon's work that so greatly moved men of the earlier age (the seventh and eighth centuries) the only certainly genuine survivor is this first hymn.

One great book of scriptural verse has come down to us: MS Junius 11, often called the Cædmonian Manuscript. It used to lie on the show shelves of the Bodleian Library, and anyone who would take the trouble to walk up the winding stairs could go and look at it – where it is now I don't know. It was written – I mean penned by the scribes – about A.D.1000; but though it contains matter that is very old (though dressed up in later spelling) it does not represent Cædmon's work.'

J.R.R.T., *passages from lectures on Old English verse*.]

the oddest facts in Old English literature; and it is only made the odder when we observe that *Beowulf* is a very rare name indeed. In Old English it only occurs in this poem, and in *biuulf* the name of an abbot (otherwise unknown) inserted in the *Liber Vitae* (or list of benefactors) of Durham.

The question is bound up with *Scyld* and *Scéfing*, with all the traditions enshrined and blended in the *exordium*, and with the general interpretation of the poem. But I will indicate these points.

The oddity of the appearance of the rare name *Beowulf* given to two distinct persons in this one poem can only be explained as:

(a) *mere accident*: these two characters in tradition just happened to have the same name, and the author could not help himself;

(b) *error*: the names became assimilated by scribes, since the poet made the poem;

(c) *deliberate*: the poet gave this name to the two characters, or assimilated their names, on purpose: for some object of his own, or because of some theory he held.

(a) is highly improbable. Moreover, there is fairly conclusive evidence that the character in the mythical genealogy should have the mythical monosyllabic non-heroic name *Beow* 'barley' going with *Scéaf* 'sheaf'.

Was *Beow* altered by the poet to *Beowulf*? Or is it a scribal blunder? *Beow* would scan much better at both occurrences in the poem of Beowulf son of Scyld; but as much licence is allowed with proper names that is not conclusive.

There is no trace outside our poem of a Beowulf in connexion with Scyld or Sceaf. But neither is that conclusive: since our poet is not merely repeating, but is using and reshaping old traditions for his own ends. Nowhere else are Scyld and Sheaf combined; or the mysterious arrival in a boat, with a glorious departure in a ship to an unknown destiny, added. The funeral with which the poem ends deliberately echoes the funeral with which it begins. That is a point of art. But it cannot be made to cover a *deliberate* assimilation of names also. For various reasons:

(1) Because the poet, though a poet and willing to modify and select his material to suit his purpose, respected old traditions, especially dynastic ones: and this legendary sequence *Sceaf – Beow* was well-known in his day, and remained so for a long time.

(2) The similarity of names would *not* help his artistic purpose, but *blur* it. The second funeral 'echoes' the first, but they are thus 'compared' only to mark their complete contrast. The first marks the departure of a strange half-divine restorer, who leaves a once-forlorn people under a glorious house. The second, the fall of a last defender of a people's liberty, leaving them without hope.

(3) And of course finally, because the first funeral was not that of Beow/Beowulf but of Scyld.

Our manuscript is c.1000, something like 250 years after the poem was made. It no doubt remained a famous poem – so that even scribes employed to make a new copy might well know the general content and that its hero was *Beowulf* before ever they took up the pen. But knowledge of the legendary and old dynastic matter had grown dim.

I personally believe that the poet made *Beow* the son of Scyld; and that *Beowulf* is a later alteration. Because it is certainly an *alteration* – yet a purposeless one, and therefore unlikely to be one made by the poet, an artist, a man very sensitive to repetitions and significant correspondences. Yet no one has ever been able to show that this correspondence is anything but a nuisance and a distraction. Beowulf of the Geats has no lineal connexion at all with Beowulf of the Scyldings, and never alludes to him, as he surely would when he came marching into Heorot; or else Hrothgar would, when Beowulf the Geat's lineage is under discussion.

The way out that has been sought – by asserting that the two Beowulfs are in the poem different characters, but that this is due to the chances of tradition: one and the same folk-lore hero has become divided into two – that does not attract me. I do not think that either of the Beowulfs are *historical*. The first certainly not – a mere step in a fictitious genealogy preceding the first historical name *Healfdene*; nothing more is known of him, and his only function is to hand on the realm. The second only historical, if at all, in the sense and degree that King Arthur is: an historical germ, a real person perhaps, about which practically everything that is told is borrowed from myth, folklore, or sheer invention. But the two are not on the same 'unhistorical' plane. Beow/Beowulf 'Barley' is the glorification (by genealogists) of a rustic corn-ritual *myth*. Beowulf the bear-man, the giant-killer comes from a different world: *fairy-story*.

Well, there it is. I think that the unfortunate 'chance' that placed a character in the genealogy of the Scyldings with a name that began with the same letters as Beowulf, the fairy-story hero, has with the aid of two scribes both extremely ignorant of and careless with proper names – even Scriptural *Cain* gets turned into *camp* 'battle' in line *1261 (1048) – produced one of the reddest and highest red herrings that were ever dragged across a literary trail – already difficult enough to follow.

16   *in Scedeland*; *19 *Scedelandum in*

Scedeland contains the Old English form of the very ancient name seen now in the name *Scandinavia*. Its original form was *Skaðin-* (cf. Old Norse Skaði the giantess who went on snowshoes). The old name *Skadinaujō* or *Skadinawī* = 'the isle or peninsular of *Skaðin-*' (which seems sometimes to have included what we call Norway and Sweden but probably not modern Denmark) was Latinized as *Scadinavia*: *Scandinavia* is a literary altered form.

The Old English form was *Scedeníg* (*1686; *Scedenisle* 1415), the Old Norse *Skáney* (< *Skaðney*), whence modern Swedish *Skåne*. The Norse (old and modern) forms were usually applied to the very tip of Sweden (Skåne), which anciently and indeed until modern times belonged to Denmark, and was in fact (I think) the ancient home of the Danes. *Scedelandum* here probably means more or less the same as what we mean by Scandinavia. *Scedenigge* in *1686 is definitely however the land of the Danes.

17–18 *he dwells in his father's bosom*; *21 *on fæder [bea]rme*

The manuscript is damaged at the edges and here only *rme* (with room for two or three preceding letters) is preserved. *bearm* is literally 'lap', but figuratively means 'protection, possession': it is the best filling of the gap. Cf. 32 'on his lap lay treasures' (*40 *him on bearm læg*) where *bearm* is used literally, but in a context which explains its connotation: the jewels were laid on his lap in token of his ownership and kingship. The doctrine is that a young man (a prince) should already in his father's lifetime begin the practice of that prime virtue of Northern kings, *generosity*, by giving gifts to loyal knights – gifts which are still technically in his father's *bearm*. It is the gifts and treasures rather than the young man that are in his father's lap!

[The translation (as given above) does not accord with this.]

18–19; *22–4 *that . . . there cleave to him loyal knights of his table* (O.E. *gewunigen wilgesíþas*) *and the people stand by him* (O.E. *léode gelæsten*)

This is an example of Old English 'parallelism': the verb and subject are repeated but with variations, while the object 'him' remains the same. 'Parallelism' is not *mere repetition*, nor mere verbosity or word-spinning, under the necessity of 'hunting the letter', as this simple example shows. The *wilgesíþas* are the 'beloved companions', the members of the king's Round Table, the knights of his household or *comitatus*, who stand by his side at need; *léode* is more general: chief men, people: they follow him and render service.

21; *26 ff.   The ship-burial of Scyld

[My father observed that since his purpose in these lectures was to 'assist in construing *Beowulf*' he could not discuss what light can be thrown on the ship-burial of Scyld by other northern heroic traditions and by archaeology, but nonetheless wrote on the subject as follows.]

One may say briefly that ship-burials of chieftains Norse and English did occur in historical fact (as revealed both by tradition and archaeology); and that the dating is reasonably sound. We cannot of course 'date' the fictitious Scyld – but the dramatic time of *Beowulf* is the sixth century, with a background of dimmer and older traditions of the fifth century (to which Healfdene, Ongentheow &c. belong), and that is near enough in agreement with archaeological dating of ship-burials.

The author of *Beowulf* was not a heathen, but he wrote in a time when the pagan past was still very near: so near that not only some *facts* were remembered, but *moods* and *motives* also. His source was no doubt primarily oral and literary: actual mention and description of these things in lays and stories. There must have been far more visible 'archaeological' evidence in his day in England than now. But that will not help in the case of real ship-burial (in which the ship is actually set adrift); and a man of the West Marches (as I believe our poet to have been) would not often see such mounds as those at Sutton Hoo. If he did, he would require tradition (lay or history) to explain their contents and purpose. People who dug into graves and carried off the treasures dedicated to the dead were still in those days called thieves and not archaeologists.

There is probably not much heightening of the picture (by exaggeration, for instance): granted that Scyld ended his days as a glorious, conquering king, and was given a ship-burial, he might indeed be accompanied by a great mass of costly things; and *of feorwegum frætwa gelæded* (*37; 'treasures brought from regions far away' 29) would be strictly true. The treasure in the Sutton Hoo burial, for instance, included things that had come from the eastern Roman Empire. The position of the body in the centre, by the mast, with treasure in the lap and about it, has also archaeological support.

More interesting, however, are the concluding lines, and the suggestion – it is hardly more; the poet is not explicit, and the idea was probably not fully formed in his mind – that Scyld went back to some mysterious land whence he had come. He came out of the Unknown beyond the Great Sea, and returned into It: a miraculous intrusion into history, which nonetheless left real historical effects: a new Denmark, and the heirs of Scyld in Scedeland. Such must have been his feeling. For almost certainly we must attribute to him the choice of ship-burial for Scyld Scefing. The miraculous arrival in a boat he derived from ancient traditions concerning the mythical culture-hero Sceaf. It was he that rounded it off by using traditions of ship-burial to make a moving and suggestive 'departure'. At any rate nowhere else do we find this ending for Scyld or Sceaf.

In the last lines 'Men can give no certain account of the

havens where that ship was unladed' we catch an echo of the 'mood' of pagan times in which ship-burial was practised. A mood in which what we should call the *ritual* of a departure over the sea whose further shore was unknown, and an actual belief in a magical land or other world located 'over the sea', can hardly be distinguished – and for neither of these elements or motives is conscious symbolism, or real belief, a true description. It was a *murnende mód* filled with doubt and darkness.

The lines are precious. It is very rarely that we have any *written text* so near to 'archaeological' time in the North. Not more than a century divides *Beowulf* from Sutton Hoo.

[I give here the conclusion of the brief prose tale of Sheaf, written by my father for *The Lost Road*, of which I have given the opening passage in the note to line 3, *Scyld Scéfing*. The closely associated alliterative poem *King Sheave* did not reach his departure.

But it came to pass after long years that Sheaf summoned his friends and counsellors, and he told them that he would depart. For the shadow of old age was fallen upon him (out of the East) and he would return whence he came. Then there was great mourning. But Sheaf laid him upon his golden bed, and became as one in deep slumber; and his lords obeying his commands while he yet ruled and had command of speech set him in a ship. He lay beside the mast, which was tall, and the sails were golden. Treasures of gold and of gems and fine raiment and costly stuffs were laid beside him. His golden banner flew above his head. In this manner he was arrayed more richly than when he came among them; and they thrust him forth to sea, and the sea took him, and the ship bore him unsteered far away into the uttermost West out of the sight or thought of men. Nor do any know who received him in what haven at the end of his journey. Some have said that that ship found the Straight Road.

But none of the children of Sheaf went that way, and many in the beginning lived to a great age, but coming under the shadow of the East they were laid in great tombs of stone or in mounds like green hills; and most of these were by the Western sea, high and broad upon the shoulders of the land, whence men can descry them that steer their ships amid the shadows of the sea.]

So ends the *exordium* proper, giving the background of mystery and antiquity behind the renowned Scylding house. In the manuscript the 'section' or 'canto' numeration begins with 'I' at *Đá wæs on burgum* (*53, 41). But we have not really yet reached the action. Another passage follows, 41–69 (*53–85), giving a further account of the 'Arthurian' court of Heorot, glorious and doomed, gnawed already by the canker of treachery. The members of the 'house' are touched on, and their external political relations; and the building of the 'hall' Heorot. This is apt and skilful. It is a necessary transition from the remote antiquity we began with, and it gives the real 'scene' against which the action is to take place. Both the politics (the relations of Danes and Swedes, 48–9, *62–3) are important, and the actual *hall*. It is within that nexus of political relations and royal policies that the Anglo-Saxon poet sees and places his tale; just as much as he sees and locates his monster in the famous *building* Heorot. The significance of much that follows is lost if we do not realize that to put Grendel into Heorot is like telling a ghost-story localized in Camelot (in romantic effect) and in the Tower of London (in historicity). And if we do not realize that the Danish house was allied with the mortal enemies of the Geats: with the Swedes.

153

44; *57   *Healfdene*

We here meet for the first time the name *Healfdene*, Norse *Halfdanr*. The name was not used in England as a 'given' name, although it is here preserved in English form. It thus can only be the knowledge of Healfdene Scylding that causes the viking King *Healfdene*, who attacked England in 871 and later, to be given an exact rendering of his Norse name [in the Anglo-Saxon Chronicle] when the other chieftains' names all appear in oddly garbled forms like Sidroc.

Halfdanr became an extremely popular Scandinavian name. But its use and popularity seem to go back to the ancient fame of *Halfdanr Skjöldungr*, the equivalent of our character. Though Scylding legend has been very much dislocated in Norse, and Halfdanr is often remembered only as a figure in isolation, it is notable that the very epithets we meet here in *Beowulf* are also attached to him in Norse: he is named *hæstr Skjöldunga* ('highest': which may originally have meant 'tallest' or 'most glorious'); he is *Halfdanr gamli* 'Healfdene the Old' ('aged and fierce in war' 45, *gamol ond gúðréouw* *58), reputed to have lived to a great age, and to have held his power until a natural death (cf. *þenden lifde* *57, 'while he lived' 45, which we perceive to mean 'to the end of his life') – although he had, as Saxo says, lost no opportunity of exercising his *atrocitas* (cf. *gúðréouw*).[1]

---

1   ['Saxo Grammaticus (the lettered), the earlier books of whose *Historia Danica* are a store-house of Scandinavian tradition and poetry, clothed in a difficult and bombastic, but always amusing Latin' (R.W. Chambers). Saxo was a Dane; he flourished in the

We may at least conclude that a commanding figure in ancient Danish legend was 'Halfdane', and that there is a connexion between the Norse and English traditions; indeed they both have the same *historical* basis.

48–9 *[a daughter] I have heard that was Onela's queen, dear consort of the warrior Scylfing;* *62–3 (manuscript reading) *hýrde ic þæt elan cwén Heaðo-Scilfingas healsgebedda*

There is no lacuna and no sign of confusion in the manuscript; but that it is corrupt is shown (a) by *62 being metrically deficient, and (b) by the absence of a verb after *þæt*. At least we may be sure that *wæs* is part of what has dropped out between *elan* and *cwén*. We know also that more has gone, because *62 still does not scan with the addition of *wæs*, and *Elan* is an impossible name – as an almost certain first guess it is a genitive parallel to -*Scilfingas* (*as* = *aes* = *es*). We may therefore assume fairly safely that the missing part was (*a*) a woman's name, (*b*) *wæs*, (*c*) a man's name ending -*elan*. Also that the woman's name and her husband's obligingly alliterated: but we don't know what was the initial letter, as a princess's name did not necessarily begin with the dynastic letter (cf. *Fréawaru* sister of *Hréðríc* and *Hróðmund* sons of *Hróðgár*).

latter part of the twelfth century, but of his life scarcely anything is known. Concerning *Haldanus* he wrote that the most remarkable thing about him was that 'though he had made use of every opportunity that the times afforded for the display of his ferocity, his life was ended by old age and not by the sword.']

To aid our further guessing we have *Scilfingas*. This was the name of the great Swedish house. This alliance may have been, and probably was, connected with the not far past enmity between Danes and Geats (you could not be friends with both Geats and Swedes!) – cf. 1554–8 'Thou hast accomplished that between these peoples, the Geatish folk and spearmen of the Danes, a mutual peace shall be, and strife and hateful enmities shall sleep which erewhile they used' (*1855–8). The fact that the most famous of the Scylfings was Onela son of Ongentheow (2197, 2463; *2616, *2932) is so remarkable that any other name would have to have very strong evidence. But there is no other trace of this marriage of Onela.

65 (*81) ff. *The hall towered high . . . awaiting the warring billows of destroying fire . . .*

Here we have a reference to the doom in store for Heorot, the glorious hall. It is characteristic of our poet (and of most Anglo-Saxon poets who have left any traces) to put in this dark note of doom immediately after telling of the hall's new-built splendour. The 'doom' is of course derived from lays or tales in which the destruction of Heorot by fire was an event (in the past).

'The murderous hatred between father-in-law and son-in-law' (67–8, *84) refers to the feud between a people called Heathobeardan and the Scyldings. My view is that in the expansion of Danish power, represented by the rise of Healfdene (*héah ond gúðréouw*), islands not originally

Danish had been occupied. Cf. the lines about Scyld at the beginning (3–4). The site of Heorot had a religious significance.[1] It had moreover previously been held or controlled by the Heathobeardan: it was the struggle for the sacred site that so embittered the strife. It is in keeping with Hrothgar's character (as depicted) that he should seek to end this feud not by war but by a political marriage between Fréawaru and Ingeld, the young heir to the Heathobeard kingship, who had survived his father's downfall. It appears that the marriage was about to take place at the time of Beowulf's visit; that it did take place; that the 'policy' was unsuccessful; and Ingeld attacked Heorot.

Heorot was burned, but Ingeld was utterly destroyed by Hrothgar and his nephew Hrothulf. Heorot then evidently did not endure long. It was built after the crushing defeat of the Heathobeardan: to that (I think) *heraspéd* in line *64 ('fortune in war' 50) refers. Grendel very soon invaded it. The twelve years during which Hrothgar endured the assaults of Grendel (118, *147) is long enough to allow Ingeld to grow from a child to a dangerous young prince old enough to lead a war of revenge. Whether this is history, or derived from his legendary sources, it seems clear that our poet has here worked out the chronology pretty well, and placed Beowulf's visit where he should in the political time-scheme.

---

1   The religious connexions were with the culture gods, in Norse terms Njöðr and Frey (Yngvi-Frey). Hence we find the names *Fróda* and *Ingeld* as Heathobeard names. But also after the Danish seizure of this site we find the name *Fréawaru* given to Hrothgar's daughter; and the Danes claim the title 'Friends of Ing'.

He is thus able to exhibit Beowulf's political sagacity by making him foresee and foretell events (that hearers knew would actually happen.) [See 1697–1739, *2020–69.]

67   *the time was not far off*; *83 *ne wæs hit lenge þá gén*

This is not a 'crux' of sense. The general sense is clear: Heorot was still glorious, but it was doomed to be burned. *All* the history of Heorot was in the mind of poet and audience; but the poet was conscious of *dramatic* time (as throughout). The ultimate doom of the dynasty of Healfdene and the great hall built by Hrothgar cast a shadow over the court of Heorot in Old English – as later a shadow lay on Arthur and Camelot. The question really is: what is *lenge*?

[After a lengthy analysis of the historical linguistic possibilities my father wrote that he thought it most probable that the poet wrote *longe*, noting that the passage has many minor errors. See the Notes on the Text, p. 108, line 67.]

The time was 'not long', because at the time of Beowulf's visit the marriage of Hrothgar's daughter to Ingeld was not far off, and the story of what happened (told as a prophecy by Beowulf) suggests that the trouble broke out soon after the marriage.

82–3   *a fiend of hell*; *101 *féond on helle*

The Old English *féond on helle* is a very curious expression. It implies, of course, that Grendel is a 'hell-fiend',

158

a creature damned irretrievably. It remains, nonetheless, remarkable; for Grendel is not 'in hell', but very physically in Denmark, and he is not even yet a damned spirit, for he is mortal and has to be slain before he goes to Hell. There is evidently a confusion or twilight in the thought of the poet (and his age) about these monsters, hostile to mankind. They remain physical monsters, with blood, able to be slain (with the right sword). Yet already they are described in terms applicable to evil spirits; so here (*102) *gǽst*.[1] Whether *féond on helle* is due to a kind of half-theological notion that one of the accursed things, of misshapen human form, being damned carried their hell ever with them in their hearts and spirits – or whether it is due to taking over a 'Christian' phrase carelessly (*féond on helle* just = 'fiend, devil') – is difficult to decide. The latter would demand that Christian phraseology was already well-developed and fixed when *Beowulf* was written. The phrase went on. In Middle English *fend in helle* is still used just as 'devil'. Wyclif uses *fend in helle* of a very living and bodily friar walking about England. (It is to be remembered that *féond* properly = 'enemy' only, and still when undefined bears that sense in *Beowulf*.)

---

1 [In all the texts of the translation this is rendered 'creature', 83. Against his reference here to *gǽst* my father later pencilled a note suggesting that there may be a confusion with *gæst*, *gest* 'stranger'. This, and the meaning of *féond on helle*, were discussed by him in Appendix (a), *Grendel's titles*, to *The Monsters and the Critics* – where he said of the word *gǽst* that 'in any case it cannot be translated either by the modern *ghost* or *spirit*. *Creature* is probably the nearest we can now get.']

86–92; *106–14

[My father's remarks are introduced thus: 'An important passage for general criticism. See my lecture [i.e. *The Monsters and the Critics*; see p. 170]. Here (since our attention is primarily to the *text*) we may note the following.']

My view is that *106–14 is certainly genuine, the work of the effective poet, maker of *Beowulf* as we have it. It shows that study of the Old Testament which is characteristic of him. His comparison of the old native legends of strife and heroism, and Scripture, had presented him with two problems, or aroused in him two lines of thought.

(1) Where do the monsters come in? How can they be equated with the Scriptural account of antiquity? And he saw also the parallel between the legendary strife of men of old with these implacable misshapen enemies lurking in dark dens, and the strife of Christians with the fallen devils of hell [*pencilled here later*: quite another plane of imagination].

(2) What are we to think of the nobility and heroism of the heathen past? Was it all just evil, damned?

To his ideas on this second more difficult question (in his day a much more living and controversial issue) we shall soon be coming in lines 134–50 (*168–88). I think that he attempted to equate the noble figures of his own northern antiquity with the noble figures, sages, judges, and kings of Israel – before Christ. They too were 'damned' owing to the Fall, even if they were members of the chosen people. The redemption of Christ might work backwards. But in the Harrowing of Hell why should not (say) Hrothgar be among the rescued too? For the people of Israel could also fall away in time of trial to the worship of idols and false gods. For that reason I think that when Anglo-Saxons made *Sceaf* the son of Noah born in the Ark, it was not mere genealogical fantasy, a mere trick to make their kings' lines go back to Adam. (For that is not particularly glorious. If you make your genealogical tree too long it merges into that dim long-rooted tree upon which all men grow. Any serf in Æthelwulf's house could claim descent from Adam.) It was rather a process, due to a line of thought closely related to the ideas of the *Beowulf*-poet. It gave the northern kings a place in an unwritten chapter (as it were) of the Old Testament.

[The following passage is more easily understood if the O.E. text (*104–16) and the translation (85–94) are set out together:

             fífelcynnes eard
105 wonsǽlí wer   weardode hwíle,
     siþðan him Scyppend   forscrifen hæfde
     in Cáines cynne –   þone cwealm gewræc
     éce Drihten,   þæs þe hé Ábel slóg;
     ne gefeah hé þǽre fǽhðe,   ac hé hine feor forwræc
110 Metod for þý máne   mancynne fram.
     Þanon untýdras   ealle onwócon,
     eotenas ond ylfe   ond orcnéas,
     swylce gígantas,   þá wið Gode wunnon
     lange þráge;   hé him ðæs léan forgeald.
115 Gewát ðá néosian,   syþðan niht becóm,
     héan húses . . .

85   [Grendel] unhappy one, inhabited long while the troll-kind's home; for the Maker had proscribed him with the race of Cain.

That bloodshed, for that Cain slew Abel, the Eternal Lord avenged: no joy had he of that violent deed, but God drove him for that crime far from mankind. Of him all evil broods were born, ogres and goblins and haunting shapes of hell, and the giants too, that long time warred with God – for that he gave them their reward.

92

Then went Grendel forth when night was come to spy on that lofty house . . .]

Our poet's answer in the first case he found in the book of Genesis. The misformed man-mocking monsters were descendants of Cain. And the reference to the 'giants' of old clinched the matter for him. The blending is clearly observable: he begins with northern words *eotenas, ylfe* (two classes of non-human but human-shaped creatures), and ends with the word *gigantas* borrowed from the Latin version of Scripture [Genesis VI.4].

Even so – and this is the point really pertinent to my present task – lines 86–92 (*106–14) have the air of an *insertion* or *addition*. Not an interpolation: that is, they seem to me to bear the impress of the style, rhythm, and thought of the 'author'. Yet they do interrupt the simple sequence of narrative – and syntax. Observe that there is no subject at all to *gewát* *115 ('went forth' 93, [where 'Grendel' is added in the translation]). It is difficult to resist the strong suspicion that it once followed immediately on *weardode hwíle,* *105 ('inhabited long while' 85). Read the passage omitting *106–14, 86 ('for the Maker . . .')–92, and you will feel the force of this.

I think that in all this early part of *Beowulf* our poet is sticking very close to some old material already in verse; hardly doing more in parts than work over it. One of the things he did in this process was to insert this passage 86–92 (*106–14) which expresses his philosophy of the northern monsters.

Or of course he may, in the long process of composition which must lie behind the final construction of so large and complex a poem, have improved and enlarged his own earlier, simpler, more plain fairy-story drafts. Such things do happen. In either case you get a very good but nonetheless separable and intrusive passage. You can find similar things in, say, Chaucer. *The Nun's Priest's Tale* is obviously based on old material, and obviously much elaborated by Chaucer. You can here and there lift whole chunks and say 'Ha! Master Geoffrey, you stuck that in. You think it an improvement, do you? Well, perhaps it is. Perhaps.'

90–1 *haunting shapes of hell*; *112 *orcnéas*

The O.E. word occurs only here. *orc* is found glossing Latin *Orcus* [Hell, Death]. *neas* seems certainly to be *né-as*, plural of the old (poetic) word *né* 'dead body'. This appears also in *né-fugol* 'carrion bird'. Its original stem in Germanic was *nawi-s*: Gothic *naus* (plural *naweis*), Old Norse *ná-r*.

'Necromancy' will suggest something of the horrible associations of this word. I think that what is here meant is that terrible northern imagination to which I have ventured to give the name 'barrow-wights'. The 'undead'. Those dreadful creatures that inhabit tombs and mounds. They are

not living: they have left humanity, but they are 'undead'.
With superhuman strength and malice they can strangle men
and rend them. Glámr in the story of Grettir the Strong is a
well-known example.

107–8   *Nor was it longer space than but one night*; *134–5
Næs hit lengra fyrst, ac ymb áne niht

The attack on two successive nights is probably a detail
surviving from the 'fairy-story' element. *ymb áne niht* 'after
one night' means in Old English 'on the next day (or night)'.

[The translation seems to be at odds with this.]

123–7; *154–8   Here we have a reference to legal arrange-
ments in the case of *fæhþ* ['feud'].

[It is convenient again here to set out the Old English text and the
translation together:

<blockquote>
                       sibbe ne wolde
155   wið manna hwone   mægenes Deniga,
      feorhbealo feorran,   féa þingian,
      né þǽr nǽnig witena   wénan þorfte
      beorhtre bóte   to banan folmum;
</blockquote>

123   truce would he not have with any man of the Danish host,
nor would withhold his deadly cruelty, nor accept terms of
payment; and there no cause had any of the counsellors to look
for golden recompense from the slayer's hands;]

For the expression *féa þingian* cf. *470 *Siððan þá fǽhðe féo
þingode* (379–80 'Thereafter that feud I settled with payment').

The verb *þingian* is found in *Beowulf* in this expression with *féo* in these two occurrences, and also at line *1843 (1545), where it has its very frequent sense of 'make a speech' ['discourse' (verb) in the translation]. Other senses are 'intercede for, supplicate', and 'arrange, settle a matter'. The link in these diverse senses is the noun *þing*, from which the verb is derived. Its basic sense is 'an appointed time', hence 'a meeting', hence 'debate, discussion'. The development of the colourless sense 'thing', already achieved in Old English, is very similar to the development of Latin *causa* 'argument, legal case' > Italian *cosa*, French *chose*. The terms of a settlement of a *fǽhþ* would be discussed at a meeting of the representatives of the two sides. Hence *fǽhþe féo* (dative) *þingian* means to come to terms at a *þing* concerning the 'wergild' to be paid by the offending party.

In its bare essentials *fǽhþ* was the condition of being *hated* (outside friendly intercourse) because of an act (or series of acts) of hostility by one side (family, tribe, people) against another – usually, of course, the act was the wounding or slaying of some person. Obtaining redress or wreaking revenge was a duty that then devolved upon the next of kin of the slain man. Dealt in this way, by 'vendetta', *fǽhþ* might become a state of permanent war between great families (or peoples), as in the case of the Swedes and Geats, and could reach no settlement except by the extermination of one side: as finally seems to have been the fate of the royal house of the Geats.

But a system of mitigating law grew up – especially among the families of a single united group (tribe or nation). The

offending party could 'settle the feud' by payment, and vari-
ous elaborate scales of value were drawn up. This payment
was called *wergild*: each man according to his status had a
price or *wer*. Of course settlement of this kind depended on
the willingness of both sides to accept the arrangement and
abide by it. Good relations (and the honour of the injured)
could only be restored by *redress*. If that was refused or
unobtainable, or the injury too great, *honour* required
revenge. Early legend, saga, and history contain only too
many cases of refusal of wergild (to pay it, or to accept it);
and of revenge being later taken despite the legal settlement,
so that the *fæhþ* began anew.

What is implied here is that there was never any hope of any
such settlement. Grendel was an 'alien', not recognizing the
authority of Hrothgar or of any human law. Nor was it pos-
sible to hold any conference with him, and arrange terms: and
indeed he would not have been willing to offer any. Nay, he
piled *fæhþ* upon *fæhþ*, killing fresh Danes whenever he could.

The literal translation of lines *154-6 is: 'peace he would
not have with any man of the host of the Danes, (would
not) remove the peril to life, (would not) settle the feud with
wergild.'

126　*golden recompense*; *158 *beorhtre bóte*

beorht means 'bright, clear of light and sound, loud or
shining'. Though (like Latin *clárus*) the application of the
word to persons or their deeds, when we should say 'glori-
ous, splendid, magnificent', is natural and not unusual, the

application here is startling and unusual. 'They could not expect a shining (brilliant) recompense' is a very strong *litotes*. It implies 'they could not in fact expect the very shabbiest, they could expect nothing at all.'

130   *sorcerers of hell;* *163 *helrúnan*

Old English possessed a word *hel-rún*, also weak *hellerúne, hel-rúne*. This occurs in glosses equated with *hægtesse, wicce* 'witch' and with such Latin words as *Pythonissa* ('diviner'). Probably here we have a masculine counterpart (as *wicca* beside *wicce*), whether formed for the occasion or not. Outside Old English we have Old High German *helliruna* 'necromancia', and the extremely interesting though corruptly preserved Gothic word, half-Latinized, *haliurunnas* in Jordanes' history of the Goths, which he says means *magas mulieres* (see below).

To discuss the full implications of this word would take too long. Its elements are *hell* 'Hell' (Gothic *halja*), and *rún* 'secret'. The first word is ultimately related to *helan* 'conceal' (Latin *céláre*); hence it means the hidden world, the underworld, Hades, the Realm of the Dead. In paganism 'the hidden, mysteries' lead inevitably down into the darkness.

rún is a word (probably ultimately meaning 'whispering') implying any secret knowledge handed on privately. It occurs also in Keltic, Old Irish *rún* 'secret', Welsh *rhin* 'secret, mystery, enchantment'; and was very probably derived by Germanic from Keltic. It may have a good sense – so in *1325 *rúnwita* 'one who knew my secret counsels, my confidant' is equated with *rædbora* (1106–7 'my counsels were his and his wisdom mine'). But a *hel-rúne* was one who knew secret black knowledge – and the association of *hell* with the dead shows that the gloss in O.H.G. 'necromancia' is very close. The special association of 'necromancy' with women is very ancient, and very tenacious. The 'Weird Sisters' of *Macbeth* are good illustrations of the immemorial dark imagination of *helrúnan*.

The word is not used here casually, however, not just as an archaic pagan word to give a dark colour to the picture.

The witch or 'necromancer' was like Grendel an outcast, and again like Grendel balanced in the imagination between the human and the monstrous or demonic. Though veritable human beings could go in for dark and abominable lore (and have secret associations), there was an ill-defined border between such folk with their acquired powers, and actual demonic beings: 'weird sisters'. So Wulfstan[1] couples *wiccan* (witches) *and wælcyrian* (valkyries).

With regard to Grendel the story told by Jordanes (derived evidently from lost Gothic lays and legends) is particularly interesting and illustrative. King Filimer (an ancient king of the period of Gothic migration south to the Sea of Azov), he relates, expelled from his camp women who practised magic arts: *magas mulieres quas patrio sermone haliurunnas is ipse cognominat*, that is 'the female magicians, whom he himself

---

1 [Wulfstan: eminent scholar and ecclesiast, Archbishop of York, died 1023.]

(Filimer) calls in his ancestral tongue (Gothic) *haliurunnas*'. This is probably a corruption of *haliarúnas*, Latin accusative plural of *haliarúna*, Latinized from Gothic *haljarúna* = O.E. *hell-rún*. The women banished into the desert there met the evil spirits of the waste, and from the unholy marriage of witches and demons sprang the loathsome race of the Huns.

Here we have another point of contact between Scripture and Germanic legend. A kind of reverse parallel to the deduction drawn from Genesis IV and VI that the giants and monsters were descendants of Cain, the outlaw [see the note to 86–92]. And Grendel the descendant of Cain is reckoned among the *helrúnan*. It is more than likely that dark ancient legends, concerning the origin of imagined evil beings, and of actual outlaw-folk and hated enemies of alien race, were associated in pagan Old English with the ancient word *hell-rún*, like that far-off echo of Gothic legend preserved in the garbled history of Jordanes.

Truly it is said that 'men know not whither *helrúnan* go in their courses.' Darkness goes with them. Their secret and malicious purposes are unfathomable, except that they are perilous, and hostile to Man beyond hope of peace. Where did the weird-sisters dwell, and by what strange devices did their paths cross Macbeth's, to his undoing?

135–50; *170–88   [A note on 134–5, *168–9, follows on p. 181.]

The whole of this passage offers one of the most interesting sections, and *the* most difficult, for the general criticism of the poem. It cannot adequately be dealt with apart from consideration of the poem as a whole, and especially of its 'theology'; or apart from theories concerning its mode of composition. I have already treated this particular point, after a fashion, in an appendix to my lecture: *The Monsters and the Critics.* [For other references to the lecture see the note to lines 86–92, p. 160 above, also pp. 305, 309, 337.] I will here attempt to give in brief summary my present views.

Beowulf is a work, as we have it, of a single hand and mind – comparable to a play (say *King Lear*) by Shakespeare: thus it may have varied sources; minor discrepancies due to imperfections in the handling and blending of these; and may have suffered some 'corruption' (e.g. occasional deliberate tinkering or editing, and many minor casual errors) in the course of tradition between author and our copy. But it makes a unified artistic impression: the impress of a single imagination, and the ring of a single poetic style. The minor 'discrepancies' detract little from this, as a rule.

But in this case we have something more serious to deal with. A flat contradiction of one of the main leading ideas of the poem. The shock is comparable to what we should feel if we suddenly heard Lear ridiculing the Fourth Commandment or Cordelia praising Goneril and Regan.

What is the leading idea and what is the contradiction?

The 'leading idea' is that noble pagans of the past who had not heard the Gospel, knew of the existence of Almighty God, recognized him as 'good' and the giver of all good things; but were (by the Fall) still cut off from Him, so that in time of woe they became filled with despair and doubt – that was the hour when they were specially open to the snares of the Devil: they prayed to idols and false gods for help.

The sources of this idea were probably, first, the Old Testament in itself, or in the versified Cædmonian form; and second, actual report and knowledge of contemporary Northern pagans. The old idea that the author of *Beowulf* was just confused in his head, and that all he had was a few bits of Old Testament story which he had remembered while actual Christian teaching was beyond him, is of course patently absurd. The poem belongs to the time of that great outburst of missionary enterprise which fired all England, when the English were busy with the conversion of Frisia and Germany, and the reorganization of disordered Gaul: to the days in fact of St. Wynfrith (or Boniface), the apostle of Germany, and martyr in Frisia, the Englishman who has been held to have had a greater influence on Europe's history than any later Englishman. The poem most closely connected with *Beowulf* is *Andreas* – a missionary romance. *Beowulf* is *not* a missionary allegory; but it comes from a time when the noble pagan and his heroic ancestors (enshrined in verse) were a burning contemporary topic and problem, at home and abroad.

You must observe two things: the mere fact that the poet wrote a poem about the pagan past shows in general that he did not belong to the party that consigned the heroes (northern or classical) to perdition. Pagan past – certainly. The poet was well aware of it. He knew that Denmark and Sweden were still in his own day heathen. Therefore his picture of Hrothgar and Beowulf is deliberate. What is more, their monotheism is due to clearly held theory about facts – and is not due to a mere rigid piety: a sort of unintelligent Christian censorship. Piety and censorship of that sort would not have allowed the poem to be written at all.

What then did the author do with his material, descending from the not very remote pagan English past? Less, I think, than may be supposed. Points of contact between pagan belief and Scripture (thus especially the Old Testament which told him the *truth* about Man before Christ) particularly interested him. He linked and commented on them: as in 86–92 (*106–14). But he cut out the names of the heathen deities. Why? Because he believed they were lies; and because he believed that people like Hrothgar knew it, and only had recourse to heathen gods and their idols when under special temptation by the Devil. The heathen gods, whether mere vain fictions, or fictions grafted on the memories of dead kings of old, were deceits of the Evil One. He is speaking to you in his own person when he says in *176–8 that 'they besought the Slayer of Souls to help them in their misery' [translation 140–1 'implored the slayer of souls to afford them help against the sufferings of the people']. He is not accusing the Danes of direct conscious Satanism; but stating that in fact by praying to idols they were praying to the Devil.

So far so good. A reading of the whole of *Beowulf*, and a scrutiny of every line and expression of theological import, shows in general that this clear rational theory was consistently carried out. Now for the contradiction. Here is a translation of *170–88.

That was great torment to the lord of the Scyldingas, an anguish of heart. Many a man of might sat often communing, counsel they took what it were best for stouthearted men to do against these dire terrors. At times they vowed sacrifices to idols [in their heathen fanes >] in pagan tabernacles, with prayers implored the Slayer of Souls to furnish help to them against the people's sufferings. Such was their wont, the hope of heathen men: of hell they were mindful in their hearts' thought; the Author they [knew >] comprehended not, the Judge of Deeds, nor had they heard of the Lord God, nor verily had they learned to praise the Guardian of the Heavens, the King of Glory. Woe to him that through [fiendish malice >] (probably) the malice of fiends / shall thrust down his soul into the fire's embrace, to look for no comfort nor any change! Joy to him that is permitted after his death-day to [go seek >] find the Lord, and in the father's bosom to seek for peace!

[If this text is compared with lines 135–50 in the full translation of *Beowulf* it will be obvious that my father had the latter in front of him. A curious point is that the later pencilled change in the present text of *fanes* to *tabernacles* was made also to the typescript C (line 140 in the full translation), while *fiendish malice*, which stood in the present text as written, was in the typescript C a pencilled emendation of *rebellious malice*.]

A few notes on this are required.

*180 *(ne) cúþon* and *181 *(ne) wiston* [in the passage translated above 'knew (> comprehended) not' and 'nor had they heard of']. *cunnan* and *witan* are properly distinct like Latin *cognosco* and *scio*. For reasons that appear later – to reduce as far as possible the discrepancy of the passage – I have given this distinction full weight, translating *wiston* 'had heard of'. *cunnan* is properly 'know (all) about, understand (the nature of)', in the sense that you know persons and places; *witan* 'know facts'. So that strictly *Metod híe ne cúþon* (*180, 143) might mean no more than 'they had little or no knowledge about Metod (the power that orders and governs the world, God or Providence)'. But *ne wiston híe Drihten God* (*181, 144) can only mean 'they did not know of the existence of God at all, did not know of His being even.' Actually I doubt if this distinction is really present in this passage, which I regard as you will see as a late interpolation: both sentences probably really mean 'they did not know that God existed'. The distinction between *cunnan* and *witan* became obscured, except that *cunnan* became more and more limited to the sense 'know how to do (a thing)', whence our 'can'; while *gecnawan* 'recognize' slowly extended its sphere, until in modern English it covers both *cunnan* and *witan*, and 'I wot' has become obsolete.

bið *183, *186 (in *Wá bið þǽm* 'Woe to him' and *Wél bið þǽm* 'Joy to him' in the passage translated above). Both these expressions are general or 'gnomic' and not strictly 'future'. I have therefore omitted *bið*, since the modern 'woe to him' has this general reference. *bið* is in Old English quite distinct from *is*. The latter is purely 'present indicative', denoting actual contemporary facts: *seo sunne is hát* can only mean 'the sun is now at this moment hot, I can feel it, it is a warm

174

day.' *seo sunne bið hát* means (a) 'the sun will be hot', or (b) 'the sun is hot – it is one of the classes of hot things'. 'All that glitters is not gold' requires *bið* in Old English if it is a proverb: *ne bið eal þe glitnað gold. Nis eal þe glitnað gold* could only refer to a collection of bright things actually before you, and would mean 'Here are some bright things, but actually they are not all of gold, some are brass.'

slíðne nið *184 ['through fiendish malice' 146; '(probably) through the malice of fiends' in the translation of the passage given above]. This expression is not as simple perhaps as it seems – indeed it may even possibly assist in 'dating' the passage, and marking it as one belonging to a later period than that of the main body of the poem.

The word *slíðe* occurs in all the Germanic languages – with a general sense 'grim, disastrous, fearful'. That sense will suit elsewhere in verse, e.g. in *Beowulf* *2398 *slíðra geslyhta* (2018 'cruel slaying'). It only occurs in religious contexts here and in *Elene* 857 (*on þá slíðan tíd* used of the Crucifixion).[1] But the word had, nonetheless, some special connexion with pre-Christian religion, or mythology. In Old Norse *slíðr* is not only an adjective, but also the name of the river that flows about the realm of Hel, Goddess of the dark underworld. This makes an interesting parallel to

---

1   [The reference is to the Old English poem *Elene*, one of several poems known to be the work of a poet named Cynewulf, from his having interwoven into passages of his verse the *names* of the Runic *letters* that spell out his name.]

the Greek name Στυξ 'Styx' in relation to στυγειν ['hate, abominate'] and στυγερός ['hated, hateful']. It would seem likely that the word retained a 'heathen' flavour in Old English, and meant 'devilish'. This seems borne out by the following curious facts. Outside verse it is only found in a Psalter gloss (actually Eadwine's Canterbury Psalter). Here the adjective *slíðe, slíðeleca,* and the noun *slíðness* are four times used to gloss *sculptile, sculptilia,* which in the contexts mean 'idols'. It must be admitted that when in *Beowulf* we meet *slíðne níð,* precisely in an anathema on idolaters, there seems more than probably to be a connexion. This can most easily be explained by assuming that *slíðe* had acquired the sense of 'devilish, diabolical' – partly through some ancient associations with heathen *hell,* maybe; and partly by the line of development that gave a diabolical sense to such words as *scaþa, féond, bana,* etc. The gloss in the Psalter is thus only approximate and means 'fiends' or 'fiendish things', not 'carven images'. The *slíðe níð* of *Beowulf* means 'diabolic malice', and we perceive that it applies probably *not* to the malice of the damned themselves but to the malice of the *gastbona* ('the Slayer of Souls') who deluded and ruined them. But we perceive also that it is probably a piece of later 'Christian' diction, unlike the use of the word elsewhere in *Beowulf* or older Old English verse – and one that has, in verse, only one possible parallel, a use in a signed poem of Cynewulf, *Elene* [as mentioned above], while Cynewulf has, on reasonably good grounds, been suspected of tinkering with *Beowulf* elsewhere [see pp. 309 ff.].

Let us now return to the 'contradiction'. This resides in the words 'nor had they heard of the Lord God' (144). This is quite unlike the minor discrepancies to be observed in *Beowulf* (and in many other major works of literary art). What is the explanation? Can the theology of the Danes (and even of the *witan* ['wise men, counsellors']) have differed from that of their wise king? Is that what the poet means? It would not be an impossible notion. The 'wise men' of both peoples, Danes and Swedes, were doubtless 'conservatives', and likely to be tenacious of heathen practice. It is the *snotere ceorlas* ('wise men') of the Geatas who are said in line 166 (*204) to 'inspect the omens', like Roman *auspices*. It is the Danish *witan* here who are specifically accused of vowing sacrifices.

But a little consideration will show that this is no way out. The lines do not merely say that the *witan* were obstinate heathens, who had recourse to idols in time of stress and temptation – that would be no discrepancy: they declare that they were *wholly ignorant of God* and his existence. But it would be quite impossible for any *wita* to associate with King Hrothgar for a day and remain in such a state. Even the *scop* in Heorot sang the praise of the Ælmihtiga, 75 ff., *92 ff.

Then was the poet a dolt? There are then only two possible alternatives. (i) The poet made a bad blunder – i.e. right at the beginning of his poem, in a crucial key-passage, he wrote words which are flatly inconsistent with the whole of the rest of his poem; and he never revised them. (ii) The text has suffered alteration since it left his hands.

In the end readers of *Beowulf* will choose (i) or (ii) for

themselves. I personally choose (ii) – for the following reasons in brief:

Beowulf as a whole is strikingly consistent, and shows every sign of being carefully worked over, so that references forward and backward are all linked up. That this major discrepancy should have been left untouched is difficult to believe – even if, indeed, he could ever have made the blunder at all (say, in some early draft, before his ideas had clarified); it is much more likely that he started out from the very beginning with his general idea of the 'good pagan' already formed.

Turning then to *interpolation* or *rewriting*: we find that there is evidence, quite independent of the present passage, that *Beowulf* did prove attractive to some rewriter at theological points. But if interpolation or rewriting has occurred at one such place it is likely to have occurred elsewhere where theological interest was specially prominent. We shall therefore look (a) for any signs, now discoverable, in the present passage, of another voice and hand; and (b) for any reasons that may have moved this rewriter specially at this point. As to (a): we have already observed that in *þurh slíðne níð* we have a trace of another and later diction. Beyond that we have only judgements based on style and rhythm: notoriously subjective, and liable to be as unconvincing to others as they are convincing to those who make them. To me at any rate I can only record that the last part, at least, of this passage speaks with a quite different 'voice' to the rest of the verse in which it is imbedded. As to (b): I can best make clear my view by sketching briefly what I think happened here in the history of our text.

At this point *heathen customs* were specially mentioned in the original material used by our poet – for Heorot and its site had in the ancient traditions about the Scyldings a special association with a heathen cult. [With the following Note cf. pp. 329 ff. in the discussion 'Fréawaru and Ingeld'.]

(*Note*. Thus *æt hærgtrafum* *175 (139–40 'in their heathen tabernacles') is an ancient element – not understood by the scribe at all, and so (a) retained with its dialect vowel *hærg* for West Saxon *hearg*, and (b) corrupted to *hrærg*. The full elucidation of this point belongs to consideration of the feud with the Heathobeards. But it seems clear to me that that feud was largely concerned with the possession or control of a centre of a 'cult', and a fane. The cult was one connected with the fertility religion that later in Scandinavia was associated with the names Njǫrðr, Frey, Yngvi-Frey. And after the Scyldings became masters of this centre we observe the Danes taking on names reminiscent of that cult: Hrothgar is called (*1044) *eodor Ingwina*, 'Defence of the clients of Ing' (850–1 'warden of the Servants of Ing'); his daughter is *Fréawaru* (1700, *2022), 'Protection of Fréa = Frey'; and what is more, Sceaf and Beow belonging to corn-myth became blended with Scyld in Hrothgar's ancestry.

hærgtrafu only occurs here. And I think it is probably a very old element. It means 'heathen tabernacles' (*hærg* is a heathen fane or altar, surviving now only in old place-names such as Harrow-on-the-Hill; *træf* a tent). It is therefore all the more remarkable that the *place* of the seat of the Skjoldungar in Old Norse should be Lejre (as the name is in modern Danish) < *Hleiðr* (genitive *Hleiðrar*) or *Hleiðrar-garðr* – for this name seems to be an ancient name for a *tent* or *tabernacle*: at least it can most easily be related to Gothic *hleiþra* 'tent'.)

Now our poet edited his old material. He appears to have kept in the reference to *blót* [Old Norse, 'sacrifice, sacrificial feast'] or *wígweorþung* (*176; 139 'sacrifices to idols') at this point. Why? It was there, and it was quite consistent with his theory to leave it in, for he knew well enough that these old pagans (a) had heathen customs, such as *augury* mentioned in 166 (*204), and (b) had false gods, to which in time of trial and despair they might have recourse. But he only put in as much as was consistent with his theory and belief and conscience, and he made a comment – that by sacrificing to idols (when so tempted) they were turning to the Devil. And that was what caused the later trouble. The later 'Christian' did not find this comment long enough or strong enough. I think we can hear the 'voice' of the original poet clearly enough at least as far as *hæþenra hyht* (*179, 'the hope of heathens' 142). Somewhere after that point the new stuff has been (skilfully) attached, possibly at the expense of a line or two of the original. *Helle gemundon in módsefan* *179–80, 142–3 may be from the original poet – 'they remembered hell in their hearts': such is the natural drag down in pagan times. Once past this corner all would be easy for the original poet. His 'editing' of his older material would usually involve no more

than silence concerning the names of false gods (when he rec-
ognized them: apparently *Ingwina* was not clear to him, or
may have been taken as genealogical only), and inner change
of the reference of words. For example, in *381-2 (306-7)
Hine hálig god ús onsende is in the context of the poem not
necessarily a Christian but it is at least a monotheist expres-
sion. Yet it could have stood in a pagan lay at this point. Both
hálig and *god* are pre-Christian! If Hrothgar had offered *blót*
to Fréa in his distress, and had then seen a young champion
arrive unexpectedly, he could still have well exclaimed *Hine
hálig god ús onsende* in the original pagan material.

[In this set of lectures my father had in fact passed over the problem
presented by lines 134-5, *168-9, despite his words that follow here.]

134-5; *168-9

Now we must return to the *crux* which we have left
behind unsolved. This couplet is perhaps the most difficult
in *Beowulf*. But that in itself is a warning. In its own style
and diction *Beowulf* is not an obscure poem, far from it: it
is on the whole, once you know the words, easier to read
than other Old English verse. It is legitimate, therefore, at
the outset to suspect that we are faced by either *corruption* or
alteration of the original text.

But the couplet does not appear to be corrupt: no one has
seriously attempted to find relief in emendation, at any rate
no emendation worthy of consideration has ever been pro-
posed. The *crux* is one of translation.

[I give here the Old English text and the translation in the full text together, as fully as is needed to follow the argument.

  164 Swá fela fyrena féond mancynnes,
     atol ángengea oft gefremede
     heardra hýnða; Heorot eardode,
     sincfáge sel sweartum nihtum;
  168 nó hé þone gifstól grétan móste
     máþðum for Metode, né his myne wisse.
     Þæt wæs wræc micel wine Scyldinga,
     módes brecða.

131–6 Thus many a deed of evil that foe of men stalking dreadfully alone did often work, many a grievous outrage; in Heorot's hall bright with gems in the dark nights he dwelt. Never might he approach the precious Throne of grace in the presence of God, [Who took no thought of him >] nor did he know His will. That was great torment to the Scyldings' lord, anguish of heart.]

The difficulties are these: what are the references of *hé* *168, *his* *169? *hé* = Grendel, Hrothgar, *Metod, gifstól, maþðum*? Also the exact sense of *grétan*, of *maþðum*, and of *myne wisse* are all in doubt.

Now at first sight it looks as if *hé* was Grendel, and the *gifstól* was Hrothgar's throne, and a contrast is intended between the normal behaviour of a loyal thane in the hall and the conduct of the wicked intruder who did not recognize the lawful authority of the king. And in favour of *hé* = Grendel is the fact that Grendel has been the subject since *164, 131. But before we can test this assumption we have to consider the doubtful words.

grétan means fundamentally 'hail, address, greet', but in Old English, through the usages 'accost, address oneself to' it may be used (as a *litotes*) for 'assail'; or it may come to mean or imply 'set hand to, touch' (as in *gomenwudu gréted* *1065, 'the harp was touched to mirth' 868–9). But we perceive that the most natural sense of *gifstól grétan* is not 'touch' but 'hail, address the throne (of gifts)'. *maþm* means a gift, and so can of course repeat or refer to the *gif*-element in *gifstól*; but it cannot refer to the whole *gifstól* – it cannot mean 'the throne'. *Maþm* is a thing given in exchange or as reward ('a precious thing' only secondarily); and kings, even in fairy-story, do not give away their thrones. It is however a thing that a king on his throne might give, so it seems clear that *grétan* is used in two slightly different senses: to address (approach), and to lay hands on, touch.

myne is a noun related to *munan* as *cyme* ['coming'] is to *cuman*. *munan* means 'think of, have in mind or purpose'. *myne* thus means 'thinking of (a person or thing) – intention, will – recollection'. Actually elsewhere it is mostly recorded in a good sense, so that contextually it may mean 'good will (towards), kind thought (of)'. Now *witan* in Old English can be used with verbal nouns in the sense 'know, feel': as *witan ege* 'feel fear, fear'. So *witan myne* could be taken to mean 'have thought or memory (of).' But the usual sense in verse is purpose, wish, and, if an accompanying genitive is present, it is subjective not objective (as in the frequent *módes myne*). So that clearly *ne his myne wisse* is most likely to mean 'and did not know his purpose/wish'. But it might mean 'and did not have thought for/of him'.

But it must be observed that unless a fresh *hé* is put in – by a direct emendation – before *his* – the subject of *wisse* must be the same as the subject of *móste*; as the line stands the subject cannot possibly be God.

With these preliminaries it will at once be found that the throne cannot be Hrothgar's. 'Grendel could not touch (or approach) the bountiful throne, receive a gift in the presence of (*or* because of) God, and knew not His purpose (*or* took no thought of Him).' This certainly would not be *módes brecða* (*171) to Hrothgar, even if it were true. But could it be? Why could Grendel not approach the throne, when he was in sole control of Heorot all night? There was no magical or divine protection over the throne any more than over the hall or its inhabitants, and no doubt Grendel could have sat in the king's throne and gnawed bones there (which would be *módes brecða* perhaps). And it is no solution to reply that what is meant is that Grendel could not come before the throne and get a *maþum*, like an honest *þegn*. For he could have done so, if he wished. Lines *154–8 (123–7) declare that he did not wish to do so. Had he desired peace or truce the Danes would have welcomed him. It was not *Metod* but Grendel's wickedness that cut him off from the *dréam* [e.g. *Beowulf* *88, 'the din of revelry' 72]. And in any case we see how ill *for Metode* fits into any such attempt at a rendering.

It becomes plain therefore that the language is theological. *gifstól* is God's throne, and is an example of the frequent use of heroic language with theological import; *gif-* (and its equivalent *maþum*) refers to divine *grace* or *mercy*. So *giefstól* = God's throne in [Cynewulf's poem] *Crist*, line 572.

Try again. 'Never (*or* in no wise) could he have recourse to the gracious throne and its bounty in the presence of God (*or* because of God, i.e. because God did not allow this); and he knew not His will.' Grendel certainly is under God's curse, as a descendant of Cain; but that idea does not come in here, because unless you insert a new *hé* (as I have said), *ne his myne wisse* cannot be twisted to have any such sense as 'nor did He (God) have thought of him'.

Indeed, is this remark certainly applied to Grendel? No. Indeed (I think) it is certainly not. The fact that Grendel was cut off from mercy has been dealt with, and is not particularly interesting at this point. It certainly was not part of Hrothgar's torment. No, to my mind it is clearly Hrothgar who is referred to. To begin a new matter with *hé* and only introduce the new name later (*wine Scyldinga*) is a frequent practice of the *Beowulf* poet. It is specially clumsy here, perhaps, for the shift in reference of *hé* (after *eardode* 'dwelt' *166 = Grendel) is sudden. But this shift is nothing like so awkward as the attempt to make the couplet (*168–9) part of Hrothgar's *wræc*, as it must be if *hé* still refers to Grendel.

The suddenness of the shift is, I think, due to the fact that this little couplet (dealing with grace and the position of heathens with regard to God) is an interpolation or elaboration probably by the same hand as altered the following passage. Notice that it is – a very rare thing in *Beowulf* – *detachable* without damage to metre, and with improvement in coherence. For though doubtless inability to pray for mercy would be *módes brecða* to Hrothgar, it is fairly clear that *módes brecða* really refers to the ravages of Grendel and the death of his thanes. To my mind it seems plain that *Swá fela fyrena* *164 (131, 'Thus many a deed of evil') once stood much closer to *Swá ðá mælceare* *189 (151, 'Even thus over the sorrows of that time').

The excision of the couplet *168–9, and of *180–8 (143 'nor knew they the Creator'–150) would much improve the whole sequence,[1] even if we assume that (say) one and a half to two and a half lines of the 'untinkered' poem after *180 are now removed and lost. We will translate therefore:

He (Hrothgar) could not in any way (*or* ever) approach the throne of grace, receiving a gift before God, and he did not know His will. This, though not the possible alternative, 'and he did not take thought of Him', would not be wholly inconsistent with the main poem. But in fact it is more likely to come from the hand of the man who wrote *Metod híe ne cúþon, ne wiston híe Drihten God*. [See further pp. 309–12.]

151–2   *Even thus over the sorrows of that time did the son of Healfdene brood unceasingly;* *189–90 *Swá ðá mælceare maga Healfdenes singála séað*

séað [past tense of *séoðan*, modern English *seethe*]: cf. *1992–3 *Ic ðæs módceare sorhwylmum séað* (1674–6 'On this account did care about my heart well ever up in surging sorrow'). The Old English poets describe the emotions

---

1   [To make this clearer to the eye, in addition to the brackets enclosing lines 134–5 (the translation of *168–9), which my father entered on the typescripts, I have inserted brackets to enclose also lines 143–50 (the translation of *180–8.)]

– especially of great grief, [?] injury, or frustrated wrath – in terms of a boiling pot. The *wylmas* (hot upswelling surges) rise and burn the *hreþer* or inwards. The word *wylm* (*wælm*, *welm*) is related to *weallan* 'boil, surge' (intransitive). It is of course usually used literally of bubblings, gushings, surges, and only of emotions in such compounds as *sorg-*, *bréost*, *cear-*.

(*Note.* Except in *Beowulf* *2507-8 *hildegráp heortan wylmas, bánhús gebræc*, of Dæghrefn crushed to death by Beowulf. But here it is really physical: *heortan wylmas* = *heart's throbs* = *throbbing heart*. [Translation 2107-9: 'a warrior's gripe it was that quenched his beating heart crushing his frame of bones.'] The word survives for instance in Ewelme (near Oxford), which is not named after two trees but from O.E. *ǽ-welm* 'out-gush', the name of a spring.)

The verb *séoðan* also meant 'boil', but unlike its modern descendant was transitive, meaning 'set to boil, cook (by boiling)'. It thus implies a protracted and conscious and introspective process – which we by a different metaphor (but still one referring to keeping things 'hot') call 'brooding'.

163–4 *With that voyage little fault did wise men find;*
*202-3 *Ðone síðfæt him snotere ceorlas lýthwón lógon*

lýthwón: adverb, 'very little'. This habit of 'understatement' (because it may become a habit, and that is a 'linguistic idiom' no longer having any special effect) is very common in Old English. Here all that is required for one engaged in reading the text is to realize that the literal 'found very little fault with that journey' does not mean that *their objections were not important though they made some*; it does not even mean *they found nothing to say against it* (as in modern English 'he little knows what's coming to him' = 'he has no idea') *and said 'Very well, go if you wish'*. It means *they applauded the project*. Just as the *unwáclícne* 'not mean or shabby' of the funeral pyre of Beowulf (*3138; 2636 'not niggardly') means 'with lavish splendour'.

How you would render this in modern language is less important than appreciation of the actual implication of the Old English words. Sometimes the original understatement will fit, sometimes not. In Old English understatement is not a mere colloquial habit, though it is, as it were, a linguistic mood. It comes very frequently at points of 'high colour' – where later (mediæval) romancers would tend to heap up words and superlatives – as though the poet (and the linguistic mood that he inherited) suddenly realized that shouting merely deafens and that at times it is more effective to lower the voice.

[At this point my father 'recommended to the attention' of his audience the feast in Heorot on the night of Beowulf's arrival, *491–8.]

Then for the Geatish knights together in company a bench was made free in the drinking-hall. There to their seats went those men stout of heart, resplendent in valour. An esquire his office heeded, he that bore in hand the jewelled ale-goblet, and poured gleaming out the sweet drink. Ever and anon a minstrel sang clear in Heorot. There was mirth of mighty men, no little assembly of the manhood of Danes and Weder-Geatas.

[If this is compared with the same passage in the full translation of the poem, 398–405, it will be seen that my father had it in front of him, for this version differs from it in only a very few points. This has been observed earlier, p. 173.]

Heroic, restrained, moving – relying on the effect of the metre and one or two 'laden' words full of implication: *deall*, *duguð*. [*þrýðum dealle* *494, 'resplendent in their strength' 400; *duguð unlýtel* *498, 'no little assembly of the tried valour' 404.]

(*Note. deall*: a poetic word (preserved only in Old English verse) – meaning as near as we can get to 'resplendent', since it evidently properly referred to outward and visual richness and brightness; but it is here by that compressive art of Old English poetry applied to *þrýð* 'strength', so that those acquainted with the idiom, or acquiring an understanding of it, can with the maximum economy receive a picture of tall, physically admirable men of such a mien that appraising eyes passed over their costly armour to their stature and bearing.

duguð: a word meaning 'proven worth', but already long applied to the *body* of older and war-tried men as contrasted with the *iuguð*: the youths, esquires, and men of mere promise; so that *duguð unlýtel* conveyed a vision of many proud and stern faces in the torch and fire light.)

It is just a glimpse of 'description' interspersed with actions and the clash of persons – briefly repeated in *611 12 (*Dær wæs hæleþa hleahtor, hlyn swynsode, word wæron wynsume*; 497–8 'There was laughter of mighty men, the din of singing; sweet were the words'). But it may be contrasted with the New Year's feast at Camelot in *Sir Gawain and the Green Knight*. There the author is suddenly aware that he must get on with the action: '*Now wyl I of hor seruise say yow no more*', he cries, '*for vch wyʒe* [everyone] *may wel wit no wont þat þer were*' (*Gawain* 130–1). But how much better to say less and not say so! Yet he is relatively modest. For the full vulgarity of shouting and overstatement you must look at the feast when in the alliterative *Morte Arthure* Arthur entertains the embassy of Rome [see *The Fall of Arthur*, 2013, p. 80]. Leaving aside the disgusting and incredible description of the food, for the *þegn* (*494, 'an esquire' 401) or the gracious queen Wealhtheow, performing her ancient rite of presenting the ceremonial cup to the king and afterwards honouring the chief guest (498 ff., *612 ff.), we have Sir Cay, the king's chief butler, busy with Arthur's goblets – sixty of them! (*Morte Arthure* 170–219).

This Old English understatement – allied though it is to the taste of the time, and to a mood of language that preferred compression and brevity (as in the *kenning*) – is frequent enough. I might have commented on it earlier: e.g. on *Nalæs hí hine lǽssan lácum téodan* (*43, 33–4), literally 'they did not array him with less gift-offerings' = 'they arrayed him with far more' – but with an additional catch: he came without any gifts or accoutrements whatsoever. He was *féasceaft funden* (*7), 'destitute' ('forlorn' 5), alone, a child, in a small boat – with (according to some surviving traditions) only a corn-sheaf beside him.

Both these passages illustrate two points: *one*, that the 'meaning' of the poet cannot be arrived at by a mere bald *literal* translation, or by warming it up with modern diction, without appreciating the idiom; and *two*, that we constantly need to know more than we do (tackling *Beowulf* direct and without any previous knowledge). So in *43 we need some idea of the 'Sheaf' tradition; here [i.e. 163–5, *202–3] (probably) some of the folk-lore out of which in part Beowulf as a character came. Though the poet finds it necessary to add 'dear though he were to them' (164–5) (since Beowulf is now in the position of sister-son to the king [Hygelac; see 300–1], a position of traditional love and affection) the eager applause with which Beowulf's desire to go away on an adventure [was greeted] is very likely derived from a fairy-tale situation in which men were glad to be rid of the strong loutish youth. Cf. *2183 ff. *Héan wæs lange, swá hyne Géata bearn gódne ne tealdon*, etc. (1835 ff. 'Long was he contemned, for the sons of the Geats did not account him worthy', etc.).

165–6   *they observed the omens*; *204 *hǽl scéawedon*

Tacitus in his *Germania* [chapter X] says that the Germanii paid the greatest attention to 'auspices' and 'lots': *auspicia sortesque ut qui maxime observant.* Not that in fact they appear to have differed in this from other 'Indo-European' peoples, or the Romans of an earlier period, as the word *auspex* 'bird-observer' for omen observing shows, and *aus picium* (whence our 'auspicious occasion' in which as here in *Beowulf* the 'omens' are assumed to be good).

It is interesting to consider why the author left in this reference to heathen practice, without comment.

171–82; *210–24

A good passage of description. The long march to the sea is compressed to *fyrst forð gewát* ('Time passed on', 171). For a moment the vision is of a cliff-top, the boat is seen below half drawn up prow foremost on the sand; we see the men busy lading it, then pushing it with oars or poles out into the water. The wind fills the sails, and it is off swiftly, as marked by the foam at the prow, like a white gull, which gives an impression of increasing distance, catching the gleam of far off cliffs and mountains in a strange land.

Compare the description in Cynewulf's poem *Elene*, 225–35[1] of Elene's sailing to the Holy Land, in which the effort to deal with a far more important occasion has led only to a piling up of poetic vocabulary for ships and the sea with no real affective picture at all.

[In his prefatory essay *On Metre* to the revised edition (1940) of the translation of *Beowulf* by J.R. Clark Hall (reprinted in *The Monsters and the Critics and Other Essays*, 1983) my father chose this passage, the voyage of the Geats to Denmark, as the exemplifying text in Old English, together with an alliterative translation: this I have cited, for comparison with his prose translation (171 ff.), in my introductory note to the latter, pp. 9–10.]

---

1 [On Cynewulf see the footnote on p. 175. The subject of this poem is the discovery of the true Cross by St. Helena, the mother of the Emperor Constantine.]

181–2; *223–4

[My father expended a great deal of time and thought on certain passages in *Beowulf* that go by the name of *cruces*: when the text is peculiarly hard to interpret for one reason or another and where competing emendations lie thick on the ground. In this case his discussion of the line runs to many pages of a closely-reasoned examination, much too long to be included here; but the matter will be seen to be of interest when considering the relative dating of his writings on *Beowulf*. Here therefore I cite his initial statement of the problems, and give a brief indication of his favoured solutions, omitting his closely argued and convincing discussions.]

þá wæs sund liden, eoletes æt ende (reading of the manuscript)

A 'summing-up' remark, or 'concluder' at the end of the journey. Though it begins in what we call the middle of a line, *Þanon* *224 ('Thence'), following *ende*, is really at the head of the next 'chapter', or 'sub-chapter'. The 'concluder', though its general purport is clear: 'the boat had come to the end of its journey', contains two difficulties: *liden* and *eoletes*.

[For the unknown word *eoletes* he accepted the emendation *eoledes*, given the meaning 'water-journey, voyage'. Of *liden*, the past participle of the verb *líðan*, he wrote as follows:]

liden. The at first sight obvious translation: 'then was the sea traversed' seems a little weak and obvious even for a 'concluder', which is usually more weighty and pointed even if repetitive; and it meets with the difficulty that the verb *líðan* is elsewhere in Old English always intransitive (it is practically always used of faring by or journeying over water). I think that this objection is fairly strong, if not decisive.

[He thought also that 'a pictorial objective ending mentioning the *boat* with which the passage began (*flota* *210) would be much better than a mere 'passive' statement – and more probable. His conclusion was to accept the suggestion of an unrecorded noun *sundlida* 'seafarer, ship' (comparing *ýðlida* of the same vessel, with *ýð* 'wave', *198, 161): 'then the ship was at the end of its sea-journey'. But he accepted also a further emendation, to *sundlidan* (dative), as more idiomatic and nearer to the manuscript reading: 'then for that ship the journey was at an end.'

In the earliest text of his prose translation of the poem he translated the words *þá wæs sund liden, eoletes æt ende* 'The waters were overpassed; they were at their sea-way's end'. This he corrected later to 'Then for that sailing-ship the voyage was at an end'. It will be seen that this is the rendering that he came to as he wrote his commentary. This was the wording in the typescript copy ('C'); in this text my father crossed out *voyage* and replaced it with *journey*. This is therefore the translation given in this book.

It may also be mentioned that in his article *On Metre* (referred to in the note to 171–86 above), in his Old English text of the passage he printed the words as *þá wæs sundlidan* and credited the emendation in a footnote.]

184   *their mail-shirts they shook;* *226 *syrcan hrysedon*

[This is another case where my father came to oppose his treatment of it in his translation as originally made, which read 'their mail-shirts clashed'. In Klaeber's edition the verb *hryssan* (past tense *hrysedon*) is glossed 'shake, rattle' and is regarded as being here (exceptionally) intransitive, and the phrase *syrcan hrysedon* as 'asyndetic', i.e. dropped into the larger sentence without conjunction. He wrote:]

hrysedon is transitive: so always where elsewhere recorded. In any case the verb means 'shake roughly', not 'rattle', so that [the notion of an] asyndetic interpolation of *syrcan hrysedon* with *syrcan* as subject, sandwiched between two past tense plurals of which the subject is the Geats, is both unnecessary and improbable. The men must have done the shaking. They had probably not worn their hauberks while sailing (they were no doubt part of the *beorhte frætwe* (*214, 174 'their bright harness') that they carried aboard and put in the hold), and now unrolled them and shook them out before putting them on at once (being now in an alien land). In any case, and certainly if they had worn the mail-shirts, they would need some attention after a sea-passage in an open boat, though this one is represented as taking less than two days.

189–90 *anxiety smote him*; *232 *hine fyrwyt bræc*

fyrwyt (better spelt *firwit*) is usually glossed 'curiosity, inquisitiveness', which makes the frequency of the expression *hine firwit bræc* sound very strange (Klaeber says 'One would like to know the origin of this quaint expression'. Not too difficult to perceive!) But the phrase was no doubt coined for special urgent occasions; while 'curiosity' or 'inquisitiveness', which now usually imply an attitude which may be quite frivolous, is not a good gloss. *firwit* often approaches 'care, solicitude, *anxiety*'. It is an emotion of one seeing or hearing anything that puts one on the alert, and requires immediate enquiry or action, or of one anxiously awaiting very important news. (The 'passive' treatment of the person, and the 'active' of the emotion, is in keeping

with the general depicting of emotion in Old English.) So in
*1985 *hyne fyrwet bræc* (1668–9 'eagerness pierced his heart')
refers to Hyglelac's impatient desire to hear about Beowulf's
adventure; in *2784 the same phrase (2342 'Anxiety pierced
his uplifted heart') refers to the great anxiety of the man who
had been into the dragon-den to know whether Beowulf was
still alive to see the booty before he died.

Here the coastguard suddenly sees a number of strange
men mooring a ship and bringing out warlike equipment. He
is seriously alarmed. 'Anxiety deeply troubled him to learn'
is perhaps a fair rendering. He had means of raising an alarm
if necessary. He had men near at hand (*maguþegnas* *293,
'my young esquires' 236). Though he fiercely brandished
his spear, and spoke in hostile terms (cloaked in courteous
expression) he could not alone have resisted the landing of
fifteen men. He might, if his suspicions were justified, hope
to escape to summon aid, since he was mounted. You need
not picture him riding up to within easy spear-cast! His chal-
lenge was shouted in a high clear voice from a fair distance.

202–3 *no hall-servant is he in brave show of weapons*;
*249–50 *nis þæt seldguma wæpnum geweorðad*

The compound *seldguma* occurs only here. The context
shows that it means someone of inferior rank. So *nis þæt
seldguma* etc. 'that he is no ordinary man' is a way of saying
'he must be a man of high rank'. It is with this *positive* inten-
tion that *wæpnum geweorðad* ('in brave show of weapons')
goes, and the guard does not mean (as the word order might

now suggest) 'This is no humble man just dressed up in good arms'. 'Doubtless this is a man of rank, with his noble weapons' is nearer to the sense.

[Thus my father had rejected his translation 'no [minion >] hall-servant is he in brave show of weapons'.]

The difficulty is to explain *seldguma*. Clearly one would expect it to mean 'a man with a seat in the hall', that is one of the warriors usually in a king's household, a variant of *geselda*: for which see *1984, where Beowulf is actually called *sinne geseldan* in relation to Hygelac (1668 'the companion at his side'). *Seldguma* would seem to be just what Beowulf is. Though a kinsman of the king he was young, not war-tried (though the hero of many adventures of youthful daring and strength), and not one of high rank in the court (one of the *witan*). The explanation is probably that we are underestimating the guard's praise. At home Beowulf may have seemed just one of the *geogoð*, though a notable one; to a stranger with a fresh and seeing eye he looks a king's son or a young chieftain. 'This is not just one of the king's knights, but his stature, fair countenance, and peerless mien, if I am not deceived, (show him to be a prince).'

But the implication of this praise is partly hostile and suspicious: such a crew and leader are out on a big business of some kind. What is it?

205 *false spies*; *253 *léasscéaweras*

léasscéaweras: 'lying-observers', i.e. spies with treacherous intent. The guard is being hostile and as insolent as the situation allowed. It is to the use of such opprobrious words that the word *hearm* 'insult' refers in line *1892, when on their departure the guard greeted Beowulf and his companions as friends: *nó hé mid hearme . . . gæstas grétte* (1587–8 'not with unfriendly words . . . did he hail the guests').

213; *263   *Ecgtheow*

Ecgtheow does not alliterate with *Beowulf.* It is notable that though Beowulf is quite plainly in part a non-historical fairy-tale character, he is by the author given a father and other close kin. There were clearly traditions about these names – especially about Ecgtheow (cf. 370 ff., *459 ff.) – which the author did *not* invent; his allusive references being certainly to things that (many of) his audience would know about. Cf. also the kinship with *Wígláf* son of *Wíhstán* of the *Wægmundingas* (see 2365–6, *2813–14).

Ecg- names are common, but *Ecgtheow* is not found else-where (except in Old Norse *Eggþér*, and then only as *glaðr Eggþér* herdsman of the giants, who sat and played the harp on a mound); and is therefore hardly likely to be purely fictitious. There are two possibilities: (1) that while Ecgtheow and the Wægmundingas had their place in historical legend-ary tradition, our author intruded Beowulf into this family to give him the princely place that his treatment of the char-acter required; (2) that there were traditions of a person 'X' in history who carried on or tried to carry on the Geatish kingdom against the Swedes after the ending (in Heardred) of the Hrædling dynasty; with this figure the folk-tale had been blended (for reasons not now discoverable) probably at a period before, even long before our author composed his poem.[1]

The first of these seems very improbable. If traditions about, say, Ecgtheow and his feud and taking refuge at the Danish court (see 370–5) were still remembered unconnected with 'Beowulf', what would such an audience think of the procedure? And if we suppose that Ecgtheow was chosen because of his Danish connexion to make [plausible?] the acceptance of a Geat in the (not very friendly) court of Heorot, what of the Wægmundingas? Some of the things said about them are odd. Wiglaf, kinsman and last staunch companion of Beowulf, is called *léod Scylfinga,* *2603, 'liege of the Scylfingas', the Swedish dynasty;[2] and we learn that his father Weohstan/Wihstan had been one of the knights of Onela the Swedish king and the actual slayer of Eanmund the rebellious nephew of Onela, whose brother Eadgils had taken refuge with Heardred of the Geats, and who (in revenge for Heardred's death at Onela's hands) was later supported by Beowulf and helped to kill Onela and become king of the Swedes.[3] This seems just the sort of confused situation

---

1 [Heardred was the son of Hygelac. The Hrædling dynasty: the descendants of Hrethel (Hrædla), father of Hygelac. On the forms *Hrædla, Hrædling* see the note to 358–9, pp. 238–9.]

2 [In the complete translation, 2186, *léod Scylfinga* is translated 'a lord of Scylfing race'.]

3 [The sons of Ongentheow King of the Swedes were Ohthere and Onela (see the note to 48–9). Eanmund and Eadgils were the sons of Ohthere. When Onela became king his nephews fled the country and took refuge with the king of the Geats, who was

and the sort of family, with divided allegiance and possibly estates on both sides, out of which a man might come who was able to maintain a measure of Geatish independence after the end of their dynasty – at any rate during the reign of Eadgils. Since his precarious situation was short-lived he would be a figure about whom 'legend' might gather (in lieu of authentic genealogical lore), especially if this was helped by accidents of similarity: e.g. he was of obscure origin; he was large and strong, and uncouth – he may even have had a name or nickname referring to one of such tales.

232–3 *A man of keen wit . . . will discern the truth in both words and deeds;* *287–9 *sceal scearp scyldwiga gescád witan, worda ond worca*

sceal basically means 'is bound (to do), has an obligation (to do).' Hence its use as a future equivalent, as we can say 'it's bound to rain if I don't take an umbrella'. So here it is not, I think, an expression of a duty or necessity arising from office or function, but 'gnomic'. The exchange of what we should call 'platitudes', received opinions about the way things go in the world, was more honoured in heroic circles

---

now Heardred, the son of Hygelac slain in Frisia (2003–4). Both Heardred and Eanmund were slain in Onela's subsequent attack, the slayer of Eanmund being Wihstan, Wiglaf's father (2194–5); Beowulf then became king of the Geats. Afterwards, with the aid of Beowulf, Eadgils Ohthere's son went north and slew Onela, his uncle, becoming himself king of the Swedes (2012–16). See the note to 303–4, at end.]

than in (say) modern academic ones. (The ultimate 'gnome' is propounded at the end of Beowulf's address to Hrothgar: *Gǽð á wyrd swá hío scel!* *455, 'Fate goeth ever as she must' 367.) Had the coast-guard been expressing an opinion on a *particular* situation he would have said: 'a man in my position has to keep his wits about him and recognize a liar when he meets him.' What he does say, in effect, is: 'a man of discernment will naturally be able to recognize an honest man' – that he is a man of discernment (or he would not be in his position) is understood.

We use *will* (not *shall*) in such 'general' statements if we use an auxiliary at all. Thus the 'gnome' *draca sceal on hlǽwe* is not 'a dragon shall be in a grave-mound', which in our usage would imply the wish or purpose of 'I' the speaker, but 'a dragon will be found in a grave-mound', because such is its nature, or 'dragons are found in graves'. Translate therefore: 'A man of acumen, who considers things properly, will naturally show discernment in judging words and deeds.'

246–8; *303–6

['It would take far too long,' my father said, 'to discuss this matter, and criticize the many editorial variations'; but he would 'give you in brief my view dogmatically.' I give it here with some slight reduction, and begin with the passage in the form of the unemended manuscript and in the translation.

Eoforlíc scionon
ofer hléorberan   gehroden golde,
305   fáh ond fyrheard,   ferhwearde héold
gúþmód grummon.   Guman ónetton . . .

246 Figures of the boar shone above cheek-guards, adorned
with gold, glittering, fire-tempered; fierce and challenging
war-mask kept guard over life. The men hastened . . .]

This is a well-known crux of translation and text since
at least *gúþmód grummon* must be corrupt. The passage
puzzled the scribe, either because it was already corrupted
or in places hard to read, or because he could not make
much sense out of it, or for both reasons combined. One of
the signs of this is the retention of a number of 'dialectal',
i.e. not West Saxon forms, which would probably have been
altered if the scribe had felt more confidence: *scionon*, *beran*
for *bergan* (W.S. *beorgan*); *ferh* for *feorh*.

The principal difficulty is in *gúþmód grummon*, and here
my solution is not (I think) found elsewhere. First of all, I
think the whole passage is an example of the 'representative
singular', frequently used in description. For example, sol-
diers march by (each accoutred more or less alike) – helmet
shines, crest tosses, spear glitters, hauberk clinks. But this pas-
sage is even more selective: only a helmet is described: prob-
ably the most notable and fearsome item (to an onlooker) of
the array of a fully armed Northern warrior of the heroic age.
(A similar method is used in 261–2, *321–3, where the hauberk
is selected.) The seemingly awkward change in verbal num-
bers *scionon* – *héold* is due to a change in syntactic subject,
not in visual object: only one helmet is described, but *each*
had more than one *eoforlíc*, a 'boar-likeness', representative
of the boar as a symbol of ferocity, also in heathen times of
religious or magical import. The representation of a boar as a

helm-crest is an undoubted archaeological fact, but not more than one such per helmet.

Nonetheless, a single helmet could be said to have more than one 'boar-likeness'. This is actually said of Beowulf's helmet, which is described (1211–12, *1453) as being 'set (plated) with *swínlícum* [dative plural]' by the smith who made it. The *eoforlíc* are therefore not 'crests' but representations of boars, of men with boar-heads or tusked masks, placed on a decorative band *just above the cheek-guards* [reading *hléorberga* for *hléorberan*] as is actually said. Then what is the subject of *héold*? A new singular subject, but also a part of the helmet, related to the *eoforlíc* is required. It cannot be found in line *305; therefore it must be concealed in the corrupt *gúþmód grummon*. I therefore propose to read *gúþmód gríma*. I suppose a process of corruption not necessarily all accomplished in one stage, by which *gríma* was assimilated (by a process often exemplified in inattentive corruption) to *gruman* before *guman* (*306). Since this meant nothing it was later turned into the real word *grummon* '(they) roared or raged' which might seem to a puzzled scribe vaguely to fit the context, but in fact does not.

The *gríma* was a mask or vizor (partly) covering the face. That the helmets of this company had such *gríman* is assured, since Wulfgar at the door of Heorot says so: *grímhelmas* *334, *heregríman* *396; 'your masked helms' 271, 320. That these were or might be of fierce or horrifying shape, designed (like more primitive war-paint) to frighten off assailants (and so act as life-guards) is shown by the frequent use of *gríma* for a bogey, or terrifying apparition.

It is true that *gúþmód gríma* 'the war-spirited mask' would appear to require transfer of an epithet proper to a warrior to his armour. This is not a grave difficulty: arms can be described as *fús* or *fúslíc*, that is 'eager to advance, eager for battle'. But the *gríma* or mask probably more or less represented a *face*, human or animal, and *gúþmód* was the expression of this face.

288–496; *356–610   The speeches at court

With these speeches we make further and fuller acquaintance with 'courtesy' of word and bearing as conceived by the poet, modelled doubtless on the best contemporary manners. Wulfgar was not a 'servant', but an officer of the court. It was his duty to assess the merit of strangers at the door and to advise whether they should be admitted.

290–1   *well he knew the customs of courtly men*; *359 *cúþe hé duguðe þéaw*

Duguð is properly an abstract noun related to *dugan* 'be of worth, service', etc.; so its basic sense is 'worth, usefulness, value'. This sense it retained; but it also developed special applications. No doubt partly assisted by the rhyme with *iugoþ, geogoþ* 'youth', it became used for the age when a man was of most service, his prime. Then naturally it could be used (like *iugoþ*) for the body of all men, or all the men in a given place, who had *duguþ*. It thus can often mean 'host of (fully-grown and war-tried) men'. This is always its sense in *dugoþ ond iugoþ*. But it is often its sense when it stands alone; then it often means 'host (of warriors), splendid host'. It is not often possible to determine whether the sense in a given passage is most closely allied to this branch 'glorious host', or to the older sense 'worth, value, excellence'.

So it is in *duguþe þéaw*. This may be 'the manners of manly virtue, of fitness and worth', or 'the manners of the *duguþ*, the knights and well-trained men of the court'. In any case 'the correct manners for a knight' is meant.

When at last the stage is set, and the two main 'heroic' characters at last come together, Hrothgar and Beowulf, we have to consider more carefully the various threads out of which this poem is woven.

It had two fundamental materials. 'Historial' legend and Fairy Story. The 'historial legend' is derived ultimately from traditions about real men, real events, real policies, in actual geographical lands – but it has passed through the minds of poets. How far the historical realities of character and event have been preserved (more than some suppose, I fancy) in this way is a different question. The Fairy Story (or Folktale if you prefer that name) has at any rate been altered: for in this case it has been welded into the 'history'. And not, I think, for the first time by our poet. Beowulf and the Monster were already grafted onto the court of Heorot before ever he made this poem. But however it was done, by one poet or a succession of them, it caused great changes not only of detail but of tone. And it did not leave the history unaffected. You have only to consider how different is magic, faerie, and the like when it takes place in the court of Camelot in the time of Arthur, that are placed in history and geography, from a mere fairy-tale; and how different is the atmosphere of Arthur's court for all its atmosphere of 'history' because of this fairy-element, to understand what I mean. And then – above it all, working on this powerful blend, is the latest poet, our poet, the Mallory of the Heorot legends, with his contemporary ideas of virtue and courtesy, and his theology, and his own particular apprehension (often of dramatic cast) of the characters: his Hrothgar, his Beowulf. Only if we keep these three things in mind shall we really understand these conversations and speeches, Wulfgar, Beowulf, Hrothgar, Unferth. Behind the stern young pride of Beowulf, on the surface credible enough, lies the roughness of the uncouth fairy-tale champion thrusting his way into the house. Behind the courtesies (tinged with irony) of Hrothgar lies the incredulity of the master of the haunted house; behind his lament for his vanished knights lurk still the warnings given to frighten off the new-comer, with stories of how everyone who has tried to deal with the monster has come to a bad end.

I shall analyze the first speech of Beowulf to Hrothgar, and Hrothgar's reply, in a moment, to show what I mean – and specially so as to make a guess at what Hrothgar really meant at the end of his reply.

Of course, care is taken to make Beowulf fit the 'historial' background. His father is made to have been a refugee at the Danish court. He himself is a nephew of the ruling king of Gautland,[1] grandson of the late king Hrethel. The very political relations between Gautland and Denmark are used to provide a machinery by which Hrothgar can know something about him – and so reveal it to us indirectly. Yet the fairy-story element peeps out through every chink. What did the diplomatic exchanges between the courts of Denmark and Gautland enable Hrothgar to learn? That the king's nephew was a man to keep his eye on, enjoying considerable popularity; likely to become a power in the land later, older than the king's own son Heardred, but apparently so far loyal, and not likely to try to seize the throne? Yes, but not here. Here we learn only that the king's nephew possessed the pure fairy-story characteristic of having *thirty* men's strength in his hands!

At least that is so in the part of the poem we are considering. But the interweaving of 'history and politics' is continual. The emissaries evidently did bring back political news as well as tidings of 'faerie'. Policy is not forgotten. The folk-tale champion is also the prince of a real kingdom. Policy is one of the strands of Hrothgar's long sermon (1426 ff., *1700 ff.) – against misplaced pride and unjust ambition. The dynastic situation in Gautland is plainly alluded to in Hrothgar's farewell speech 1546–53, *1844–53. And this very element, noble loyalty, which is part of Beowulf's character as a political person, is brought suddenly into connexion with his most folklore-like talent (his strength of grip) in Beowulf's own speech. We learn that his contest with

---

1 [*Gautar* is the Old Norse form of O.E. *Geatas.*]

Grendel is to be a gripping-match, no courtly affair of arms. 'Folk-tale here!' we may cry. But Beowulf, as he is now conceived, has his answer ready. Grendel does not know how to use civilized weapons. I will take no unfair advantage, not as I hope ever to keep the esteem of my liege-lord, Hygelac! (350 ff., *433 ff.).

And then we come to a new and very fascinating character, Unferth. To which book does he belong? The Book of Kings, or Tales of Wonder? It is very difficult to decide – for Unferth is the actual link between the two worlds. He is balanced precisely between them.

His function in the story as we have it is clear enough. He is an important person in the Danish court. He is a *þyle* [see p. 138, footnote], and as such it is his place to know all about people. His character (envy) and his function (knowledge of men and realms) are made the machinery by which we get further information to complete our picture of Beowulf the Strong; and the 'flyting' [contention, wrangling] that ensues is made to bring Beowulf to the point of a 'vow', made before the court , that he will at once (*ungeára nú* *602, 'ere long' 488) tackle Grendel. He cannot back out of that, and Hrothgar is at last really convinced. His *wén* (*383, 'hope' 308) becomes certainty, for now Beowulf's determination is beyond doubt (495–6, *609–10).

But if we look closer and consider other details we shall find much to ponder. My own view is that Unferth is a composite character – in this tale a figure produced by the contact of the two elements: courtly and fairy story. He is thus very similar to Beowulf himself, and like him is not (evidently) entirely fictitious. He had a father Ecglaf (see the note to 406), and he had brothers. The story that he slew them [477–8, *587] – a very startling fact or accusation – can hardly have been invented for this occasion. There was, we must suppose (it is natural and not peculiar to Old English legend), a tendency, in a period when genealogies, often long, and the interrelations of families, were still a part of native lore and learning, for figures of fiction – derived from folk-tale, or merely from poetic-dramatic treatment of 'history' – to become blended with minor more or less historical characters. It is to the dramatization by poets of historial legend, rather than to folk-tale, that on his fictitious side Unferth belongs. His name is significant because it is 'significant', that is: has a name suitable to his function. Unferth means Unpeace, Quarrel; and the first thing we hear of him is that he unloosed a spell for the creating of strife (407; *onband beadurúne* *501). The name was made for the figure: a sinister figure in the renowned court of Heorot. It does not occur elsewhere (and even in our text is always written *Hunferð*, a not uncommon name, in spite of the alliteration). It does not occur in Scandinavia, though Unferth is here a great person in a famous Danish court.

Evidently he is largely a creation, an element in the ominous situation at Heorot, as it was dramatized by English poets: a literary relative of those wicked counsellors that have the ear of aged kings. In poems dealing with Heorot as such, with the doom of the Scyldings, with the old king, his young heir Hrethric, and the powerful figure of Hrothulf [son of Halga, Hrothgar's brother], the scheming nephew in the background, it is likely enough that Unferth had a part to play, quite apart from his appearance in *Beowulf*. So far he comes out of 'historial' legend, with perhaps some actual historical features attached. But here he comes out of the Tales of Wonder, not the Book of Kings. The things he knows and reveals about Beowulf come out of northern legend.

[In the passage that follows my father was touching obliquely on the intricate matter of the relationship of an episode in *Beowulf* (the descent of the hero into the mere where the monsters dwelt) to the story found in Scandinavian folk-tales, and in particular that in the Icelandic *Grettis Saga*. That these narratives are related is universally agreed; and remote as they are in all the circumstances, an extraordinary linguistic connexion survived. This lies in the word *hæftméce*, found nowhere else in Old English, applied to the sword Hrunting, and the Icelandic word *heptisax*, found nowhere else in Norse, defined in the text as a broadsword with a handle (haft) of wood – but in the saga with a different significance in the story.]

What is more, he is the possessor of the curious weapon *Hrunting*, the *hæftméce* (*1457, 'that hafted blade' 1215), which evidently played a definite part in the fairy-story of the descent into the magic cave. Not in 'the general folk-tale', but in a particular northern form of it from which our *Beowulf* derives; for in the Icelandic form the *heptisax* reappears (though with a different function). I suspect that on this side Unferth represents the traitor, who after leading the hero to the cave, deserts him, leaving him to his fate (e.g. cutting or letting go of the rope by which he descended). Of that in our tale nothing is left save the fact that the *hæftméce* on which

Beowulf had depended failed him altogether. The desertion is glossed over and obscured: nothing is left of it save the fact that the Danes assumed that all was over with Beowulf and went home (1341–3, *1600–2).

This is guesswork. And all the more difficult because doubtless the alterations that have been made on both sides, the courtly and the fairy-story, as a result of their fusion, are the result of a process, not of one poet's work. Nonetheless, I do not think we can understand the 'flyting' of Beowulf and Unferth, or fully appreciate the *use* our poet has made of the situation, without considering such matters.

But in *Beowulf* as it is, it is even more interesting to consider the dramatic use that the author makes of Unferth, a use all the more effective because he did *not* have to invent him: he was already there in Heorot, stories of which were well-known to the author's audience.

The men of the Geats were sitting on a bench together (398–9, *491–2); Beowulf himself was in an honourable place (as we learn in his report to Hygelac, 1690–2, *2011–13) beside Hrothgar's young son: thus not far from the king himself, and near to Unferth, who sat at the king's feet (406–7, *500). Unferth's outburst is thus not bellowed at Beowulf from a distance – a savage discourtesy which would not have been tolerated by Hrothgar. He spoke clearly, with malice, but not at first outward discourtesy, certainly not with violence. (His chief object was the ears of the king and the chief people nearby.) Correctly read, his words should begin in an outwardly polite tone, so that they might be taken at first by hearers to be courteous, even admiring. In more or less modern terms: 'Are you the great Beowulf, the one who had that famous swimming match with Breca?' Since clearly Breca (historical or not does not here matter) was a famous character in tales of swimming and sea-hunting, this would sound complimentary enough, and men near would prick up their ears. Note then with what art the tone is shifted. It was a mad prank. Then comes the lie (as it is meant to be taken): 'Breca beat you, he was the stronger'. This would be said in a matter of fact tone – befitting one who just reports facts (which it was the function of a *þyle* to know and remember). Breca's position as an independent chieftain is added to make the lie more convincing (423–6, *520–3). Only at the end (426–31, *523–8) does Unferth's tone become more malicious and menacing or contemptuous. But at no point does he shout or bluster.

On the other hand, Beowulf shows resentment at once. He begins with an accusation that Unferth has drunk too much. He continues in a louder and more combative tone and style than Unferth had yet used, by giving his own account. Read aloud, it is almost impossible not to feel and not to represent the rising passion of Beowulf, as he recalls the events. And then being now fully heated with wrath, he turns on Unferth personally. Each sentence rises to a new point of scorn and anger, until at last forgetful of all courtesy he speaks in contempt of Danish courage, and vows to oppose Grendel with Geatish valour.

The 'flyting' is a memorable passage, very good even by modern standards, though we may tend to criticize it: for instance, in the somewhat repetitive references to the swimming in the sea. Yet it must be remembered that though 'dramatic' this is not drama, but narrative poetry (or mouth-filling rhetoric). In the economy of the tale it has, of course, a narrative function: Unferth touches off the spark of Beowulf's passionate (but not savage!) nature, and brings him to the point of a public vow to challenge Grendel at once. From that he cannot recede. More, we now really meet and know Beowulf and his character. Steadfast, loyal, chivalrous (according to the sentiment of the author's time), but with a smouldering fire. He is on the good side: his enemies are wild beasts, monstrous and evil creatures, or his king's and people's foes. But when roused he is capable of violent and superhuman action. If he does not wholly follow the sober counsels of wisdom,[1] he satisfies their most important prescription. He speaks *gilp* (proud vows) in the heat of his heart but he performs his vow – even to his last day, when it cost him his life.

300 *while he was yet a boy*; *372 *cnihtwesende*

It is not easy to imagine how Hrothgar knew Beowulf as a 'boy' – whatever precise age that may mean. If Beowulf had ever before been to Denmark to Hrothgar's court – e.g. with his father when Ecgtheow was a refugee – it is odd that he never alludes to this. If Hrothgar ever paid a visit to the

---

1 [My father made a reference here, but by line-numbers only, to passages in the Old English poem known as *The Wanderer*. These counsels are cited in translation in the note to 329 ff.]

(on the whole) hostile court of Hrethel, that also would be curious; and also is not mentioned.

It is possible that the poet merely wanted to introduce some facts about Beowulf and found the speeches of Hrothgar a convenient and dramatic method, without considering the details of his machinery very closely. But I do not think that is really the case. It would have been easy to bring on any other character (e.g. one of those who had been on the mission to Geatland (303–4, *377–9) to give the required information. More likely is it that Beowulf had already been given a place in the legends of Denmark and Geatland before our poet handled the tale; and is here (in his manner) merely giving selections from and allusions to other accounts. I think that Beowulf is meant to have been at Hrothgar's court as a young child. He may not remember much about it or the causes of his father's holiday abroad; but *sóhte holdne wine* (*376) says Hrothgar: 'he has come back to visit a friend who has not forgotten him' [cf. the translation 302–3, 'seeking a friend and patron']. In that case *Đonne* 'Then'(*377) is clearer – '*Then later on*' when Hrothgar got a chance of learning more he heard that the little lad had grown up to be a champion wrestler. [Cf. the translation 303–6, 'Voyagers by sea . . . have *since* reported that he hath in the grasp of his hand the might and power of thirty men.']

301   *his only daughter*; *375 *ángan dohtor*

Real kings have 'only daughters'; and this only daughter was not quite of the kind frequently met in fairy-tale, the only daughter who is also an only child, with whom the lucky suitor eventually obtains the kingdom too. Hrethel's daughter is however nameless. She is also the link between Beowulf and the kingdom of the Geats, which Beowulf (though not his father) does in the end obtain. She may be not unfairly regarded as a fairy-tale element – we do not know Ecgtheow's story or how he won the hand of King Hrethel's daughter, though there probably was a tale to it – yet she may be fictitious: a mere link forged later between legend and the historical dynasty of Hrethel and his three sons, the last Geatish actors in the ancient feud between Swedes and Geats.

As a matter of history this feud seems to have ended more or less in favour of the Swedes, with the extinction of the separate line of Geatish kings and the union of the territories in one kingdom. In some ways an earlier counterpart of England and Scotland; but with a difference. The crown and capital remained in the North; the king called himself king of Swedes and Geats (in Latin Suio-Gothorum); and to a certain extent separate laws and customs lived on in the southern land. About the last figures in the ancient Geatish dynasty and their fall legend evidently gathered early. If there was any historical basis for Beowulf, the last king whose fall presaged the end of the people's independence (as is clearly foreshadowed in the poem *Beowulf*), it must be in some character, not of the direct royal line, who for a while maintained a precarious position afar the Swedish invasion in which the last legitimate king, Heardred son of Hygelac, was slain, the father having lost his own life and his fleet in the rash raid on the Low Countries. [See the note on 213.]

But even if Beowulf has that much history behind him he is in the main a figure of fairy-story who has crept into the place of this far off and forgotten Hereward the Wake: a monster-slayer, and a dragon-slayer. And even of the eldest son of Hrethel, Herebeald, the story told (the accidental arrow) has a smack of legend, whatever we may think of the historicity of the death of William Rufus. And there is too much of the *ánga dohtor*. Not only does Hrethel present his only daughter to a champion Ecgtheow; but his son Hygelac presents his only daughter to a champion Eofor (2518–9, *2997).

It seems probable that there has been duplication here. In some way the tradition of the marriage of the king's only daughter to a champion has become attached to both Hrethel and the next king Hygelac. Possibly the stories of Ecgtheow and Eofor are in some ways duplicates. In any case the 'only daughter' who was given to Eofor (together with a rich reward in land or money, 2514–16) for the slaying of the Swedish king Ongentheow cannot have been a child of Hygd 'the very young' (1619), who was Hygelac's wife at the time of our story, and who was the mother of Heardred, a man much younger than Beowulf. [See the note to 1666–7.]

303–4   *gifts and treasures for the Geats*; *378 *gifsceattas Géata*

gifsceattas Géata must be taken as meaning 'gifts for the Geats', as is seen by *þyder to þance* *379. The political situations are not clear. In general coldness, if not hostility, would appear to have been the relations between Danes and Geats.

Natural enough: they were neighbours. Also there was a matrimonial alliance between the Swedish Scylfing house and the Danish Scylding house. Hrothgar's own sister according to that account had married a Scylfing prince; and if the probable guess that he was none other than Onela is right [see note to 48–9] she was the wife of a prince who had a mortal feud against Hygelac son of Hrethel – at the very moment when Beowulf arrived in Denmark – the nephew and devoted knight of Hygelac, conqueror and 'slayer' (by the hands of his vassal Eofor) of Onela's father! Hrothgar hints that there had been hostility which Beowulf had now put to rest.[1] Hostility fits the situation well enough. Where then does the taking of gifts over sea fit in? Note that to þance does not necessarily mean 'in thanks', but 'to gain or express goodwill'. [Cf. the translation, 304: 'in token of good will'.]

Conceivably it is a mere piece of machinery contrived so that Hrothgar can hear more about Beowulf. But other methods which do not run counter to the general situation could easily have been thought of: see the note on 300,

---

1   In his farewell speech Hrothgar says (*1855–63): 'Thou hast achieved this, that between the peoples, Geats and Danes, mutual peace shall be, and the strife and cruel enmity shall cease, that they before waged; that while I rule this wide realm, treasures shall be exchanged, and many men shall with good will greet one another over the sea where the gannet bathes, many a ring-prowed ship over the deep shall bring gifts and tokens of friendship.' This would naturally be interpreted that right down to Beowulf's arrival there had been tension and even war between the two realms.

   [With this passage compare that in the complete translation, 1554–62.]

while he was yet a boy. It is therefore quite possible that the poet was alluding to something quite specific and definite in the traditions about the relations of the three royal houses: an exchange of courtesies on some particular occasion, such as Hygelac's marriage. Courtesies of that kind – not necessarily implying any change of diplomacy or 'foreign policy' – were not uncommon. In Old English times the English kings sent gifts *to þance* to many notable persons. Alfred for instance sent gifts as far away as to the Patriarch of Jerusalem.

But I do not agree with the usual editorial reading of the situation that Danes and Swedes were hostile naturally, while the relations of the Danish and Geatish royal houses were excellent. This view can only be held by ignoring the matrimonial alliance that is deliberately and pointedly alluded to by the poet as the very background of the political situation at Heorot (48–9, *62–3), and by blurring over the clear meaning of Hrothgar's farewell words. It is due also to overvaluation of the Norse sources which reflect a *later situation.* After the downfall of the Hrethlingas and the absorption of Geatland, Danes and Swedes as powerful and aggressive neighbours naturally became hostile, and remained so into modern times. But in *Beowulf* we hear clear echoes of an earlier political situation, while Geatland was independent, at times ascendant, and the direct neighbours of the Danes. These (probably quite historical) traditions have, however, been somewhat altered by the intrusion of 'legend': Beowulf and Ecgtheow. Cutting across the politics is Hrothgar's personal, almost avuncular, interest in the son of Ecgtheow, grandson of the Geatish king Hrethel.

The situation presented by the poet is not however necessarily confused and contradictory. It is certainly a leading trait in the character of Hrothgar *as depicted* (and likely enough was true to his character in history) that he was a cautious diplomatist, preferring to solve his external problems by negotiation. This trait is the essential machinery in the Heathobard tragedy – by which Hrothgar's daughter Freawaru was married to the Heathobard prince Ingeld, heir to the bitterest of all the feuds against the Scylding house. And note: it was just at the time when danger had become acute again that Hrothgar tried with a stroke of policy (*rǽd* 2027) to avert war (1703–5, *2027–9). Ingeld, saved when his father was destroyed, had now grown up and reached the age when honour would require him to think of avenging his father. So it is possible enough, and in accord with Hrothgar's *political* character (quite apart from Ecgtheow and his son) that it was just at the moment when the Geats became really dangerous that Hrothgar would try a policy of appeasement. Now that moment would be after the disastrous death of the old Swedish king Ongentheow and the accession of Hrethel's third and very warlike and ambitious son Hygelac.[1]

There is evidence, external to *Beowulf*, that Ohthere, son of the slain king Ongentheow, did in fact only rule a very

---

[1] A legitimate deduction from his military success in the Swedish war, turning defeat into crushing victory; and from his great (historical) raid into the Frankish realm, which in itself reflects (a) ascendancy over the Swedes and absence of fear on his northern borders, (b) friendship with the Danish king, and (c) power and greed.

restricted realm, that he was buried in Vendel in Sweden and not in the great mounds of the kings at Old Uppsala, and that during his reign the Geats were in the ascendant, probably controlling much of Swedish territory. That was the situation until Hygelac made his rash and fatal raid into Frisia. At some appropriate time during that situation (Hygelac's accession, or his marriage, or the birth of his heir) it would be quite in the Hrothgar manner to send a mission bearing gifts to the Geats *to þance* – to suggest that friendship between the two houses was possible and might be profitable.

Hrothgar need not have forgotten his sister; but she would, on this reading, be merely the wife of Onela, the second son of Ongentheow, a prince of a diminished house, merely the brother of a small king who had in any case two sons (Eanmund and Eadgils). The Swedish revival came with the downfall of Hygelac – but that was far in the unforeseen future at the time alluded to in lines 303–4, (*377–9). The accession of Onela, his driving out of his brother's sons, his invasion of Geatland (while it lay under the disaster of the loss of its king, army, and fleet, and his slaying of the last Hrethling, Heardred, occurred after Hrothgar's time. [See the note to 213, p. 199, footnote 3.] Then, when Sweden became dominant, and by the absorption of Geatland became the powerful and aggressive neighbour of Denmark, began that 'essential hostility' between the Danish and Swedish kings, reflected in Norse legend and history, and indeed enduring far into medieval and modern times.

305–6   *the might and power of thirty men;* *379–80 *þrítiges manna mægencræft*

Cf. 'thirty knights (Grendel) seized', 98, *123. An exaggerated fairy-tale number in both places: in neither by itself very significant, so that variation would have mattered little. There is no metrical necessity favouring *þritig* in either place (for a skilled writer), and it is a fair deduction that the identity of number was meant to be significant and to be noted (by the author's audience. Very likely also, within the tale, by Hrothgar's court.) Grendel was capable of killing thirty fighting-men at once (and carrying off at least most of their remains); Beowulf was as strong as thirty men. It was an equal number, with possible hope in it.

þritig is again mentioned in connexion with Beowulf, 1988–90, *2359–62: he escaped from the great defeat by the Franks by *swimming*, bearing off thirty suits of armour.

320–1   *Leave here your warlike shields;* *397 *lǽtað hildebord hér onbídan*

Note the prohibition of weapons or accoutrements of battle in the hall. To walk in with spear and shield was like walking in nowadays with your hat on. The basis of these rules was of course fear and prudence amid the ever-present dangers of an heroic age, but they were made part of the ritual, of good manners. Compare the prohibition against *drawing a sword* in the officers' mess. Swords of course also were dangerous; but they were evidently regarded as part of a knight's attire, and he would not in any case be willing to lay aside his sword, a thing of great cost and often an heirloom. But against this danger very severe laws existed protecting the 'peace' of a king's hall. It was death in Scandinavia to cause a brawl in a king's hall. Among the laws of the West Saxon king Ine is found:

Gif hwá gefeohte on cyninges húse, síe hé scyldig ealles his ierfes ond síe on cyninges dóme hwæðer hé líf áge þe náge.

'If any man fight in the king's house, he shall forfeit all his estate, and it shall be for the king to judge whether he be put to death or not.'

In spite of the verbal courtesies, until the two sides felt quite sure of (a) their welcome, (b) the errand of the strangers, the attitude was like that of a general receiving emissaries from another army, and of men visiting an enemy camp. Too often had desperate men made their way in for the prosecution of a blood-feud. Too often had men found themselves suddenly surrounded by armed foes in a hostile hall. So Beowulf sets a guard over their shields and spears (323–5).

329   *Hail to thee, Hrothgar!*; *407 *Wæs þú, Hróðgár, hál!*

Wes hál, usually with *þú* inserted, is the usual polite formula of greeting in Old English. They wished you good health on meeting you; we merely enquire after the symptoms: 'how do you do?' From *wes heil* the formula, altered under the influence of Norse and Norse drinking customs is derived our noun *wassail*. I know of no evidence that *wes hál* was specially associated with drinking-pledges in Old English. In *617 indeed the formula used by the Queen was apparently not *wes hál*, but *béo þú blíðe (æt þisse béorþege)* or the like [so *bæd hine blíðne æt þære béorþege* *617, 'wished him joy at the ale quaffing' 501–2].

329 ff.; *407 ff.

Beowulf at once reveals himself as proud and confident. But not 'boastful'. To say that Beowulf is 'boastful' is due to a misapprehension of the situation, and to a lexicographical difficulty. Beowulf's speech is certainly a *gilpcwide* (*640, 'proud utterance' 519), which you will find glossed 'boastful speech'. But the gloss is false. Do people like to listen to 'boasting'? Yet the poet says that the Queen was delighted with Beowulf's *gilpcwide*. And when the lexicographers come to *gilpgeorn* they feel themselves obliged to gloss it 'eager for glory' (and not for vainglory). The trouble is that while the Old English words *gielpan* and *gielp* were neutral, good or bad according to the situation, but normally good (since vainglory was not admired), we have not a neutral word, or one leaning to good. *Boast* is derived from a Middle English word meaning mere noise, while *vaunt* contains Latin *vanum* 'empty'.

But *gielp* did not mean 'empty brag': that was *idel gielp* and contemptible. It meant proud speech, or exultation. And these things were not despised in certain circumstances. To

223

utter a *gielp* after you had achieved something may seem to us to approach near to our 'boasting', but it had to be moderate and *true*. To utter one before the event was a serious matter, involving a promise to perform, the breaking of which meant ignominy. Advice on this point will be found in *The Wanderer* 69–72 and 112–13: 'A wise man . . . must never be too eager for *gielp*, until he has full knowledge; a man shall pause when he utters a *béot* (another word often rendered 'boast', but more properly rendered 'vow'), until, moved though his heart be, he knows clearly whither the thought of his mind is leading.' And later: 'Good is he that keeps his word; and never shall a man too rashly reveal the fierce emotion (O.E. *torn*) of his breast, unless he has already perceived how to accomplish the remedy with valour.' That is, he must not say 'I will kill you for that', unless he means to do it, and sees a way commensurate with his means and will to do so.

The situation here is, of course, of a young man who has come a long way to do a difficult and dangerous task, that has so far defeated old and better men. He has already 'sent in his card', and though the poet has only in his selective way made Beowulf mention his errand to the coastguard, it is plain from Hrothgar's words (306–9, *381–5) that a hint of it was given also to Wulfgar. He therefore needs credentials. He at once gives them. And note, he does not beat on his chest and bellow and offer to show off his strength in the primitive manner that from some commentators one would gather he shows.

334–5   *as soon as the light of evening is hid beneath heaven's pale*; *413–14 *siððan æfenléoht under heofenes hádor beholen weorþeð*

[I give here my father's discussion of the manuscript reading *hador* and the proposed emendation *haðor* in a slightly more concise form.]

The word *hádor* is an adjective meaning 'clear, bright', nowhere else used as a noun. It is used of sound (voice) at lines *496–7 (*Scop hwílum sang hádor on Heorote*), 403 'the minstrel sang clear in Heorot'); otherwise it is almost always found in reference to the sky (or sun and stars). But that association is in description of *brightness*; this on the other hand is a description of the coming of a (sinister) darkness, of the 'hiding' of sunlight, itself already dim compared with day.

Primarily for this reason I greatly prefer *haðor*. It also seems nonsense to say that the evening-light is hidden *under* the brightness of the sky. The noun *haðor* (like *hádor* a poetic word, but rarer) is found elsewhere in the form *heaðor* '(place of) confinement'. In *Beowulf* it occurs in the verb *geheaðerod* *3072, 2582, with the sense 'shut in, enclosed in'. *under* was very frequently used in describing position within, or movement to within, a confined space, especially of enclosures or prisons, 'within four walls'. Cf. *1037 *in under eoderas* (*eoderas* being the outer fences of the courts), 845 'in amid the courts'.

It must be remembered that men still in 800 A.D. retained more closely and vividly a 'flat-earth' imagination. We retain many items of flat-earth geocentric diction: the sun rises and sets, men go to the ends of the earth, and so on. Educated men knew then, at any rate as a matter of school-learning, that the earth was round, but that did not affect the images of poetry (nor very much the actual feelings of poets). The wide earth was lit by day by the sun; night came when it sank beyond the fences or rim of the earth, and went slowly down into the dark underworld, through which it journeyed until next morning it rose above the eastern fences again. I suppose it would be hard to find (in Europe) anybody who now thought of the sun or moon descending into darkness or wandering during night through dim abysses under the world – in so far as people think of such things at all: night is not very important, and urban men hardly look at the sky at all.

I think *haðor* here has a sense similar to that of *eoderas* (see above). Cf. *eodera ymbhwyrft*, line 113 in *Juliana* [a poem by Cynewulf], the whole encirclement of the earth within the 'horizon' – the boundary fence; also in the poem *Exodus* 251, *leoht ofer lindum lyftedora bræc*, 'above the shields [of the host] light burst through the sky-fences'.[1] The sky is there not the sun but 'the pillar of fire' which is imagined in the poem as a kind of miraculous sun or ball of fire by night.

---

1 [In my father's own edition of *Exodus*, published by Joan Turville-Petre in 1981, p.57, he noted: '*Lyft-edoras* is probably "borders of the sky", i.e. the horizon; *eodor* means both "fence (protection)" and "fenced enclosure, a court". The phrase should therefore mean "broke through the fences of the sky".']

We may therefore, reading *haðor*, translate *under heofenes haðor beholen weorþeð* 'is hidden within heaven's fences'.

[At the end of his discussion my father later wrote the following in pencil:]

The translation I offered 'hid beneath heaven's *pale*' is a (perhaps not very laudable) effort to find an English word or words that might be connected with light, or with fences.

338–9 *when I returned from the toils of my foes, earning their enmity;* *419–20 *ðá ic of searwum cwóm, fáh from féondum*

This would probably not be difficult if we knew the tales alluded to. I do not believe that *searu* could have the sense 'battle'. The Germanic *sarwa-* is of unknown or uncertain ultimate etymology, but evidently meant *skill* (the skill of a smith or artificer), any device which required skill to plan and make. It was specially applied to 'arms' upon which much cunning and skill was expended – no doubt particularly to the ring-mail, costly and difficult to make. But it could still be used of contrivance, skill, cunning, as in *1038, 846; *2764, 2324; also of evil devices, plots, machinations, or actual snares, though this is not exemplified in *Beowulf*, except in *searoníð* 'cunning malice'. Cf. the derived verb *syrwan, besyrwan* to plot against, trick, ensnare.

Here the choice is, I think, between emendation to *on searwum* 'in my war-gear', or [retaining *of*] escaped from the 'snares' (evil devices) of my enemies. The latter is much more likely (especially in dealing with *eotenas* of whom

Grendel was one; cf. 581–2 'he purposed of the race of men someone to snare', *sumne besyrwan* *713.) In any case *on searwum* is a frequent phrase, and would not be likely to be altered to *of.*

Old English *fáh* is not properly (though usually) translated 'hostile' here: *fáh* does not mean 'hostile' but 'hated' – it properly describes the *state* of the *offender* with respect to the *injured.* So the implication here is that Beowulf had given his foe 'something to remember' – he had ravaged the *eotena cyn.* Translate: 'when I returned from the snares (?*or* clutches) of (my) enemies, earning their hatred.' See the Notes on the Text, p. 112, 338–9.

338–43; *419–24

It is sometimes said that there is a discrepancy between this passage and other accounts of Beowulf's youthful exploits, the Breca episode, 447 ff., *549 ff., especially 466–7 'it was my lot with sword to slay nine sea-demons', *574–5 *mé gesǽlde þæt ic mid sweorde ofslóh niceras nigene.* But even if the reference in both places were to the same exploit there would not be any actual discrepancy. For one thing, as this, the earlier passage, goes in our text, it refers already to more than one exploit. Beowulf claims to have accomplished many: 'on many a renownéd deed I ventured in my youth' 330–1, *hæbbe ic mǽrða fela ongunnen on geogoðe* *408–9, and he is only giving a selection. It would not be good policy to refer to the same events again when challenged, the same evening, by Unferth.

Nor would it be according to the author's practice. When his narrative involves repetition he gives different details on each occasion. We do not hear about Beowulf being placed in an honourable seat in the hall, beside Hrothgar's son, nor about his daughter Fréawaru, until Beowulf reports to Hygelac (1689 ff., *2009 ff.). But there is no discrepancy. We learn more, in due course.

It may be useful then to look at the earlier account more carefully. If so, we shall see that *Géatmæcgum* (*491, 'the young Geatish knights' 398) does not include Beowulf himself [see the Notes on the Text, p. 114, 398]. *mæcg* though often used loosely, as most 'man'-words, was properly a boy, a young man, and is often so used, and never of a leader. So here it does not include the man who is called *se yldesta* (*258, 'the chief' 209), and *aldor* of the company (*369, 'the captain' 298); and in *829 (674) *Géatmecga (léod)* is not a tribal name (as in *Weder-Géata léod* etc.) but refers to the specific band led by Beowulf. And the placing of Beowulf in a special seat near to the king is not only a natural courtesy to the sister-son of a neighbouring king, but it explains Beowulf's proximity to Unferth, 'who sat at the feet of the lord of the Scyldings'. Unferth does not shout out his challenge down the hall, but speaks his words as to a neighbour, with no doubt the king's ear specially in mind [see p. 211].

If we compare Beowulf's two speeches we shall observe that the first [that addressed to Hrothgar] refers to an exploit against *eotenas* (which are not water-beasts) and another against *niceras*.

[I give here the Old English text of the former together with my father's translation:

> selfe ofesáwon, ðá ic of searwum cwóm
> 420 fáh from féondum, þǽr ic fífe geband,
> ýðde eotena cyn, ond on ýðum slóg
> niceras nihtes, nearoþearfe dréah,
> wræc Wedera níð – wéan áhsodon –,
> forgrand gramum;

337 they had themselves observed it, when I returned from the toils of my foes, earning their enmity, where five I bound, making desolate the race of monsters, and when I slew amid the waves by night the water-demons, enduring bitter need, avenging the afflictions of the windloving Geats, destroying those hostile things – woe they had asked for.]

It was no doubt Beowulf's reference to *niceras* (water-beasts) that evoked Unferth's special reference to the match with Breca. But the events are not the same: the earlier is an attack in revenge against monsters who have injured the Geats – and 'asked for trouble' (*wéan ahsodon*); the second is primarily a swimming and endurance match, to which the water-beasts are incidental.

The writing of the verbs *geband*, *ýðde* without conjunction marks the second as relating to the same action as the former: 'on the occasion when I bound five, ravaging the ogre-kind'; but the interposition in line *421 of *ond* (of which as a conjunction joining sentences the author is sparing) clearly marks what follows as a separate or additional matter: best appreciated now by stressing 'and': 'and I slew nicors in the waves by night.'[1]

I think it highly likely that *fífe* 'five' in line *420 is an error for *fífel* neuter plural 'monsters'. This word was practically forgotten, and is only preserved in one of the fragments of the Old English poem *Waldere,* but occurs in *Beowulf* *104 in the compound *fífelcynnes eard* (86 'the troll-kind's home') of Grendel's home, which shows connexion of *fífel* with *eoten*. This word seems to have represented the *eoten*-kind in their huge, clumsy, lumpish and stupid side: so Old Norse *fífl* 'clown, boor, fool'. But in any case *geband* is not *ofslóh,* so that even retaining the numeral *fífe* there is evidently no direct connexion with *574-5, *ic mid sweorde ofslóh niceras nigene* (466-7).

These references are allusive and obscure, and even to people who knew the words (*fífel, eoten, nicor*) familiarly, as we must suppose the audience which the author had in mind did, they can only have been of interest *as allusions to known tales.* Two deductions are legitimate:

(1) that entertainment in the hall (by *scop,* or *þyle,* or unofficial performer) was not limited to genealogies and legends of great kings, lords, and heroes, but included 'fairy-tales', and stories of marvels, and magic. Nor was such matter beneath

---

1 [In the light of these considerations my father changed the translation from its original form in the typescript C 'when five I bound, *and made desolate* the race of monsters, and when I slew amid the waves' to 'where five I bound *making desolate*', and he also underlined the 'and' in 'and when I slew'.]

the attention of the highest, of kings.[1] (2) that *definite* stories associated actually with a character called Beowulf were already known when our author wrote; so that allusions to them were sufficient.

I would myself make a further deduction, though that is far less certain; that such folk-tales were more or less nameless, but some had been *attached* to the name Beowulf already – that is, Beowulf was originally independent of them, and it is not therefore necessary (or probable) that the name is derived from the deeds or character of the folk-tale hero.

348–50   (Beowulf's request to Hrothgar) *that only I may, and my proud company of men, this dauntless company, make Heorot clean;* *431–2 *þæt ic móte ána [added: ond] mínra eorla gedryht, [MS ond] þes hearda héap, Heorot fælsian.*

It is possible to view *[ond] mínra . . . . . héap* as an addition to show Beowulf's courtesy to his companions, and to fit the courtly presentation of the story, in which in a more primitive form Beowulf would have met Grendel alone. The words certainly fit the story as told, for all the Geats sleep

---

1   Consider the remarkable passage 1767–74, *2105–13, when Beowulf reports that Hrothgar himself, at the feast celebrating the death of Grendel, performed and apparently gave specimens of most 'genres' of entertainment: (i) harp-playing, (ii) recitation of lays, historical and tragic, (iii) telling wonder-stories [*syllíc spell* *2109] correctly (that is, according to received form), (iv) making an elegiac lament on the passing of youth to old age.

in the hall, but only Beowulf wrestles with Grendel. But I do not think that the author meant or implied more than just what he said. For one thing, it is possible, indeed likely, that in the form of the *sellíc spell* nearest behind this version Beowulf had companions and/or competitors in the hall when Grendel came.[1] For another, more careful consideration of the text will lead, I think, to re-interpretation of *ána*.

If this were an auctorial addition to accommodate the story of a lone 'bear-man' champion to Beowulf a prince with a retinue, it would be extraordinarily poor stitching. There is in the manuscript no connecting link before *mínra*; but one is essential: *gedryht* and *héap* are nominatives, but different from *ic*. They are, however, themselves parallel and equivalents, and should not and certainly would not have had a connecting *ond* as in the manuscript. This has been misplaced and should be before *mínra*. If one insists on *ána* in the full sense, 'I myself *solo*', this remains, as I say, poor stitching, indeed almost absurd: 'I beg that I all alone, and my troop of men etc., be permitted to rid Heorot.' The perfunctory reference to his men becomes too obviously an afterthought to be either modest or indeed polite.

The solution lies, I think, in consideration of *ána*. This is not, as seems still universally stated, a weak adjective agreeing

---

1 See my 'reconstruction' or specimen *Sellíc Spell* which I hope to read later. I think that Beowulf had one (or two) companions, also eager to try the feat. Beowulf took the last turn. And [that] will explain his passivity while Grendel kills and devours 'Handshoe' (1745–9, *2076–80), evidently the *slǽpendne rinc* of *741 ('a sleeping man', 604).

with (and thus solely applicable to) a singular noun. It is an adverb, which usually qualifies a singular noun, but does not necessarily do so. It can be found qualifying a group, separated from others. So the nearest translation of *431 is 'that I only and my company be permitted' (and no others) – i.e. the hall is to be cleared of all Danes.[1] The verb *móte* naturally agrees with the adjacent *ic*, and this is placed first, because Beowulf is the *leader*, and as is plain from the beginning any hope of success depends on his personal strength. It is obvious that he, if anyone, will be actual victor over Grendel. So Hrothgar hands the hall over to *him*, 532–5, *655–8. But the *gedryht* was not supposed to be functionless, a mere escort of honour, and possible witnesses of the contest. Nobody (not even Beowulf) *knew* the outcome, within the tale; nor should we, if we could come to it without knowing the tale, and with a fresh appetite undulled by literary experience. The author has done what he could to make the issue doubtful: see especially 353–67, *438–55. What if Beowulf got into grave difficulties, or was overcome and slain? His companions would be in a like case to, say, Byrhtnoth's *heorðwerod* [the men of his household]: they would have to fight on without hope, to avenge their leader, and redeem their honour (and Hygelac's). They are plainly informed of that (though of course they knew it before they set sail) by Beowulf himself

---

1 Part of the point, I think, of the *ic ána* passage, in which Beowulf asks Hrothgar to leave only Geats in the hall, is that some at least of the bravest of the Danish warriors would have wished to remain also, for saving of Danish honour, after such a challenge by aliens.

in 356–9, *442–5. Grendel will devour them all – if he can. And they very much feared that he could, and would. See 564–9, *691–6.

They started out, of course, with great confidence in Beowulf, though the rumours of Grendel had been terrible (119 ff., *149 ff.). I do not think it at all fanciful to suppose that 'they had learned that a bloody death had ere now . . . swept away all too many of the Danish folk' (567–9; *híe hæfdon gefrúnen* etc. *694 ff.) refers to what they had learned since arrival. Not only Unferth would be nettled by Beowulf's proud (and contemptuous) words, especially 483–8, *595–601. And even if Beowulf had been milder, it would still be natural for the men in the hall to give the strangers the most horrible picture of Grendel and his ferocious deeds, for the saving of their faces. The young men went to bed with the gloomiest forebodings – not relieved by their leader's sudden boast, to meet Grendel unarmed!

351 ff.; *435 ff.   [Beowulf will not bear arms against Grendel]

Sometimes noted as 'ingenious rationalization', i.e. of the feature of primitive story that this wild-man or bear-boy only fought like an animal. But it is far from certain that such a feature does lie behind *Beowulf*, and in any case it must lie a long way back before our author, and before the attachment of 'folk-tale' to an actual character (with a kin).

Beowulf is not in fact represented as incapable of weapons. He goes fully armed. In youth he and Breca set out with naked swords (439, *539), and Beowulf kills a water-monster with a weapon (452–3, *556–7). Eventually he kills nine *niceras* with his sword (466–7, *574–5). Later he possesses a famous sword with a name, Nægling (2252, *2680). He was, however, terribly strong, and could (like indeed any heroic warrior!) fall into a mad rage. In the battle in which Hygelac fell Beowulf slew Dæghrefn the Frankish champion (slayer of his lord Hygelac?) with his hands,[1] probably throttled him or broke his neck. For Beowulf does not hug or crush. His strength is specially in his hands and finger-grip. [*Added later*: But the words used of the slaying of Dæghrefn (2107–9, *2507–8) could apply to a deadly embrace in which Dæghrefn's body was crushed, though they need not do so.] In his rage he is likely to break his sword by the sheer violence and strength of the blow: 'too strong that hand, that as I have heard with its swing overtaxed each sword' (2254–6, *2684–6).

Actually, if one approached the poem without bias from previous folk-tale records, *Beowulf* would seem to derive from the imagination of a coast and island people, familiar with the sea, rather than forest and mountain; and he would seem more akin to – that is to say, to derive his legendary qualities from – sea-beasts. His greatest prowess

---

1 [After these words my father cited the Old English text, line *2502, [ic . . . Dæghrefne wearð] tó handbonan, in his translation 2103 'my hands were Dæghrefn's death'. But subsequently he struck out the words tó handbonan and wrote in the margin: 'handbona means "actual slayer" and can be used of killing with weapons. So in *2506 it is necessary to say (after using handbona) ne wæs ecg bona "no sword-edge was his slayer",' 2107.]

is in swimming, and *niceras* are his special foes: not very bear-like.[1]

We may assume that the wizard/troll-like aspect of Grendel, which enabled him to render *human* weapons useless against himself, was supposed to be unknown to Beowulf. The idea is used later to explain why his men could not help him (647–55, *794–805). But a 'magic' or giant-made sword was found effective in Grendel's cave.

358–9 *the Gothic knights, the strong band of Hrethmen*; *443–5 *Geotena léode . . .. mægen Hréðmanna*

These lines are very interesting – not for the poetry and narrative; but because accidentally, by the loss of so much Old English literature, every reference to old names of the heroic past is of special antiquarian interest. But enquiry is often made more difficult because by the time our late copy of *Beowulf* was made the ancient traditions were already

---

1 The white bear (*ursus maritimus*) might seem a connecting link; but the 'polar bear' seems not to have been known, even in Scandinavia, until the settlements in Iceland (end of the ninth century) and Greenland (end of the tenth century). It was then called *hvítabjörn*. Traditionally, the first *hvítabjörn* was brought to Norway by Ingimund the Old c. A.D. 900. In any case one is reminded rather of tales from the northern isles about demonic sea-creatures, sometimes of seal-form, that may molest the dwellings of men near the sea, begetting offspring on women, or carrying them off. Some such ravages may well be referred to in the *Wedera nið* [*423, 'the afflictions of the windloving Geats' 341–2] that Beowulf avenged [see note to p. 230, 338–43]. [Against the latter part of this note my father wrote that references were required but that he could not at that time recover them.]

becoming dim, and since they were obscure to copyists refer-
ences to them were liable to corruption. Copyists of all times,
in any case (and the two that made the *Beowulf* manuscript
were no exceptions) are apt to bungle proper names.

So here, as far as can be discovered, *Geotena* is not the
correct form of any Germanic or tribal name; and the ques-
tion is, which known name will explain the scribal *Geotena*
most credibly. A great deal of ink has been spilled on that
question. But to my mind most of it had been better left in
the bottle, and can now be washed out, since it has been used
largely in aid of what can only be described as the 'Jutish
lunacy' – 'the Géatas are the Jutes'. Once you admit that
queen-bee into your bonnet it will lay a hive of maggots
there. I will not enter here into a discussion with those to
whom this sad thing has happened. Even so, a great deal may
be said. I will attempt to give a summary of the chief points.

The manuscript has *mægen hreð manna*. Old English
scribes usually do not join compounds, so we are free to join
them up or not, as seems fit. I approve the joining *mægen
Hréðmanna* as a national name.

(1) *hréþ* is an Old English verse word (occurring by
itself twice elsewhere). Variant forms *hróþ* and *hróþor* are
also found. Also a verb *hréðan* 'exult, triumph'. The basic
sense was one of 'sound': 'exultation, (shouting) in triumph'.
The noun could form the first part of personal names: thus
Hróþgar, Hréþric, Hróþulf. Norse sources show that these
figures of Danish tradition really contained this element
hróþ, but it was not applied to *Scyldingas* or Danes in general.

(2) An element *hréþ-* (never *hróþ-*) is, however, specially associated with 'Goths', O.E. *Gotan*. Thus *Hréðgotan* in the Old English poem *Widsith* and in Cynewulf's poem *Elene* [footnote on p. 175]. In this sense ('Goths') *hréþ* can stand alone: so *Hréþa here* [army] = Goths in *Elene*.

(3) But this use of *hréþ-* is found to be a later alteration (in English) of a different element: O.E. *hrǽd* (Germanic *hraidi*): (a) because *hrǽd* occurs in *Widsith*: *Hrǽda here* = *Hréþa here*; (b) because this O.E. *hrǽd-* corresponds to Old Norse *hreið-*, as in *Hreiðgotar*. In Norse this was later altered to *Reiðgotar* owing to the special association of the Goths with riding, and cavalry.

(4) Now we find the same element, and the same variation, among the Géatas. The oldest member of the Geatish royal line mentioned in *Beowulf* is *Hréþel*, but his name is also found in the forms *Hrǽdles*, *Hrǽdlan*.

This is significant, because many other points connect the Goths (*Gotan*) and the Géatas (Old Norse *Gautar*). (a) The *Géatas/Gautar* occupied an area in the south of what is now called Sweden. The Goths came from Sweden, and their name survives in Gotland, the large island off its east coast. (b) The two names are beyond doubt connected in origin: *got/géat* are in ablaut-relationship,[1] just as e.g. *goten*, past participle 'poured', is with *géat*, past tense singular of the same verb. (c) The name *Gautr* is in Old Norse a frequent name for the god Óðinn (Woden), whose cult was especially connected with

---

[1] [*ablaut*: a term used of the alternation in the vowels of related word forms, as e.g. *drink*, *drank*, *drunk*.]

Goths. (d) *Gaut* appears in Gothic traditions at the head of the Gothic royal line of the Amalungs, to which Theodoric belonged. (e) I would add finally that Óðinn/Wóden was evidently originally a wind- or storm-god. We note that the *Géatas* are called *Weder-Géatas* or simply *Wederas*: Wind-Géatas, or Wind-folk; while the only plausible (and indeed clearly correct) etymology of the *hrǽd/hreið* element is to connect it with Old English and Old Norse *hríð* 'storm'. (This is probably seen also in the Old English name for the month of March: *hrǽdmonað*, *hredmonað*, and also twice *hreðmonað*.)

It thus becomes very curious that we have here in one passage the name *Hréðmanna* and the form *Geotena* – not *Géata*. Quite briefly, it seems to me that much the most likely explanation of this is that in the text originally there stood *Gotena*. Probably, because the author derived the names from traditions recognizing the original identity of Goths and Géatas. Possibly, because the word *hréð-manna* (or *hrǽd-*) suggested 'Goths' to some intervening scribe or editor, while such old heroic words were still better remembered than in c. A.D. 1000. Our actual *Geotena* is thus a blend between *Géata* the word expected and *Gotena* the word in the copy. Just below we have a similar error in line *461 (373), manuscript *Gara*, where *Géata* was expected but the text had *Wedera*.[1]

---

1 [The original text of my father's translation (356–9) of *443–5 was 'Methinks he will . . . devour without fear the Geatish folk, as oft he hath the proud hosts of your men.' This depends on the interpretation of the text as *mægenhréð manna*. In a note to the present commentary on this matter he remarked that *mægenhréð* 'might-triumph of men' occurs nowhere else; and 'even if this

359–64; *445–51

This insistence on the expense of keeping Beowulf, or of providing him with a fitting funeral is curious. Warriors and champions were, of course, expensive. They ate and drank much. In times of peace it was their chief occupation, in the intervals of other sports, horse-races, horse-fights, betting, rivalries and quarrels: if he kept a poor table, a king would soon earn a bad nickname (such as *matar-illr* 'food-shabby' in Old Norse). They had to be richly rewarded for deeds of valour: not to be free-handed in such cases was the worst fault in a king after the murder of kin or comrades.

If engaged from among men of other tribes or lands they had to be paid for heavily (cf. 2099, *2496).[1] All the same, when Beowulf offers (at a feast in which he is being honourably entertained and welcomed) the consolation to the king that feeding him will no longer be a matter of anxiety (*sorgian* *451 – a strong word, always referring to 'cares' which cause painful thought), this has a very odd ring. It sounds like an echo of the underlying folk-tale. At least (derived from this) it must already have been part of the character of Beowulf,

---

is supposed to mean "triumphal force [i.e. troop] of men" it is a singularly unhappy way of referring to men who have actually been killed and eaten.' The later text was pencilled in on the typescript C. (See the Notes on the Text, p. 113, 356–9.)

[1] Like football 'stars' acquired to strengthen a team, but with this distinction: the champion got the money or other payment, not the chieftain or people whom he had left. Unless of course, like Ecgtheow, he had got into trouble (a feud), in which case his adherence could be obtained by settling his debts (see 379–80, *470).

as already known to the author's audience, that he was a prodigious eater: even perhaps as much more voracious than the norm as was his thirty-fold strength greater. Humour is not obvious in *Beowulf* – it would indeed be out of place if obtrusive – but a careful reading will often detect irony in what is said, either within the tale itself or appreciable by its hearers. A fleeting smile might well here pass over the face of a listener (well versed in old tales), and a fleeting thought come: 'the king did not realize what Beowulf's upkeep would have cost!'[1]

359–60   *in burial to shroud my head;* *446 *hafalan hýdan*

This here means 'give me funeral rites', but the whole ceremony is indicated only by one item (a preliminary rite or custom); covering the head of the slain. This was not expensive. But the full rite of honour envisaged was burning on a pyre, with costly accompaniments. (Beowulf expressly reserves his corslet, which is not to go to the pyre, but to be returned to Hygelac.) Cf. the reference to Æschere, killed by Grendel's mother, 1782 ff., *2124 ff., where it is said that the Danes could not lay him upon a pyre because he had been eaten[2] – all save his head, 1185, *1420–1. There is possibly an

---

1   Actually, as the time-scheme is presented, Beowulf was only 'fed' by Hrothgar for three days: the day of his arrival, followed by the match with Grendel; the day of the feast of victory, followed by the coming of Grendel's dam; the day of the assault on Grendel's lair, followed by the final feast. Beowulf left early next day.

2   [This is not actually stated: it is said only that 'She had borne away that corse in her fiend's clutches beneath the mountain stream'.]

irony therefore in *hafalan hýdan*. Beowulf did not realize that his head might be the only thing left of him.

367   *Fate goeth ever as she must!*; *455 *Gǽð á wyrd swá hío scel!*

It is a difficult matter to determine in any given passage containing *wyrd*: (1) how far it was more than grammatically 'personalized'; (2) what precisely it 'means', that is, how far it had, or retained, for speakers or hearers any conscious ingredient of what we may call mytho-philosophical reflection in evidently well-known formulæ. But such questions would require too long an answer for this place. The matter of *wyrd* only concerns the criticism of *Beowulf* in particular in so far as it is concerned with the 'theology' of the author, and that requires a special disquisition or lecture, examining the references to Scripture, to heathendom, to God, or to 'Fate' in the poem. Anyone who is sufficiently interested in the poem, or in the mind and imagination of the period, can of course do that for himself. I would issue two warnings, obvious but often neglected.

(a) There is a dramatic element in the poem. It is most strongly seen in the conception of the characters of Beowulf and Hrothgar and their presentation. It is important to note whether 'theological' expressions occur in a speech by Beowulf, by Hrothgar, by some other 'character', or are used by the poet himself addressing his audience directly.

(b) Expressions involving *Fate*, *Fortune*, etc. are at all times liable to become formulæ, the content of which has evaporated. They become items of colloquial diction. Off-hand you cannot, if a man says 'fortune favours the brave', from that deduce his temper of mind, his beliefs or philosophy, if he has any, nor whether he would write *fortune* with a capital F, and has, even as a fancy, any imagination of a 'person', existing independently of himself and his inherited phrases, turning a wheel up or down in fits of caprice.

Most of the expressions concerning *wyrd* are tautologous, manifestly, or verbally concealed. Not because people were too stupid to perceive this, but because drawing attention to the inevitable tautology expresses a resigned or 'fatalistic' mood. This expression *gǽð á wyrd swá hío scel* is hardly more than a grammatical variation on *che sará sará* 'what will be, will be'. Note that *wyrd* is a *feminine* noun, and it is more than probable that, if we translate the inevitable *hío* of Old English by the word *she*, we shall be greatly exaggerating the conscious degree of personification in the formula. *wyrd* is grammatically simply the verbal noun to *weorðan*, 'turn out, become, happen'. The verb is here omitted, or *gán* 'proceed' is substituted; but in *2525–6 *unc sceal weorðan . . . swá unc wyrd getéoð* the tautology is verbally manifest: 'to us it will happen . . . as happening appoints' [translation of the poem, 2122–4, 'to us . . . shall it be done . . . even as Fate . . . decrees to us'].

In many phrases *wyrd*, grammatically personalized, thus practically functions as a substitute for the passive, with 'unnamed' agent: *572 *wyrd oft nereð . . . eorl þonne his ellen deah*, 'a man will often be preserved if his courage does not fail' [translation of the poem, 465–6, 'fate oft saveth a man not doomed to die, when his valour fails not']; *1205 *hine* *wyrd fornam*, 'he was destroyed' [996 'fate took him']; *2574 *swá him wyrd ne gescráf*, 'as was not appointed for him' [2163 'for him fate decreed it not'].

But here I am deliberately minimizing. It is far from the whole story: *wyrd* means 'a happening', event, and it can still be used as just that: *3029–30 *hé ne léag fela wyrda né worda* 'he did not conceal anything of what had occurred or been said' [translation 2546 '. . . of what had chanced or had been said']. But it has other meanings, such as Death (so *2420 *wyrd ungemete néah*, 2037 'the fate very nigh indeed'); and can be spoken of as a 'power' or an ordinance in itself, or as subordinate to, or even equated with Metod or other words commonly used as synonyms of God, even with God. (The clearest case of 'subordination' is *1056, *nefne him wítig God wyrd forstóde*, 861–2 'had not the foreseeing God . . . fended fate from them' – if *wyrd* does not simply mean 'death'). See further the note to 465–6.

369   *for my deserts*; *457 *For gewyrhtum*

[In place of the meaningless reading of the manuscript *fere fyhtum* my father accepted the emendation *for gewyrhtum* 'because of my meritorious deeds'.]

It may be observed that Beowulf himself had made no mention of this motive of gratitude (335 ff., *415 ff.). He had said that the counsellors of his realm had urged him to go because he was a strong man, successful in fights with monsters. Hrothgar's reply is intentionally made a little cool, and tinged with irony, in contrast to his hopeful welcoming

to Beowulf's arrival in his reply to Wulfgar (306–8; *381–4).
Though it is in accordance with the poet's economy only to
introduce information about Ecgtheow gradually, the abrupt
way in which the indebtedness of Beowulf's father to himself
is at once introduced in Hrothgar's answer makes it an obvi-
ous reproof, even if smilingly spoken.

Hrothgar's thought may be represented thus: 'He should
have mentioned his father and all that I did for him. He
looks as strong as reports have made him, and he is very
self-confident. Like these young men, I doubt if he realizes
the terror of Grendel; and certainly he has no pity for my
shame.' He replies, in modern terms: 'My *dear* Beowulf!
How good of you to come to this country, where we once
had the honour of receiving your father and helping him in
his troubles. *Some may* remember his killing of Heatholaf.
Your people were glad to get rid of him after that, and he
took refuge here. But that, of course, was long ago, when I
had only recently succeeded my dear brother. I settled the
matter at some cost of treasure, and your father swore alle-
giance to me. As for Grendel, it is *painful* to be reminded of
the shame he has put me to. But rumours can hardly have
equalled the truth: he has killed hosts of men, many of them
knights of great fame and courage. Over and over again all
that has been left of them in the morning has been pools of
blood in the hall. Well, well: take a seat now, and something
to eat and drink. (It is not night yet.) In due time you can
turn your mind to adding to your triumphs – if you are
keen to try it.'

377 Heorogar; *467 Heregar

The correct form of the name appears to have been *Heorogar* [*heoru* 'sword'], as in 47 (*61) and 1813 (*2158, *Hiorogar*). Variation in the form of personal names, even well-known ones, by which the first element preserves the alliteration but is changed into some other more or less similar element, is frequent. It is nonetheless a form of error, of scribal origin: the actual names of individuals no doubt had one correct form only, for formal use. Confusion of *heoro-* and *here-* was specially easy, since they looked much alike, while both belonged to a similar sphere of meaning. *here* 'army' remained in use, but *heoru* as a separate word was virtually obsolete even in verse; it occurs once in *Beowulf*, *1285 (1070). It was still very frequent in verse-compounds, but most of them show that the actual meaning of *heoru* was forgotten, and *heoro-* imparts only a vague sense of 'grim, cruel, blood', or seems actually to be taken to mean *here-* (war-host).

386–7 God may easily . . .; *478 God éaþe mæg . . .

The exact sense and implication of this is not certain. The strictly literal equivalent is 'God can (has the power) easily to do this.' It may seem unreasonable to object that to the Almighty degrees of ease or difficulty are inapplicable; nonetheless I doubt if *éaþe* here has the (in the situation rather absurd) sense 'easily, without difficulty': *éaþe* very frequently and *mæg* in many cases are used of possibility and probability (in circumstances) rather than of facility and personal ability.

In that case *éaþe* will be nearer to 'well' as in 'he may well come', 'it may well be that', and *mæg* to 'may', so that a nearer rendering would be 'God may well do this' – the unknown element being not God's *power* but His *will*. In any case in emotion and purpose this is *a cry for pity*, though it is not put into the form of a prayer. It is, if you like, a pious *statement*, which God may hear, and (maybe) will be moved by.

395–7; *489–90   [The concluding words of Hrothgar's first speech to Beowulf]

[I give first the Old English lines, *489–90, as they appear in the manuscript. My father discussed at length the problem of the passage and his solution of it in his lectures on the textual '*cruces*' in *Beowulf*, and more briefly in his general commentary. In this case I include here from the former his discussion of what the king is *likely* to have said to Beowulf (with this compare the note to 369), before turning to his interpretation of the Old English words (this latter being given in abbreviated form).

> Site nú tó symle   ond on sǽl meoto
> sigehréð secgum   swá þín sefa hwette.]

It would now be proper to make some preliminary conjectures concerning what Hrothgar is likely to have said at this point. His speech in general is an antistrophe to Beowulf's opening address. What Beowulf said in précis was this: 'I have come a long way to pit myself against Grendel. I have already had experience in monster-fighting. I hope to be successful, but (modestly) of course one never knows.' The last part is expressed with elaborate courtesy: 'God will decide. Grendel will of course eat us Geats, if he can. In that case

248

you will be troubled with me no longer, and will not have to feed me. Send my corslet back to Hygelac, it belonged to his father. Things will go as fate orders.'

Under the cover of the elaborate speech and courtesy there is heard the proud confidence of a strong young champion; and also further back and fainter the voice of the fairy-story: the 'unlikely lad', the lumpish and greedy bearboy, who is a trouble to keep and feed, but who is now offering to earn his keep (or put an end to it) by trying his hand against the monster that has so far defeated all comers.

What does Hrothgar answer? First he politely points out that he has a right to accept Beowulf's offer: he had befriended his father.[1] This is not derived from the fairy-story, but is part of the cement which has been devised for fixing the fairy-story element firmly in its place in the background of 'historial' legend. A passage follows which is more closely derived from fairy-story: the would-be champion is warned of the terrible power of the monster, 381–95, *473–88. Into this is inserted *God éaþe mæg* . . . [see note to 386–7], which seems to have been added to define Hrothgar's attitude to *wyrd* (*wyrd* says the king, 'but only because God has allowed Grendel to do this'), and as an answer to Beowulf's words 355–6 and 367 (*440–1, *455). Then Hrothgar winds up with the obscure words that we have to interpret. Keeping, as far as possible, in mind the old fairy-story element, and the courtly

---

1   [Added later:] There is a tinge of irony here: 'You have come *feorran*? [*430; 'from so far away' 348] 'Not too far for your father when he needed help. Not too far, then, to come and pay the debt.'

background, and the situation in this story as this poet has chosen to tell it – what is Hrothgar most likely to have said?

Undoubtedly the most likely thing is this: 'Many have feasted here and vowed to meet Grendel. Each time blood in the hall was all that remained of them next morning. But do you sit down *now* and feast. Later you can turn your mind to your boast / or to battle, if you have the heart for it.' It is to be noted that it was only later when Beowulf reaffirmed his vow that Hrothgar rejoiced, and decided that the young man really meant it (495–6, *609–10). [See note to 290–1, p. 208.]

Hrothgar might, of course, have said other things. For instance: 'Listen to and ponder the glorious songs of my minstrels (they will uplift your heart).' A minstrel does in fact begin to sing (403, *496). Or he may have said: 'Speak freely to men in the hall, telling tales of victory, not excluding your own feats, such as you have alluded to.' This might be felt to give special point to Unferth's outburst. As soon as he could get a hearing, after the *scop* had finished, the *þyle* put in his word: it was his place to know all about people. But he was angry. Hrothgar (on this view) had invited the stranger to tell men all about his adventures.

Among these alternatives – which are the most likely, and indeed the only senses (I think) which, even with torture, the manuscript words can be forced to yield – the first remains overwhelmingly more probable. The minstrel does sing with a clear voice, but only as the normal accompaniment of a feast: his song is not reported or made significant. The malice of Unferth needed no presidential courtesy to whet it. Indeed his outburst really comes in better as a more violent and discourteous form of Hrothgar's warning (according to the first alternative above). 'Yes,' he says in effect, 'you heard what the king said: blood on the benches in the morning. You are a fine fellow, no doubt, but not as fine as you think you are. You have not always come off best. And you will not come off best with Grendel – if you do later find you have the heart to sit up for him.'

There are more extant solutions and proposals concerning this troublesome passage than there are words in it, – to mention only the better.

The central difficulty is *meoto*. There is only one certainty: *Site nú tó symle ond . . .* shows that another imperative singular must follow. This can only be extracted from *on sǽl* or *meoto*. Examination of the possibilities shows that *onsǽl* cannot be an imperative singular, nor *meoto* a noun (which it would have to be if *onsǽl* were a verb). If then *meoto* is an imperative singular it must stand for or be a slight error for *meota* in dialectal form (left unchanged as usual when the scribe like the editors could not identify the word): i.e. the imperative singular of **meotian* = West Saxon **metian*. Now such a word would have an excellent etymology: it would correspond exactly to Gothic *mitón* 'deliberate, ponder, consider'. What is more, it actually occurs in the Old English poem *Genesis*, line 1917, imperative singular *geþanc meta þíne móde*, of which the sense is 'ponder the thought in your mind'; *on sǽl* then means 'in due time'.

A subsidiary difficulty is *sige hréð secgum*. In this the

object of *metal/meota* must be found. *sigehréð secgum* 'victory for men' is possible. But to my mind it seems plain that *sige Hréðsecgum* 'victory for the Hrethmen' [see the note to 358–9] is meant. (For the addition of a word meaning 'man' to a tribal name note that this occurs immediately afterwards in *Géatmæcgum* *491, 398.)

Beowulf is to turn his thoughts to winning a victory for the Geats, where so many others have failed. In this case Hrothgar is actually recalling Beowulf's expression *mægen Hréðmanna* (*445, 359): 'I expect that he will if he can manage it, as he has done to men before, eat the troop of the Hrethmen' says Beowulf, modestly. 'When the time comes contrive victory for the Hrethmen, if your heart has the courage' rejoins Hrothgar. The phrase is similar.

Finally, *hwette* is here present subjunctive (of the yet unrealized future), 'according as (= if) your heart may egg you'. *hwettan* is a strong word, (to whet, incite egg on), and quite unsuitable to most other interpretations of the passage.[1]

406 *Unferth, son of Ecglaf;* *499 *Unferð, Ecgláfes bearn*

Quite contrary to his usual manner the author suddenly produces Unferth 'out of his hat', without warning and with his full style: name and patronymic. This exceptional procedure must be significant. Certainly it shows that Unferth

---

1 [For the successive alterations made to the translation in this passage see the Notes on the Text, p. 114, 395–7.]

son of Ecglaf was already a well-known figure in the court of
Heorot before ever our author wrote his *Beowulf*. No visit
to Heorot would be complete without a glimpse of him – it
would be like going to Camelot and never hearing of Sir Kay.
The audience was waiting for his appearance, and now would
be eagerly attentive. He had a traditional temper of mind
and behaviour already attached to him (as rough discourtesy
was attached to Kay): envious, intelligent, but malicious and
'worm-tongued'. What would he say?

Less certainly, but probably, this was how he usually
made his appearance: a watchful man, sitting 'at the feet of
the king', unobtrusively, hardly noticed at first by strang-
ers, listening to all that was said, and careful to wait before
speaking, until his entry would be most effective. The patro-
nymic was important, because it was connected with sinister
traditions about his dealings with his kin – that belonged
to him personally, quite apart from his connexion with the
Grendel-story.

Whether he has an historical 'kernel' (likely enough) or
not, Unferth belongs primarily to the politico-dynastic side
of the English traditions concerning the Scyldings and the
court of Heorot. But when tales of the Grendel-kind became
attached in legend to Heorot, it was probably inevitable,
from his position there, that he should become involved in
them also. It seems unlikely that our poet was the first hand-
ler of the Heorot-story to make this link. In that case some
contact or clash between Beowulf, the bane of Grendel, and
Unferth must already have become part of the tradition. But
it is probable that the clash and 'flyting' was made much

more important than it had been, by our author. He evidently took much trouble with it; he made it into one of his major set-pieces, and did not disappoint the interest he had aroused with his lines 406–7 (*499–501).

The originality of the author of our *Beowulf* was probably not shown at any point by sheer invention (even of minor characters or events), but by (1) making the *centre* the Grendel theme, previously only one of the accretions to the Heorot-story, and to it incidental: its two main pivots had been the Heathobard feud; and the ambition of Hrothulf and the ruinous kin-strife after Hrothgar's death. (2) enriching the whole poem with references to other cycles of story. Not only to the Geatish-Swedish feud, which the placing of Beowulf as his central character naturally involved; but to important items in English (Offa) and Jutish and Frisian story (Hengest); as well as occasional references to Swedish, Danish and Gothic tradition, or other minor peoples (Wendlas, Wylfingas, Helmingas, etc.). So that (as we still feel, though our sight is now blurred and the landscape darkened) his poem is like a play in a room through the windows of which a distant view can be seen over a large part of the English traditions about the world of their original home.

Ecglaf may sound like an invented counterpart to Ecgtheow. But the resemblance is probably purely accidental – supporting rather than casting doubt on the view that the 'historical' placing of the two characters (Unferth and Beowulf) were processes independent of their passing contact. An invented similarity would have been made more of.

452 ff.; *555 ff.   [Beowulf's fight with a sea-beast]

A good example of the difficulty of understanding *Beowulf* (and of translating it). The obstacles are often, as here, of two kinds. The author is referring to things or actions very well known to himself and his audience, and therefore has no need to be precise; but we may be quite unfamiliar with them. He can therefore afford to be literary or 'poetical' in what he says: that is, not put things in an obvious way; but his and his contemporaries' notions of literary style may be quite alien to our taste or habit. We may thus get (or feel we are getting) a crabbed line or two, about something which we dimly see or not at all.

We are, or at any rate I am, not familiar, as actor or onlooker, with savage infighting with a sword. Nor indeed with swords in their variety. But it does not take a great effort of imagination to get some idea of Beowulf's predicament. He was seized by a sea-beast of great strength, and no doubt held close. It took great strength to resist the grip sufficiently, to prevent himself being gored or bitten; but he had only one hand; the other held a naked sword (439, *539). That is a weapon at least two feet long. Only by a great effort could he retract this so as to level the point (453, *orde* *556) at his enemy; there would then be little if any striking-distance, and to thrust this through the tough hide would require very great strength of hand and arm. It was a great feat. But it is recorded (hardly 'described'!) in the words: 'fast the grim thing held me in its gripe. Nonetheless, it was granted to me to find that fell slayer with point of warlike sword; the battle's onset destroyed that strong beast of the sea through this my hand' (451–4). The great strength of hand in this one terrific jab is (or was for the poet's audience) emphasized by the curious impersonal expression; the desperate effort to make a moment's opportunity for the jab is (simultaneously with Beowulf's 'sportsman's modesty' of expression) exhibited in *hwæþre mé gyfeþe wearð . . .* (*555), 'Nonetheless it was granted to me . . .' (452). I suppose that in modern terms the nearest would be 'Yet a chance came for me', or 'Yet I found a chance to get my sword's point into the beast'.

465–6   *Fate oft saveth a man not doomed to die, when his valour fails not;* *572–3 *Wyrd oft nereð unfægne eorl, þonne his ellen déah*

(Cf. the note to 367, *Fate goeth ever as she must!*) This as it stands is about as completely an 'illogical' reference to Fate as could be devised. Fate often preserves (from Fate?) a man not at the time fated to die, when his courage does not fail – preserves him from what – death (already fated)!

This requires a considerable note to elucidate. To go to the kernel of the matter at once: emotionally and in thought (so far as that was ever clear) this is basically an assertion not only of the worth in itself of the human will (and courage), but also of its practical effect as a possibility, that is, actually a denial of absolute Fate. It is no doubt a 'saying' not first devised by our author, but a saying that would appeal to and be likely to come from such a character as his Beowulf, young, strong, fearless. I myself think that it is a saying ultimately from popular rather than 'heroic' or aristocratic language: and that its 'illogicality' is much reduced if, in that light, we realise that *wyrd* is (or was) not philosophic Fate, but fortune or chance, and *unfǽgne* probably does (or did) not mean 'not doomed to die', but 'undaunted by circumstances, not unnerved'. 'Fortune (as oft is seen) saves an undaunted man, when his vigour does not fail' does not seem so absurd.

As for *ellen*, 'vigour' is about right: it is not a purely poetic word, though most used in heroic verse. Though it sometimes appears in contexts where 'strength' might fit, it does not mean 'physical strength', not the bodily instrument but the strength and heat of spirit driving a man to vigorous action. Not limited to modern 'courage/valour', since it was not solely exhibited in situations of danger or the conquest of fear. Basically *ellen* referred to the competitive, combative spirit of proud individuals. A runner in a race must show *ellen*. Even Unferth's envy and malice showed *ellen*.

As for *wyrd*, 'the turn of events, how things go', this sense is found in 'heroic poetry' (e.g. in *Beowulf*, *hé ne léag fela wyrda né worda*, 'he did not conceal anything of what had occurred or been said' [cited in the note to 367]). But it is not there the usual sense; and a meaning equivalent to 'chance' or 'fortune' must be regarded as mainly belonging to more popular language, less concerned with high destinies.

As for *unfǽge*: *fǽge* is a difficult word, but in all probability was in origin a popular (even agricultural) word without reference to doom or Fate: 'ripe (to fall), gone soft, rotten'. Even in heroic poetry the sense '*doomed* to die' is rather contextual than contained in the word itself, and in many cases

'near death' is all that it really means. In popular language a
fǽge man was not so much a man 'doomed' as a man without
(or who had lost) pith or vigour, whose *ellen ne déah*. *Unfǽge*
is only found in this apophthegm (*572–3) and again in *2291
[translation 1929–30 'one whose fate is not to die']. In the
apophthegm the popular sense 'not enfeebled' will fit well, as
we see. In *2291 the precise sense is less certain, since it refers
to the man who raided the dragon's hoard and so roused him
to fury, and was instrumental in causing Beowulf's death.
But unfortunately, both from the tantalizingly allusive way
in which this story is told, and from the grievous damage to
the manuscript which has made the account of the raid on the
hoard illegible (*2226–31, 1875–8), we are in doubt about the
tale and the character of the man. If he was a man who showed
resolution, and at least the will and courage of desperation in
his dreadful feat, then *unfǽge* in *2291 may agree with *573. I
think this is probable. He had actually gone forward to this
place with cunning stealth (*dyrnan cræfte* *2290, 1928), step-
ping close to the dragon's head. So a resolute man by the grace
of God (*Waldendes hyldo* *2292–3, 'the favour of the Lord'
1931) may well escape unharmed!

We learn that the raider did not plunder the hoard of his
own accord (*Nealles mid gewealdum* *2221, 'By no means
of intent' 1869): he was a fugitive slave who had commit-
ted some crime (*synbysig* *2226, 'a man burdened with guilt'
1873–4) and fled from *heteswengeas* (*2224, 'the lashes of
wrath' 1872–3) probably implying being killed rather than a
frightful beating. If as seems most likely the next words are
ærnes þearfa 'lacking any shelter', then, as what can be read of

the badly damaged passage suggests, he did not know until he got inside that he had entered a dragon's lair and hoard. *ðám gyste gryrebróga stód* *2227 ('upon the trespasser dire terror fell' 1875–6); but this does not make him a feeble coward. He showed desperate courage. In spite of his appalling situation, he saw how he might turn it to his advantage. Evidently he did not give way to panic, nor shriek (as one *fǽge*) which would have been the end of him. He seized a great gold-plated goblet (1922, *fǽted wǽge* *2282) and made off, took it to his master, and with it bought his pardon. The act of a pretty tough man. One deduces that his crime had been a violent one, and also that the *fǽted wǽge* was of immense value! That later he is called *hæft hygegiómor* (*2408, 'a captive with gloomy heart' 2026) and is forced to go *héan* and *ofer willan* ('in shame' and 'against his will') as guide back to the lair, does not detract from this at all. He was now accused of rousing a dragon who had burned and ravaged the land, and destroyed the king's house and throne: he might well now be *hygegiómor*.

Since *unfǽgne* (*573) is the first occurrence of *fǽge* in *Beowulf*, I append a note on this word, with special reference to the assertion of its 'original meaning' (above, p. 257).

It seems to me that the etymologists are here probably right. *fǽge* derived from Germanic **faigī* did not in origin mean 'fated'. It probably meant, as I have said, 'ripe' or 'over-ripe' (of fruit, etc.) > 'rotten, crumbling' > (of men) 'near the end of their time, at the point of death' This is really the sense in this passage in the Old English poem *Guthlac* (which is hardly less 'illogical' in appearance than *Beowulf*

*572–3): *Wyrd ne meahte in fǽgum leng feorh gehealdan . . . þonne him gedémed wæs* ('Fate could not any longer keep life in the man than was ordained for him'). Saint Guthlac was dying of a mortal disease and was 'at death's door'. However, *fǽge* had a curious sense-development. It partly remained on the old level; but it was also affected by two things: current (vague and hardly philosophical) notions of Fate, especially as governing the time of a man's death; and actual observation of the moods and behaviour of men. When used of men it moved from the sense 'rotten, etc.' > 'soft, sluggish, inert, poor-spirited'. But this might be blended with the observation in what seems to them to be an inevitable situation – especially if their notions of 'Fate' are held strongly enough to make them 'fatalistic': they 'throw in their hand', yield to circumstances, make no effort to save themselves; or in some cases act wildly and irrationally, becoming 'fey', and making disaster certain by their own actions. It is to this 'loss of nerve' – a form of *cowardice* (in the Germanic view a loss of *ellen*, though not mere *timidity*, which would seek flight, if possible) – that *fǽge* and *unfǽge* often refer. The links in the sense-development (which must go far back) are now largely lost. But that the sense 'spiritless, unnerved, *ellenléas*' existed in Old English, apart from passages where 'Fate' is mentioned, is seen in the formula *(ne) forht ne fǽge* 'neither timid nor irresolute'.

512 ff.   *fair words he said: . . .*; *630 ff. *[Béowulf] gyddode . . .*

   gyddode 'uttered a *gidd*'. This is often translated 'lay, song', but though it could refer to things 'sung', its meaning was wider. It meant any form of words (short[1] or long) of composed or premeditated style, or speech on a formal occasion. In the last case the rhetorically skilled would no doubt be able *impromptu* to adorn words with alliteration and other graces, but the essential thing that made a *gidd* was probably the use of a reciting *tone,* which we should probably call 'sing-song' rather than 'singing' – rhetoric ('making a speech'), recital (of a tale), and in later times reading aloud (as e.g. in vernacular addresses or sermons) were probably far more alike then than now. A colloquial conversational tone was probably not admired. On the other hand the natural rise and fall of the voice and its emphases were not disregarded or distorted as in modern singing: they were, rather, enhanced, the pace slowed, and the enunciation more 'orotund'. The *gyddum* of *151 (121 'in songs') implies that knowledge of the troubles of Heorot was not just popular rumour or talk, but that formal 'tales' – in verse or otherwise – had been composed on the topic. Here it may be noted that Beowulf's *gidd* (513–19, *632–8) exactly fills seven lines, is natural and straightforward in construction, and very little altered or 'adorned' to fit into verse: probably not very different from the actual words that a man of courtly breeding could produce on such an occasion *impromptu.* [See further pp. 347–8.]

---

[1] For example, it could apply to proverbs or platitudes of received wisdom. Such pronouncements as that in 465–6, the subject of the last note, were a *gidd.*

524–30; *644–51

[I give here the Old English text of this passage together with my father's translation as given in this book.

644   oþ þæt semninga
         sunu Healfdenes   sécean wolde
         æfenræste;   wiste þǽm áhlǽcan
         tó þǽm héahsele   hilde geþinged,
         siððan híe sunnan léoht   geséon meahton
         oþðe nípende   niht ofer ealle,
         scaduhelma gesceapu   scríðan cwóman
         wan under wolcnum.   Werod eall árás.

524   until on a sudden the son of Healfdene desired to seek his
      nightly couch. He knew that onslaught against that lofty
      hall had been purposed in the demon's heart from the hours
      when they could see the light of the sun until darkling night
      and the shapes of mantling shadow came gliding over the
      world, dark beneath the clouds. All the host arose.

In a lengthy discussion in his lectures on the textual *cruces* in *Beowulf*
he wrote that 'the general meaning of the passage is in brief clearly:
"Hrothgar knew that Grendel would come (as every night) at the
determined time, i.e. when darkness came."' He was now opposed
to Frederic Klaeber's interpretation, that 'lines *648 ff. plainly mean:
"from the time that they could see the light of the sun, until night
came" . . . The king knew that fight had been in Grendel's mind
all day long: Grendel had been waiting from morning to night to
renew his attack on the hall.' He believed that *648–9 should not be
taken in this way to refer to Grendel's thought and purpose, but on
the contrary must give the time and reason for Hrothgar's sudden
departure, followed by the break-up of the assembly (*Werod eall
árás*). In that case (he wrote),'*siððan* means "as soon as" > shading as
it often does into "since" = "because"; *oþðe* does not mean "until";
and *geséon meahton* is probably corrupt.' On this last point I cite his
text in full.]

However the rest is construed this last must refer to a sign of oncoming night (for Grendel's determination was to come after daylight, as much as Hrothgar's desire to leave the hall was then aroused). Unless *híe sunnan léoht geséon meahton* can be made without emendation to be such a sign, a negative *must* have been omitted.[1]

I used to suggest that the words meant 'they could see the sun shining into the hall, because it had sunk so low that it was on a level (say) with the west windows'. But even if it were a matter of common knowledge that Heorot was so placed and built as to make this possible, it would be very far-fetched and to an Old English poet an unnatural thing to say; while the *opðe* clause which continues and elaborates the picture refers to common observation of sunset and nightfall out of doors.

The *ne* has been omitted: without it the line has a very much louder 'false ring' than with it. 'Logical' scholars are always very shy of admitting that a negative has been omitted; to insert one makes a great logical difference! But looked at either palaeographically or psychologically omission is a likely event that may easily happen. *ne* is a small word. In such a case as this it follows *n*. Phonetically it was reduced to *nə*, *n* in colloquial pronunciation, and was in fact often hardly audible or indeed phonetically omitted – hence the habit, already growing strong in Old English, of reinforcing pre-verbal *ne* with another negative adverb: *ná*, etc.

---

1 [Klaeber took the view that the emendation *geséon [ne] meahton* 'has a false ring; one would expect, at least, something like *leng geséon ne meahton*' ('could see (the sun) no longer').]

[With regard to the meaning of *opðe* 'or' my father noted: 'It is undoubted that *opðe* can be used sometimes not for 'or' as an exclusive alternative, but to introduce an alternative (and more emphatic) mode of expression, or to add some point implied but not previously said.' Here he would translate it 'or to say more', 'and what is more'. He proposed the following translation:]

until suddenly Healfdene's son (Hrothgar) was eager to go to his bed at evening, knowing that it was due time for the monster to come on a raid to the high hall, since they (he and all people in that place) could not see the light of the sun, and more, darkling night over all, shapes of mantling shadow were coming stalking gloomy under the clouds. All the host arose.

[It will be seen that he had now rejected the translation (lines 527–8) 'from the hours when they could see the light of the sun until darkling night . . .', but he did not change the typescript C in this respect.]

549   *esquire*; *673 *ombihtþegne*

The *ombihtþegn* must have been one of the Geats. Nothing is said about the differences of rank and function among the fifteen Geats when they set out. But it is gradually made clear to us that (whatever folk-lore research may say about supposed origins) the conception that the author had, and evidently expected his audience to have, of Beowulf was that of a 'prince': a young man of high rank in his own court, sister-son of a powerful king, in addition to his personal valour. He thus has a *þegn* attached to his personal service, as 'esquire'. The duty of such a man was to care for the arms, and produce them when required. The word 'esquire' is derived from Latin *scútum* 'shield' (*scútárius* 'shield-bearer' > Old French *esquier*), which with the development of heraldry, and of panoplied knights on horseback, became both a more personal and symbolic thing, and also larger and heavier. Here the *ombihtþegn* has as special care the costly and ornamented sword – the most precious and personal item of armament. This is brought into connexion with Beowulf's vow to eschew weapons: immediately after handing over his sword he repeats it; but as Old English *sweordbora* = esquire shows, the sword was in any case at that date the chief care of such a person.

555–6 *Nought doth he know of gentle arms*; *681 *nát hé þára góda*

[My father argued that the meaning of this was 'Grendel does not know what is right and proper (for a knight), so as to answer me with stroke of weapon'. 'The word *þára* does not refer back to anything previously said, but is an example of the definite article used of what is well-known, or customary – similar to our use of 'the' with an adjective (now usually singular) as in 'the good' = 'what is good' – but *góda* is here the genitive plural of the noun *gód*.' He made no mention in this note of his translation 'gentle arms' (556), used in the sense 'noble, honourable', which is found in both texts.]

567 *Nay, they had learned . . .*; *694 *ac híe hæfdon gefrúnen . . .*

How had they learned this? [that a bloody death had ere now in that hall of wine swept away all too many of the

Danish folk.] Clearly the line does not refer to the reports of Grendel that had reached Geatland. The band did not set out on a 'forlorn hope' or a suicidal venture. As the story is told the Geatish *witan* supported Beowulf in his desire to pit himself against Grendel, and believed the feat to be within his measure. Success, and the hope of return, depended for his companions primarily on Beowulf, and they cannot have despaired of his ability from the outset. The reference is thus evidently to conversation in the hall. Though, as I have suggested [see pp. 211, 229], Beowulf's companions were probably not sitting with him, near the king, but together on a bench further down the hall, they certainly heard Hrothgar's (intentionally alarming) account of Grendel's raids, 381–95, *473–88. If they heard it, they would not be much impressed by Unferth's sneer, 427–31, *525–8, but it can hardly be doubted that their Danish neighbours and companions in the hall had further elaborated the gruesome tale, for the saving of Danish 'faces'. Indeed after Beowulf's speech, which though primarily addressed to Unferth steadily rises in anger and loudness of utterance to the challenging conclusion, there would, one feels, be quite a number of Danes willing to make the companions of the cocky young Geatish captain shudder at the thought of a night in Heorot.

569–70   *a victorious fortune in battle*; *697 *wígspéda gewiofu*

[The conclusion of this note is very rough and hastily written, and I have introduced a short passage attempting to repair an apparently broken text.]

wígspéda gewiofu is a remarkable phrase. It means evidently: '(had granted to them) destinies of victories', apparently plural because a grant was made to each man individually (Hondscioh being left out of account [see 1745 ff., *2076 ff.])

The word *gewife* is a verbal derivative, of which the original meaning was 'product of weaving (together)'. It is only found, however, as seen above in the figurative sense of 'design, fate, fortune'. It is remarkable that this apparently 'mythological' (or allegorical) word should only be found in *Beowulf* among literary texts, although other words belonging to the same region of thought (e.g. *wyrd*) are frequently used. This probably indicates that the pictorial 'figure' of weaving, in connexion with 'fate', was obsolescent, and soon ceased to be current.

Klaeber says: 'As the context shows, the concept of the 'weaving' of destiny (by the Parcae, Norns, Valkyries – here he gives references to Grimm and others) has become a mere figure of speech'. Personally, I doubt very much that the use of 'weave' in this connexion had ever been anything more. There has been a great deal of mystification, inaccuracy, and fanciful 'web-weaving' in all discussions of 'mythology', supposed primitive or common Germanic mythology not least; and the works cited by Klaeber are no exception. Grimm (*Deutsche Mythologie*) in particular provides a wonderful nexus of citations and references, but I think that anyone approaching his treatment of the 'Fates', and kindred matters, critically will feel that in general his 'evidences' do not support his theories, even when they do not actually disprove them. His great work is now, alas! antiquated, inevitably: it is vitiated (1) by his, naturally for his time, inaccurate linguistics; (2) by his desire to see as much 'heathendom' as possible everywhere; (3) by his refusal to give weight to the fact that *nothing* got written down in Germanic languages until people acquainted with Greco-Latin learning got to work; and (4) by confusing matters that, though maybe akin, are nonetheless different in origin, purpose, and imagination: e.g. the Fates and Valkyrjur; or weaving and spinning.

Let us take one prime point: *weaving*. Though related activities, *weaving* and *spinning* are quite distinct operations (of wholly different imaginative suggestion). What is more: *weaving* needs a more or less elaborate machine (loom) and tools; it was not a specially female operation – it remained largely a masculine craft down to Bottom and beyond. The picture of three old sisters sitting at a loom (or three looms?) to determine the length of a man's life cannot have been a primitive notion. On the other hand spinning (the production of threads) was far more ancient, and was specially associated with women (as still the 'distaff side' and 'spinster' remind us). [The Greek names of the Fates (*Moirai*, Latin *Parcae*) were *Clotho*, *Lachesis*, and *Atropos*. Clotho is 'the Spinner' who spins the thread of life;] Lachesis 'allotting, lot' is this thread's determined length; but Atropos [the 'unturnable'] simply represents the inexorability of the allotment, which no human will can alter. In any case the allegory deals primarily with length of *human life*, and is not a general 'historical' allegory at all. We do not know about ancient Italic 'mythology'. But the Italic 'weaving' words do not appear ever in any such area of thought. The literary uses are derivative from Greek. Latin *Parca* was originally singular. According to Walde, with probability, it is the name of a divinity concerned with *birth* (*parere*) – the ancestress, so to say, of the fairy godmother at christenings!

569 ff.; *696 ff.

[The commentary here is more easily followed from the Old English text, which I set out here together with my father's translation.

Ac him Dryhten forgeaf
wígspéda gewiofu, Wedera léodum,
frófor ond fultum, þæt híe féond heora
ðurh ánes cræft ealle ofercómon,
700 selfes mihtum. Sóð is gecýþed,
þæt mihtig God manna cynnes
wéold widerherð. Cóm on wanre niht
scríðan sceadugenga. Scéotend swǽfon,
þá þæt hornreced healdan scoldon,
705 ealle bútan ánum. Þæt wæs yldum cuþ,
þæt híe ne móste, þá Metod nolde,
se scynscaþa under sceadu bregdan,
ac hé wæccende wráþum on andan
bád bolgenmód beadwa geþinges.

569 Yet God granted them a victorious fortune in battle, even to those Geatish warriors, yea succour and aid, that they, through the prowess of one and through his single might, overcame their enemy. Manifest is this truth, that mighty God hath ruled the race of men through all the ages.

There came, in darkling night passing, a shadow walking. The spearmen slept whose duty was to guard the gabled hall. All except one. Well-known it was to men that, if God willed it not, the robber-fiend no power had to drag them to the shades; but he there wakeful in his foe's despite abode grimhearted the debate of war.]

It should be noted that there is not a break or 'jerk' at *bregdan* *707 [a reference to the punctuation in Klaeber's text: *bregdan; -*]: *ac* refers precisely to what is there said, even though *he* is of course the 'one' (*ánum* *705) who alone kept awake and watchful. *Þæt wæs yldum cúþ* is not a mere tiresome repetition of the same idea as that already expressed in *700 ff., *Sóð is gecýþed* . . . The poet's moralizing may not be according to our taste, generally, or in this particular place. I would prefer that he had not inserted *Þæt wæs yldum cúþ* . . . *under sceadu bregdan* into his remarkable description of the approach of Grendel. Nonetheless the insertion has a point. It is part of the characterization of the hero Beowulf, and goes with *Wyrd oft nereð* etc. [see note to 465–6]; and at the same time it reinforces *696–9 (above): the reflexion that God works through men and their powers (which He provides). *Sóð is gecýþed* is an 'exclamation' of the author to you, who are supposed to share his religion, though possibly not to have reflected much upon it. But we then re-enter the story: *Þæt wæs yldum cúþ* means 'it *was* then generally recognized', and so by Beowulf himself. *But* he believed in *ellen* [see note to 465–6 at p. 257], and he did not merely lie down 'resigned'; his strength was God's gift ('God's grace to him' 546–7, *Metodes hyldo* *670), and he meant to use it, even if in the last resort the issue was in God's hands. It was part of his *ellen* that his heart was not filled with fear, but with wrath; anything more that he had learned about the monster since his arrival had made him hate Grendel more, and more resolved to overcome him.

[From this point the text continues for several further pages, I think clearly written at the same time as the preceding note, but these were separated off later by my father with this title:]

Excursus on references to the power of God as ordainer of events (Metod) in *Beowulf* with special regard to *700–9, [572–9]

[There is also a typescript of this text, headed only EXCURSUS, a copy of the manuscript of remarkable exactness and scarcely any deviation from it in any detail. That an amanuensis could do this seems almost as unlikely as that my father would copy a text of his without making the smallest alteration.]

There can be no doubt that, like the author of *Sir Gawain and the Green Knight*, the author of *Beowulf* was deeply interested in the contemporary 'code' of the aristocratic class, its values and assumptions; and his whole story is told with these in mind, and with a critical attitude towards them. Also, like the later poet, he vividly realized the story he was telling (monster and all) as such, and told it very well,[1] moralizing apart, with an equally clear grasp of character in his actors. But the difference between the two poems is, of course, very great. First of all they deal with wholly different points of morality and 'code'; secondly, the later poet seldom addresses his audience, or comments. He was dealing with a problem much simpler, from the point of view of literary handling, addressing a 'Christian' audience, members of a religion established many hundreds of years, and was not concerned

---

1 At any rate in the first part. The second part perhaps less so: in any case it is too much interrupted by the weight of history outside the immediate event.

with its foundations, but with an excrescence or 'heresy' that was or had been current and 'fashionable'; he was criticizing the picture of the 'man of honour' as it still appeared in the minds of men of birth and breeding. The tale he told, partly by its inherent character, and partly by his skill in shaping his version, was much more suitable to his purpose, and the 'moral' or 'morals' arose naturally from the actions and speeches of his characters. His personal intrusions are rare, and mostly those of a simple narrator saying 'I will now tell this', or 'I will pass over that' – with one major exception: the long passage 624–665,[1] where the picture of the author's 'perfect knight' is set up , and his 'values' described.

But the author of *Beowulf* was writing for a society in which Christianity had not long been established, a few generations perhaps, but kings and nobles knew and honoured the names of their pagan ancestors, not so far back. Their *scops* and *þyles* remembered and recounted still histories and tales, greater and less, out of a time of pure heathenism. Christianity had done little, in the noble class, to soften the sentiments behind the code of honour. Physical courage (and sheer strength of body), pride and a fierce individualism which would brook no humiliation, and the duty (and pleasure) of revenge, were the chief features of 'the man of honour'. The fundamental tenets of One God, creator and ruler of all, inscrutable maybe in His decisions in this or that case, but still 'benevolent' to Men, and each man, and of a life hereafter, had

---

1 [*Sir Gawain and the Green Knight*, translated by J.R.R. Tolkien, stanzas 27–28.]

not dethroned Fate, inexorable, unconcerned with good or ill in deeds, and the opposition to it of unbending pride, self-will, with the reward of *dóm*: glory, the praise of *men* (not of the Judge), now or hereafter. Fate and glory never have, of course, been completely dethroned, but it is a matter of degree.

The vividness of the 'sentiment' and its powers over actions and *approval of actions* among a warlike noble class till in (say) the early ninth century is one that can hardly now be appreciated. The story that the poet chose to tell (and all its background in personal and national feuds and hatreds) was *threaded through with it*. And so still was the very language that he had to use. It was a good tale, much of it already known and popular with the kind of men that he addressed. But as is clear enough he retold it with a purpose. This 'purpose', and shift of valuation, which he had in mind might in brief be represented thus:

'There is One God, supreme ruler of the world, and true King of all mankind. By Him all events (*wyrd*) are governed; [*added later to the manuscript* for He is the Metod, the Ordainer]. From Him proceed all good things and gifts (including courage and strength). This has always been so. It was so in the days of your fathers' fathers. What is more, they knew it, even as all the descendants of Adam, unless seduced by the Devil, or falling into despair in evil times. Good and wise men of those days feared God and thanked Him.

'Here is the great warrior Beowulf. You admire him. He was worthy of it. God gave him an astonishing gift of more than human strength – he recognized it as a gift. As a boy he was of course rash and heedless, and enjoyed showing off his strength. But now he comes to manhood. He is still proud and self-confident, not unnaturally in one so indomitable, but he is aware of God. You will observe that though he is eager for glory, and the approbation of good men, self-aggrandisement is not his main motive. He may earn glory by his deeds, but they are all in fact done as a service to others. His first great deed is the overcoming of a monster that had brought untold misery on Hrothgar and his people: Grendel, a *féond mancynnes*. His other deeds are done as a service to his king and his people: he dies in their defence. Beowulf does not come first with Beowulf. He is loyal, even to his own disadvantage. Loyalty you also admire, though it is today less practised than courage and emulation.

'He was the king's cousin. When Hygelac threw away his life and most of his fighting force in a rash raid into Frankish territory, he left only a boy heir, Heardred. Beowulf was the chief noble and greatest warrior in the kingdom, but he (unlike Hróðulf whom stories make much of) did not attempt to set him aside, though a desperate struggle with the Swedes was imminent. He succeeded to the throne only when the Swedes had slain Heardred; he helped to re-establish the kingdom; and he died in ridding it of a monster greater and more terrible than Grendel.

'This then is a story of a great warrior of old, who used the gifts of God to him, of courage, strength and lineage, rightly and nobly. He may have been fierce in battle, but in dealing with men he was not unjust, nor tyrannical, and was remembered as *milde* and *monðwǽre* [in the last lines of the poem]. He lived a long while ago, and in his time and country no news had come of Christ. God seemed far off, and the Devil was near; men had no hope. He died in sorrow fearing God's anger. But God is merciful. And to you, now young and eager, death will also come one day, but you have hope of Heaven. If you use your gifts as God wills. *Brúc ealles wel!*'[1]

But to present this 'message' in his day the poet had constantly to point his story, by reminder of God as Ruler, Giver, and Judge. He may have done this more than necessary, or more than we feel is necessary, in places even unseasonably, but he did not write for us. There can be little doubt that what he wrote made a powerful impression in his time, and continued to be read long after. A reward (which he can hardly have expected) was granted him: that his work should be the major piece of Old English verse that has survived the wrecks of time – still profitable for men to read in its own right, quite apart from its acquired value as a window into the past. A punishment for its small defects (which he did not deserve) is that ignorant men, even of his own faith, should scoff at it, or call it 'small beer'. That his work cannot now be read at all without trouble, nor understood and valued in detail without sustained effort, is due under God to *wyrd*, the doom of men to live briefly in a world where all withers and is forgotten. The English language has changed – but not necessarily improved! – in a thousand years. *Wyrd* has swept away to oblivion nearly all its kin; but *Beowulf* survives: for a time, for as long as learning keeps any honour in its land. And how long will that be? *God ána wát.*[2]

---

1 [*Beowulf* *2162, 'Use all the gifts with honour' 1816.]
2 [God alone knows.]

627   *a ghastly fear;* *769 *ealuscerwen*

The general meaning of the passage is clear, and the contextual meaning of *ealuscerwen* is defined within fairly close limits: it must mean something like 'horror'. But it is a good example of the difficulty that is sometimes met in discovering the etymology and original significance, and the contemporary meaning and associations, of a word that (by chance, probably) occurs only once in Old English. 'On all the Danes, on dwellers in the town, on every bold heart, on every man, fell *ealuscerwen.*' We note that, as usual, the narrator inserts into the middle of description of what is happening *inside* the hall a brief 'snapshot' of what is happening *outside.* There is a terrible din in Heorot. It is heard in all the houses of the royal *burg* clustered in the neighbourhood. The Danes, however *céne* they may be, hearing it feel *ealuscerwen.* Then the noise, after a lull while Beowulf and Grendel wrestle, bursts out afresh, and the Danes feel *atelíc egesa* (*784, 'dread fear' 639–40). *ealuscerwen,* therefore, probably means something like *atelíc egesa* 'horrible dread'.

But how does this word, a compound that has as its first element *ealu* 'ale' arrive at such a sense? Does *ealu* here mean 'ale'?

Yes, it does – that is, whether it meant 'ale' originally or not, *ealu-* was thought to be identical with the ordinary word *ealu* 'ale'. This is shown by a passage in the poem *Andreas* [an apocryphal legend of St. Andrew]. This passage (*Andreas* 1524–7) describes the overwhelming of the heathen, cannibal

Marmedonians by a miraculous flood: *fámige walcan / mid ǽrdæge eorðan þehton; / myclade mereflód; meoduscerwen wearð / æfter symbeldæge* ['the foaming waves at dawn covered the earth; the flood of water grew great; there was *meoduscerwen* after the day of feasting']. We cannot doubt that the expressions 'mead'-*scerwen* and 'ale'-*scerwen*, both describing 'woe' or 'horror' are related. *Andreas* clearly imitates *Beowulf* in places. This may be one of the places. In that case, the comparison would only show that the poet of *Andreas* knew *ealuscerwen* from *Beowulf*, took *ealu* as 'ale', and produced a variation *meoduscerwen*, relying on his audience's knowledge of *Beowulf*.

But the situations in *Andreas* and *Beowulf* are not in fact similar. And we may go further: unless in *ealuscerwen* it was clearly felt by listeners to Old English verse how the sense 'ale' was related to the total sense 'woe/horror' of the compound, it would be frigid, not to say ridiculous, to coin a mere imitative variation with 'mead'.

So the problem of interpretation is really unaffected by the relations of *Andreas* and *Beowulf*, or the question whether *Andreas* was merely imitating *Beowulf*, or whether both were drawing in common on the inherited stock of Old English verse-words, and Old English descriptions of fear and disaster – following after mirth and feasting. The key to the problem is, therefore, in *scerwen*.

[My father thought it probable that *scerwen* was an abstract noun derived from a verb *scerwan*, recorded only in a compound form *be-scerwan* 'deprive'. Probably related verbs without the *w*-element, as O.E. *scerian*, *scirian*, have the meaning 'allot, assign'. But noting that words that have the sense 'take away, deprive, rob' can add the prefix *be-* with change of construction rather than of sense, he concluded that a possible meaning of the element *scerwen* was 'tearing away, robbing, depriving', and gave it as his opinion that *ealuscerwen* and *meoduscerwen* both basically mean 'cutting off, deprivation of ale or mead.']

They got their sense of 'horror and woe' not just crudely because an announcement in an ancient English hall 'no beer tonight' would have caused horror and woe (or even panic), but because *ealu* and *meodu* were symbols of the mirth and pleasure of peace, and life at its brief and passing best. Thus at the opening of the poem Scyld is said to have 'denied the mead-benches' to his foes. This does not mean that he marched in and pulled away the seats from under his enemies; but that the whole life and peace and honour, each in their separate halls, of the kings and lords that opposed him was overthrown.

If this interpretation is correct then actually the use in *Andreas* is nearer to the original simpler use, and the use in *Beowulf* remoter; and the occurrence of these two *hapax legomena* [words only once recorded] in *Andreas* and *Beowulf* is not evidence of the direct relationship of the poems. *meoduscerwen æfter symbeldæge*: a rude end to mirth after joy: that is the kind of phrase in which 'deprivation of mead or ale' got its sense of grief and horror. In *Beowulf* there had been a feast, but the description of it is many lines away. And 'a rude awakening' does not in fact suit the context too well. The coming of Grendel was expected. His raids had endured twelve years. What caused the *ealuscerwen* was his hideous cries and the din of the grim battle in the hall.

But other explanations fit even less well. For instance, 'allotting of ale' [see the editorial note above] – used ironically, as 'a bitter drink'. Again the *Andreas* passage is much more suitable: the heathen are being drowned. But I still think this explanation impossible. *meodu* and *ealu* are good symbols and cannot just be used to mean the opposite. The *Beowulf* usage would be incredible. Had *meoduscerwen* meant 'dealing out of mead' then in such a context any Old English poet would have put in a negative, or a bad adjective, as indeed we see later in the same passage in *Andreas*, *Þæt wæs biter béorþegu*, 1533, 'that was a bitter beer-drinking'.

687–8 *had dragged his footsteps, bleeding out his life*; *846 *feorhlastas bær*

'bore his life-tracks' – what does this mean? Probably, 'dragged a trail marked by his life-blood'. *feorh* means vitals or life-principle, and any part or element in which this resides. Cf. *2981 *wæs in feorh dropen*, 2503 'he was stricken mortally'; and for a passage where *feorh* seems plainly to signify 'blood' cf. *1151-2 *Ðá wæs heal roden féonda féorum*, 944–5 'then was that hall reddened with the life-blood of their foes'.

691–2 *doomed to die he plunged*; *850 *déaðfæge déog*

[The word *déog* does not occur elsewhere. My father examined the attempts to identify it or to correct it, and concluded that 'the best that can be done' is to suppose it to be a corruption of *déaf* 'he (had) dived', past tense singular of *dúfan*.]

705–10; *867–74 [Passage concerning verse-composition]

This is an interesting (and in Old English unique) reference to the *manner and mode* of alliterative composition. (Compare the equally interesting passage 1767 ff., *2105 ff., describing Hrothgar's personal performance as narrator and singer: that deals with the *kind and content* of 'literary' compositions.) This passage has, of course, attracted attention, and has been the subject of varied translations and interpretations: some of them in my view erroneous, especially those that compare the *Beowulf* passage with the famous passage in *Sir Gawain and the Green Knight*, lines 30–6. They should, however, be compared; and lines 42–4 of the prologue to Chaucer's *Parson's Tale* also.

[*Beowulf* *867 ff.   Hwílum cyninges þegn
               guma gilphlæden, gidda gemyndig,
               sé þe ealfela ealdgesegena
     870   worn gemunde, word óþer fand
               sóðe gebunden; secg oft ongan
               síð Béowulfes snyttrum styrian,
               ond on spéd wrecan spel geráde,
               wordum wrixlan;

translation 705–10
     At whiles a servant of the king, a man laden with proud memories who had lays in mind and recalled a host and multitude of tales of old – word followed word, each truly linked to each – this man in his turn began with skill to treat in

poetry the quest of Beowulf and in flowing words to utter his ready tale, interweaving words.

Sir Gawain 30–6	If ȝe wyl lysten þis laye bot on littel quile,
	I schal telle hit astit, as I in toune herde
	with tonge,
	As hit is stad and stoken
	In stori stif and stronge,
	With lel letteres loken,
	In londe so haȝ ben longe.

translation (J.R.R.T.),	....
stanza 2	as it is fixed and fettered
	in story brave and bold,
	thus linked and truly lettered
	as was loved in this land of old.

The Parson's Prologue	But trusteth wel, I am a Southren man,
42–4	I kan nat geeste 'rum, ram, ruf,' by lettre,
	Ne, God woot, rym holde I but litel bettre;]

The consideration of the two (contemporary) Middle English passages and their comparison belongs primarily to Middle English studies, and has as its centre the use of *lel letteres* in *Sir Gawain* and *by lettre* in the *The Parson's Tale*: the origin of our modern (and inaccurate) term 'alliteration'. It was a use arising, evidently, from a contemporary 14th century competition and debate between 'alliteration' and 'rhyme' as *structural* devices in verse. There was no such competition or debate in Old English times. Rhyme, of course, pleased or excited the attention of poets' ears, and vocalic rhyme, and consonantal rhyme, (*flōd/blōd* or *sund/ sand*), was used on occasion; but as an adornment or special effect, not structurally. Alliteration was taken for granted. We therefore must not hasten to assume that it is referred to in *Beowulf*: it might be, but it is *prima facie* not likely that it was.

There is at first sight a similarity between the expression *with lel letteres loken* and *word óþer fand sóðe gebunden* that has not escaped notice. This similarity is sometimes increased by treating *word óþer fand sóðe gebunden* as a parenthetic statement, supposedly of this sort: 'one word led to (found) another truly linked (to it)'. But this fails, before we need to consider *sóðe gebunden*: (a) because *cyninges þegn* *867 is left without a verb – *secg eft ongan* clearly begins a new sentence; and (b) because though *word óþer* is good Old English for 'one word x another word', the use of *fand* (with *word* as subject) in the supposed sense is very dubious in any context. In a literary context, expressly referring to poetic composition, the verb *fand* must certainly have as subject 'minstrel/ poet' who 'finds, invents, makes'. There can be no doubt that punctuation with a semi-colon at *gebunden* is correct. The subject is the *þegn*, *guma gilphlæden* who versed in old lays and lore is said now to have contrived 'other words' – i.e. a new poetic eulogy not in his previous repertoire as such, though as we see he made extensive reference to his *ealdgesegena* (*869), concerning Sigemund and Heremod.

However, in any case, and with any punctuation, *sóðe gebunden* cannot, I believe, refer to 'alliteration', nor be compared with *lel letteres loken*, as is often supposed (cf. Klaeber, note to line *870 f.: 'for the true alliterative "binding", *sóðe gebunden*, cp. *Sir Gawain and the Green Knight* 35: *with lel*

letteres loken'.) If it is translated 'truly bound', a false simi-
larity (for speakers of modern English) is created between
it and 'loyally'[1] locked (= linked), because *treowe, trewe,*
true 'dependable, true' is more or less equivalent to *leël, lel*
(leial, loial). But if modern English has confounded *verus* and
fidelis, sannr and *tryggr, wahr* and *treu,* Old English had not
yet done so: O.E. *sóð* is not an equivalent of *treowe, triewe.*
Its normal and central sense is *verus,* (what is) true in fact, in
reality, (what is) in accordance with verity. The sense of *sóðe*
gebunden cannot be in line *871 'actually and in fact bound',
but it must be related to that basic sense. *Sóðe* is probably not
the adverb, but instrumental of the noun (= later *mid sóðe*);
in any case the binding or linkage [?present] is not one of
external rule, but of reference to 'truth' (verity): justly. That
is, it is a linking not of *metre* but of *diction*: most probably
an allusion to the propriety of synonyms or equivalents used
in the Old English 'linked' verse style, which should share a
real and just correspondence with the thing or action spoken
of – another aspect of the feature of alliterative verse later
described as *wordum wrixlan* (*874). *sóðe gebunden* describes
the truth and propriety of the terms used, *wordum wrixlan*
the actual variation of words (with different sounds and
metrical effects). It is with such questions of the propriety
and homogeneity in the use of synonyms and 'kennings' that
much of the Old Norse *Skáldskaparmál* is concerned.

---

1 'loyal' here means 'dutiful, doing what is required (at the required
time) as a 'loyal' servant would. So in the Towneley play of *Noah*
(15th century): 'This forty dayes has rayn beyn; it will therefor
abate full *lele.'*

The close parallelism of the passages in *Beowulf* and *Gawain* thus disappears. The concern of the old courtly minstrels with their far more polished and sophisticated art was with style; the fourteenth century alliterative poets were concerned primarily to conserve their native *rum-ram-ruf*. But it remains of great interest that the two most gifted authors using the 'alliterative' English verse whose work has been preserved should both feel moved to make an allusion to their verse medium.

[My father's translation of lines *870–1, cited at the beginning of this note, 'word followed word, each truly linked to each', interprets the Old English words in the manner that he here strongly opposed, but the text of the translation was not subsequently modified.]

708 ff.; *871 ff. [Síð Béowulfes: The Quest of Beowulf]

It is obviously impossible to discuss in full these two references to heroic 'matter' in the poet's eulogy of Beowulf: Sigemund and Heremod, in the compass of a 'note'.

Points that might be emphasized are these. (1) The résumé of the content of the eulogy, Sigemund and Heremod, is a story (or stories) within a story (the eulogy) within a story (*Beowulf*). It is therefore 'cursory' to us, who would like to know more; but no doubt it picks out the 'high lights' for those who *knew*: every phrase had a point.

(2) The reported lay does not end until line 747 (*915). Sigemund and Heremod were linked in men's imagination, if only as supreme examples of the *wrecca* (see the note to 731, *898). The end is indeed 'cursory', where the conclusion

284

is brought back to Beowulf again. We may surmise that the minstrel said, or would have said in real life, more than 'He there, Beowulf, has proved more satisfactory to mankind and to his friends; the other was possessed by wickedness.' But the beginning is simply missing – because this *is* only a story within a story, and *sið Béowulfes* has been recounted to you.[1]

(3) The Sigemund story survives as a part of the most renowned and long-lived Germanic legend – the Völsunga saga / Niebelungenlied complex – and there is therefore plenty still left to invite (and perplex) comparison. The difficulty of the Heremod legend is of the opposite kind. Probably for the very reason given here (734–5, *901–2), because Heremod's fame was eclipsed by Sigemund's, this legend has been lost, except for allusions – though when *Beowulf* was written it was evidently still well-known in England.

(4) In content and structure the reported précis illustrates the manner (of which *Beowulf* itself is a sufficient example) of *gilphlæden* poets in composing such eulogies or lays celebrating the virtues of a chosen hero – no doubt approved by their audience: they drew on *ealdgesegene* for the adornment and for the pointing by contrast of their account of the central figure (For these O.E. words see p. 280).

(5) But this is a lay within a lay – that is a *fictional* adornment or pointing of the *Beowulf* story by its author. Our author then (not the supposed contemporary poet) was

---

[1] *Béowulfes sið* may well have been the actual name by which the earlier lay (or lays) dealing with Beowulf's coming to Heorot was known.

the actual selector of the illustrations, of Sigemund and Heremod. His choice, therefore, was very unlikely to be random: it had point for his purposes in his poem as a whole. Various reasons can be guessed.

This last point deserves a little more consideration. How far you may feel these 'reasons' to remain 'guesses', or to discover truth, will depend on the degree of respect you have for the artistry (or at least for the thoughtful care) with which *Beowulf* was composed. This respect is, I think, increased by study. Here are some of the reasons which may be surmised, or perceived.

(a) Sigemund and Heremod were both *wreccan*, as is implied in *898–901, *Sé wæs wreccena wíde mærost . . .* (731 'He was far and wide of adventurers the most renowned . . .'). This word is interesting and important, and is quite inadequately represented by the usual dictionary glosses. Beowulf was not (as his tale is here told) precisely a *wrecca*, but his exploit had this in common with the deeds of *wreccan*: it was not done in the course of duty, but in a spirit of adventure; and it was accomplished away from home, in the service of the king of another people.

(b) Sigemund was also a monster-slayer (718–19, *883–4). But his most renowned exploit was performed alone (723, *888), like Beowulf's wrestling with Grendel.

(c) More important still, I think, Sigemund fought and slew a dragon. On this major point see further the note to 710–34, (noting here, however, that if you believe (as I do not) that our poet, either in 'error' or on purpose, was attaching to Sigemund a dragon-slaying that did not belong to him this point is not weakened, but reinforced). Now I think that *Beowulf* is threaded through with 'irony', with remarks, references, and allusions, for the full understanding of which *the whole poem* must be taken into account: both what is said or has happened, and what will happen, must be considered. Thus when the minstrel is represented as singing his eulogy, Beowulf had only wrestled with Grendel, but before his exploit is complete he will have to dare to go absolutely alone into the cave of a monster, and there defeat her. What is more, before his life is complete, he is to fight and slay a dragon, and die in the victory. Sigemund was (or is represented as) the pre-eminent dragon-slayer (not – certainly in the older layers of legend – a frequent exploit!). Evidently in extolling Beowulf Hrothgar's minstrel had equated him with Sigemund; but he did not know this: that Beowulf was to face a dragon at the end – with different motive (Sigemund's is represented as plunder, 726–9, *893–6) and result. We shall probably never know whether this 'irony' was introduced for the poet's own satisfaction (and for the more perceptive of his hearers or readers, when they had heard his whole poem through), or was immediately recognizable (i.e. because the ending of Beowulf and/or the Geatish kingdom in a dragon-fight was already part of the legend before our extant poem was made). But it seems to me impossible to believe that it is accidental: that Sigemund, as a dragon-slayer, was made the chief figure of comparison, without any reference to the end of Beowulf (either as planned by our poet, or as already enshrined in legend).

(d) Heremod is introduced because these two great

figures, Sigemund and Heremod, in tales of *wreccan* were already associated; because he was a Dane and this is a song made by a minstrel of Hrothgar's court, and his legend evidently closely concerned the rise and origin of the line of Healfdene. Heremod's disastrous decline and fall had ended the previous dynasty and left the interregnum (alluded to in lines 12–13, *14–16). And of course, because his decline into wickedness[1] made a good ending 'by dark contrast' to the character of Beowulf. Irony is again present: for the bard was singing of a young man, and though in eulogy he might attribute all kingly virtues to his hero, he could not know that Beowulf would (as the author knew) end with the praises: *manna mildust ond monðwǽrust, léodum líðost ond lofgeornost.* Contrast the words of the sage old fatherly king, who again alludes to Heremod (1435–49, *1709–24), but addresses a young man in the flush of his double triumph, and presents to him Heremod as an exemplary *warning.* 'Learn thou from this, and understand what generous virtue is!' *Ðú þé lǽr be þon, gumcyste ongit!*

Hrothgar was an old and wise king, and such a warning was permissible. He had nothing further to gain, and had already rewarded Beowulf with royal courtesy and with princely gifts – to which he was about to add 'twelve precious things' at their parting (1566, *1867). It is quite possible that the minstrel was not so single-minded. Members of his craft

---

1 The unkingly crimes of avarice and ungenerous hand, and of treachery and murder of men of his own court, are charged against him in 1436 ff., *1711 ff.

were accustomed indirectly, or more often directly, to suggest that the virtue of open-handedness in reward of services rendered might well be practised at once – with possibly good effect on future compositions. Beowulf could not (in view of the gifts and gold that he had received)[1] plead like Gawain *that he had no men wyth no maleȝ with menskful þingeȝ* (1809; 'no bearers with baggage and beautiful things', stanza 72), and could only offer courteous thanks for services. He rewarded the coast-guard with a sword (a very great gift). So much that was customary is omitted, that we can hardly doubt that the *guma gilphlæden* was also 'remembered'.

(e) A last point: it is possible to see in the curious repetition of the 'dark picture' of Heremod (by the minstrel and by the king) a trace of an older, more historical, tradition concerning the dynasty of Heorot: of Healfdene and his sons. It is like listening to an insistence on the wickedness of Richard III at a Tudor court. The absence of any historical ancestor between Healfdene and the mythical Beow is (in addition to his peculiar name) sufficient indication that he was a 'new man' and at best had no direct or clear descent from preceding kings; and no doubt, like other successful interlopers, once securely settled by force he was eager to justify his position by reference to the disorder and misery that preceded him – and later

---

1   It would of course be understood that he would present much of this wealth to his own lord Hygelac on his return. It is in fact recorded that he gave Hygelac all the first four gifts (1807 ff., *2152 ff., where we learn that the corslet had been Heorogár's, and was in fact specially sent to Hygelac), and also four of the horses; and gave Wealtheow's necklace to Queen Hygd.

by the fabrication of a genealogy (which resembles a Tudor play with Arthurian origins).

710–34; *874–900   [The sketch of the Sigemund story]

[In this note my father turned to the question of the attribution of a dragon-slaying to Sigemund rather than his son; another discussion of his on this subject is recounted in *The Legend of Sigurd and Gudrún*, 2009, pp. 351–6.]

I find it impossible to believe that a 'dragon-slaying' is here attributed to Sigemund in 'error'. 'Error' in this connexion needs consideration. What can it mean? When used with regard to a purely legendary feature, such as a dragon-slaying, it must imply that the critic imagines that there was (somewhere, sometime) a legend of Sigemund, 'true' or at least original or authentic, aberrations from which are 'erroneous'. But that supposition is itself erroneous: with regard to any ancient legend or legend-complex. Such things never in fact existed except in actual poems or stories told by actual individuals, using, re-telling, re-handling what they had already heard or read. But in the case of the author of *Beowulf* his version could be 'aberrant': that is, it could omit matter which *in his time* was normally included in a tale of Sigemund the *wrecca*, or it could add incidents that had not so far been usually added to the tale. (In which case, of course, such incidents would certainly be drawn from other similar tales.) Is this likely in the present case?

No. First, it is highly unlikely that in a précis of the Sigemund story included for a specific purpose, and

represented as the lay of another minstrel, the author of
Beowulf would alter the tale in a major point from what was
in his time current.

Secondly, this is admittedly the oldest reference to the
Sigemund story that is now extant, even in point of manu-
script date. It is thus antecedently probable that its diver-
gence from later forms of the tale is due to 'archaism': it is
later accounts that are in 'error', that is to say, have altered
the story.

No certain conclusion, of course, can be drawn from the
absence in the Old English précis of any reference to the
son of Sigemund or his connexion with the Burgundians
and the sons of Gifeca. In such a précis for such a purpose
the author of *Beowulf* would naturally end the reference to
Sigemund with his supreme feat. It is, however, *probable*
that the Völsung story (*Wælsinges gewin* *877, 712–3) had not
yet been connected with the Burgundian saga; *possible*, that
Sigemund had not yet been provided with a son, other than
Fitela.[1] The Burgundian–Attila matter was however well-
known in England, as references in the old poems *Widsith*
and *Waldere* show. It is a well-known tendency in tales that
are popular and long re-told for them to be enlarged, until
they become 'cycles', taking up or being linked to other sto-
ries with which they at first had slender connexions, or none

---

1   If, as seems most probable, under the words *eam his nefan* (*881)
    'mother's brother to nephew' [translation 716–17, 'of such matters,
    brother to his sister's son'], which is correct if incomplete, lies the
    same story as in the *Völsunga Saga*, in which Sinfiötli was the son
    of Sigmundr and his sister.

at all. One of the methods used in this process is to provide
the original hero with a son, either a newly invented one, or a
character in another story. In either case the son will tend to
have similar adventures, with variation, to those of his father.

This seems to me to have taken place in the case of
Sigemund. But the 'dragon-slaying', the supreme feat which
made its achiever the most renowned hero of the North,
could not be duplicated. It was therefore taken over by the
son. But it does not fit him so well. It is indeed unnecessary
to his tragic story, and in German it is practically forgotten.
Sigemund, whatever historical 'kernel' his story contained,
belongs to an older, more primitive (indeed more savage)
past, in which *eotenas* and *dracan* are more appropriate. In
the *Völsunga saga*, a 'cento', made of different sources and
different lays, one is conscious of this division. It may also
be observed that while Sigemund's name remained fixed, his
son's, sharing the prefix *Sige-*, is not fixed: in Norse sources
it is *Sigurðr* (which would be O.E. *Sigeweard*), in German
sources *Sigfrit* (*Siegfried*), which would be O.E. *Sigeferþ*.
That the name of the original dragon-slayer and prime hero
should not be fixed in form would be strange.

731; *898   *wrecca*

In the social and political Germanic world of the early
centuries of our era were founded the divergent develop-
ments of this word: on one side to our 'wretch', on the other
to German *Rocke*, 'valiant knight, hero' (of old). Both lines
were fully developed in Old English.

wrecca means in origin an 'exile', a man driven out from the land of his home – for any reason: crime, collapse or conquest of his people or princely line, economic pressure or the desire for more opportunity, and often (if he was of high birth) dynastic struggles among members of the 'royal family'. In *2613 *wræcca(n) wineléasum* (2194 'a lordless exile') is applied to Eanmund the son of the previous Swedish king Ohthere, driven out by his uncle Onela. In *898 (731) *sé wæs wreccena wíde mærost* it is seen on the other hand that a *wrecca* might win great renown. Cf. *The Fight at Finnsburg* 25 where Sigeferþ boasts of his status: *Sigeferþ is mín nama, ic eom Secgena léod, wreccea wíde cúð* [known far and wide]. The term is also applied to Hengest, *1137 ('the exile' 932). It may mean then no more than the immediate fact that Hengest had now under necessity become nominally Finn's 'man', and accepted lodging and 'keep' from him, though in a foreign land. But Hengest was probably already a *wrecca*, an 'adventurer', a man who with his *héap* or personal following had, though a Jute, taken service with Hnæf. Except then in not being 'legally' an exile, Beowulf was himself for the nonce of the *wrecca*-class. With a personal following chosen by himself (*héap* *400, 323; *432, 349) he had gone off, in time of peace at home, in search of adventure and profit, and offered his service to the king of another people. Ecgtheow, his father, had been in all senses a *wrecca*, being driven out from his own land because of his deeds (372–4, *461–2), and taking service with the Danish king ('oaths he swore to me' 381, *472).

But, of course, in 'real life' the position of a *wrecca* was unhappy. Only a man of commanding character and great courage could long survive in a state of outlawry, still less win renown or wealth. Most such men lived 'wretchedly' or perished; while many of them were no doubt justly outlawed or exiled, and were men of evil character. Hence already in unheroic language a *wrecca* meant a 'wretch' – either a miserable unhappy homeless man, or a despicable and wicked one.

769–71 *Lo! this may she say, if yet she lives, whosoever among women did bring forth this son among the peoples of earth*; *942–6 *Hwæt, þæt secgan mæg efne swá hwylc mægþa swá þone magan cende æfter gumcynnum, gif héo gýt lyfað*

The 'exclamatio' *Hwæt* ff. has been regarded as a reminiscence of Scripture. But there is not in fact any close verbal resemblance between Hrothgar's words and Luke xi.27: Blessed is the womb that bore thee . . . The 'exclamatio' nonetheless has the appearance of an addition, that does not fit the situation. Hrothgar knew all about Beowulf's parentage, and he himself says (300–1 ff., *373–5 ff.) that Beowulf's mother was the only daughter of Hrethel. Yet here he says: 'whatsoever woman bore this son, if she yet lives.' The difficulty cannot be resolved by making the exclamation 'general'. It is cast in the present indicative. A general expression would take the form (in this situation when Hrothgar knew the facts): 'Lo, any woman whatsoever who had borne such a son might praise God for this favour': *mæg* and *gyf héo gýt lyfað* ('may' and 'if yet she lives') do not fit. The natural way of taking *ðone magan* ('this son') is demonstrative indicating Beowulf (here present).

[Added later:] It is possible that praise of the victor's mother was an old element in the folk-legend of the 'strong man' and has not been fully assimilated to his historical background.

783–5 *Yet rather had I wished that thou might see him here, Grendel himself, thy foe in his array sick unto death!*; *960–2 *Úþe ic swíþor, þæt ðú hine selfne geséon móste, féond on frætewum fylwérigne!*

This is frequently misinterpreted, even by those whose business it is to know Old English grammar and syntax: e.g. the old J.R. Clark Hall crib has: 'I heartily wish that thyself (*sic!* for *ðú hine selfne*) couldst have seen him' – i.e. 'I wish (now) that you (Hrothgar) had been there then!' That (Old English grammar apart) is both a foolish and insolent remark. It is nonetheless retained in C.L. Wrenn's revision of Clark Hall.

Actually Beowulf says: 'I would have liked far more that you should be able to see Grendel himself.' And he means (deprecatingly): 'I am very sorry only to have an arm to show you; I should have preferred to have presented you with Grendel himself complete – and dead.'

Úþe swíþor: *úþe* is past tense subjunctive (of *unnan*) used in an unfulfilled or unrealizable wish: = 'I should have been more greatly pleased'; *móste*, also subjunctive (because it also refers to something merely thought and not a fact), is past tense by the sequence of tenses normally practised (as in Latin) by O.E. – and by modern English: so 'I should have been happier, if he had been here now – *or* were / was here.' Translate then: 'I should have been better pleased that thou shouldst have seen him himself, thy foe in his war-gear, lying felled' (literally 'felling-weary', *fyl-wérigne*, that is *weary* (= dead) after being laid low).

on frætewum is probably carelessly used, since warriors fallen in battle were usually *on frætewum* unless stripped. But it is dangerous to attribute such 'carelessness' to this author. The picture Beowulf had in mind was of Grendel complete, but dead. He did not wear 'armour' like men, but he had the equivalent of weapons in his hands, each finger of which (as we are soon to learn) had a long tearing nail like steel. Now Grendel is not there entire, and part of his *frætwe* has been already torn off.

785–6 *I purposed in hard bonds swiftly to bind him upon his deathbed*; *963–4 *Ic hine hrædlíce heardan clammum on wælbedde wríþan þóhte*

As *wæl-* shows, this does not mean that Beowulf thought of catching him alive and binding him. It is a poetic periphrasis (of a kind more admired then than now) for 'kill him with my hand-gripes', elaborated in 786–7 (*965–6) 'that by the grasp of my hands he should be forced to lie struggling for life'.

789–90 *I did not cleave fast enough for that*; *968 *nó ic him þæs georne ætfealh*

This is appropriate modesty, and more or less true. If Beowulf had been even stronger than he was, he might have held the ogre in such a way that he could not have got away by leaving one arm. It may be observed that Grendel only put one hand out to grasp Beowulf (*746, *748; 608–10); so that Beowulf never had hold of more than one hand before Grendel pulled away and tried to escape.

791–2 *Nonetheless he hath left behind upon his trail his hand and arm and shoulder*; *970–2 *Hwæþere hé his folme forlét tó lífwraþe lást weardian, earm ond eaxle*

Cf. *lífwraðe* *2877 'life-support' = defence against death (2419 'succour of his life'); so here *tó lífwraþe* = 'as a defence against death' = 'so as to save his life (by escape)'. If Grendel's arm had not broken off Beowulf would have throttled him. Though there is no suggestion in the actual account of the wrestling (608 ff, *745 ff.) that the casting of an arm was in any way willed by Grendel, as a last desperate trick to escape, the use of *swice* *966 'tricked, cheated' [*bútan his líc swice*; 'had not his body escaped me' 787–8], and the present lines, certainly suggest that this notion was once part of the tale.

[It will be seen that the words *tó lífwraþe* were left untranslated in the original typescript B(i), and the omission was not subsequently repaired.]

lást weardian 'to guard the track', very frequent in verse = 'to remain behind'.

797 *the great Day of Doom*; *978 *miclan dómes*

Note the reference to Doom's Day (called in Old English *(se) micla dóm, dómdæg* and *dómes dæg*), here actually made by Beowulf himself. Here Grendel is regarded as a 'man' with a soul that survives death – cf. 693 'yielded up his life and heathen soul', *851-2 *feorh álegde, hǽþene sáwle* – as a descendant of Cain. Ignorance of Germanic beliefs untouched by Christian teaching (as they inevitably were before they could be written down) makes it impossible to say whether references to a Last Day are purely Christian or not. *Hell* was a native word. Punishment of the wicked is certainly contemplated in Old Norse (more or less) 'heathen mythology', and the poem *Völuspá* reserves a place of torment for them; though Hell, like Hades, was the 'hidden land' of all the dead – apart from the Odinic conception of Valhöll.

803-5 (of the nails on Grendel's hand): *At the tip was each one of the stout nails most like unto steel, grievous and cruel were the spurs upon the hand of that savage thing. All agreed . . .* *984-7 (MS) *foran æghwylc wæs steda nægla gehwylc / style gelicost hæþenes hand sporu hilde/[verso of page] hilde rinces egl unheoru æghwylc gecwæð . . .*

The manuscript is plainly to some degree corrupt. In my opinion there is far too much *hwylc*: my suspicion is chiefly aroused by the first *æghwylc* in *984 which is *not* required for sense, and is in the same manuscript line as *gehwylc*. The latter is in its right idiomatic place; the former is not.

The attempt to keep the manuscript readings (except for the repeated *hilde*) leads to a punctuation of this sort: *foran*

gehwylc wæs, steda nægla gehwylc, stýle gelícost . . . 'in front
(i.e. at the tip) each (of the fingers) was, each of the places
of the nails, like unto steel'. This carries no conviction. It is
the nails themselves, anyway, sticking out at the ends of the
fingers like spikes, that are like steel; not the 'places of the
nails'.

Now a way out of this difficulty has been found by emen-
dation of *steda* to *stíðra*, genitive plural, 'stiff'. Cf. *1533 *stíð
ond stýlecg* applied to the sword Hrunting (1282 'steeledged
and strong'). No reason for the corruption of so well-known
and contextually intelligible a word as *stíðra* into *steda* can be
seen. The resulting metre is scarcely credible. The correction
of this by cancelling *gehwylc* cancels the wrong word, as I
have suggested above. Old English seldom violates idiomatic
word-order; and where an emphatic adverb usurps the first
place in a sentence, as does *foran* here, the subject should
follow the verb. In consequence *æghwylc* *984 must be either
a *misplaced anticipation* or a *corruption by anticipation* of a
word that is not noun or adjective, i.e. not the subject. The
former alternative implies that a word, more or less parallel
to *nægla gehwylc*, has dropped out after *wæs*. The latter is on
all counts more probable. I should select as the real word that
has been corrupted by anticipation into *æghwylc* is *æghwær*
'at each point'.

The corollary of this decision, which retains *gehwylc*,
is that *steda* can only be replaced by a word scanning one
long monosyllable or two short syllables, and so produc
ing a normal E-line. Far the most probable emendation is
to my mind *stede-nægla*. The corruption of *stede* into *steda*,

by anticipatory assimilation of word-endings, would be an example of one of the commonest errors of transcription, especially in inflected languages. The word *stede-nægl* does not occur elsewhere, but it would bear an obvious sense: a fixednail, a nail driven into wood so as to stick out like an iron spike. It would be the equivalent of *stedigra nægla*.[1]

We thus arrive at:

foran æghwær wæs
stedenægla gehwylc   stýle gelícost

'At each tip each of the standing nails was like a steel spike.'[2]

egl. Since Grendel's nails have been likened (i) probably to iron spikes fixed in a wooden post, (ii) to spurs, it is unlikely that the word *egl* here is to be identified with *egl, egle*, a word meaning an awn of barley. It is far more likely that it is an error for *eglu*, neuter plural of the adjective *egle* 'grievous, repulsive'.

The final translation of the passage will thus run so: '(They gazed upon the hand set above the high roof, beholding the demon's fingers.) At the tip at every point each of the

---

1   *stedig* 'fixed moveless' is only recorded in the derived sense 'sterile', but it must have existed in the original sense, as the ancestor of our 'steady', because there is a verb derived from it, *stedigian,* 'bring to a stand, stop'.

2   [The translation 803–4, cited above, which goes back to the first typescript, 'At the tip was each one of the stout nails most like unto steel', shows the emendation of *steda* to *stiðra*.]

standing nails was like steel, spurs on the hand of the savage warrior, horrible and monstrous were they.'

813–15   *Sorely shattered was all that shining house within, from their iron bars the hinges of the doors were wrenched away;* *997–9 *Wæs þæt beorhte bold tóbrocen swíðe / eal inneweard írenbendum fæst / heorras tóhlidene*

[For the original text of the translation here see the Notes on the Text, p. 116]

If we look at the context and sense of these lines, we perceive that not only is *fæst* superfluous metrically, but destroys the sense. The poet is speaking of the smashing up of Heorot, not of its strength. It would seem evident, though remarkable, that this passage has been corrupted by reminiscence of *773–5: *þæs fæste wæs / innan ond útan írenbendum / searoþoncum besmiþod* (631–2 'stout was it smithied within and without with bonds of iron cunningly contrived'). There *fæste* is required; and it is from that passage that *fæst* has crept into the text of line *998: it should be removed. We should then read, punctuate and translate thus: *Wæs þæt beorhte bold tóbrocen swíðe / eal inneweard, írenbendum / heorras tohlidene;* 'the shining house was all broken up within; the door-hinges were wrenched away from the iron bars.'

Here the *írenbendum* are the transverse iron bars that go across the door, partly serving to strengthen it and bind together the separate planks or timbers, and partly to carry on their ends the rings or hooks (which fit into or over the hooks on the door-post) – the *heorras*. What is described is probably the forcing of the door outwards in Grendel's efforts to escape, so that the bars bearing the rings were wrenched off the hooks on the posts (the other part of the 'hinges').

817–18   *No easy thing is it to escape – let him strive who will*;
*1002–3 *Nó þæt ýðe byð tó befleonne – fremme sé þe wille*

The general context indicates that it is *death* that is not easy (i.e. impossible) to escape; but *þæt* is indefinite 'it', and does not refer to any previous or following words. A rough modern equivalent would be 'escaping is not easy'. *fremme* does not mean 'try it'; but in order to match 'not easy = impossible' the poet says 'let him who wishes to, achieve it'.

1393   *a mighty sword and old*; *1663 *ealdsweord éacen*

Cf. 1307–8, *1560–1: the sword was so large that no other man but Beowulf could have wielded it. But *éacen* probably means more than this: it had an 'added' [the etymological sense], i.e. supernormal power: as is indeed shown by the fact that it slays monsters who had put an enchantment on all ordinary mortal swords: cf. 654–5, *801–5.

1395–6   *[I slew . . .] the guardians of the house*; *1666. . . *húses hyrdas*

We cannot take a mean grammatical refuge from the charge of 'inconsistency' in the story, by treating this as a 'generic' plural, like *mécum wunde* *565, *bearnum ond bróðrum* *1074. For one thing, they are not good parallels: *mécum* implies sword-thrusts [so in the translation, 461]; *bearnum ond bróðrum* is probably an ancient grammatical 'dual' idiom. [The translation, very oddly, retains the plural, 'of brothers and of sons', 877.] But where is the discrepancy? Grendel received a mortal wound in the wrestling in Heorot and apparently had died miserably on his bed before Beowulf reached his lair. But in *1618–19 we read of Beowulf: *Sóna wæs on sunde sé þe ær æt sæcce gebád / wíghryre wráðra, wæter up þurhdéaf* (1357–9 'Soon was he swimming swift, who had erewhile lived to see his *enemies* fall in war. Up dived he through the water'). Here (*1666) he says that he slew when he got a chance 'the house's *wardens*'. In *1668–9 (1398–9) he says that he carried the hilt away from his *enemies*. Surely only an obstinate desire to find fault could find 'discrepancy' in this, or signs of 'another version of the story'! *1618–19 and *1668–9 are both perfectly true, and in accordance with the story told. At the moment when Beowulf dived back up again he had in fact survived the fall in battle of both his foes, and he did carry the hilt away from the house of Grendel and his dam where both lay dead. In *1666 there is no real discrepancy if we consider (*a*) that *sléan* means 'smite' and Beowulf did in fact cut off Grendel's head 'when he got a chance' (*þá mé sæl ágeald*, *1665), and (*b*) that though 'dead' this was necessary for the final laying of his fell spirit. Consider the trouble that Thorhallr had with

Glámr the *dead* thrall, until Grettir cut his head off and laid it by his thigh.[1]

1416–97; *1687–1784

The whole of this passage is very important for the general criticism of *Beowulf*. We have in 1416–25 (*1687–98) a passage describing the ancient sword-hilt that is most interesting and important – especially with reference to the dating of *Beowulf*, and the blending and fusion of Scripture and pagan northern legend. The archaeological interest is only secondary: for if no swords with runic inscriptions naming their owners had ever been found, the poet plainly describes one, and it is the connexion made between the *eotenas* of the North and the *gigantes* of Scripture that is really significant.

We then have Hrothgar's sermon. In this we have Christian (virtually medieval) motives woven together with the pagan 'exemplum' of Heremod. The use of Heremod as a 'dark contrast' – a 'caution' – by Hrothgar links together the praise after the second deed with that after the first, where Heremod is also introduced.

The 'Christian' part of the sermon is very interesting. It serves to complete (before we finally part from him) the portrait of the patriarchal Hrothgar. But (as we shall see) it raises in very special and acute fashion the questions (*a*) whether our

---

1 [The story of Glámr can be readily found in R.W. Chambers, *Beowulf, An Introduction,* where extracts from the Grettis Saga, with translations, are given.]

'*Beowulf*' has been tinkered with since it was composed: that is, touched up by another poet – I am not speaking of mere scribal corruption and copying; (*b*) whether it was known and imitated by other poets still extant; and (*c*) whether Cynewulf is concerned in either or both of the two preceding processes.

On the question of the *fusion* of Scripture and northern mythology, of Cain-Grendel and the Giants, I have already said what I think in *The Monsters and the Critics*.

The main Scriptural source of the reference to Giants is Genesis vi.4 (possibly connected with iv.22 and the reference to Tubal-Cain (sixth generation in descent from Cain) 'instructor of every artificer in brass and iron'). But as I have said elsewhere the main defect of our criticism is ignorance of the *native* mythology. In Old English we have nothing to go upon, save these same scant and already blended references which we are trying to understand. Outside, we have chiefly Old Norse (preserved late). I do not doubt that English tradition agreed in what one might call the philo sophical principle with Old Norse: the essential hostility of the monsters – even those in more or less human form (giants and trolls) – to the 'humane', or human-divine. But of its more specific details, which would help to explain the fusion, we are ignorant. Did native tradition contain some Flood tradition which would help to explain 1418–19 (*1689–91)? Probably it did.[1] But if so it is lost now – except

---

1 Flood traditions are spread all over the world. Old Norse does not preserve any – the very beautiful reference to the earth rising newly green out of the sea, and the waterfalls pouring off it, while

in *Beowulf* *1689 ff. Such references as *eald enta geweorc* ['the ancient work of giants'] (not confined to *Beowulf*) and *ealdsweord eotonisc* ['old giant-forged sword'] are in themselves enough to show that there was in England an ancient imagination of 'giants', and that on one side they were (in the language of Genesis vi.4) 'mighty men which were of old, men of renown', and also the makers of mighty works beyond human compass. To them were attributed not only wonders of geological origin, nor only relics of bygone masons and smiths, but also works conceived only in the imaginations of poets: human works enlarged and endowed with added power: *éacen*; things of wonder and magic. Yet they hated men, and were enemies. If with Cain, the outlaw and murderer, you associate the ogre-traditions of the North, it is then clear that such references as Genesis iv.22 concerning Tubal-Cain and craftsmanship in brass and iron will fuse with the *ealdsweord eotonisc* tradition. You will find in Grendel's lair *enta ærgeweorc* *1679, ('the work of trolls of old' 1408–9), a sword both of superhuman size and supernatural power, work of the *giganta cyn*, a relic of the Flood: truly an *ealde láfe* (*1688, a 'relic of old days' 1417).[1]

---

the eagle that fishes on the mountain sides flies over it, is not quite in point: in the *Völuspá*, at any rate as we have it, that scene seems to refer to the future after the destruction at the end of the world.

[1]   It is particularly to be observed that the word *gígant* is only used in Old English verse of 'Scriptural' giants in *Beowulf* *113, 91 (Cain's offspring), *1690, 1419 (the Flood), and in the Old English poem *Genesis A*, 1268 – except of the sword in Grendel's lair, which is *gíganta weorc* (*1562, 1308–9).

It is plain that the whole business of fusion, at the upper or mythological end – where contact was closest, Scripture itself being more 'mythological' in its mode of expression – was intricate. But this at least we can say: the fusion (at any rate, that which we find in *Beowulf*) is certainly not that of a pagan who remembers a few items from early sermons. It is the product, as I have said elsewhere,[1] of deep thought and emotion. It is indeed the product of *learning*, of a man or men who could *read* Scripture, who had with their eyes read the Latin words: *Tubalcain qui fuit malleator et faber in cuncta opera aeris et ferri* – and *Gigantes autem erant super terram in diebus illis* [*Genesis* iv.22 and vi.4]. (The very word *gígant* is derived from Latin and equated with *eoten* and *ent*.)[2]

When we pass on to Hrothgar's sermon, we need not overdo the 'learning'. We need not see in *swigedon ealle* 'all were silent' (*1699, 1426) a reminiscence of [the opening lines of] *Æneid* Book II: *Conticuere omnes intentique ora tenebant. Inde toro pater Æneas sic orsus ab alto* ['All were still, and held their gaze intent upon him. Then from his lofty couch father Æneas thus began'].[3] You do not need to read

---

1 [In *The Monsters and the Critics*, p.20 in the collected essays, 1983.]
2 [This subject is continued into a discussion of what the *Beowulf*-poet, even if he could not read Latin, might learn from Old English scriptural poetry, concerning Tubal-Cain the great ancestral metalsmith, or God's punishment of the giants by the Flood (citing the early incomplete poem known as *Genesis A*, 1083 ff. and 1265 ff.)]
3 [It is hard to believe that such a suggestion was ever made, and perhaps it never was.]

Virgil in order to imagine a silence when a venerable king begins a solemn discourse! But we need not, on the other hand, be unduly surprised to find that together with the Bible the poet shows knowledge of a definitely Christian homiletic tradition with an allegorical or symbolic mode of expression – to us 'mediaeval' in flavour.

Yet there is, all the same, something odd here. 'Blending' is naturally again observable. We have the purely Germanic, northern, story of Heremod alluded to, with special reference here to his unprincely crime of greed: *nallas béagas geaf Denum æfter dóme* *1719–20, 'He gave not things of gold unto the Danes to earn him praise' 1443–4. This is neatly paralleled later, in the picture of the generalized 'fortunate man' destroyed by pride, and success corrupted into avarice: *gýtsað gromhýdig, nallas on gylp seleð fætte béagas* *1749–50, 'his grim heart fills with greed; in no wise doth he deal gold-plated rings to earn him praise' 1468–9. Although it would be possible to view this as produced by a homiletic interpolator expanding the moral of *1719–20, I do not personally doubt that the homiletic elaboration of the moral is mainly due to the 'author', that the same hand wrote both *1719–20 and *1749–50, and designed them to echo one another.

There are, however, two things to note. Firstly (a point that does not in itself prove any 'tinkering' by later hands): the 'sermon' or *giedd* is artistically too long, and also is not throughout suitable; it is too 'Christian' in colouring for the good *pre-Christian* patriarch, Hrothgar. This stricture applies especially to the reference to 'conscience' (*sáwele* *hyrde* 'guardian of the soul'), and the allegorical shafts of the evil one (*bona* (*bana*) 'slayer'), *1740–7, 1460–7 – even if we accept as 'Beowulfian' the passage *Wundor is tó secganne* (*1724, 1450) to *hé þæt wyrse ne con* 'he knows nothing of worse fate' (*1739, 1460–1), and also (say) *1753, 1472 onwards, in the course of which the theme of the end of youth and fortune is further elaborated – cf. the close parallel especially to *1761–8, 1479–84 provided by *The Seafarer* 66–71.[1]

But that is not all. There is a quite exceptionally clear – convincing, in fact inescapable – connexion between Hrothgar's sermon *1724–68, 1450–84, and the Old English poem *Crist* 659 ff. and 756–78. The resemblance is one both of *matter* and *turns of expression*, e.g. *þonne wróhtbora . . . onsendeð* of his *brægdbogan biterne strǽl* [*Crist* 763–5, 'when the author of evil . . . sends forth a bitter shaft from his deceitful bow'; beside *Beowulf* *1743–6 *bona swiðe néah, sé þe of flánbogan fyrenum scéoteð. Þonne bið on hreþre under helm

---

1 [In a footnote at this point my father wrote: 'See my lecture Appendix (b).' This is the substantial writing headed *(b) 'Lof' and 'Dom'*; *'Hell'* and *'Heofon'* following the text of *The Monsters and the Critics*, in which he cited, without translation, both the passage from *The Seafarer* and Hrothgar's words referred to here (but with the words *eft sona bið* misprinted as *oft sona bið*); of the latter he said that this was 'a part of his discourse that may certainly be ascribed to the original author of *Beowulf*, whatever revision or expansion the speech may otherwise have suffered.' I give here the passage from *The Seafarer* in translation: 'I do not believe that earthly riches will last for ever. Always one of three things hangs in the balance until man's final hour: sickness or old age or violence of the sword will wrest his life from the doomed and departing.']

drepen biteran strǽle (1463–6).] Indeed it would hardly be too much to say that the 'sermon' from *1724–68 (1450–84) reads and rings often more like the author of *Crist* than that of the author of the rest of *Beowulf*.

The author of *Crist* (certainly of the runic passage (797 ff.) and so almost certainly of what precedes it) was Cynewulf.[1] Among the 'signed' works of Cynewulf are *Elene* and *The Fates of the Apostles*. In these poems there are numerous parallelisms of expression with *Beowulf*. So there are also in other poems: e.g. *Guthlac* (probably not by Cynewulf) and *Andreas* (certainly not). From them we can deduce no more than that *Beowulf* was known and admired by later poets[2] – in itself probable enough. But the feeling (independent of research) that the sermon is overloaded, and partly discrepant in tone and style, is on quite a different footing. I do not doubt that Cynewulf knew and admired *Beowulf* and echoed it, and I am perfectly certain that he did not in general revise or rewrite it: the style, temper, and mind are quite different from his. But I think that Klaeber hits off the conclusions that must be drawn. In the first place, the king's address forms an organic element in the structure of the epic; and that the king should deliver a sermon of 'high sentence' is entirely in keeping with his character as imagined and depicted in the poem, and with the moral and serious

---

1 [See the brief editorial note on Cynewulf's 'signatures' on p. 175.]
2 Not infrequently the only certain deduction is that all the authors were 'Anglo-Saxons' writing within a common literary tradition: a thing we knew already.

temper of *Beowulf* as a whole. But in the second place the most reasonable interpretation of the exact situation and resemblances is, nonetheless, that Cynewulf's own hand has retouched the king's address: has in fact turned it from a *giedd* into a genuine homily.

Why? Because at this point there was the nearest point of contact between the two authors and their thought. Whatever we may think of his taste – I think it, as exhibited in his signed poems, bad at worst and poor at best – Hrothgar probably interested him, and especially the sermon. It was too good an opportunity to be missed – and he took it: not of course observing (it was far beyond him) that by making more explicit the moral, and adorning it with the homiletic allegory of his own day, he was damaging a great work (and one in the long run more profoundly significant and instructive than his own overtly 'Christian' verse).

I think it is indeed likely enough that there are other 'Cynewulfian' touches of improvement in the text of *Beowulf*. The most nearly certain one is *168–9 (134–5).[1] This is not only unsuitable (and obscure because its thought, which runs on 'grace' and damnation, is not really in harmony with the context) but easily detachable; and not only detachable, but its excision an obvious improvement in verse texture and sense.[1] But detachability is not a certain criterion – not if we are really dealing with Cynewulf. He was an eloquent man with a rich *wordhord* and a skilled word-craftsman. He could manage joints all right.

---

1 [These lines are discussed at length on pp. 181 ff.]

Thus if we pass from the general (and I think practically certain) conclusion that a later author has been at work here, to the question of exact detail – what did he do? – we shall not reach any clear result. It is not so much a question of 'interpolation' only as of actual rewriting, which might intricately blend old and new.[1]

1583; *1887

Here ends the 'First Part' of *Beowulf*, with pregnant words, and a moving contrast of Age and Youth. Whether or no (as some have thought) this part was originally meant to be the whole poem, and the second part a later enlargement by the same author, in the economy of the whole poem as we now have it the structure is fairly clear.

The First Part depicts the *rise* of Beowulf, his emergence as a full *hæleþ*: his coming of age, and acquisition of *blæd*, fame and fortune, glorified by the strength and hope of youth. And it is hinted that Beowulf escaped the temptation of *blæd*: he did not fall into arrogance, or greed. But the First Part also foreshadows the coming of old age, the bitter wisdom of experience. It makes it very poignant to find the young proud Beowulf so much like Hrothgar so soon as the Link or Interlude of his return home (1584–1851, *1888–2199) is over. The first words that he speaks are reminiscent: 2041–3 'In youth from many an

---

1 ['However, here is my opinion' my father wrote at this point, and there follows his detailed discussion of the probabilities in different passages; this I have excluded, since it is lengthy, and difficult to follow amid the abundant twofold line-references.]

onslaught of war I came back safe, from many a day of battle. I do recall it all'; *2426–7 *Fela ic on giogoðe gúðrǽsa genæs, orlegh-wíla; ic þæt eall gemon.* Compare Hrothgar, 1485–9, *1769–73. The contrast of Youth and Age – Age and death the inevitable sequel of Youth and triumph seen in the Rise (part I) and Fall (part II) of Beowulf is made far more vivid by thus setting Youth before Age for its judgement.

And finally for us – and I do not doubt also for the poet and his contemporaries – the whole poem is dignified by the connexion with the great Scylding court, the golden House of Heorot glorious and doomed. It gives it what one might call an Arthurian atmosphere and background.

1623   *The fierce mood of Thryth . . .;* *1931 *MS *mod þryðo wæg . . .*

[I give here the passage concerning Hygd, wife of Hygelac king of the Geats, in which these words (one of the most beaten grounds in Old English textual criticism) occur, both in the original text (*1929–32) and in the translation (1621–4).

                    næs hío hnáh swá þéah,
1930   né tó gnéað gifa   Géata léodum,
        máðmgestréona,   mod þryðo wæg
        fremu folces cwén,   firen ondrysne

1621   Yet no niggard was she, nor too sparing of gifts and pre-
        cious treasures to the Geatish men. The fierce mood of
        Thryth she did not show, good queen of men, nor her
        dire wickedness.

In the first part of his very long note my father was concerned to defend his view, shared by several editors of *Beowulf*, of how the words

313

of the manuscript here underlined should be emended and interpreted on textual and linguistic grounds alone (i.e. without reference to the legend of Offa: see 1637 ff., *1949 ff.).]

If we knew no more about Offa and his bride than we do about Hygd it is perfectly clear that we have here another case of *praise by contrast* (compare the way Heremod is introduced, 734, 1435; *901, *1709). We should also by this parallel be led to look for a name (of Offa's queen) at the beginning of a reference to her. Only in *mod þryðo wæg* is there any chance of finding one.

Though transition can be abrupt in *Beowulf* – the transition at 734, *901 is abrupt enough – it is unlikely that Hygd is no more referred to after *máðmgestréona*. It is *possible* only if we read *Módþryðo wæg* with *Módþryðo* as a proper name. The sequence will then be 'Hygd was good, she was not mean. Módþrýðo (once) showed, good queen of her people (as she became later), dreadful wickedness.' The placing of the name abruptly at the very beginning is at least nearly sufficient to give the required sense of 'on the other hand'. But it leaves *fremu folces cwén* very odd indeed – this is not explained until 1634 ff. (*1945 ff.). Moreover among the 150 or so names in Germanic ending in *-þrýþ* (*-truda, -druda, -þrúðr*, &c.) there is nothing elsewhere corresponding to *Módþrýðo*.

[After a further discussion concerning the formal historical difficulties in the assumption of a proper name *Módþrýðo* my father emphatically rejected it, and said that *mód Þrýðo wæg* 'seems the only possible interpretation of the manuscript'. He took *Þrýðo* to be the name *Þrýðe* with the Anglian (Northumbrian) ending *-o* in oblique cases, corresponding to West Saxon *-an*, this *-o* being 'retained by the scribe since he was at sea as to the sense of the passage'. The meaning is therefore 'the temper of Þrýðe (Thryth)'.]

But *mód Þrýðo wæg* makes us say: 'Hygd was good: she showed the temper of Þrýðe, good queen, her grievous wickedness.' This is the opposite of the natural intention of contrast. We are driven to assume that *ne* has fallen out. For the *ne* at the beginning of the contrast see *1709 (1435). In defence of the emendation *mód Þrýðo [ne] wæg* we must observe: *ne* (or any negative particle in any language) appears in *logic* to be overwhelmingly important, exactly reversing sense, so that it is difficult to conceive of its omission. As a matter of fact (i) it is in *writing* a small easily omitted word on mere mechanical grounds, especially as scribes do not follow the detail of sense (and the scribe here, as always when faced with legendary names, was plainly at sea); (ii) even in speech it is often reduced to a very fugitive element in spite of continual linguistic renewal, and even then is sometimes accidentally omitted.

[With these remarks on the dropping of negative particles cf. p. 263. – The meaning of the passage as emended thus is given in this note: 'Hygd was not mean. The mood of Þrythe she, good queen of her people, did not show: her grievous wickedness.' It will be seen that this is very close to the wording in my father's translation given at the beginning of this note.]

Following this discussion he turned to the intricate question of the legends of the wife of Offa – there being two kings of that name: Offa king of Mercia in the eighth century, ('Offa II'), and Offa king of Angel (the ancient home of the Angles in Schleswig), ('Offa I'), supposed to be the far distant ancestor of Offa of Mercia. I cite here only his concluding remarks on the subject of 'Offa's wife'. Following from his consideration of the view that the story of the wicked wife of Offa II originally belonged to Offa of Angel he continued:]

This I think is enough to show that in 'historial legend' Offa of Angel, the reputed (and probably actual) ancestor of Offa of Mercia had a matrimonial legend. That his wife was called Þrýþ (or Þrýðe), Latinized later as *Drida*. Of her the original story was of the *Atalanta* type: the perilous maiden who destroys all weakling suitors, but is at last conquered by a strong man, and then becomes a good wife.

Why is it put in here? Of course – according to the method we have already observed in Sigemund and Heremod – as a method of enhancing and pointing praise or blame. Yet it is more 'dragged in', or so it appears at first sight, than any other of the 'episodes'. Sigemund and his dragon-victory have an organic and ironic fitness as a comparison with young Beowulf who is to be slain by a dragon. Heremod is a Dane and connected with Sigemund on the one hand, and on the other a good concrete illustration of the vices that Hrothgar is preaching against. The *Fréswæl* [the 'Finn episode'] (as I have laboured to show) is closely connected with the Scyldings, and the house of Healfdene.

Now the connexion (even with the replaced negative advocated above) between Hygd and Þrýðe is somewhat abrupt. Still it cannot be shown that the Offa passage in *Beowulf is* later than the rest, or contemporary with Offa II. The idea that it is a covert contemporary allusion is certainly to be dismissed. Not only because it is far from covert if contemporary with a king called Offa: its author if he escaped with his head would soon have found himself a wandering minstrel looking for a new patron. But because in history Offa's queen was like Hygd and not like Þrýðe at all.

If the Offa-story is an elaboration and addition at all, it is one made by the author himself. Why he thought it fitting – and he probably did feel it to have some kind of fitness (such as we can see in Heremod and Finn and Sigemund): he was not as has been supposed a mere dragger-in of old tales – we can probably not now discover in our ignorance of that great nexus of interwoven 'historial legend', concerning English origins, and the great royal and noble houses, which he possessed.

1633–4 *he of Hemming's race [Offa] made light of that*; *1944 *Húru þæt onhohsnode[c] Hemminges mæg*

[My father thought it probable that Hemming was Offa's maternal grandfather. The translation depends on the etymology proposed for the unrecorded *onhohsnode*. The common rendering 'put a stop to it' assumes the existence of a verb unrecorded in Old English *(on)hohsin(w)ian*, derived from *hohsinu* 'hamstring' ('*hock-sinew*'), supposedly here in a figurative sense 'to stop, restrain'. In the course of a long and detailed discussion of cognate forms in other Germanic languages my father rejected this as 'a violent and unlikely metaphor', and noted that 'nowhere have we found anything but a literal meaning to "hamstring" a horse.' 'What has this got to do with the tale?' he said, teasing the proponents of this etymology, 'even the racing Atalanta was not vanquished by being hamstrung!' [Atalanta in Greek mythology was a huntress who would marry no man who could not defeat her in a race, and if a suitor defeated her he was put to death.)

He himself favoured, very hesitantly, another proposed etymology, that of an unrecorded verb *(on-hoxnian)*, related in some way to Old English *husc, hux* 'scorn, derision' and the verb *hyscan*; hence his translation 'made light of that'. He concluded the note with a translation of the passage in a different style:]

Nonetheless the descendant of Hemming (Offa) laughed at all this, and men in the hall (gossiping over their ale) added that she committed fewer (i.e. no more) crimes from the moment that she became the gold-decked bride of the young warrior.

1666–7   *to the hands of mighty men*; *1983 MS *hæ[ð]num tó handa*

[In the manuscript the word reads *hæ num*, the third letter, ð, which can still be read, having been erased by the scribe. In my father's translation he added at the time of typing a footnote to *mighty men*: 'or *Hæðenas*, name of a people'.]

What does the manuscript mean, and what is the reason for the erasure? It is easy to rewrite the text and substitute *hæleðum*. But it is quite incredible as a solution, and does not explain the manuscript. The erasure (never put right) shows that the scribe was bothered – and it is more than likely that we have once again a *proper name* belonging to heroic tradition. Since the scribe first wrote *hæðnum*, had he really been preparing the way for a correction *hæleðum* (incidentally a common word that he nowhere else bungles) we should expect him to have erased either *n* (so as to insert *le* before ð over the line) or both ð and *n*.

Also, there is a proper name *Hǽðne*. It occurs in the poem *Widsith* (line 81), *(ic wæs) mid Hæðnum*. As far as *Widsith* goes, these people can hardly be doubted to be the Old Norse *Heiðnir*, later (with regular loss in Old Norse of ð before *n*), *Heinir*, dwellers in the *Heiðmörk* (modern

Hedemarken) in Norway on the Swedish border. The erasure may be due (1) to its being identical in form with *hǽðen* 'heathen', a word of special evil associations in A.D.1000 (the scribe's time) and not good associations for the virtuous Hygd – but why not then erase the whole word? Or (2) to the existence in Old English of a form *Hǽne* (with a similar change to that seen in Old Norse or to actual knowledge of the later Norse form). (1) is hardly likely without (2). I should restore *Hǽðnum*.

Editors ask: why should this folk appear in Hygelac's hall? The answer is probably provided by *Widsith* 81 and a consideration of other stories. The *Hǽðne* were Hygd's own people, and just as Danes were in the Heathobard court as retainers of the Danish queen Freawaru daughter of Hrothgar (1697 ff., *2020 ff.), so *Hǽðne* were at the court of Hygelac in attendance on Queen Hygd.

Widsith line 81 reads: *(ic wæs) mid hæðnum ond mid hæleþum ond mid hundingum*. Quite apart from comparison with *Beowulf* a likely emendation of *mid hæleþum* is *mid hæreþum*: the corruption of a proper name to a common noun of similar form is well evidenced (cf. *Cain* to *camp*, *1261, *Eomer* to *geomor* *1960, etc. in *Beowulf*). But when immediately before *hæðnum* in *Beowulf* we find *Hæreðes dohtor* (1664, *1981) the connexion between *Widsith* 81 and *Beowulf* becomes extremely probable.

The *Hærede* are the Norwegian tribe *Hǫrðar* (stem *harud*), cf. Hardanger-fjord – incidentally there is a reference in an entry in the Anglo-Saxon Chronicle (787) to the first coming of the Norsemen in three ships 'from Hereða land'. The use of the stem of a tribal name as a proper name among neighbours is a common phenomenon: as modern Scott, Inglis, Walsh. The actual relation of *Hæreð* father of Hygd (presumably a prince of the *Hǽðne*) to the *Hæreþe* cannot now be discovered.

Though the passage is obscure (because we do not know what the poet assumes to be known) and also corrupt, we do observe that Hygd had, or was given by our author, a *place* in the real geographical northern world. Her name is odd (nowhere else recorded in itself, and there is no other record of the name of Hygelac's queen): it alliterates with her husband's, and is etymologically related to it: *Hygd* (cf. *ge-hygd* 'thought') / *Hyge-lac*. But it also alliterates with her father's name. I think that the fact that it has an 'abstract' look is fortuitous. Women's names were frequently made from abstract words; occasionally they occur uncompounded, as *Hild* 'war', *Þrýþ* 'strength'. After all, *Hyge-lac* might be interpreted as 'play of mind', yet he is no abstraction: there can be no reasonable doubt that he is an historical Geatish king of the sixth century called *Hugila(i)k*.

It cannot, however, be denied that our poet's account of Hygelac is a little peculiar, and not free from suspicion of being confused with that of Hrethel (and *vice versa*).

He is a *geongne gúðcyning* (*1969, 'the young warrior-king' 1654), at the date of Beowulf's return. His wife is *swíðe geong* (*1926, 'very young' 1619), and so probably not long married, though long enough to have shown herself a generous patroness. Her son Heardred is too young to govern when Hygelac falls in Frisia (1996–2001, *2370–6). Yet when Hæthcyn son of Hrethel fell before King Ongentheow of Sweden, we learn that Hygelac (the surviving son) came up with reinforcements (2471–4, *2943–5) and Ongentheow fell to the sword of Eofor, Hygelac's thane. Eofor was rewarded with land and treasure (2514–16, *2993–5) and the hand of Hygelac's *only daughter* (2518–19, *2997). Cf. 'to Eofor he gave his only daughter . . . for the honouring of his house' with Hrothgar on Beowulf: 'His sire of old was called Ecgtheow; to him Hrethel of the Geats gave as bride his only daughter' (300–1, *373–5). Two only daughters in the family each given to (somewhat obscure) retainers![1]

The usual calculations make Hrethel roughly contemporary with Healfdene (fifth century) and Hrethel's three sons and one daughter therefore roughly contemporary with Healfdene's three sons and one daughter (see 46–9, *59–63), so Hygelac ought to be about the same age as Halga the third son of Healfdene, and not much younger than Hrothgar. Yet Hrothgar is represented as an old man bowed with years and full of regretful reminiscence; while Hygelac is a *bregoróf cyning* (*1925, 1618) actually called 'young' (1654, *1969), with a very young wife.

This contrast can be partly explained by the nature and limits of 'historial legend'. The main lines of the traditional characters of ancient historical lays were very much dependent on the circumstances of their *death*. A character once

---

1   [On this see the note to 301.]

fixed tends to appear thus at all times when he comes on the stage. Arthur is usually young and eager for novelty. Victoria becomes indelibly fixed by the great act of living and reigning so long as an old and widowed queen. In 'historial legend' of the Anglo-Saxon kind any young knight who visited the court of England within, say twenty or thirty years of her death would be likely to find upon the throne a small but venerable figure in black, with white hair. Hygelac on the other hand died in the field as a still vigorous warrior, leaving his heir a minor.

Nonetheless it soon becomes apparent that 'his only daughter' married to Eofor after *Hrefnesholt* [Ravenswood, 2464, *2935] cannot be the daughter of Hygd. Hygd must be a second wife. And the more we try to separate Hygelac from Hrothgar in age (and the younger we make Hygelac die) the more impossible is it for him to have a marriageable daughter to give to Eofor. In fact almost the only difficulty in working out a satisfactory chronology to fit the *Beowulf* statements is *either* Hygd's extreme youth *or* the only daughter. Something seems to have gone a bit wrong with the 'history' of Hygelac.[1]

---

1 [I omit here my father's further and detailed speculations on the chronology, taking it up again with what he considered a 'reasonable' chronology. On the inclusion of Beowulf he remarked: 'Whether "historical" or not does not matter; Beowulf has been fitted into the dynastic chronology by the poet presumably not without some thought, or by traditions older than the poet.' In the following he changed the dates a good deal, and I give the final ones.]

425		Birth of Healfdene
440	~	Ongentheow
455	~	Hrothgar
465	~	Onela
465	~	Hrothgar's sister
475	~	Hygelac
495 *or later*	~	Beowulf

Ongentheow was slain at *Hrefnesholt* at the age of 65 in A.D. 505. Hygelac was then 30. If he had a daughter she was a child of about seven.

Beowulf visited Heorot c. 515. Hrothgar was then actually old, being 60.

Hygelac married Hygd (a second wife?) about 510; he was 35 and Hygd only about 18. Heardred was born about 511. Hygd was still only about 23 at the time of Beowulf's return. Hygelac was 40.

Hygelac fell in Frisia c. 525 at the age of 50. Heardred was a minor (about 14): Beowulf was then a tried warrior of 30.

It is a possible explanation that the tradition of the *ánge dohtor* really belongs to Hrethel; but that the intrusion of Beowulf (unhistorical at any rate as an actual member of the Geatish royal house) by our poet, or the blending of 'historial legend' and folk-story in the traditions he knew, has confused matters. It is very likely nearer to 'history' that it was Hrethel's *ánge dohtor*, Hygelac's sister, that Hygelac gave in marriage to Eofor. (Ecgtheow has replaced Eofor and caused duplication of the 'only daughter'.)

FREAWARU AND INGELD

1697–1739; *2020–69

In these lines we have the fifth[1] of the main 'episodes' in *Beowulf*, and the most difficult and important after Finn and Hengest. In a sense it is not an 'episode', or allusion, but an essential part of the Danish half of the scene, as the references to the Swedish-Geatish wars and the fall of Hygelac are of the Geatish half.

The purposes of the passage are clearer than in any other case: it completes the picture of Heorot; it links the Danish and Geatish halves of the scene (for this reference to the troubles of the court of Heorot is actually spoken in Hygelac's hall), and it gives a peculiarly realistic touch to the whole background. Beowulf reports to the king (in the manner of an ambassador) what he has seen and learned concerning dynastic politics in the south. It is a most ingenious and 'historial' use of tradition, selected, as we shall see, with careful attention to chronology. Finally, it illustrates Beowulf himself. The story is all told in the future; and on the whole that device is nearly successful – if we allow a large measure of sagacity to Beowulf, not only in considering court-gossip, and judging the character of kings and queens,

---

1 Or the first continued; since the matter is alluded to already in 65–9, *81–5. The others are Sigemund; Heremod; Finn and Hengest; Offa.

but in foreseeing how old retainers are likely to behave. And it is told in this way precisely so that Beowulf should show kingly sagacity and fitness for rule, not merely great physical strength. For all knew that what he *predicted* did come to pass. This element of political wisdom combined with valour has already been alluded to by Hrothgar in 1546 ff., *1844 ff., praising Beowulf for seizing the opportunity of proposing and promising an *alliance* between Geats and Danes, who had formerly been hostile.

Altogether a very justifiable 'episode', admirably conceived for the purposes of the present poem (and quite undeserving of the strictures that have been passed on it). Its only weakness, in fact, is that the 'egging' of the old *æscwiga* (1715 ff., *2041 ff.) is too precise in detail, too clearly taken from a lay concerning what *did* happen, to be really suitable to a genuine 'forecast'.

Purely accidental weaknesses for us (for which the poet could not be blamed) are the dubious places in the surviving text, and the fact that we do not know in detail the story to which he was alluding. We know that it *was* well-known, so that an allusive reference would be quite enough for the poet's purpose. But we have to piece much scattered evidence together to make out now what it is all about.

The whole business of the Heathobards and their feud with the house of Healfdene is of the greatest importance and interest: going to the very heart of early Danish (and English) history. But I must limit myself on this occasion more or less to what is essential to the *Beowulf* reference, and in particular to Freawaru and Ingeld.

Let us first see what can be made out from the passage in *Beowulf.* From this we learn (1697–1702, *2020–5) that Freawaru was Hrothgar's daughter, and that she was betrothed to Ingeld the son of Froda: which means according to ancient Northern custom that the marriage-feast, probably at Heorot (the house of the bride's father) was imminent (at the time of Beowulf's visit) and its date already fixed: hence the talk in the hall about it was natural. We learn that Hrothgar accounted the match wise politically (*þæt ræd talað* *2027, 'accounts it policy' 1703), and hoped by it to set a long feud to rest. Note that this does not necessarily mean, though it might mean, that Hrothgar had initiated the match. Since the poet immediately passes to consideration of a people called *Heaðobeardan* and a fatal battle (1714–15, *2039–40), it is plain that Ingeld and Froda are Heathobards, and that the stage of the feud that preceded the moment chosen by the poet was a disastrous defeat of the Heathobards by the Danes. Though not explicitly stated, it seems certain that among the fathers of the present generation of Heathobards who were then slain and despoiled was the king Froda himself, Ingeld's father. It is to settle the bloodfeud which Ingeld has against him that Hrothgar favours the match.

From 1715 (*2041) we have a prophetic utterance – actually a sketch based on lays dealing with the affair as history – concerning the failure of the match and the reawakening of the feud. It is plain that Freawaru took with her to Ingeld's hall a retinue of Danes. Whether they actually behaved arrogantly or not, several of them gave offence by wearing swords (and probably other treasures) won in the old battle from the fathers of men in Ingeld's court. Strife is thus renewed. An old grim retainer (of the sort that can still be met: more zealous for the honour of the house than the master) eggs a young man, until he kills one of the Danes who wears his father's trappings. The Heathobard escapes, and the truce is broken on both sides.

The slayer is plainly *not* Ingeld (*mín wine* *2047 [translated 'my lord' 1721] can mean just 'my friend': cf. *wine mín Unferð* *530, 432–3), since it would appear plain that Ingeld's personal feud was against the Danish *king*, not just one of the young knights; and also the important lines 1735–7, *2064–6, show him struggling between love of wife and the old feud.

It would appear that a Dane or Danes retaliated by slaying a Heathobard, and then Ingeld was drawn in. Beyond that point the 'episode' does not take us. We can see that it is founded on a pretty extensive story or historial legend, slow-moving, detailed, and with many actors in the English manner, and not contracted, concentrated and intensely personal in the Norse manner.

What happened later can be guessed from the allusion in lines *81–5, 65–9, where it is clear that Heorot was doomed to flames, when a deadly feud between father-in-law and son-in-law should be re-aroused. The statement that Heorot had been so well builded that the Danes thought that nothing but fire could destroy it (635–9, *778–82) is also probably an allusion to the fact that tradition recorded its final destruction by burning.

There are two other allusions from English sources to this story. From *Widsith* 45–9 we learn that Ingeld was actually defeated at Heorot and the might of the Heathobards there destroyed. Combined with *Beowulf* *81–5 this shows that Ingeld must suddenly have taken up the feud again and made a descent on Hrothgar, that Heorot was destroyed by fire, but that nonetheless the Heathobards were utterly defeated. Ingeld must have been slain. What was the fate of the hapless Freawaru we do not know.

The other 'English' allusion is found in one version of a letter from Alcuin [a celebrated Northumbrian theologian and man of learning] (A.D. 797 – close, that is, to the probable date of the composition of *Beowulf*) – to Speratus Bishop of Lindisfarne. Alcuin says: *Verba dei legantur in sacerdotali convivio; ibi decet lectorem audiri non citharistam, sermones patrum non carmina gentilium. Quid Hinieldus cum Christo?* [In the rectory of the monks the words of God should be read; there it is fitting that the reader be heard, not the harper, the discourse of the Fathers, not the songs of the pagans. What has Ingeld to do with Christ?] This interesting passage tells us no more for our present purpose than that Ingeld's name was probably pronounced *Injeld*, and that lays concerning him must have been extremely popular for him to be thus singled out as the typical pagan hero. For general criticism it tells us a good deal more. Alcuin is rebuking monks for listening to native English lays sung to the harp, and for still taking an interest in pagan kings who are now lamenting their sins in hell. This rebuke is, of course, evidence of the existence at once of a stern and uncompromising reforming spirit, and of laxity (probably culpable laxity for monks). But it shows at any rate the possibility of the combination of Latin and vernacular learning in the eighth century. There is also a *via media* which, no less Christian than Alcuin, yet does not consign all the past to oblivion (or to hell), but ponders it with increased insight and profundity. This is the way of the poet who wrote *Beowulf.* More regretfully he refers to the men of old being ignorant of God.[1]

In tradition Heorot seems to have been remembered specially as a centre of pagan worship. We may suspect that this is of importance in the feud and battles that raged round this site, that the feud was indeed a battle for the possession of a sanctuary [on this see the note on *æt hærgtrafum,* pp. 179–80.] But beyond this the purely English evidence will not take us.

[My father wrote here: 'To consider the Norse sources would take us too far afield', but having said this he proceeded to do so (and added the words 'in full' after 'Norse sources'). I give this section of 'Freawaru and Ingeld' in a somewhat abbreviated form.]

We touch in this conflict, and in the legends about it, on something very old and central to the nearly forgotten history of the Germanic North in heathen times. All but the final stages are already dim and remote in early Old English traditions. In Norse the whole matter has been confused and distorted by the adoption and 'Danification' of traditions that were not in origin Danish (nor Scandinavian?) but belonged to the peninsula and islands of what we may call (for lack of a better word) the Anglo-Frisian peoples, expelled or absorbed by the Danes in the early centuries of our era.

---

1 [It is difficult to know how to interpret this observation, in the light of the discussion in the note to 135–50 (*170–88).

In particular the naif attempt of later chroniclers to accommodate them all in a unilinear Danish royal line has had many ridiculous results: not least the conversion of old wars of peoples into parricide and fratricide among Skiöldung kings and their sons. In addition all that relates to the older heroic world has in Norse been overlaid and obscured by the specially Scandinavian sub-heroic period or Viking-age. An age that was in many ways, though later, not an advance but a relapse into violence and barbarism: a triumph of Oðinn and the ravens,[1] of bloodshed for its own sake, over the gods of corn and fruitfulness [the Vanir]. This is symbolized in surviving Norse mythology itself by the war of Oðinn and the Æsir with Njörðr [the father of Frey and Freyja] and the Vanir.

The Heathobards are specially associated with peace.[2] With the name of *Fróda*, in Norse *Fróði*, *friðr* ['peace'] is peculiarly joined. In the background of tradition lies the great peace, the *Fróðafriðr*, in which there was corn in plenty and no war or robbery.[3] Now the later Scandinavian sources have obviously doubled and trebled, and even more greatly multiplied, the number of Frothos and Ingelli (Ingjalds) in their Danish

---

1   And of the warrior lord of hosts, descendants of Ódin, with his tombs and dead and Valhöll of the mighty slain, over the priest-king and the temple and the farmer and master of flocks.

2   Although in *Beowulf* and in *Widsith* as opponents of the Danes they bear the prefix *Heaðo-*. This probably means 'war'. But this is an 'epic addition', relating to the Danish conflict, and also enabling them to alliterate with the H~ of the Scyldings' names.

3   So it is said of Fróði by Snorri Sturluson in the *Skáldskaparmál* 43 that in the time of the *Fróðafriðr* no man did harm to another, and there were no thieves, so that a gold ring lay for three years beside the highway on Jalangsheath.

line, merely in the effort to accommodate varying stories. But Heathobard tradition must nevertheless have contained at least two Fródas: one the historical father of their last king Ingeld, and one the remoter (perhaps mythical) ancestor: the Fróda of the Great Peace. The tradition of the Great Peace may be no more than a legendary way of symbolizing a powerful rule, in which (say) the Heathobards were leaders of a confederacy with some religious centre; or it may be in origin mythological: a representation as a dynastic ancestor of the God of the cult and of the Golden Age. Both may well be combined.

Our story refers to the time of the beginnings of Scandinavian expansion and trouble in the islands. Just as the story of Hóc and Hnæf and Hengest reflects the incursion of Danes into Jutland and the peninsula, the Heathobard story depicts their seizure of Seeland, the centre of that world and the seat of its cult. And Seeland has remained ever since the heart of Denmark. There are still Hleiðr – now the village of Leire, and Roskilde, the Canterbury of Denmark, as well as the modern commercial capital Copenhagen: *Kaupmannahöfn* ['haven of the merchants']. It was not a religious war: the Odinic cults of Viking times (which now bulk so large in our imagination of the North) had hardly arisen. It was an attempt to seize the centre of the Anglo-Frisian world, and to conquer it – and it succeeded, and was no doubt a prime factor in the westward migration. The conquests legendarily ascribed to Scyld (the eponymous ancestor) belong doubtless in history to Healfdene or his real father.[1]

---

1 [With the following passage in the text cf. pp. 179–80.]

And we see the Danes of this house taking on the cultus: they are called *Ingwine*. The third son of Healfdene is *Halga* 'the holy', and Hrothgar's daughter is named after Frey 'the lord': *Freawaru*. It is probably not by chance nor by mere invention of our poet (though the precise form of blending is only found in the *exordium*) that we find in the ancestry of the house of Healfdene, blended with the heraldic military eponym Scyld, the corn hero *Sceaf*, and *Beowulf* I, certainly an alteration (or corruption) of *Beow* 'barley' [see the note to line 14]. And we may note that in *Widsith Sceafa* 'Sheaf' is king of the Langobards. The connexion of Langobards and Heathobards is most probable. The Heathobards cannot be identical with the Langobards or Lombards, who had already migrated far from the North in the second century B.C. But they may represent the people from whom the Langobards sprang. There are many instances of names remaining in the North in the old homes while migrant elements (such as Rugii, Goths and Vandals) bore the names far away south.

The struggle for the control of Seeland and the sanctuary and holy site of Hleiðr (where the great hall of Heorot was built) give point to the bitter feud. Coming down to the end of the struggle (remembered in historical or semihistorical legends and lays) we may infer (I think) that the Danes remained in possession while Healfdene lived; and that this old fierce king lived to a great age and died untouched by avenging swords. The tradition of his *atrocitas* and of his great age – exactly answering to the Old English epithets *gamol ond guðreouw* [see the note to line 44] – is still attached to him in Norse, even when he is quite cut off from all his true connexions. Even the Old English adjective *héah* is echoed.

But the Heathobards were not destroyed, and there was evidently a period in which they recovered. It is possible that among the stories in the late Norse sources there linger traces of ancient tradition, when we hear of the ill-treatment of Hróarr and Helgi by King Fróði. Heorogar is only remembered in English. We learn that he died a long way back when Hrothgar was young (375–9, *465–9). His death is almost certainly connected with Heathobard revival. Whether Hrothgar's assertion that even in youth he ruled 'a spacious realm' (376–7, *ginne ríce* *466) be true or not, it is probable that the Danes lost control of Hleiðr. But the Heathobards were again heavily defeated, this time clearly by Hrothgar. The note of senility and desire for peace (produced by the poet's painting of him as an old man at the end of a long reign) must not delude us into regarding him as mere peacemaker and consolidator of an inherited power. There are many hints to the contrary. His warlike youth is alluded to (847–50, *1040–2). He had to fight to re-establish himself when he succeeded his brother Heorogar. In particular it may be noted that it was after a great victory that he set up his seat and built Heorot, 50 ff., *64 ff. – *þá wæs Hróðgáre herespéd gyfen*. This, I think, was clearly the great battle (alluded to in the Freawaru episode) in which Fróda was slain. Hrothgar retook Hleiðr and again became lord of a confederacy (as Healfdene, and in legend Scyld, had been). On this coveted site he built his great hall.

We cannot expect perfectly consistent chronology in an epic based on many lays concerning matters some three hundred years before; and certainly the conception of Hrothgar as an old and venerable king has disturbed it. So too doubtless has the intrusion of the legendary Grendel. As far as our poem goes, we learn that there was a period (undefined) in which Hrothgar dwelt in Heorot in splendour. How soon Grendel came to disturb this we are not told (though the suggestion is that it was soon): precision is not to be expected when fairy-story intrudes upon historial legend. But we are told that Grendel raided Heorot for twelve years (118, *twelf wintra tíd* *147, = 'many a year' 122–3, *fela misséra* *153).[1] Now if I am right in supposing that Heorot was built after the overthrow of Froda (and that the poet was referring in line

---

[1] During which time recourse was had to heathen sacrifice. I believe on various grounds that that passage *175–188 (139–50), in particular *180 ff. (143 ff.), has been touched up and expanded [see the note to 135–50]; but ultimately the discrepancy between the patriarchal, god-fearing Hrothgar and this account is due to the material. Heorot was a site associated specially with heathen religion: *blót* [Old Norse: worship, sacrificial feast]. The actual legends or lays descending from pagan times, which our poet used, probably made a considerable point of the *blót* to gain relief at this juncture in the story. *Hleiðr* (*Hleiðrargarðr*) is (I think) to be connected with Gothic *hleiþra* a tent or tabernacle. In which case it is practically identical in sense with *hærgtrafum* *175 (140). [See pp. 179–80.]

It is to be expected from the fact that the English traditions are far older than the Norse that they should have preserved far better the individual *names*, but should have lost the geography from which they were now removed; while Norse far later has confused names and relations but has preserved the geography: English does not mention Seeland or Leire; Norse has forgotten Heorogar and Heorot.

50–1, *64–5 to the battle mentioned in 1714–15, *2039–40) this period will be just about right. It looks as if the poet knew from tradition how long a time elapsed between the building of Heorot and the marriage of Freawaru, and therefore could give (and had to give) a fairly precise number of years. If Grendel haunted Heorot, it must be before the last outbreak of the Heathobard feud and the destruction of Heorot, and the haunting must occupy a slightly shorter time. This also dictated the placing of Beowulf's visit (and the end of the haunting) at a time just before the Heathobard affair. [See the note to line 65 ff.] We see thus that the allusion of Beowulf to Freawaru's betrothal has also a chronological fitness and purpose. At the date of his visit Ingeld is betrothed but not married. That he did not fall with his father in the battle indicates that he was at the date of the battle very young. Fifteen years (about) have since elapsed (including twelve years of Grendel's hauntings): he was then about ten, he is now about twenty-five. This fits excellently.

Note. The reasonableness and historical air of the chronology when we are considering the traditions concerning Heorot and the Heathobards is only enhanced by the contrast with the inexactitude in 1485, *1769, where (in order to point the moral of pride going before a fall with the example of Grendel, and in order to heighten his picture of the venerable age of the patriarchal king) the poet makes Hrothgar say that he had enjoyed *hund misséra* (literally 50 years, ['a hundred half-years']) of prosperity before Grendel came. Whether applied to the period before the building of Heorot, or to the first peaceful glory of Heorot, or to both, this is of course impossible.

Now we come to the actual story of Freawaru and Ingeld. Comparison of the quite independent English and Norse traditions shows that two things are common to both and therefore 'original': the egging of the old retainer, and the love motive. But the Norse (as seen in e.g. Saxo) is altered: it may be called dramatic and intense, if you will. Rather it is theatrical, and certainly brutalized. It may be a dramatic gain to make Ingeld the object of the 'egging', and to make him the slayer and truce-breaker.[1] But certainly such an Ingeld: a profligate whose 'repentance' was shown by murdering the guests at his board, would not have become the hero of English minstrelsy. But that we here have that very rare thing in ancient northern legend (and almost unique thing in

---

1   [On Saxo see the note to line 44. In his grotesque account the story of Ingeld (Ingellus) is radically changed. His father Frotho was treacherously slain, but 'the soul of Ingellus was perverted from honour'; and Saxo describes this debauched monster of gluttony and sloth in a slow torrent of denunciation. Ingellus married the daughter of Swerting his father's murderer, and treated his sons as dear friends. But learning of this state of affairs the ancient and somewhat gruesome warrior Starkad came to the hall of Ingellus and delivered so devastating a condemnation of his conduct that there was roused in Ingellus a spirit of revenge, and he sprang up and slew the sons of Swerting as they sat at the banquet.

My father's remarks were evidently made in response to Klaeber's observation: 'Compared with the *Beowulf*, Saxo's version marks a dramatic advance . . . in that Ingellus himself executes the vengeance, whereas in the English poem the slaying of one of the queen's attendants by an unnamed warrior ushers in the catastrophe.']

what survives in ancient English): a love-story, is clear from the survival of this element (however transmuted) in Norse as well as English. In Norse the love of Ingeld becomes, in the fierce and brutalized Viking atmosphere, degraded, a sign of softness and wantonness; no man should ever have given way to it and been forgetful of the duty of murder. Not so in English. The love is a good motive, and the strife between it and the call of revenge for a slain father is held to be a genuine tragic conflict – otherwise Ingeld's story would not be heroic at all, and certainly not one that any minstrel would have sold for a single dragon (let alone a Shylockian wilderness).[1] But the love referred to is passionate love, not the mere reverence for queen and consort and the mother of the royal children. The general suggestion of the tale in (Norse and English) is that the tragedy occurred soon after the marriage. And this brings us to a point in the story that the English evidence does not explain. How was the love of Ingeld and Freawaru brought about – in the story? – not in history (where the match may well have occurred, and have been purely 'political' on both sides).[2] Was the story here 'romantic': a chance

---

1 [The reference is to *The Monsters and the Critics*, p. 11, where my father quoted Professor R.W. Chambers in his edition of *Widsith*, p. 79: 'in this conflict between plighted truth and the duty of revenge we have a situation which the old heroic poets loved, and would not have sold for a wilderness of dragons'. The reference to Shylock is to *The Merchant of Venice*, III.i.112: 'I would not have given it for a wilderness of monkeys.']

2 It has been noted above (p. 326) that *þæt ræd talað* (*2027) does not prove the match to have been devised and planned by Hrothgar, but only that he saw the political advantage of it.

meeting, a disguised prince spying out the enemy's stronghold; or more realistic: an embassy, an invitation to Heorot under safe conduct, and a feast in which the beautiful princess captivated Ingeld's heart, as *eorlum on ende ealuwæge bær*? (*2021, 1698–9). We cannot tell. The last is, I think, (for Old English) probable. It is possible that 'myth' has here again touched 'historial legend', just as the traditions of the golden age gathered about the name of Fróda (see pp. 330–1). For it is impossible not to be struck by the fact that the pair of lovers: *Fréawaru* and *Ingeld* both bear names including a Frey-element (*Frea* and *Ing*); and that Frey fell hopelessly in love with the daughter of his enemies: Gerðr the daughter of the giant Gymir. Yet this does not prove either Ingeld or Freawaru or their love wholly 'mythical'. History has a way of resembling 'myth': partly because both are ultimately of the same stuff. If no young man had ever fallen in love at first sight, and found old feuds to lie between him and his love, the god Frey would never have seen Gerðr. At the same time such a love is more likely really to arise in a people and family whose traditions are of Frey and the Vanir rather than of Odin the Goth.

1708 ff.; *2032 ff.

[My father's discussion of the difficult lines *2032 ff. in the episode of Freawaru and Ingeld is best understood if the Old English text is set out together (in Klaeber's punctuation) with his translation as given in this book.

> Mæg þæs þonne ofþyncan   ðéodne Heaðo-Beardna
> ond þegna gehwám   þára léoda,
> þonne he mid fæmnan   on flett gæð:

2035   dryhtbearn Dena, duguða biwenede;
       on him gladiað gomelra láfe,
       heard ond hringmǽl Heaða-Beardna gestréon,
       þenden hie ðám wǽpnum wealdan móston,
       oð ðæt hie forlǽddon tó ðám lindplegan
2040   swǽse gesíðas ond hyra sylfra feorh.
       Þonne cwið æt béore se ðe béah gesyhð,
       eald æscwiga, se ðe eall geman . . .

1708 This, maybe, will in that purposed time displease the
Heathobardish king and each knight of that folk,
when one walks down their hall beside the lady, a
noble scion of the Danes amid their host (*passage
corrupt and doubtful*). On him will gaily gleam
things prized by their sires of old, a stout sword ring-
adorned once treasure of the Heathobards, while yet
their weapons they could wield, until they led their
comrades dear and their own lives to ruin in the clash
of shields. Then will one speak at the ale, seeing that
costly thing, a soldier old who remembers all . . .

I am unable to explain the phrase in line 1708 'in that purposed time.']

*2034 Here as in *2054 we have MS gǽð. It is the rather
absurd convention not to emend this but mark it with a
circumflex gêð: though emendation is just as much required
here as in the case of any other scribal substitution of unmet-
rical synonyms or dialectic equivalents. We require gangeð.

*2035 This line – the only really difficult and dubious
one in the episode – admits of very many interpretations (if
emendation is allowed), and even if the silly ones are dis-
carded there is still an unfortunately wide choice. No one
could call Klaeber's note *2034 ff. crystal clear! However,
matters can be a little simplified if you start with a prefer-
ence for reasonable syntax, and a belief that this was also

preferred by the poets. Here is a shot at translating the context:

'It may then give offence to the king of the Heathobards and to all the lords of that people on that occasion when he walks into the hall with the lady, a noble scion of the Danes ?amid a company of tried warriors? (reading *bi werede* [*werod* 'company'] for *biwenede*): on them will gaily gleam the heirlooms of old men (i.e. of the previous generation, the fathers of those present), hard and ring-adorned, the Heathobards' own possessions, while still they were permitted (*sc.* by fate) to wield those weapons, and until they led to ruin in the clash of shields their dear comrades and their own lives. In that time there will speak at the drinking an old retainer, who sees a ring (?), one who remembers it all, the slaying of men with spears: grim will be his mood ...'

It is clear from this that *swords* are the chief cause of trouble.[1] This at once introduces several difficulties.

he *2034: who is it? And also how can (if, as they should, *he* *2034 and *him* *2036 apply to the same person) 'he' wear more than one sword?

dryhtbearn *2035: meaning, and number?

beah *2041: what is this? Can it possibly be a sword?

---

1 For the use (frequent) of *láf* (*2036) as 'sword' (the pre-eminent heirloom) cf. *795 *ealde láfe* 'his ancient blade' 648, and *1488 (1243); for the use of *hringmǽl* as 'sword' cf. *1521 *hringmǽl* 'the weapon ring-adorned' 1272, and similarly *1564, 1311.

To take *dryhtbearn* first: this cannot refer to Ingeld: this is not a wedding feast, but plainly a scene in the land of the Heathobards. It does not refer to Freawaru. *Dryhtlic* can certainly mean 'noble' and is applied to Hildeburh (*drihtlíce wíf* *1158, 'that royal lady' 950), but this is derived from *dryht* 'court, the assembled warriors of a king'. As first element of a compound it retains its proper sense: a *dryhtbearn* is a young member of a *dryht*, a young knight or soldier.

But there is a difficulty of number: *he* singular, followed by *dryhtbearn*, *him* plural (from the logic of the situation and from *biwenede* *2035 which must, if kept, be a past participle plural). Even if we take *he* to be used like *sum* (as it occasionally is in Old English) 'a man', the change of number is harsh.

There is one further difficulty. The sense of *biwenede* 'treated, entertained' is evidenced in line *1821 (*bewenede*, 'cherished' 1528). But the use of the genitive plural *duguða* instrumentally = 'splendidly' is not either evidenced or likely.

Emendations are clearly called for: the very difficulty of the passage, in spite of the fact that the general situation is not in doubt, is sufficient to suggest that the text is corrupt in one or more points.

I think one must choose between *duguða bi werede* 'among a company of the tried warriors' and *duguðe* (or *duguðum*) *biwenede* 'nobly entertained'. The latter alteration makes the further emendation of *he . . . gangeð* *2034 to the plural *hie gangað* very desirable. I would thus read *þonne hie mid fæmnan on flet gangað, dryhtbearn Dena duguðe biwenede: on him gladiað . . .* 'when they with the lady pace the hall, young Danish knights of the escort nobly entertained: on

them gaily gleam,' &c. It is clear, I think, that the change to
hie gangað is a striking improvement resulting in a natural and
stylistically normal sentence – if we keep *biwenede*.

　　beah *2041: The answer is no. *beah*, which means a torque,
a spiral arm-ring, or corslet cannot = 'sword'. The difficulty
here may perhaps be caused by our ignorance of the specific
detail of the English story. The Danish lord singled out by
the *æscwiga* (*2042) may well have had also an heirloom-ring
or jewel upon arm or neck.

　　Still, the *æscwiga* later only mentions 'sword' (*dýre íren*
*2050, 'his prizéd blade' 1721–2). *beah* is very likely a cor-
ruption, for instance of *bá* 'both': both the hated Danish
lady and her knight. But this would require *bi werede*, for
we should have to keep *he* in line *2034. Then we should take
him *2036 plural as referring to *duguða* the Danish chivalry.
Thus: 'when he with the lady paces the hall, a young knight
of the Danish court in the armed company of their chivalry:
on them gleam the heirlooms of their fathers'.

　　On the whole I lean to this – with or without alteration
of *beah*. '*he*' may well in the story (as told by the lays that
our poet knew) have been a named man, with a specific part
to play; just as the name of the *æscwiga*, and of the young
Heathobard and his father, were all probably known. But –
and this point has, I think, usually been missed – the device
of giving this to Beowulf as a *prophecy* had forced the poet
to vague anonymity. However shrewd a young man Beowulf
might be, he could not possibly guess (without extensive
knowledge of the Heathobard court) which old retainer

would 'egg', and which Heathobard would take vengeance. And he could not yet know what young Danes would be chosen to go! Notice the namelessness of *he* and *æscwiga*, and *þín fæder* and *hyne* (*2048, *2050; 1721, 1723), in contrast to the almost gratuitous name Withergyld (*2051) when Beowulf is referring to the bygone battle which he *could* know about! We see at once that Withergyld cannot be the father [i.e. of the 'young warrior', *2044, 1718–19] or anything more than one of the 'lords of the Heathobards', famed as having fallen with Froda.

1746; *2076   ['Handshoe']

With the MS *Þær wæs Hondscio hilde onsæge* cf. *2482–3 *Hæðcynne wearð . . . gúð onsæge* (2087–8 'upon Hæðcyn . . . war fell disastrous'). The sense is therefore '(death in) battle fell on Handscioh', and the emendation to *hild* necessary and certain. The scribe probably (as some editors since) could not believe in a man named Handshoe = Glove, and so took the line to mean 'a glove (i.e. the *glóf* of *2085, 'pouch' 1753) fell with war (hostile intent) [*hilde*] upon the doomed man.'

There is however no need to doubt the name. It does not occur elsewhere in Old English, but is evidenced in German, e.g. in the place-name *Handschuhes-heim*, and is paralleled by the Norse name *Vǫttr* 'glove'. At the same time we gather that there were many stories and named characters associated with the courts of Hrothgar and Hygelac in Old English of which we only get hints in *Beowulf*. Here we must suspect a fairy-tale element: that a man called 'Handshoe' should go into a 'glove' is remarkable enough[1] (and has a Grimm sound!) – and not less so when we observe that *Handshoe* is only recorded here, and only here is *glóf* used apparently as a 'bag'.

In fact Grendel's 'bag' must here be meant to be 'glove'. As originally conceived Grendel was so large that a man could go inside his glove. Compare the adventure of Þórr inside the giant Skrýmir's glove in *Gylfaginning*.[2]

1767 ff.   *There was mirth and minstrelsy . . .*; *2105 *Þǽr wæs gidd ond gléo . . .*

This passage is obviously both interesting and important for literary history. The author of *Beowulf* has a poet's special interest in his craft. Compare the reference to the technical side of verse in *867–74 [see the note to 705–10]. Here we evidently have a reference to *forms* of composition: 'genres'; and to *matter*. Unfortunately the extremely scanty records of Old English verse and prose make it difficult to interpret the passage clearly.

---

1   [Handshoe plays an important part in my father's *Sellic Spell* (pp. 363–9).

2   [In the story told by Snorri Sturluson in *Gylfaginning* §44 Thór and his companions, seeking shelter for the night, came in the darkness upon a great hall, with an entrance at the end as wide as the hall. Inside they found a side chamber where they passed the night. But in the morning Thór saw that the side chamber was the thumb of the giant Skrýmir's glove.]

What is preserved is (a) in verse: mainly scholarly polished verse *written*, and preserved in careful book-hand in a few survivors of the costly books of ancient England. Except for the major example of *The Battle of Maldon* – clearly of a freer, hastier, and more topical kind, with looser metrical laws, but probably representing a kind that was practised at all times – and a few scraps (such as verses in the *Chronicle*, or the charms), what we have gives only an indirect glimpse at the minstrelsy of the English hall. Caedmon's Hymn is all that we have preserved that is certified as extempore.[1]

(b) in prose: we have no tales, no 'sagas', little or nothing of the work of the *þyle* [see the note to line 3] – except the gloss *þylcræft* = *rhetoric*, and probably early royal genealogies, and probably the matter behind some of the entries for the early years of the Chronicle (such as those on Hengest and Horsa). Again there is one exception: the compressed 'saga' episode about Cynewulf and Cyneheard in the *Chronicle* entry for the year 755, which stands out (in manner and matter) as *derived from* (not actually one) a told tale.

Points that we can note, nonetheless, are as follows. The fact that the king himself plays and recites. For England we have little evidence (except the late tale, apocryphal and impossible, concerning Alfred's visit to the Danish camp); but that nobles and kings practised minstrelsy is well known

---

1   The verses are justly taken as a sample – in style and diction and metre. The miracle is not in their excellence, but in a good piece of standard accomplishment coming from the dull shy cowherd. See further p. 143, footnote.

in Scandinavia. Indeed the Norse *skáld* was usually a man of a great house, and also a warrior.

Note. Beowulf expressly says that this took place on the night after Grendel's defeat, and before Grendel's mother came. He places it after the King had given him gifts. It refers therefore to the time described previously between *1063 and *1237, 867–1025. But there is no mention there of Hrothgar's singing or harp-playing. This is not necessarily a 'discrepancy'. It is an obvious method of enlivening the double account, to tell some things in the narrative and others in the report. 'Discrepancy' would only be present if it were impossible to fit in Hrothgar's performances [i.e. into the earlier account of the occasion]. A northern feast lasted long. Hrothgar's performances (not all at a stretch: *hwílum* . . .*hwílum* *2107–13, 1769–74), can hardly have occurred at *1063–5, 867–9 when only singing and playing in the presence of (*fore*) Hrothgar is mentioned. It is *Hróðgáres scop*, not the King, who sings of the *Fréswæl* (*1066, 870). But it can have occurred at *1160, *Gamen eft ástáh* (952–3 'Merry noise arose once more'), and in the long interval, after Wealhtheow's perambulation, passed over briefly, *1232–3 *Þær wæs symbla cyst, druncon wín weras*, 1021–2.

[I give here the original text *2105–13 and my father's translation 1767–74 of the passage in which Beowulf describes to Hygelac the performance of Hrothgar at the feast.

2105   Þǽr wæs gidd and gléo;   gomela Scylding
               felafricgende   feorran rehte;
               hwílum hildedéor   hearpan wynne,

gomenwudu grétte,   hwílum gyd áwræc
sóð ond sárlíc,   hwílum syllíc spell
2110   rehte æfter rihte   rúmheort cyning;
hwílum eft ongan   eldo gebunden,
gomel gúðwiga   gioguðe cwíðan,
hildestrengo;

1767   There was mirth and minstrelsy: the aged Scylding,
full of ancient lore, told tales of long ago; now did
he, once bold in battle, touch the harp to mirth,
the instrument of music; now a lay recited true and
bitter; or again, greathearted king, some wondrous
tale rehearsed in order due; or yet again, warrior of
old wars, in age's fetters did lament his youth and
strength in arms.]

We know little or nothing of the relation of harp-playing
to verse, and recitation. The nature of Old English verse,
such as that of *Beowulf*, makes it unlikely that it was 'sung'
in the modern sense.[1] The words *feorran rehte* *2106 (1769)
seem to refer to relating lays or tales of ancient days: the
same words *feorran reccan* are used of the *scop* who sang a
'Creation' lay (*91, 74). In *2107–8 we note that the *harp* is
mentioned, as distinct from *feorran reccan*, and from *gyd*,
syllíc spell, and from the concluding 'elegy'.

gyd: (early West Saxon *giedd*, other dialects *gedd*) is a
word of wide or vague application in Old English verse.[2]
It seems able to be used of any formal utterance, discourse,
or recitation. Thus Hrothgar calls his discourse or sermon a

---

1   It is in essential structure rhetorical, recitative, allied to *speech* –
though dignified, sonorous, and measured.
2   A distinct discussion of the word is found in the note to lines 512
ff., p. 260.

gyd *1723 ('considered words' 1447), while Beowulf's formal words when handing over the gifts to Hygelac are called *gyd* *2154 ('appointed words' 1810). But from various uses, and connexion with *gléo* (as *gidd ond gléo* *2105), it is plain that it can mean what we would call a *lay*. Note that the lay of Finn and Hengest is called *gléomannes gyd* *1160 ('the minstrel's tale' 952). It is thus fairly plain that *gyd . . . sóð ond sárlíc* *2108–9 refers to a tragic heroic lay (dealing with historial legend): such as the *Fréswæl*.[1]

spell: it is thus very interesting to see *gyd* contrasted as *sóð* with *syllíc spell* 'a marvellous tale'. Not that *spell* means a 'fairy story' – it means just an 'account', report, story. The minstrel's song about Beowulf's feat is a *spel* *873 ('tale' 710). But here there is plainly a distinction in *matter* between the *sóð* and the *syllíc*, which is probably not unlike the distinction we should draw between the 'historical' and the 'legendary' (or rather, marvellous, mythical). Sigemund and his dragon might be a case – a dragon was *sellíc*: cf. *sellice sædracan* *1426 ('strange dragons of the sea' 1189); but all that lost matter (which we call fairy-tale) of which only traces remain from the North – such as Grendel, and occasional hints in the Elder Edda, and of course more in the Edda of Snorri Sturluson, as in the tales about Thór – is probably meant. Yet

---

1 *gyd* is frequently joined with *geomor* 'sad' : as *151 *gyddum geómore* ('sadly in songs' 121), *1118 *geómrode giddum* of Hildeburh's lamentation (914), and so would be equally applicable to the 'elegy' or lament with which the King concludes (*2111 ff.). Note that the lament of the old man for his son is called a *gyd* (*2446, 2059 'a dirge').

note *rehte æfter rihte* *2110. It was not just a wild invention, but a known tale properly unfolded.

cwíðan: Here we have the 'elegiac' strain of lament – of which Old English provides us with more examples: there are traces in *Beowulf* itself. The passage (for instance) *2247 ff. *Heald þú nú, hrúse* . . ., 1892 'Keep thou now, Earth . . .' is in the manner of a set lament – and is actually offered as the lament of the last survivor of a race of kings. Cf. *2444 ff. *Swá bið geómorlíc* . . ., 2057 ff. 'In like wise is it grievous . . .', though this is not presented as an actual lament. The most successful and moving lines of *Beowulf* itself, *3143, 2639, to the end, are a lament. And parts of *The Wanderer* and *The Seafarer* naturally come to mind. Indeed the likeness of Hrothgar's words *1761–8 (1479–84) to part of *The Seafarer*, already noted [see p. 309 and the editorial note], is so close that we are justified in deducing that the kind of poetic utterance our author had in mind in *2112 [referring to Hrothgar, see p. 347] was not unlike: *yldo him on fareð, onsýn blácað, gomelfeax gnornað, wát his iúwine, æðelinga bearn eorþan forgiefene*[1] (*The Seafarer* 91 ff.); that in fact such lines derive from a very ancient variety of Northern poetic expression. But the special situation of the English – a people amid the ruins, cut off from the old lands, the lands of the heroes of their ancient songs, and gradually as their knowledge grew feeling themselves indeed to be in the Dark

---

1 [Old age comes upon him, his countenance grows pale, grey-haired he grieves, knowing his friends of past days, sons of princes, given to the earth.]

Ages after the departure of the glory of Rome[1] – gave a special poignancy to this feeling, and special pictorial vividness to it. Both of the passages from *Beowulf* cited above are filled with the vision of deserted and ruined halls; *gesyhð* . . . *wínsele wéstne, windge reste réte berofene, rídend swefað, hæleð in hoðman* *2455–8, 'he sees . . . the hall of feasting, the resting places swept by the wind robbed of laughter – the riders sleep, mighty men gone down into the dark' 2064–7. So also is *The Wanderer.* Nobody would have better understood or been better able to play Hrothgar's part than Alfred – who won his mother's praise for *poemata saxonica* – the lays of his northern heroic fathers – and yet felt himself almost alone in the Dark Age, attempting to save from the wreck of time some sparks surviving from the Golden Age, from Rome and the mighty *Cáseras* and builders of the fallen world.

1857 ff. *then into Beowulf's hands came that broad realm* . . .; *2207 ff. *syððan Béowulfe brade ríce on hand gehwearf* . . .

At *Beowulfe* we begin on folio 179r a sadly dilapidated page, mutilated as usual at the right edge, but also faded

---

1   Dagas sind gewitene
     ealle onmédlan   eorþan ríces;
     nearon nú cyningas   ne cáseras
     ne goldgiefan   swylce iú wǽron   *The Seafarer* 80–3

[The days are gone, all the pomp and pride of earth's kingdom; there are now no kings or emperors or givers of gold as once there were.]

350

badly, and 'freshened up' where visible by some later (and unauthorized) hand: the hand of someone either ignorant of Old English or much at sea as to the drift of the passage. A pity: here the poet leaps straight into the dragon-story and the thrilling adventure of the fugitive hiding in a cave by chance, discovering it to be a treasure-hoard, and nearly stepping on the dragon's head (*2290, 1929) in the dark as he rummaged about. And this is badly spoilt; *2226–31 (1875–8) are practically unintelligible. Allowing for the Old English manner this is a very moving treatment of this 'fairy-tale' situation – remarkable for the 'sympathy' shown by the author for both the wretched fugitive and the dragon. But it is characteristic of that manner that the narrative is not 'straight'. First we hear of the dragon. Then, that 'someone' got into the barrow, and took a cup. Then, that the nearby folk soon learned of the dragon's rage. Then we hear more of the intruder: he was a fugitive slave (master unknown). Then some precious details of his experience in the barrow are lost; but it is not until *2289–90 (1929) that we get the detail that he had trodden close to the worm's head. It is also characteristic of our poet (and of Old English as we know it as a whole) that the scene in the barrow passes at once into *an elegiac retrospect* on the forgotten lords who placed their gold in the hoard, and then died one by one until it was left masterless, an open prey to the dragon.

But this is *not* inartistic. For one thing, it occupies the 'emotional space' between the plundering of the hoard, and the curiously vivid and perceptive lines on the dragon snuffling in baffled rage and injured greed when he discovers the theft: lines which gain greatly from the concluding words of the interjected 'elegy': *ne byð him wihte ðý sél* *2277 ('no whit doth it profit him' 1918) – the last word on dragon-hood. Also, of course, the feeling for the treasure itself, and this sense of sad history, is just what raises the whole thing right above 'a mere treasure story, just another dragon-tale'. The whole thing is sombre, tragic, sinister, curiously real. The 'treasure' is not just some lucky wealth that will enable the finder to have a good time, or marry the princess. It is laden with history, leading back into the dark heathen ages beyond the memory of song, but not beyond the reach of imagination. Not till its part in the actual plot is revealed – to draw the invincible Beowulf to his death – do we learn that it is actually enchanted, *iúmonna gold galdre bewunden* *3052 ('the gold of bygone men was wound about with spells' 2564), in which the quintessence of 'buried treasure' is distilled in four words, and accursed (*3069–73, 2579–84).

So this passage rivals the *exordium* on ship-burial (*32–52, 25–40) as that very rare thing, an actual poetic expression of feeling and imagination about 'archaeological' material from an archaeological or sub-archaeological period. Many such mounds existed in Scandinavia, and even in England in the eighth century, already ancient enough for their purpose and history to be shrouded in mist. Here we learn what men of the twilight time thought of them. And, of course, the writing and the elegy are good in themselves, and not misspent – since the ashes of Beowulf himself are now to be laid in a barrow with much of this same gold (though much also is to melt in the fire, *3010–15, 2530–4), and pass down into the oblivion of the ages – but for the poet, and the chance relenting of time: to spare this one poem out of so many. For this, too, almost fate decreed: *þæt sceal brond fretan, æled þeccean*: that shall the blazing wood devour, the fire enfold. Of the others we know not.

*

SELLIC SPELL

Introduction

The only general statement by my father about his work *Sellic Spell* that I have found is the following very rushed note in pencil, difficult to read:

> This version is *a* story, not *the* story. It is only to a limited extent an attempt to reconstruct the Anglo-Saxon tale that lies behind the folk-tale element in *Beowulf* – in many points it is not possible to do that with certainty; in some points (e.g. the omission of the journey of Grendel's dam) my tale is not quite the same.
>
> Its principal object is to exhibit the difference of style, tone and atmosphere if the particular heroic or *historical* is cut out. Of course we do not know what precisely was the style and tone of these lost Old English things. I have given my tale a Northern cast of expression by putting it first into Old English. And by making it timeless I have followed a common habit of folk-tales as received.

As far as *Beowulf* goes I have attempted to [?draw] a form of story that *would have made* linking with the Historial Legend easiest – especially in the character of Unfriend. And also a form that will 'explain' Handshoe and the disappearance of the companions in the tale as we have it. That the third companion 'Ashwood' is in any way related to the coastguard is a mere guess.

The only daughter comes in as a typical folk-tale element. I have associated her with Beowulf. But here the original process was evidently actually more intricate. More than one tale (or motive of tales) was associated with the Danish and Geatish royal houses.

This was certainly written after the final text of *Sellic Spell* was achieved, as is shown by the reference to 'the journey of Grendel's dam' (i.e. her attack on Heorot, absent from the final text) and by the name 'Unfriend' (which only displaced 'Unpeace' on the typescript D). A note written on the same page at the same time may be mentioned here:

Bee-wolf: to my mind the most likely etymology is a kenning - quite apart from the evident surviving 'bearish' characteristics of Beowulf (e.g. Dæghrefn).

(On Dæghrefn see the commentary on *Beowulf* p. 236).

The formation of the text

The textual history of *Sellic Spell* is simple to set out, but extremely complex in detail. There is an initial manuscript, which I will call 'A': but this remained my father's working text, in which he developed the story in stages, rewriting many passages and introducing new material at different times, but (as it seems) not necessarily reverting to earlier stages to accommodate changed elements in the narrative. Thus A as it stands is a confusing and (at first sight, at any rate) inconsistent patchwork. But in the nature of the case the 'imagined story' offered such a multitude of choices as to give great scope to his tendency to withdraw from too ready an appearance of finality.

There is also a partial, roughly written manuscript 'B', in which the story of the attack of the monster on the Golden Hall was developed from the account in A into a new structure. This was not written into A, but aspects of it were entered as marginal additions and alterations; and I think it virtually certain that my father intended manuscript 'B' to be a very lengthy rider to the manuscript A. On this view the whole evolution of *Sellic Spell* was in fact reached in this one, overburdened manuscript; and from it was derived directly a good manuscript 'C', lightly emended here and there, setting out clearly the final form of the story.

The manuscript C was closely followed by a careful typescript 'D' that in all probability I made at the same time as my typescript of the translation of *Beowulf*; and that in turn by a professional typescript 'E', an exact copy of D as corrected, and with a very few further authorial alterations.

It seems to me that to set out in full detail the textual development would be uncalled for, but that a more brief account may be found interesting. I give here therefore, first, the final text of *Sellic Spell*, as represented by the typescript E, but follow it with a comparison of the earliest and latest versions, and the Old English text.

*

The name Sellic Spell

This is taken from line *2109 (1772 in the translation), when Beowulf, recounting to Hygelac his fortunes at Heorot, described the performance by Hrothgar at the feast that followed the rout of Grendel: *hwílum syllíc spell rehte æfter rihte rúmheort cyning*, 'or again, greathearted king, some wondrous tale rehearsed in order due'. *syllíc* and *sellíc* are different forms of the same word. In a hasty note on the typescript E my father wrote:

> Title taken from the enumeration of the 'kinds' of stories to be recited at a feast (*Beowulf* *2108 ff.): *gyd* heroic lay 'historical and tragic'; *syllíc spell* 'strange tales'; and 'elegiac lament'.

See further the commentary on *Beowulf* pp. 347–9.

In his lecture on lines 348–50 in the translation (see p. 233), when expressing his belief that 'in the form of the *sellíc spell* nearest behind [the poem] Beowulf had companions and/ or competitors in the hall when Grendel came', he added a note: 'See my "reconstruction" or specimen *Sellíc Spell* which I hope to read later. I think that Beowulf had one (or two)

358

companions, also eager to try the feat. Beowulf took the last turn.'

As can be seen from documents of which my father used the blank sides, the work on *Sellíc Spell* belongs, largely at any rate, to the early 1940s.

*

§ 1 SELLIC SPELL: THE FINAL TEXT

Once upon a time there was a King in the North of the world who had an only daughter, and in his house there was a young lad who was not like the others. One day some huntsmen had come upon a great bear in the mountains. They tracked him to his lair and killed him, and in his den they found a man-child. They marvelled much, for it was a fine child, about three years old, and in good health, but it could speak no words. It seemed to the huntsmen that it must have been fostered by the bears, for it growled like a cub.

They took the child, and as they could not discover whence he came or to whom he belonged, they brought him to the King. The King ordered him to be taken into his house, and reared, and taught the ways of men. He got little good of the foundling, for the child grew to a surly, lumpish boy, and was slow to learn the speech of the land. He would not work, nor learn the use of tools or weapons. He had great liking for honey, and often sought for it in the woods, or plundered the hives of the farmers; and as he had no name of his own, people called him Bee-wolf, and that was his name ever after. He was held in small account, and in the hall he was left in a corner and had no place upon the benches. He sat often on the floor and said little to any man.

But month by month and year by year Beewolf grew, and as he grew he became stronger, until first the boys and lads and at length even the men began to fear him. After seven years he had the strength of seven men in his hands. Still he grew, until his beard began to show, and then the grip of his arms was like the hug of a bear. He used no tool or weapon, for blades snapped in his hands, and he would bend any bow till it broke; but if he was angered he would crush a man in his embrace. Happily he was sluggish in mood and slow to wrath; but folk left him alone.

Beewolf swam often in the sea, summer and winter. He was as warm as an ice-bear,[1] and his body had the bear-glow, as men called it, so that he feared no cold.

There was a great swimmer in those days and his name was Breaker, and he came from Surfland. Breaker met the lad Beewolf on the beach one day, when Beewolf had just returned from swimming in the sea.

'I could teach you how to swim,' said Breaker. 'But, maybe, you do not dare to swim far out into deep water.'

'If we start swimming together,' said Beewolf, 'it will not be I that turn home first!' Then he dived back into the sea. 'Now follow me, if you can!' he cried.

They swam for five days, and never once could Breaker get ahead of Beewolf; but Beewolf swam round Breaker, and would not leave him. 'I am afraid that you may grow tired and be drowned,' he said; and Breaker was angry.

Suddenly the wind rose and blew the sea into hills, and Breaker was tossed up and down, and borne away to a distant country. When after a long journey he came back to Surfland, he said that he had left Beewolf far behind and had beaten him at swimming. The nixes[2] were disturbed by the storm, and they came up from the sea-ground. They saw Beewolf and were enraged; for they thought that he was Breaker and had roused the storm. One of them seized Beewolf and began to drag him down to the bottom: the nixes thought they would have a feast that night under the waves. But Beewolf wrestled with the beast and killed it; and in the same way he dealt with the others. When dawn came there were many nixes floating dead upon the water. Men wondered greatly at the sight of the monsters when they were cast ashore.

The wind fell and the sun rose, and Beewolf saw many capes jutting out to sea; and the waves bore him to land in a strange country far to the North, where the Finns dwelt. It was long before he reached his home again.

'Where have you been?' they asked him.

'Swimming,' he said; but they thought that he looked grim and bore the marks of wounds, as if he had wrestled with wild beasts.

In time Beewolf became a man, but he was greater than any other man of that land in those days, and his strength was that of thirty. It happened one night that as he sat as usual in a corner, he heard men talking in the hall, and there was one who told how the king of a far country had built himself a house. The roof of it was of gold, and all the benches were carven and gilded; the floor shone, and golden cloths were hung upon the walls. There was feasting in that house, and laughter of men, and music; and the mead was sweet and strong. But now the house stood empty as soon as the sun had set. No man dared sleep there; for an ogre haunted the house, and all that he could catch he devoured, or bore them away to his den. All night the monster was master of the Golden Hall, and no one could withstand him.

Suddenly Beewolf stood up. 'They need a man in that land,' he said. 'I will go and find that King.'

Folk thought such talk was foolishness; but they did not try to dissuade Beewolf; for it seemed to them that the ogre might eat many men who would be missed more.

Beewolf set off next day, but on his way he fell in with a man. 'Who are you?' said the man, 'and whither are you going?'

'Beewolf I am called,' he answered, 'and I am looking for the King of the Golden Hall.'

'Then I will go with you,' said the other; 'and my name is Handshoe.' He had that name because he wore great gloves of hide upon his hands, and when he had those gloves on him, he could thrust rocks aside and tear great stones asunder, but without them he could do no more than other men.

Handshoe and Beewolf went on together, and they came to the sea, and took a boat, and set sail; and the wind bore them far away. At length they saw the cliffs of a strange land before them, and tall mountains standing up from the foaming sea. The wind drove their ship against the land, and Handshoe leaped ashore and drew it high upon the beach. Hardly had Beewolf set foot upon the sand, when a man came down to meet them. He did not welcome the strangers. He was a grim fellow with a great ashen spear that he brandished fiercely. He demanded their names and their business.

Beewolf stood and answered him boldly. 'We are looking for the King of the Golden Hall,' he said. 'For he has trouble of some kind with an ogre, if the tales be true. My name is Beewolf, and my companion is called Handshoe.'

'And my name is Ashwood,' said the man, 'and with my spear I can put to flight a host of men.' Then he shook his tall ashen spear, so that it whistled in the wind. 'I, too, am going to the Golden Hall,' said he; 'it lies nor far from here.'

Then Ashwood and Handshoe and Beewolf went on their way, until they came upon a straight road, broad and well-made; and they strode forward, until there before them they saw the King's house standing in a green dale; and all the valley was lit with the light of the golden roof.

When they came to the doors of the hall, the guards would have stayed them, and questioned them; but Ashwood brandished his spear and they fell back; and Handshoe set his gloves to the great doors and flung them open. Then the three companions strode into the hall and stood before the King's seat. The King was old, and his beard was long and white.

'Who are you that come into my house so boldly?' said he. 'And what is your errand?'

'Beewolf is my name,' answered the young man. 'I have come from beyond the sea. I heard in my own land that you were troubled by an enemy who destroys your men, and that you would give much gold to be rid of him.'

'Alas! It is the truth that you have heard,' answered the King. 'An ogre called Grinder has haunted this house for many years, and richly indeed would I reward any man that could do away with him. But he is strong beyond the

measure of mortal men, and all whom he has met he has
overcome. None now dare to wait in this hall after night has
fallen. What hope have you that you will fare better?'

'In my arms I have strength more than most,' said
Beewolf. 'I have had hard tussles in my time, as the nixes
know to their cost. I can but try my luck with this Grinder.'

Men thought this speech bold, but not over-hopeful.

'And I can do somewhat, though it may not seem much,'
said the second. 'I am Handshoe. With my gloves I can over-
turn mighty rocks and tear great stones asunder. I can but try
whether Grinder be tougher.'

These words seemed to all more promising, though some
thought it likely enough that Grinder would indeed prove
tougher than stone.

'And I also have a power,' said the third. 'I am Ashwood.
With my spear I can put to flight a host of men. None dare
to stand before me, when I bear it aloft!'

Men thought this champion the most likely, if indeed his
weapon had the power that he claimed, and if Grinder had
not spells more strong. The King was well pleased with the
guests, and hope came to him that maybe the end of his trou-
ble was at hand. The three companions were bidden to the
feast, and seats were given to them among the King's knights.
At the pouring of the drink the Queen herself came to them
and gave to each a cup of mead and bade them be merry and
have good fortune.

'Glad is my heart,' said she, 'to see men in this hall again.'

Some of the King's men took this saying ill, and none
more ill than Unfriend,[3] the King's smith. He thought

himself of great account. He had a keen wit, and the King set great store by his counsels, though some said that he used secret spells, and that his counsels roused strife more often than they made peace. This man now turned to Beewolf.

'Did I hear aright that your name was Beewolf?' said he. 'There cannot be many with such a name. Surely it was you that Breaker challenged to a swimming-match, and left you far behind, and swam away home to his own country. Let us hope that you have become more of a man since then, for Grinder will treat you less gently than Breaker did.'

'My good Unfriend,' answered Beewolf, 'the mead has muddled your wit and you do not tell the tale aright. For it was I that won the match and not poor Breaker, though I was only a lad then. And indeed I have become more of a man since. But come, let us be friends!' Then Beewolf clasped Unfriend in his arms, and hugged him. It was a gentle hug as he reckoned it, yet it was enough; and when Beewolf let him go, Unfriend became very friendly as long as Beewolf was near him.

Soon afterwards the sun began to sink in the West and the shadows grew long on the earth. Men began to leave the hall. Then the King called the three companions.

'Darkness is at hand,' he said, 'and soon it will be Grinder's hour. Are you now willing to meet him?'

They said that they would as soon meet him that night as any other; but neither Handshoe nor Ashwood thought that he needed the other's help, and still less the help of Beewolf. They did not wish to divide the reward.

'Very good!' said the King. 'If you will not stay together, one of you must stay and try his luck alone. Which shall it be?'

'I will stay,' said Ashwood, 'for I was the first of us to set foot in this land.'

The King agreed to this, and bade Ashwood take charge of his house. He wished him good fortune, and promised him great gifts in the morning, if he was there to claim them. Then the King and all his knights left the hall. For Handshoe and Beewolf beds were prepared elsewhere. The house stood empty and dark. Ashwood made his bed beside a pillar and lay down, and though he had intended to lie awake and watchful, he soon fell asleep.

In the night Grinder arose from his lair far away over the dim moors, and came stalking down to the Golden Hall. He was hungry and had a mind to catch a man again for his meat. He walked over the land under the shadow of the clouds, and came at last to the King's house. He seized the great doors and wrenched them open. Then he stepped inside, stooping so that his head should not knock against the cross-beams of the roof. He glared down the length of the hall, and a light stood out from his eyes like the beams from a furnace. When he saw that a man was sleeping there again, he laughed. Thereupon Ashwood awoke and saw Grinder's eyes. A great fear came on him, and he leaped from his bed. His spear was leaning against the pillar nearby, but as he groped for it, it fell with a clang upon the floor. Even as he stooped, Grinder laid hold of him; and their wrestling did not last long. Grinder tore off Ashwood's head and bore him away.

In the morning, when men came back to the hall, only the spear remained, and some stains of blood upon the floor. Their fear of Grinder became greater when they saw this.

When the next evening drew near, men began to leave the hall earlier and with more haste than before.

'Soon it will be Grinder's hour,' said the King. 'Are you still willing to wait for him, seeing how Ashwood has fared?'

'I at any rate am willing,' answered Handshoe. 'And I claim the next turn, for it was I that sprang first from our boat.'

Beewolf said nothing against this; and Unfriend whispered to some that were near that the stranger seemed glad enough to leave the task to his companion. 'If this Handshoe fails,' said he, 'I do not think our Beewolf will dare to fulfil his boast.'

Now Handshoe was left alone. He thought that he understood how it had fared with Ashwood: he had not been wary, and the ogre had laid hold of him before he could use his weapon.

'I will not be caught thus,' said he; and he drew on his gloves before he lay down. He was not wholly easy in his mind, and he lay for a long time awake. Yet in the end drowsiness overcame him; but evil dreams troubled him, and he wrestled in his sleep.

In the middle of the night Grinder came again to see whether any other champion would be so foolish as to sleep in the hall and furnish him with meat. When he found that it was indeed so, he laughed aloud, and a light like flames sprang from his eyes. Handshoe awoke, and a great terror seized him. He sprang up, but his gloves were not on him, for they had slipped from his hands as he tossed in his dreams.

Before he could find them again, Grinder had him in his claws; and he tore up the champion, and stuffed the pieces into a great pouch that he carried at his belt. Then he made off, greatly pleased with his hunting.

In the morning, men found no traces of Handshoe save the gloves lying in his tumbled bed. They were now more afraid of the ogre than ever before, and some were unwilling to remain in the hall even during daylight. The King was downcast, for his troubles seemed now to have become worse than before. But Beewolf was not dismayed.

'Do not give up hope, Lord!' said he, 'for there is still one left. Third time may pay for all, as has often been seen. I still have a mind to wait for the ogre to-night. Indeed I have a great desire to have a word with this Grinder. I ask for no help but my two arms. If they fail me, then you will be rid of me at last, and you will have no need to feed me any longer, nor yet to bury me, as it seems!'

Men praised these bold words, but Unfriend said nothing. The King was well pleased, and the Queen again brought the drinking bowl to Beewolf with her own hands.

'Fate oft spareth him that fears her not,' said she. 'Drink, and be glad, and good luck go with you!'

At length the sun set, and the time came for Beewolf to keep watch. The King bade him farewell, hoping but not expecting to see him again in the morning. He promised now to give him three times the reward, if he overcame the monster.

'If Grinder is still so hungry that he ventures here again to-night,' said Beewolf, 'maybe he will find more than he seeks. If claws are his weapons and wrestling is his game, he will find one that is used to such play.'

When at last the King and all his folk had gone, and Beewolf was left alone in the dark hall, he spread his bed; but he did not lie down or go to sleep. A great drowsiness came upon him, but he sat up, wrapped in an old cloak, and set his back against a beam.

That night Grinder was seized with a gnawing hunger, and a great desire to see if there was yet a third champion so foolish as to lie in the hall. He walked swiftly under the moon, and came to the lands of men before the night was half spent. Without delay he stalked into the hall. As the doors burst open before him, he stooped forward with his hands upon the threshold, and the light of his eyes was now like two great beacons. Beewolf sat still and made no sign.

When Grinder saw that there was indeed a bed laid in the hall once again he laughed long and clapped his hands: the noise was like the clash of iron. At once he strode up to the bed and bent over it, thinking now to deal with this man as with the others. He laid his great claws upon Beewolf and pressed him backwards. But Beewolf supported the weight, and set his back more firmly against the beam behind. Then he took a grip with his fingers upon each of Grinder's arms above the wrist. Never had the ogre been so astonished in his life, for the grip of those fingers was stronger than any grip that he had ever felt before. He found that he could not use either of his hands while they held him. Suddenly his heart misgave him, and he became afraid; and very quickly he changed his mind, wishing now only to get away, out

of the house and back to his den. This was not at all the
fare that he sought. But Beewolf would not let him go; and
when Grinder drew back, he sprang up and grappled with
him. His fingers cracked, so hard did the ogre pull away.
Foot by foot Grinder struggled towards the door, and step
by step Beewolf clung to him, planting his feet against any
bar or sill that would give him purchase. The hall rang as
they wrestled. Grinder roared and yelled, and men in the
town round about awoke and trembled, and thought that all
the King's house would fall down. The pillars groaned, the
benches were overturned; boards were splintered, and the
floor was broken up.

So they came at last to the doors. Then Grinder wrenched
himself away, but only one arm could he free: Beewolf still
held him by the other. So hard then did the ogre drag one
way, and Beewolf the other, that with a great crack bone
and sinews burst asunder at the shoulder, and Grinder's
arm, claw and all, was left in Beewolf's hands. Grinder fell
backwards out of the door and vanished into the night with
a howl; but Beewolf laughed, and was glad. He set up the
great arm high above the doorway in token of victory. When
morning came, there it stood, huge and hideous, with hide
like dragon-fell, and five great fingers, each with a nail like a
spike of steel. Men looked at it in amazement and shuddered.

'That was a strong pull!' they said. 'Never sword nor axe
could have hewn off such a bough!' They were loud now in
the praises of Beewolf, accounting him the strongest of men.
Unfriend was there: he looked at the arm and found nothing
yet to say.

The King came when he heard the news, and he stood before the doors of the hall and rejoiced. 'Here is a sight that I never hoped to see,' he said. 'Wonders will never end! A young man with his naked hands has done what none of us could do with weapon or with craft. What mother's son may this Beewolf be? For he seems to have the strength of bears, not of men.'

But Beewolf made light of his deed. 'It has not fallen out as I should have wished, Lord," said he. 'No more than an arm is there to show. I would rather have given you the whole carcase, head, hide, and all. And maybe I would, if Grinder had been tougher, but he tricked me by breaking in two.'

'Yes, the task is, alas! only half done!' said Unfriend. 'For I fear that a monster so strong will not die of a wound, grievous though it may seem. When Grinder is healed, he may still do much harm with only one hand; and it may prove that his wrath and desire for revenge will make up for the loss of the other.'

The joy of the King and his men was much lessened by these words. 'What then do you think should be done, my good Unfriend?' said the King.

'I should ask Beewolf what he proposes, for he is now the great man here,' said Unfriend, louting4 low.

'If you ask me that, Lord,' said Beewolf, 'I think that Grinder should be tracked to his lair, while he is still somewhat weary, perhaps, from the wrestling that we had together.'

'But who will dare to do that?' said the King.

'I would dare,' said Beewolf, 'if I knew where Grinder might be found.'

'As for that,' said the King,' there is not much doubt. Men that walk in the wild have often brought tidings of his haunts; for they have seen him from afar, stalking in the wilderness alone. His den lies many miles away in a hidden mere, behind a waterfall that tumbles from a black cliff into shadows far beneath. Wind blows there, and wolves howl in the hills. Dead trees hang by the roots over the pool. At night fire flickers on the water. No man knows the depth of that lake.'

'It is no pleasant spot, that you tell of,' said Beewolf. 'But cleansed it must be, and that soon, if this trouble is to be ended. I will go thither. I will visit Grinder in his own home, and however many doors there may be to his house, he will not escape me!'

The King was delighted with these words, and promised to give Beewolf thrice the gifts that he had already earned, if he performed this new task. 'The gifts must wait until I return', said Beewolf. 'All that I ask now is a companion that knows the ways of your land to guide me to the spot. If it were my part to choose, I should look to Unfriend for help; for here he seems to be accounted a man of good wits.'

'Indeed Unfriend shall go with you,' said the King. 'Your choice is good; for he has travelled much, and no man knows more of the ways and secrets of this land than he.'

When Unfriend heard this, it did not seem to him that things had turned out altogether as he had wished; but he did not dare to refuse, lest he lose the King's favour and all honour in the hall. 'It will be a pleasure to show my friend Beewolf the marvels of this land,' he said; and he grinned, thinking that his wits might indeed prove of service in this venture.

The King now ordered men to bring meat and drink for the travellers; and from his hoard was brought forth a shining corslet woven of rings of steel. 'This at least you shall have,' said the King to Beewolf, as earnest of many gifts to come. Wear it now with good luck.'

It was early in the day, and the shadows were still long from the East, when Unfriend and Beewolf set off. Beewolf took with him Handshoe's gloves, and Unfriend carried Ashwood's spear; but it was so heavy that he quickly grew weary of it, and Beewolf took that too. They soon came upon the trail of Grinder, for he had spilled much blood as he went. They followed the tracks up and down dale, and left the homes of men far behind, and journeyed on over the misty moors towards the high mountains. At last they came to a path, steep and narrow, that wound among the rocks. It passed the dark doors of many caves, the houses of nixes that hunted in pools far below. Up the path they climbed, until they came to the wood of dead trees hanging by their roots, and they looked over the brink of the cliff and saw a waterfall plunging down into the black water. Far beneath them the lake seethed and eddied. There at the top of the fall they found the head of Ashwood staring at the sky.

'It seems that you have brought me to the right spot,' said Beewolf. Then he blew on a horn, and the blast of it echoed in the rocks. The nixes were aroused, and they plunged into the lake, blowing with rage. 'There are many unfriendly things here,' said Beewolf.

'Let sleeping dogs lie!' said Unfriend. 'I see no need to tell Grinder that we are come near to his doors.'

'I do not heed the nixes,' said Beewolf. 'I have dealt with others greater in the sea.'

'Yet it may prove hard to deal with many foes at a time,' said Unfriend.

'Many foes can give a man but one death,' answered Beewolf; then he stood up and made himself ready. He had on him the shirt of mail that he got from the King, and at his belt hung the gloves that Handshoe had left behind; in his right hand he held the spear of Ashwood.

'How will you get down, my friend?' asked Unfriend.

'It will not be the first time that I have dived into deep water,' answered Beewolf. 'And though this cliff be ten fathoms tall, I have seen taller.'

'And how will you get back, my friend, when all your foes are vanquished?' said Unfriend; and he smiled to himself, thinking that Beewolf was as much behind himself in wit, as he was greater in strength. 'See here, my friend,' said he. 'I have taken thought for you, and I have brought a long rope. I will make it fast at this end, and cast it over the cliff down to the water. You may trust me to wait; and when you return (as indeed I hope you will) I will draw you up.'

Beewolf thanked him. 'Your will is good,' said he, 'whatever your strength may be. If I prove somewhat heavy to draw, no doubt I can make shift to climb.' Then without more ado he dived from the cliff, and the last that Unfriend saw of him was the soles of his feet, as he clove the water.

Down went Beewolf for a long while, and found no bottom. The nixes gathered about him, and tore at him with their tusks; but the corslet of mail was cunningly forged, and they did no hurt to his body. Now Grinder had a dam, an ogress old beyond the count of years, fiercer than a she-wolf; and if her strength of limb was great, yet greater was the strength of her spells. The mere and all the lands about were under their power. There she had dwelt many ages in her cave behind the falls, and no man had dared to trouble her. There now she sat and grieved over the hurts of her son, and her heart was filled with rage. Quickly she learned that some stranger from the world above had entered her realm. In anger she came forth from her house.

When at last Beewolf came to the bottom of the lake she was ready for him. Before he could stand on his feet, she grasped him from behind, and the nixes came to her aid. Beewolf could do little against them all, being under deep water; and they dragged him away to the den of the ogress. He was tossed and battered, and well nigh all the breath was beaten out of him; for his enemies dragged him through the midst of the great eddy that boiled under the falls. The mouth of Grinder's cave was in the cliff behind the waterfall, and was only a little way under water. They dragged him inside, and then up a sloping passage that led from the door. Then suddenly the nixes fell back, and Beewolf found that he was no longer in water, and a roof of stone was high above his head. The cave was very large, and a fire burned within.

Quickly Beewolf wrenched himself free and turned and beheld Grinder's dam, the old ogress with fangs like a wolf. He thrust at her with the spear, but she was in no way dismayed, for it had no virtue in that place. With a blow of her hand she snapped the haft in two. Beewolf cast away the truncheon,⁵ but she was quicker than he. Very strong she was, there in her own house over which many spells were woven. She seized him by the shoulders and flung him on the floor beside the wall, and straightway she sat upon his breast, and drew a bright knife from her belt, and set it at his throat. Very near she came to avenging her son. But for the King's mail upon his neck that would have been the end of Beewolf.

'Heavy is this hag!' said Beewolf, and he tried to heave her off his breast. Then he gripped her by the arms as he had gripped Grinder before, and drew her suddenly towards him; and she cried out when she felt the strength of his embrace. But Beewolf rolled over, and threw her under, and thrust her to the floor; and then he sprang to his feet. Even as he did so, he saw, hanging on the wall near by, a great sword. It was old and heavy, the work of giants long ago, and no mortal man in that day, save Beewolf, could have wielded it. Swiftly he seized it, and smote the ogress such a blow upon the neck that the hide split, and the bones burst, and her head rolled off down the passage into the water below, dripping with blood. Dead she lay upon the floor, and Beewolf did not mourn for her.

As the sword fell, a light flashed up under the roof like lightning, and all the cave was brighter than day; and it seemed to Beewolf that the light came from the sword, and that the blade was on fire. He saw now that there was another chamber further in. He strode towards it, but he found that the entrance was barred by a huge stone that stood up far above his head. In no way could he stir the stone though he heaved with all the strength that he had. Then he thought of the gloves that hung at his belt, and he drew them on; and when he set his hands to the stone he flung it aside, as if it were a hurdle.

He entered the chamber, and there he saw great wealth of gold and gems that Grinder had gathered through the years. In the innermost corner there was a bed, and upon it lay Grinder. He made no movement, but if he was dead, still his eyes glared so balefully that Beewolf took a step backward. Then Beewolf raised the sword aloft and hewed off Grinder's head, and it rolled from the bed and the fire of its eyes was quenched. At the same moment the light of the sword went out.

In the meanwhile up on the cliff Unfriend waited. The time seemed long to him, and he had no wish to remain in that perilous place longer than was needful. At last it seemed to him, as he peered down, that the mist and shadows were lifted from the mere, and in a ray of sun he saw the water of the eddy far below, and it was stained red, as if with blood. He thought that maybe it was the blood of Beewolf; and the thought did not displease him, for he had not forgotten the hug. In any case it seemed to him that it was now high time to be gone. Noon of the day was past. He rose, and going to the rope he loosened the knots, so that it would slip and fall, if anyone pulled from below. Then he made off, well pleased; for he thought that, even if Beewolf escaped from the monsters, he would be wounded and weary, and if the rope failed him, he would certainly perish in the pool. In this way he hoped to be rid of the troublesome stranger who had put him to shame in the hall.

In the dark, Beewolf groped his way out from the inner chamber, and returned to the fire in the cave, and took up a burning brand. Then he saw a strange sight. The great sword that he held in his right hand was melting like an icicle in the sun. It dripped away, until nothing was left but the hilts, so hot and venomous was the blood of Grinder and his dam. The hilts Beewolf kept, and he took such treasure beside of gold and gems as he could pack in Grinder's bag; and he took also Grinder's head: and that was no light burden. Four other men would have found it all that they could carry between them.

At last Beewolf turned from the cave, and went down a passage to the doors, and plunged back into the pool. It was a long, strong swim, for Beewolf was heavily laden, and he had much ado to get under the eddy where the water fell down from the cliff. But not a nixy was to be seen in the lake. The shadows were lifted from the water, and the sun shone on it, and it looked as clear and bright as it had been gloomy before.

Beewolf came to the rope, and called; but Unfriend gave no answer. Then Beewolf caught hold of the rope-end, and began to heave himself out of the water. He had climbed only a few hands, when the rope slipped, and he fell back into the pool with a great splash. Very strange he thought it, and not at all as he had hoped.

'That fellow Unfriend,' he said, 'may boast of his skill, but for all that it does not seem that he can make fast the end of a rope. And now either a wild beast has taken him; or his heart has failed him and he has deserted me: and that is more likely.'

Beewolf swam round for a while, but there was no way up the cliff on either side of the falls, save for birds. So he turned away, and swam far along the shores of the lake; and he became so weary that he had to let go some of the treasure that he had brought from the cave; and that grieved him greatly. At last he came to a place where the banks were lower and less steep, and with great labour he dragged himself out of the water onto the flat rocks where the nixes had been used to lie in the moonlight. But the sun still shone warm from the West, and he rested there for a while.

At length he gathered up his burdens and made his way along the shore, and so climbed back to the head of the falls, and found the path by which he had come. It was a long, hard journey that he made over moor and hill back to the homes of men, and morning was on the land when he came to the tilled fields and found again the road to the Golden Hall.

The King was within, and many folk were about him, and Unfriend was telling again the tale that he had told the night before. Many would have been better pleased, if Unfriend had reported that Grinder was certainly destroyed; but there were some that did not grieve overmuch for the stranger. In the midst of the tale, and even as Unfriend was telling of the blood that boiled in the pool, the doors opened, and in strode Beewolf down the length of the hall, and the floor trembled under his feet.

No one spoke, and all sat silent in astonishment. As for Unfriend, he left his place before the King's seat and slipped away. Beewolf greeted the King, and held up by the hair the huge head of Grinder. Men gazed in fear at the sight of it, and the Queen shuddered and hid her face.

'See, Lord, what I have brought back from the deep waters!' said Beewolf. 'Here is good hunting - and not easily got! I came near my end under the waves. For Grinder had a dam, very old and wicked, the guardian of his den. The hag was not easy to master, for her spells were strong, and the spear that I took with me she broke in two. Yet I found a mighty sword hanging on the wall, and with that I made an end of Grinder and his dam. You need fear them no more. Their life is over. All who wish may sleep quiet in this house tonight and all nights after. Here are the hilts of the sword! No more remains of it, so bitter was the blood of those masters of the cave, and so unfriendly to iron.'

Then the King took the hilts and looked long at them; for they were marvellously wrought with cunning smith-craft, bound with fine wire of gold, and set with many bright gems; and upon them was written in runes the name of the great one of old for whom that sword had first been made.

'These hilts are worthy of a new blade,' said the King. 'Unfriend might perhaps fashion one that is not unfitting; for he is a cunning smith, and knows many runes beside.'

'And where is my faithful friend?' said Beewolf. 'I thought I heard his voice as I entered, but I do not see him here to welcome me. I have a mind to teach him the tying of knots.'

Then some went and dragged Unfriend out of a corner. 'Well, mannikin!' said Beewolf. 'So you got home before me? Neither heart nor wit have you, for you cannot wait for a friend, nor fasten a rope. Or if you can, then you are a treacherous knave.'

He lifted Unfriend up, and Unfriend cried out in fear, for he thought for certain that Beewolf would hug him to death. 'No, I will not kill you,' said Beewolf, 'for you are the King's man. But if I were the King I would not have you crawling in my house.' Then he beat him soundly, and let him go, and Unfriend crept out and did not enter the hall again for many a day; and there was more friendship and less strife there ever after. For Unfriend was humbled, and from thenceforth was a man of fewer words. As for Grinder's head, they took it and burned it to ashes, and scattered the ashes on the wind far from the dwellings of men.

Merry indeed was the feast that they made in the Golden Hall that night. All day the wrights and builders were busy repairing the damage: boards and wainscotes were mended, the benches were polished and set in order, and broidered cloths of many colours were hung upon the walls; and many lights were lit. When all was ready, Beewolf sat in high honour beside the King himself, and rich gifts were given to him: an axe and a fair shield; and a banner of golden cloth; and a helmet made by smiths of old, in whose work was such a craft that no blade could cleave it: a golden boar was set upon it as a crest; and a horse with a fair saddle and bright harness the King gave to Beewolf. And the Queen added gifts of her own: a golden ring of great weight she gave him, and fair raiment, and she set about his neck a necklace bright with gems. All the gold that he had got in Grinder's cave the King returned to him, in recompense for his companions, Handshoe and Ashwood, whom the ogre had slain. Twelve good men, well-armed, the King appointed to be his followers and to serve him.

Now Beewolf had become a great man indeed, and he thought that his lot had taken a turn for the better; for his treatment here was very different from his treatment at home. He lived merrily in that land for a while, and all men were his friends. Unfriend laboured long and put forth his skill, and he fashioned a great blade, and it was good. Upon it were many signs and figures, and at the edges snakes were drawn so that their bite should be deadly. With the King's leave Unfriend fitted the blade to the ancient hilts, and he gave the sword to Beewolf as a peace-offering. Beewolf took it gladly and forgave him; and he called the sword Gildenhilt and wore it ever after, and despised weapons no longer.

There was great friendship between the King and his guest, and he would have been glad to have kept Beewolf at his side; for he was old, and his sons were not yet grown to manhood, and it seemed to him that Beewolf was worth a host of men. But as time wore on a great desire came upon Beewolf to look again on his own land over the sea, and to show the folk there what honour he had earned in his travels. So at last he took his leave of the King of the Golden Hall, and bade him farewell; and the king gave him a new ship more splendid than the old boat that still lay upon the beach; and Beewolf and his men laded it with all the gold and good things that he had won; and they drew up their sails, and put out to sea.

It was not long before folk upon the shore saw white sails upon the water, like the wings of a bird that glides down the wind. As the vessel drew nearer they wondered whence it came and what might be its errand, such a fine ship as it was, with bright shields hung upon its sides, and a banner of gold. When the boat came to land, out stepped a great lord, exceedingly tall, clad in shining mail, with a high-crested helm upon his head; and twelve knights were with him. They asked him his name.

'Beewolf I used to be called, when I was at home,' said he; 'and I see no reason to change.'

Then indeed the people were amazed, and the news of Beewolf's return spread like fire. But Beewolf did not wait, and went at once to see the King, his fosterer. He strode up the hall, where once he had sat in a corner; and very different now was his bearing. He greeted the King proudly.

The King looked at him in wonder. 'Well, well! So you have returned after all!' said he. 'Who would have believed that Beewolf would overcome the ogre and set free the great Golden Hall? I never expected it!'

'Maybe not, Lord,' said Beewolf. 'But many a man has a treasure in his hoard that he knows not the worth of. You thought little of the foundling that was brought from the bear's den; yet you have earned some thanks for your fostering, such as it was.' And Beewolf gave to the King all the gold that he got in the cave, and the King received that gift very gladly.

Beewolf was now a mighty man in the land, and he fought for his King in many great wars, and gained him many victories. It is said that at times in the heat of battle he would put up his sword and cast away his shield and seize the captain of his enemies and crush the life out of him with his arms. The fear of his strength and his valour went far and wide. A great lord he became, with broad lands and many rings; and he wedded the King's only daughter. And after the King's day was done, Beewolf became king in his stead, and lived long in glory. As long as he lived he loved honey dearly, and the mead in his hall was ever of the best.

*

Notes to the text

1   *ice-bear*: A pencilled note against 'ice-bear' by my father on the carbon copy of the second typescript (E), reads:

> seems to fit – but does not. The Icelandic *ís-björn* is modern. The Old Icelandic term was *hvíta-björn* 'white-bear; but this was unknown in Europe till about 900 (after the discovery of Iceland), and so could have no part in ancient folk-legend going back beyond A.D. 500, the approximate date of Hrothgar &c.
> See further the commentary on *Beowulf* p. 237.

2   *nixes*: My father was uncertain how best to render the Old English word *nicor*, plural *niceras*, commonly translated 'water-demon' (the word he himself used in his translation of *Beowulf*). Old English

nicor, spelt *nicker*, was long known as an archaic word in English, and the related German words *nix*, *nixy* are found in English writings of the nineteenth century.

In the manuscripts of *Sellic Spell* A and C my father merely retained the Old English form *nicor*, with a plural *nicors*. This was naturally followed in the typescript D; but at this, the first occurrence of the word, my father emended it to *nickers and nixes*, but then struck out *nickers and*. At all subsequent occurrences of *nicors* he changed it to *nixes*, save on p. 362 line 6, where 'Beewolf wrestled with the nicor', he changed it to 'beast', and on p. 379 line 22, where he changed it to *nixy*.

The second typescript E has *nixes* throughout, except in the two cases just mentioned; but in most cases he lightly pencilled *nickers* above, perhaps as an alternative rather than an alteration.

3 *Unfriend*: In all the texts except E the name was *Unpeace*, but in D my father changed it to *Unfriend* throughout. In E the typist retyped *Unpeace* to *Unfriend* at the first two occurrences, thereafter *Unpeace*.

4 *louting low*: bowing low.

5 *truncheon*: used in an early sense of the word, the fragment of a spear, or the haft of a spear.

*

§ 2 A COMPARISON OF THE EARLIEST AND FINAL FORMS OF THE STORY

[I give here, in the relevant parts, the text (manuscript A) of *Sellic Spell* in its earliest form, before any significant alterations were made, so far as that can be ascertained. As this manuscript was in the first, or at any rate a very early, stage of composition there are many corrections in the detail of expression which were obviously, or very probably, made at the time of writing. In such cases I have either silently printed the corrected text, or indicated the nature of the correction if that is of interest. See further, on the nature of manuscript A, *The formation of the text*, [introduction pp. 356–7].

Once upon a time there was a King in the North of the world and in his house there was a young lad who was not like other young lads. When he was a child he was found in a bear's den up in the mountains, and the hunters took him to the king; for no one knew whence the child came or who he belonged to, and through living with the bears he could not speak. The King put him out to foster, but the foster-father had little good of him. He was a surly and lumpish boy, and slow to learn men's language. He would not work, or learn the use of tools or weapons. He was held in small account, and in the hall he was pushed into a corner and given no place among the better folk. As he grew, however, and he grew

387

marvellously fast, he became stronger and stronger, until men became afraid of him. Soon he had the strength of many men in his hands, and the grip of his arms was like the hug of a bear. He wore no sword, but if he was angered he could crush a man in his embrace.

To this point it may be observed that there was no mention of the King's only daughter; that the foundling was not fostered by the King; and most notably, that he was not named *Beewolf*, nor the reason for it. An addition to the manuscript that was very probably made at or near the time of writing, however, reads thus, following the words 'tools or weapons':

He was fond of honey, and as he had no name, people called him Beewolf.

The text continues from the point reached:

Beewolf was a great swimmer. He was as warm as an ice-bear, and his body had the bear-glow, as men called it, so that he feared no cold.

There was a great swimmer in those days, and his name was Breaker, and he came from Surfland. Breaker met Beewolf on the beach one day, when Beewolf had just returned from swimming in the sea.

From this point the original text was preserved almost word for word into the final form as far as 'as if he had wrestled with wild beasts' (p. 362, line 6). The only difference to be mentioned is the use of the word *nicors* for later *nixes*: on this see the note on *nixes*, p. 385.

After a time, when Beewolf had grown to man's size and more, news came to the land that the king of a country across the water was troubled by an ogre. Of what sort the monster was, and where he came from, no one could tell; but the tales told that he used to stalk men in the shadows and eat them on the spot, or bear them away to his den, many at a time. Rich or poor, young or old, he spared none that he could catch. Beewolf listened to these tales, but he said nothing. And more news came: it seemed that the ogre had now broken into the king's hall and devoured thirty knights. The king's hall was roofed with gold, and all the benches were gilded and carven, and the mead and ale there were of the best, but neither the king nor any of his men dared stay in the hall after the sun had set. The king had offered rich rewards to any man who would rid him of his enemy, but no one had come forward, and all the night the monster was master of the king's house.

When he heard this Beewolf stood up. 'They need a man in that land,' he said. 'I had better go .... [*illegible*]. The old folk thought little good would come of such a venture, but none ...... [*illegible*] tried to dissuade Beewolf, thinking the ogre might eat others who would be missed more. Beewolf found one man who was ready to go with him. That was a fellow named Handshoe, and he had that name because he wore gloves of bearskin on his large hands. Beewolf and Handshoe got a boat and set sail, and next day or the day after they sighted the land of the king of the Golden Hall. As soon as they stepped ashore, a man came up to them and asked their business, and there was no welcome for strangers in his looks. But Beewolf who was now grown very tall and grim stood up and spoke back proudly. 'I have come to find out the truth about the tales that men tell of this land,' he said. 'I have heard that an enemy visits your king's house by night and not a man of this land dare stay to meet him. Maybe it is idle talk, but if it is true I think I could be useful.'

'Maybe you could!' said the man, stepping back and looking up at Beewolf. 'You had better go and let the king know your errand.' He led Beewolf and Handshoe forward, until they could see the golden roof of the king's house shining before them in a green dale. 'You cannot miss the road now,' said the man, and wished them good day.

It will be seen that in the story as originally told the magical quality of Handshoe's gloves was not mentioned at this point; and the unfriendly man that met Beewolf and Handshoe on the shore had no name and no part to play beyond showing them the way to the Golden Hall. In the text that replaced this the man was still unnamed but 'He was a grim-looking fellow with a great spear that he brandished fiercely'; and when they parted, within sight of the Golden Hall, he said 'I wish you good day and good luck, though I do not expect ever to see either of you returning.'

In a short while Beewolf and Handshoe came to the door of the hall; and Beewolf brushed past the guards and strode into the hall, till he stood before the king's seat, and greeted the king.

'Hail, king of the Golden Hall!' said he. 'I have come over the sea. I have heard that you are troubled by [a creature called Grendel >] a monster that eats your men, and that you would give much gold to be rid of him.'

'Alas! it is the truth that you have heard!' answered the king. 'An ogre called [Grendel >] Grinder has harried my folk for years, and I would richly reward any man that could destroy him. But who are you and what is your errand?'

'Beewolf is my name,' said he. 'In my hands I have the strength of thirty men. [The creature that you call Grendel, that is my errand. >] My errand is to have a look at this ogre. I have dealt with folk of his kind before. And nicors also I have slain. Since there is no man in this land who dare stay to meet him, I will wait here tonight and have a word with this [Grendel >] Grinder. I ask for no more help than my two arms. If those fail me, you will at least be rid of me, and you will have no need to feed me, nor to bury me for that matter, if the tales are true.'

The king was overjoyed to hear such a speech, and hope came to him that maybe the end of his trouble was at hand. Beewolf was invited to the feast and [set beside the king's own sons >] given a seat among the king's men; and at the pouring of the drink the Queen herself came to him and gave him a cup of mead, and wished him good fortune. 'Glad is my heart,' said she, 'to see a man in this hall again.'

[The Queen's words were little to the liking of >] Some of the king's men took this saying ill, and none more so than

/ Unpeace. He thought himself of great account, for he was high in the king's favour. He had a keen wit, and the king set great store by his counsels, though there were some that distrusted him and said that he had an evil eye, and could work spells of magic, and that his counsels roused strife more often than they made peace. Unpeace now turned to Beewolf.

The scornful words of Unpeace to Beewolf concerning the swimming-match with Breaker, and Beewolf's bear-hug of Unpeace in response, scarcely differ from the final form; but as will be seen the story that then follows is radically different, though much of the text was retained in the final form.

Soon afterwards the sun began to sink in the west and the shadows grew long; and the king arose, and men hurried from the hall. Then the king bade Beewolf take charge of his house, and wished him good luck, promising him great rewards in the morning if he was there to claim them.

When the king and all the folk had gone, Beewolf and Handshoe made their beds. 'If Grinder comes tonight,' said Beewolf, 'he will find more than he is seeking. If claws are his weapons and wrestling is his game, he will find one that is used to such play, and likes it better than toying with iron tools.' Then he laid his head on the pillow, and was soon in a deep sleep; but Handshoe was not so easy in his mind, and set a drawn sword by his side.

In the night Grinder arose from his lair, far away over the dim moors, and came stalking down to the Golden Hall.

He was hungry and had a mind to catch a man or two for his meat. He strode over the land under the shadow of the clouds, and came at last to the king's house: not for the first time, but never before had his luck been so ill. He seized the great doors and wrenched them open, and stepped inside, [and as he entered >] stooping lest his head should knock against the cross beams of the roof. He glared down the length of the hall, and a light stood out from his eyes like the beams from a furnace. When he saw that there were men once more sleeping in the hall, he laughed.

Handshoe was awakened, and as soon as he beheld Grinder he seized his sword and hewed at the ogre, and did him no hurt whatever. For Grinder had set a spell upon iron and no ordinary sword would bite on his hide. He had a great glove without fingers dangling at his belt, and at once he seized Handshoe and tore him limb from limb and stuffed the pieces in his glove. Beewolf was roused from his deep sleep, and was hot with anger when he saw what became of his companion; but he lay still for a while, watching what the ogre might do next. Grinder thought he was asleep and came up to the bed, meaning to deal with him as he had dealt with the other man; and he laid his great claws upon Beewolf and pressed him down upon the bed.

From this point the original story in manuscript A of Beewolf's fight with Grinder was scarcely changed at all in the final form; but the entire narrative of his entries into the Golden Hall on three successive nights and his separate killings of Ashwood and Handshoe, before the fight with Beewolf, was lacking. Ashwood, as a presence at the Golden Hall, had not yet entered the story at all; and nor had the magical nature of Handshoe's gloves. The sentence 'Handshoe was awakened, and as soon as he beheld Grinder he seized his sword' was altered to read 'Handshoe awoke, and saw Grinder's eyes, and such a fear took him that he leapt from his bed, forgetting his gloves; and seizing his sword'; and at the same time, after the words 'stuffed the pieces in his glove' my father added 'Soon there was nothing left but Handshoe's gloves lying on the bench by his bed.' The marvellous nature of the gloves had evidently now entered in a replacement passage earlier in the A manuscript.

The original story was not changed subsequently through the speeches following Beewolf's victory; but after his words to the king, that 'Grinder tricked me by breaking,' he said. 'Yet I do not think that he has escaped with his life. He will die of that hurt, and you will be rid of him hereafter.' Unpeace said nothing at this point in the original text A (in contrast to his forebodings in the final form, which led to the expedition by Beewolf and Unfriend to Grinder's lair).

After this there follows in A a passage that my father subsequently used, without great change, at the ending of Beewolf's exploits in the lake, pp. 382–5, and this leads into a development wholly different from the final story.

Soon the wrights and the builders were busy repairing the damage in the hall; the doors were set on their hinges, and the benches were polished and set in order, and the golden cloths were hung on the walls again; and many lights were lit.

There was a merry feast that day, and Beewolf was given a seat of honour, beside the sons of the king; and as they drank the king's minstrel made a song in praise of his victory. Then the king remembered his promise, and he ordered rich gifts to be given to Beewolf: a golden corslet, and a sword from the king's treasury, and a banner of golden cloth, and a helmet made by smiths of old, in whose work was such a craft that no sword could cleave it. And the king paid Beewolf a great sum in gold besides, in recompense for his companion, Handshoe, whom the ogre had slain. And the Queen too added gifts of her own; many golden rings she gave him, and fair raiment, and set about his neck a necklace bright with gems.[1] Now Beewolf had become a great man indeed, and he thought that his fortunes had taken a turn for the better; for his treatment here was very different from his treatment at home. All men praised him, and Unpeace was exceedingly friendly.

---

1   This is a convenient place to notice a very curious addition that my father made later and hastily to the manuscript A at this point, but then struck out:

> And one ring she added. 'This may be of service at need, my friend Beewolf,' said she. 'If ever hope seems to have departed, turn it on your finger and your call for help will be answered; for the ring was made by the fair folk of old.'

When evening came and the feast was at an end, the king's men remained in the hall, as their custom had been before the haunting began; and they spread their beds, and piled their arms on the benches beside them. But Beewolf was lodged in a bower by himself and lay upon a fair bed and slept the night away, for he was weary and stiff from his wrestling.

When all men were asleep, and the night was dark, a thing befell that no man had looked for. Grinder was avenged. He was not without kin to take up the feud for him. Far away over the moorlands in her lair Grinder's mother mourned for him, until filled with wrath and grief the old ogress herself took the road. As men lay thinking of no evil, she came to the Golden Hall and crept inside. At once she laid her claws on the man that slept nearest to the door, and tore at his flesh. Men awoke at his cries drowsy and amazed; and they groped for their swords, having no time to put on helmet or mail. Seeing so many men the old ogress fled, for great as she was, she had not the strength of Grinder her son, and was not used to walking far afield to the homes of men. But she did not go empty-handed; for she throttled the man she had seized and bore him away, while all the hall was in uproar, and men were running this way and that and hewing the air. And when morning came they found that it was the captain of the king's knights that she had taken, and that was a grievous loss.

When this news was brought to the king, he was weighed down with sorrow; and sent for Beewolf. And Beewolf, seeing the king look so downcast, greeted him, and asked if his sleep had been troubled with bad dreams. 'Not dreams!' said the king. 'For evil has come to my house again. My captain has been taken, the best of my knights. Will there ever be an end of my woes? Under the shadows of night a monster has carried him off: this must be the work of Grinder's dam, and her vengeance for the hurt that you gave to her son.'

'This is news to me!' said Beewolf. 'No tale that I have yet heard ever told that two such monsters haunted your land.'

'Yet that is how things are,' said the king. '[Long ago >] At whiles / men that walk far abroad brought [> have brought] tidings to me, and told [> have told] that away over the moors they have seen two monsters stalking in the wilderness: the larger like a misshapen man, and the other like a great hag with long hair. But more of their kindred no one has ever discovered; for they dwell alone, and only a few know where their den lies. It is many miles away in a hidden mere, behind a waterfall that tumbles from a black cliff into the shadows far beneath. Wind blows there, and wolves howl in the hills. Dead trees hang by the roots over the pool. At night fire flickers on the water. No man knows the depth of that lake, and no beast will enter it.'

'It is not a pleasant spot, that is clear,' said Beewolf. 'Yet someone must explore it, if this trouble is to be ended. 'Do not despair, lord, but be merry! I will go there. I am used to swimming in deep waters, and nicors do not frighten me. I will call on Grinder's mother in her own home, and however many doors there may be to her house, she will not escape me.'

Then the king sprang up in joy, and thanked Beewolf for his words, promising him gold and jewels beyond all his former gifts, if he made good his boast.

'All I ask,' said Beewolf, 'is a companion who knows the ways of your land to guide me to the spot.'

'Unpeace shall go with you,' said the king. 'His wit is good, and he knows all tales that have come down from days of old, and he has travelled much. No man knows more of the ways of this land than he.'

When Unpeace heard of the king's choice he seemed to be willing, and indeed he dared not be otherwise, lest he lose the king's favour and all honour in the land. 'It will be a pleasure to show my friend Beewolf the marvels of this land,' he said, and he grinned.

Together Unpeace and Beewolf set off, and soon came upon the trail of Grinder and his dam, for much blood had been spilled upon the ground.

The description in the original manuscript of their journey to the cliff above the lake was preserved almost word for word in the final text, but the head that they found 'staring at the sky' was not of course that of Ashwood but that of 'the king's captain' (p. 396) who had been carried off by Grinder's dam; and there was no mention of Beewolf's taking Handshoe's gloves, still less of Ashwood's spear (see p. 394 and p. 400).

'It seems that you have brought me to the right spot,' said Beewolf; and he blew on a horn, and the blast of it echoing in the rocks aroused all the nicors, and they plunged into the lake, blowing with rage. 'There are many unfriendly things here,' said Unpeace.

'I do not heed the nicors,' said Beewolf. 'I have dealt with others greater and worse in the sea.'

'Yet it may prove hard to deal with many foes at a time,' said Unpeace. 'See here, my friend, I will give you a gift for your aid. You set no store by weapons, I know, but do not despise this one; for it may prove a strong help at need.' Then he gave to Beewolf a curious blade: upon it there were many signs and figures, and at the edges snakes were drawn that the bite of the blade should [..... *illegible* >] be deadly; but the haft was long and was made of wood. Beewolf took the sword, thinking that it was given in friendship; and now he stood up and made himself ready.

'How will you get down, my friend?' said Unpeace.

'It will not be the first time that I have dived into deep water,' answered Beewolf; 'and though this cliff be ten fathoms tall I have seen taller.'

On the sword with the wooden haft given to Beowulf by Unpeace, not present in the final form of *Sellic Spell*, see the commentary on *Beowulf*, pp. 210–11.

From this point to the end of *Sellic Spell* the final text followed the original manuscript A for the most part very closely, with only slight changes in wording here and there; such differences as there are between the two narratives are set out in the notes that follow.

The ogress, mother of Grinder, in her lair is of course introduced quite differently in A, where she was the object of the expedition:

The nicors gathered round him and tore at him with their tusks; but the corslet of mail was cunningly woven and they did no hurt to him. The old ogress in her cave soon learned that some man from the world above had entered her pool where she had dwelt many ages untroubled. She was angry and came forth from her house.

In the final text Beewolf, confronting the ogress, thrust at her with the spear that had been Ashwood's, but 'with a blow of her hand she snapped the haft in two'. In the original version, in which Ashwood was not present in the story, the sword that Unpeace had given to Beewolf reappears here:

He smote her with the sword that Unpeace gave him, and the treacherous blade betrayed him; for the edges turned upon her hide, and with a blow of her hand she snapped the wooden haft in two.

In the episode of the hugely heavy and ancient sword, hanging on the wall of the cave, with which Beewolf struck off her head, it seemed to him in the later version that the light that sprang up 'came from the sword, and that the blade was on fire'; in A he thought that it was from the further chamber, where Grinder lay, that the light had come. Here Beewolf thrust aside the gigantic stone that blocked the entry into that chamber with the aid of Handshoe's gloves, showing that (as noticed earlier, p. 394) the magic gloves had entered the story before the story in the original manuscript was completed. When Beewolf had got rid of the stone, in the original text as written, there follows a curious passage:

He entered the chamber and there he saw great wealth of gold and gems that Grinder had gathered over the years. Ashwood's great spear was standing against the wall. There were also many bones upon the floor, and these he gathered in a bag, meaning to bury them, for among them he thought were some that had belonged to Handshoe.

This passage, from 'Ashwood's great spear', was struck through. That mention is very puzzling, since there has been nothing in this manuscript, either as first written or in later additions and alterations, to explain how a spear belonging to 'Ashwood' could be leaning against the wall of Grinder's cave (see p. 398).

The treachery of Unpeace and Beewolf's arduous escape from the mere scarcely differ at all in the two versions; but a curious point is that where the final text has 'But not a nixy was to be seen in the lake' the original manuscript has 'No nicor was to be seen now in the lake, for they had all vanished when the heads of the ogres were cut off.'

In the treatment of the story of the huge sword that Beewolf found in the monsters' caverns the versions differ markedly. The description in the original version of the sword as the king examined the hilts, which were all that was left of it, was preserved unchanged; but then followed:

That treasure remained long in the hoard of the king of the Golden Hall, but whether any blade was afterwards made for it is not told.

There was thus no germ here of the final story (p. 383), in which Unfriend, now the king's smith, was appointed to make a magnificent blade to be joined to the hilts; the sword that he made he gave to Beewolf 'as a peace-offering', which he received, and named it Gildenhilt. But it is interesting to see that 'upon it were many signs and figures, and at the edges snakes were drawn so that their bite should be deadly'; for these same words were used in the original story of the treacherous sword that Unpeace gave to Beewolf as they looked down into the mere (p. 399).

In A the description of the concluding feast celebrating Beewolf's return from the mere was much less elaborate than in the final text, since the latter (pp. 382–3) was derived from the description in A (p. 395) of the first feast, held following Beewolf's fight with Grinder in the Golden Hall. This is all that was said in A:

Merry indeed was the feast that day, and now Beewolf sat in high honour beside the king himself; and rich gifts were given to him. All the gold that he got in Grinder's cave the king returned to him and more beside in recompense for his companion, Handshoe, whom the ogre had slain. And twelve good men well armed the king appointed to be his followers and to serve him.

The story as told in A of Beewolf's departure from the Golden Hall and his reception in his own country, his wedding of the king's daughter, and his becoming the king of that land in after days, was preserved without change in the final text. There is only one last detail to notice. In the A manuscript there is a pencilled addition (not found anywhere else in these papers) to Beewolf's words concerning his name (see p. 384):

'Beewolf I used to be called, when I was at home. Now some call me the knight of the golden hilts; yet I see no reason to change my old name.'

*

§ 3 SELLIC SPELL: THE OLD ENGLISH TEXT

It is not difficult to see that the Old English text of *Sellic Spell* was not written until there was a Modern English text of the work in some form in existence, even if incomplete in that form.

The opening of the original text in the manuscript 'A', given in § 2, p. 387, reads thus:

> Once upon a time there was a King in the North of the world and in his house there was a young lad, who was not like other young lads. When he was a child he was found in a bear's den up in the mountains, and the hunters took him to the king . . ..

The text of the first revision of the initial text, found in the same manuscript 'A', is very close to the final text in this opening passage (§ 1, p. 360):

> Once upon a time there was a King in the North of the world who had an only daughter, and in his house there was a young lad who was not like the others. One day some huntsmen in his land had come upon a great bear in the mountains, and tracked it to its lair and killed it, and in the lair they found a man-child.

And the Old English text begins thus:

On ǽrdagum wæs wuniende be norþdǽlum middange-
ardes sum cyning, þe ángan dohtor hæfde. On his húse
wæs éac án cniht óþrum ungelíc. For þam þe hit ǽr gelamp
þæt þæs cyninges huntan micelne beran gemétton on þam
beorgum, ond hie spyredon æfter him to his denne, and
hine þǽr ofslógon. On þam denne fundon hie hysecild.

The following example is even more striking. In § 2, p. 389, I
have given a passage from the A manuscript, as first written,
beginning:

> After a time, when Beewolf had grown to man's
> size and more, news came to the land that the king of
> a country across the water was troubled by an ogre. Of
> what sort the monster was, and where he came from, no
> one could tell; but the tales told that he used to stalk men
> in the shadows . . .

My father struck out the whole passage line by line as far
as 'thinking the ogre might eat others who would be missed
more', and wrote in rapid pencil a new text in the gaps between
the lines - this being close to the final text (§ 1, p. 362):

> One day, when Beewolf had grown to man's size and
> more, he heard men talking in the hall, and there was one
> who told how the king of a far country had built himself a
> house. The hall was roofed with gold, and all the benches
> were carven and gilded . . .

The Old English text has here:

Hit gesælde, siþþan Béowulf mannes wæstm oþþe wel máran begeat, þæt he æt sumum sæle hýrde menn gieddian on healle. Þá cwiddode án þæt sum útlandes cyning him micel hús atimbrode. Héah wæs seo heall, and hire hróf gylden; ealle bence þǽr inne wrǽtlice agrǽfene wǽron ond ofergylde . . .

I suppose that it cannot be said that this actually proves that the Old English was translated from the A manuscript, but to assert the contrary seems artificial and altogether improbable. On the other hand, if the Old English text was a translation from the tale already existing in Modern English, I am unable to explain my father's apparently contradictory statement (introduction to Sellic Spell p. 355) 'I have given my tale a Northern cast of expression by putting it first into Old English'.

The carefully written Old English text ends with the words, at the foot of a page, 'Hraþe æfter þon ongann seo sunne niþer gewítan, wurdon sceadwa lange ofer eorðan. Þá arás se cyning; menn ónetton of þǽre healle.' 'Soon afterwards the sun began to sink in the west and the shadows grew long; and the king arose, and men hurried from the hall' (§ 2, p. 392). The story here was the original form found in the manuscript A before further development: when Handshoe and Beewolf faced the entry of Grinder together.

Following the last page of the carefully written and finished Old English text are two further pages showing my father working on the preliminary stage of the version in the old language. These seem to have been written fluently, but scribbled in a very thick, soft pencil that makes the text extremely hard to decipher; however, it can be done to quite a large extent. The story in this form is taken on from Hrothgar's conferring the hall of Heorot on Beewolf; and it breaks off in the course of the fight with Grinder (a passage that was preserved in the final text, (§ 1, p. 371): 'This was not at all the fare that he sought. But Beewolf would not let him go; and when Grinder drew back, he sprang up'.

The Old English text of *Sellic Spell* now follows. I have not thought it desirable to provide a translation, because unless one translated it in a painfully literal fashion it would be misleading; and the interest of this text lies chiefly, in my view, in its demonstration of my father's fluency in the ancient tongue.

On ǽrdagum wæs wuniende be norþdǽlum middangeardes sum cyning, þe ángan dohtor hæfde. On his húse wæs éac án cniht óþrum ungelíc. For þam þe hit ǽr gelamp þæt þæs cyninges huntan micelne beran gemétton on þam beorgum, ond hie spyredon æfter him to his denne, and hine þǽr ofslógon. On þam denne fundon hie hysecild. Þúhte him micel wundor, for þam þe þæt cild wæs seofonwintre, and gréat, and æghwæs gesund, bútan hit nan word ne cúþe, ac grunode swá swá wildéor; for þam þe beran hit aféddon. Hie genómon þæt cild; ac náhwǽr ne mihton hie geáxian hwanon hit cóme, ne hwelces fæderes sunu hit wǽre. Þá gelǽddon hie þæt cild to þam cyninge. Se cyning onféng his, and hét afédan hit on his hírede and manna þéawas lǽran.

Him ne geald, swáþéah, þæt fóstorcild his fóstres léan: ac gewéox and ungehýrsum cniht gewearþ, and wæs sláw and asolcen. Late leornode he manna geþéode. Láþ wæs him ǽlc geweorc, ne nolde he ná his willes gelómena brúcan ne wǽpnum wealdan. Hunig wæs him swíþe léof, and he sóhte hit oft be wudum; oftor þéah réafode he béocera hýfe. For þam hét man hine Béowulf (and he ǽr nǽnne naman hæfde), and á siþþan hátte he swá.

Hine menn micles wyrðne ne tealdon: léton hine for héanne, ne ne rýmdon him nǽnne setl on þæs cyninges healle; ac he wunode on hyrne. Þǽr sæt he oft on þam flette. Lýt spræc he mid mannum. Þá gelamp hit æfter firste þæt se cniht weaxan ongann wundrum hrædlíce, and swá swá he híerra wéox, swá wearþ he á strengra, oþ þæt óþre cnihtas and éac weras hine ondrǽddon. Næs þá lang to þon þæt he fíf manna mægen hæfde on his handum. Þá wéox he giet má, oþþæt his earma gripe wearþ swá swá beran clypping. Nǽnig wǽpn ne bær he, and gif he abolgen wearþ, þá mihte he man in his fæþme tocwýsan. Swá forléton menn hine ána.

Se Béowulf gewunode þæt he swamm oft on þǽre sǽ, sumera and wintra. Swá hát wæs he swá se hwíta bera, and his blód hæfde beran hǽto: þý ne ondrǽdde he nǽnne ciele.

Þá wæs on þǽre tíde sum swíþe sundhwæt cempa, Breca hátte, Brandinga cynnes. Se Breca gemétte þone cniht Béowulf be þam strande, þá he æt sume cierre cóm fram sunde be þam sǽriman.

Þá cwæþ Breca: 'Ic wolde georn lǽran þé sundplegan. Ac húru þú ne dearst swimman út on gársecg!'

Þá andswarode Béowulf: 'Gif wit bégen onginnaþ on

geflit swimman, ne béo ic se þe ǽrest hám wende!' Þá déaf he
eft on þa wǽgas. 'Folga me núþa be þínre mihte!' cwæþ he.

Þá swummon hie fíf dagas, and Breca ná ne mihte Béowulf
foran forswimman; ac Béowulf wæs swimmende ymb Brecan
útan, ne nolde hine forlǽtan. 'Ic ondrǽde me þearle þæt þu
méþige and adrince,' cwæþ he. Þá wearþ Breca ierre on móde.

Þá arás fǽringa micel wind, and se blæst bléow swa
wódlice þæt wǽgas to heofone astigon swá swá beorgas, and
hie cnysedon and hrysedon Brecan, and adrifon hine feorr
onweg and feredon hine to fyrlenum lande. Þanon cóm he
siþþan eft on langum síþe to his ágnum earde: sægde þæt he
Béowulf léte feor behindan, and hine æt þam sunde ealles
oferflite. Húru se storm onhrérde þa niceras, and hie þá úp
dufon of sǽgrunde; and hie gesáwon Béowulf. Swíþe háthe-
orte wurdon hie, for þam þe hie wéndon þæt he Breca wǽre
and þone storm him on andan aweahte. Þá geféng hira án
þone cniht: wolde hine niþer téon tó grunde. Swíþe wéndon
þa niceras þæt hie wolden þá niht under sǽ wista néotan.
Hwæþre seþéah Béowulf wrǽstlode wiþ þone nicor and
ofslóh hine, and swá eft óþre. Siþþan morgen cóm, þa lágon
úp nigon niceras wealwiende be þǽm wætere.

Þá sweþrode se wind, and astág seo sunne. Béowulf
geseah manige síde næssas licgan út on þa sæ, and micle
ýþa oþbǽron hine and awurpon hine up on elþéod, feorr
be norþan, þær Finnas eardodon. Síþ cóm he eft hám. Hine
þá sume frugnon: 'Hwider éodestu?' 'On sunde nathwǽr,'
cwæþ he. Þúhte him swáþéah his ansýn grimlic, and hie
gesáwon on him wundswaþe swá he wiþ wildeor wrǽstlode.

Hit gesǽlde, siþþan Béowulf mannes wæstm oþþe wel máran begeat, þæt he æt sumum sǽle hýrde menn gieddian on healle. Þá cwiddode án þæt sum útlandes cyning him micel hús atimbrode. Héah wæs seo heall, and hire hróf gylden; ealle bence þǽr inne wrǽtlice agræfene wǽron and ofergylde; scán se fáge flór, and gylden rift hangodon be þam wágum. Þær wæs ǽr manig wuldorlic symbel, micel mandréam, gamen and hleahtor wera. Nú þéah stód þæt hús ídel, siþþan seo sunne to setle éode. Nǽnig dorste þǽr inne slǽpan; for þam þe þyrsa náthwilc seomode on þǽre healle: ealle þe he besierwan mihte oþþe frǽt he oþþe út aferede to his denne. Ealle niht rixode se eoten on þǽre gyldenan healle þæs cyninges, ne nán mann mihte him wiþstandan.

Þá semninga gestód Béowulf úp. 'Him is mannes þearf þǽr on lande,' cwæþ he. 'Þone cyning wille ic ofer sǽ sécan!'

Þás word þuhton manigum dysig. Lýt lógon hie him swáþéah þone síþ; for þam þe hie tealdon þæt se þyrs oþre manige nytwyrþran etan mihte.

Béowulf fór ánliepe fram hám: ac on færendum wege gemétte he sumne mann þe hine áxode hú he hátte and hwider he fóre.

Þá andswarode he: 'Ic hátte Béowulf, and ic séce Gyldenhealle cyning.'

Þá cwæþ se mann: 'Nú wille ic þé féran mid. Handscóh is mín nama' – and he hátte swá, for þam þe he his handa mid miclum hýdigum glófum werede, and þá he glófa on hæfde, þá mihte he gréat clúd onweg ascúfan and micle stánas to-slítan; ac þá he hie næfde, ne mihte ná má þonne óþre menn.

Fóron þá forþ samod Handscóh and Béowulf þæt hie to þǽre sǽ cómon. Þǽr begéaton hie scip, and tobrǽddon segl, and se norþwind bær hie feorr onweg. Gesáwon hie æfter fierste fremede land licgan him beforan: héah clifu blicon bufan sande. Þǽr æt síþmestan dydon hie hira scip úp on strand.

Sóna swá hie úp éodon, swá cóm him ongéan wígmanna sum; ne sægde he ná þæt hie wilcuman wæren; lócode grim-líce, and mid spere handum acweahte wódlíce. Hie gefrægn þa cuman unfréondlíce æfter hira namum and hira ǽrende.

Þá gestód Béowulf and him andwyrde módiglíce. 'Béowulf is mín nama,' cwæþ he, 'and þes mín geféra hátte Handscóh. Wé sécaþ þæs Gyldenhealle cyninges land. Wolde ic georn geweorc habban þe geþungenes mannes gemet síe. Þǽr on lande scolde man þæt findan, þæs þe we secgan hýrdon; for þam þe séo gesegen on mínum éþle gebrǽded wæs þæt féonda náthwilc þæs cyninges healle nihtes sóhte, ne nǽnig híredman his abídan ne dorstc. Gif þas word sóþ wǽren, dohte ic þam cyninge.'

'Húru þu dohte!' cwæþ se mann: stóp onbæc, and lócode úp wundriende on þone cuman (and he, Béowulf wæs þá swíþe héah aweaxen, and his limu wǽron grýtran þonne óþerra manna gemet). 'For sóþe hæfþ éow se wind on þæs cyninges ríce gelǽded. Nis nú feorr heonan þæt hús þe gé tó sécaþ.'

Þá wísode he Béowulfe and his geféran forþ ofer land, oþþæt hie brádne weg fundon: þá þǽr gesáwon hie þæs cyninges hús scínan him beforan, on grénre dene: líexte geond þæt déope land se léoma þæs gyldenan hrófes.

Þá cwæþ se wísiend: 'þǽr stent séo heall þe gé tó fundiaþ. Ne magon gé nú þæs weges missan! Háte ic éow wel faran: swá ne wéne ic ná þæs þe ic þéow siþþan ǽfre eft geséon móte!'

Þæs ymb lýtel fæc cómon hie, Handscóh and Béowulf, tó þǽre healle durum. Þǽr ascéaf Béowulf þa duruweardas: cóm þá inn gán módig æfter flóre, þæt he fore þam cynesetle gestód and þone cyning grétte.

'Wes þú, hláford, hál on þínre Gyldenhealle!' cwæþ he. 'Ic eom nú hér cumen líþan ofer sǽ. Hýrde ic þæt þé elwihta sum gedrecce. Man me sægde þæt he þínne folgaþ ǽte and þæt þú mid fela goldes þám léanian wolde þam þe þé æt him ahredde.'

Þá andswarode se cyning: 'Wálá! Sóþ is þætte þu gehíerdest. Án þyrs se þe Grendel hátte nú fela géara hergaþ mín folc. Swá hwelcum menn swá hine fordyde, wolde ic þá dǽd mǽrlíce léanian. Ac hwá eart þu? Oþþe hwelc ǽrende hæfstu tó mé?'

'Béowulf is mín nama,' cwæþ he. 'Hæbbe ic on mínum handum þrítigra manna mægen. Þæt is mín ǽrende þæt ic on þisne þyrs lócige. Wæs ic ǽr ymb óþre swylce abisgod. Niceras éac ofslóh ic. Þý nǽnig hér on lande is þe him wiþstandan durre, þý wille ic hér toniht his abídan, maþelian mid þissum Grendle swá me wel þynce. Óþerne fultum nelle ic habban búte míne earmas twégen. Gif þás mé swícen, húru þu bist orsorg mín: náþer ne þyrfe þu mé leng feormian, ne mé bebyrigan mid ealle, búte þa spell léogen.'

Þá blissode se cyning swíþe þæs þe he þás sprǽce hierde;

412

ongann wénan þæs þe his gedeorfa bót nú æt síþmestan him
gehende wǽre. Swá gebéad he Béowulfe þæt he tó symble
eode; hét settan hine onmang his híredmanna. Þá þá sǽl
gewearþ þæt man fletsittendum drync agéat, þá cóm self seo
cwén tó Béowulfe, scencte him full medwes and him hǽlo
abéad. 'Swíþe gladu eom ic on móde,' cwæþ heo, 'þe ic eft tó
sóþe mann on þisse healle geséo!'

Þás word yfele lícodon þam híredmannum, and hira
nánum ofþuhton hie má þonne Unfriþe. Se Unfriþ tealde
hine mycles wyrðne, for þam þe he þam cyninge léof wæs.
Húru he wæs swíþe gewittig mann: þý wǽron his rǽdas dýre
his hláforde. Óþre sume cwǽdon þéah þæt he drýcræftig
wǽre and galdor cúþe: oftor aweahten his rǽdas unsibbe
þonne hie geþwǽrnesse setten.

Se ilca mann wende hine nú tó Béowulfe weard, and
cwæþ him þus: 'Hýrde ic nú ǽr on riht þæt þú þé Béowulf
nemnede? Seldcúþ nama, féawum gemǽne, þæs ic wéne.
Witodlíce þú wǽre hit þe he Breca þé sundgeflit béad, and he
þá lét þé feorr behindan, and swamm eft hám tó his ágenum
earde: swá gelǽste he his béot wiþ þé. Wén hæbbe ic þæs þe
Grendel þé læssan áre dón wille þonne Breca, búte þú micle
swíþor duge nú þonne ǽr.'

'Lá! léofa Unfriþ!' cwæþ Béowulf. 'Hwæt! Þu woffast
béore druncen, dollíce gesegest eall on unriht! Eornostlíce
wæs ic hit þe mín béot gelǽste, nealles se earma Breca. Þéah
wæs ic þá giet cniht án. Sóþlíce is mín wæstm hwéne mára
núþa. Ac uton nú gefrýnd weorþan!'

Þá nóm he Unfriþ úp, ymbfæþmode hine, and clypte
hine leohtlíce (swá him þúhte). Wæs hit þéah þam óþrum

genóg, and siþþan Béowulf hine alíesde, þá lét Unfriþ swíþe fréondlíce, þá hwíle þe Béowulf wæs him néah gesett.

Hraþe æfter þon ongann seo sunne niþer gewítan, wurdon sceadwa lange ofer eorðan. Þá arás se cyning; menn ónetton of þære healle.

*

THE LAY OF BEOWULF

These two poems, or two versions of a poem, are typescripts
made by my father in the same 'midget' type as that used for
text B of his translation of *Beowulf* (see p. 1). One version
has the typed title BEOWULF AND GRENDEL, with the
number I added in ink; the title of the other as typed was
simply BEOWULF, but to this he added in ink & THE
MONSTERS, together with the number II.

That version I was the earlier, as might be guessed in any
case, is shown by the emendation in ink of the first line of
the sixth stanza *A ship there sailed on pinions wild* in version
I to *On the sails of a ship the sunlight smiled*, which is the
form of the line in the penultimate stanza of version II as
typed. Version II repeats many of the lines of version I, but is
greatly changed and enlarged by the introduction of the story
of Grendel's mother.

I have found no mention of these lays even of the slight-
est nature among my father's writings (apart from the name
'Beowulf' pencilled on an early typewritten list of his poems),
but the texts are preceded by a page on which he wrote in
ink 'Stages in the accretion of new matter to The Lay of

Beowulf'. This of course he added when the two versions were both in existence, a satiric suggestion of the importance of these poems expressed in the academic vocabulary of this branch of *Beowulf* studies.

On this cover page there is also a pencilled note 'Intended to be sung'. As mentioned in the Preface I remember his singing this ballad to me when I was seven or eight years old, in the early 1930s (but of course it may have been in existence years before that). I think it very probable that it was the first version, *Beowulf and Grendel,* that he sang.

THE LAY OF BEOWULF

I

Beowulf and Grendel

Grendel came forth in the dead of night;
the moon in his eyes shone glassy bright,
as over the moors he strode in might,
    until he came to Heorot.
Dark lay the dale, the windows shone;
by the wall he lurked and listened long,
and he cursed their laughter and cursed their song
    and the twanging harps of Heorot.

King Hrothgar mourns upon his throne
for his lieges slain, he mourns alone,
but Grendel gnaws the flesh and bone
    of the thirty thanes of Heorot.
A ship there sails like a wingéd swan,
and the foam is white on the waters wan,
and one there stands with bright helm on
    that the winds have brought to Heorot.

On his pillow soft there Beowulf slept,
and Grendel the cruel to the dark hall crept;
the doors sprang back, and in he leapt
    and grasped the guard of Heorot.
As bear aroused from his mountain lair
Beowulf wrestled with Grendel there,
and his arm and claw away did tear,
    and his black blood spilled in Heorot.

'O! Ecgtheow's son' he then dying said,
'Forbear to hew my vanquished head,
or hard and stony be thy death-bed,
    and a red fate fall on Heorot!'
'Then hard and stony must be the bed
where at the last I lay me dead':
and Beowulf hewed the demon's head
    and hung it high in Heorot.

Merry the mead men quaffed at the board,
and Hrothgar dealt his golden hoard,
and many a jewel and horse and sword
    to Beowulf gave in Heorot.
The moon gleamed in through the windows wan;
as Beowulf drank he looked thereon,
and a light in the demon's eyes there shone
    amid the blaze of Heorot.

On the sails of a ship the sunlight smiled,
its bosom with gleaming gold was piled,
and the wind blew loud and free and wild
 as it left the land of Heorot.
Voices followed from the sounding shore
that blessed the lord those timbers bore,
but that sail returned thither never more,
 and his fate was far from Heorot.

The demon's head in the hall did hang
and grinned from the wall while minstrels sang,
till flames leapt forth and red swords rang,
 and hushed were the harps of Heorot.
And latest and last one hoar of head,
as he lay on a hard and stony bed,
and venom burned him and he bled,
 remembered the light of Heorot.

II

Beowulf and the Monsters

Grendel came forth at dead of night;
the moon in his eyes shone glassy bright,
as over the moors he strode in might
    until he came to Heorot.
Dark lay the dale, the windows shone;
by the wall he lurked and listened long,
and he cursed their laughter and cursed their song
    and the twanging harps of Heorot.

The lights were quenched and laughter still;
there Grendel entered and ate his fill;
and the blood was red that he did spill
    on the shining floor of Heorot.
No Dane ever dared that monster meet,
or abide the tramp of those dread feet;
in the hall alone he held his seat
    the demon lord of Heorot.

At morn King Hrothgar on his throne
for his lieges slain there mourned alone
but Grendel gnawed the flesh and bone
   of the thirty thanes of Denmark.
A ship there sailed like a wingéd swan,
and the foam was white on the waters wan,
and one there stood with bright helm on
   that fate had brought to Denmark.

Beowulf soft on his pillow slept,
and Grendel in lust to the dark hall crept,
the doors sprang back, and in he leapt
   and grasped the guard of Heorot.
As bear aroused from his mountain lair
Beowulf grappled with Grendel there,
and his arm and claw away did tear,
   and black blood spilled in Heorot.

Merry the mead goes round the board,
and merry are men, and glad their lord,
and many a jewel and horse and sword
   he gives in gift to Beowulf.
The Danes in slumber all careless lie,
nor dream of a fiend that draweth nigh
to avenge the death her son did die
   and his blood there spilled by Beowulf.

The laughter was still and the lights were low;
the mother of trolls there wrought them woe,
with a Danish corpse she turned to go
    and shrieking fled from Heorot.
Like a shadow cast on the mountain mist,
where the winds were bleak and the heather hissed
she fled, but none could keep her tryst
    since her son found death in Heorot.

There was one who dared over mountain road
to follow her fleeing with dreadful load
to the foaming fall where she abode,
    while men made moan in Heorot.
Far over the misty moorlands cold
where the wild wolf howled upon the wold,
past dragon's lair and nicor's hold,
    and far from the lights of Heorot.

There sheer was the shore over waters frore
and withered and bent the trees it bore;
those waters black were blent with gore
    of the noblest knights of Denmark.
The flaming force there in thunder fell,
that cauldron smoked with the fires of hell,
and there the demons dark did dwell
    amid the bones of Denmark.

Quoth Beowulf 'Farewell, comrades free!
this journey none may share with me',
and his shining helm plunged in the sea
    to avenge the woes of Heorot.
The nicors gnashed his ringéd mail;
he saw their white fangs gleaming pale;
a green light burned in that deep sea-dale
    in halls more high than Heorot.

The demon lurked at her cave's dark door;
her fangs and fingers were red with gore,
and skulls of men lay on the floor
    beneath the feet of Beowulf.
At his corslet tore her claws accursed
her teeth at his throat for blood did thirst,
and the sword there failed and asunder burst
    that Unferth gave to Beowulf.

There nigh was his death in the shadowy deep,
where a corpse lay low on bony heap,
where Grendel slept in his long sleep
    and strode no more to Heorot.
A sword hung huge on the cavern's wall
once forged by ancient giants tall;
Beowulf seized it – as lightnings fall
    it fell on the foe of Heorot.

'O! Ecgtheow's son' she then dying said
'Forbear to hew my vanquished head,
or hard and stony be thy death's bed
    and a red fate fall on Denmark!'
'Then hard and stony must be the bed
where at the last I lay me dead':
and Beowulf hewed the demon's head
    and haled it back to Denmark.

Merrily mead men quaffed at the board,
and Hrothgar dealt his golden hoard,
but Beowulf wore no more the sword
    that Unferth gave in Heorot.
The moon gleamed in through the windows wan;
as Beowulf drank he looked thereon,
and the light in the eyes of the demon shone
    amid the blaze of Heorot.

On the sails of a ship the sunlight smiled,
its bosom with gleaming gold was piled,
and the wind blew loud and free and wild
    as it left the land of Denmark.
Voices followed from the sounding shore
that blessed the lord those timbers bore,
but that sail returned thither never more
    and his fate was far from Denmark.

The demon's head in the hall did hang
and grinned from the wall while minstrels sang
till flames leapt forth and red swords rang
   and hushed were the harps of Heorot.
Latest and last one hoar of head,
as he lay on a hard and stony bed
and venom burned him, and he bled,
   remembered the light of Heorot.

*